FINAL ABSOLUTION
A Novel

Patricia O'Keeffe Condon

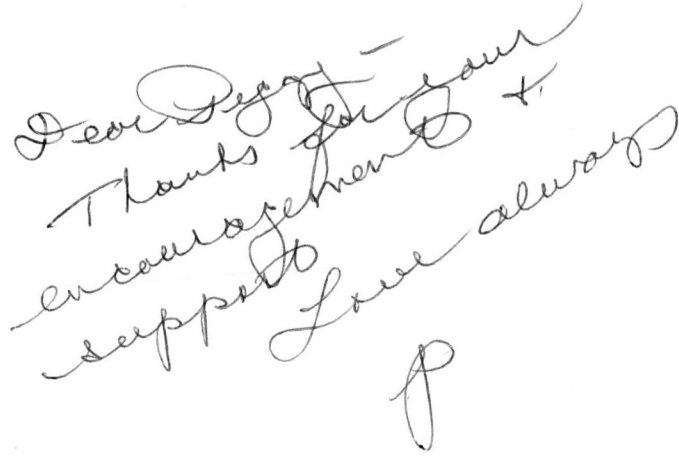

Dear Peggy —
Thanks for your
encouragement +
support. Love always
P

We are not exceptional in our beginnings: We become exceptional by refusing to accept the obstacles which destiny has placed before us.
Anais Nin

*This novel is dedicated
to the memory of
my mother
Mary Condon O'Keeffe*

CHAPTER
1

"I have breast cancer."

My mother spoke those words to me with an unmitigated sadness one day in June 1963.

I never thought of my mother dying, not even when the beast was breathing down our backs. This thing, this cancer, I vowed, would be fixed. I had just finished my freshman year at college, and I was going to be a great novelist. At nineteen who thinks their dreams are not possible? I wanted to travel, to see what the rest of the world looked like outside of textbooks. I wanted success.

As far back as I can remember, we had lived just above the poverty line, and since my mother could not work anymore, we would be living below the poverty line. Even though I had been on a full four-year scholarship at a small New Jersey college, it was impossible to return to school. I needed to work and care for her; there was no one else. I left my student days behind and with them my dreams, but it would not be permanent, I told myself. One day I would succeed, one day

I would do what I set out to do. Nothing would stand in my way.

After they had amputated her right breast, leaving a deep crater in the wall of her chest, she was especially weak, and she needed massive doses of radiation. I did not ask the doctors about her chances, fearing the answer. My mother was alive, and I intended to keep her alive; but the rawness of that implacable eventuality cut into my young soul and forced my courage and maturity. I became a caregiver. I held the basin for her when she needed it. I said the rosary when she could not pray. I studied the statistics: how many women lived, how many died in any given year, and despite the odds against her, I would not be stopped. Every day, every minute, I fought for her life. When I ran low on money, I had to decide between food and medicine. I fed her franks and beans and told her I had already eaten. I drank quarts of water so I would not feel the hunger. But then the worst happened.

The janitor, who was also in charge of collecting the rent every month, knocked on our door not more than two months after her surgery. "The rent?" He used his "rent is late" voice, loud and crude, as if we were deadbeats and had not paid our rent on time for all the eighteen years we had lived there. I still have memories of days when the entire building was without electricity and heat because someone was "rude" to him. We treated him as we treated our antiquated appliances, with great care and concern and little usage. He tried to push his six-foot frame into the living room, but I blocked his way as I attempted to shut the door behind me. I did not want him in my home. I did not want my mother to know we did not have the rent money.

"I don't have it this month, Mr. Wolochowicz," I whispered so that the neighbors would not hear me. "I'll have it soon, though. I promise."

"No! Now!" His voice ricocheted against the dingy walls of the unlighted hallway. Everyone in the building must have heard him.

"Please," I whispered again trying to hide my shame and hoping my mother would not be able to hear our conversation. "If I pay the rent now, I won't be able to buy my mother's medicine. She's in pain. She needs her medicine." Nor would I have the money to buy our food for the week, but my embarrassment and anger would not allow me to admit everything, even to the janitor.

"Next month you have rent, or you're out." He raised his voice, pointed his thick, grubby finger toward the outside, and stretched his gargantuan head in an effort to see beyond me into our apartment.

"I promise. Next month." I promised without knowing how I would accomplish that feat, and I shut the door as he scurried down the stairs.

The sea of depression that I waded through on those dark and somber days as a caregiver swelled. I became dysfunctional. I did not know how I could go on. When I slept, nightmares absolute in their horror catapulted me awake. I saw myself penniless, a beggar in the street, hungry and dirty. I prayed for God's intervention, I prayed he would provide. I had heard my mother praying such for almost twenty years—"*God will provide*"—and somehow he did, because always we had a roof over our heads and food in our bellies. But this was different. My mother's medical bills were devastating, and I had reached the point of feeding her or medicating her. I had never had to make life-threatening decisions, and my brain was creating static; it was difficult to remember if I had fed her or given her her medication. The threat of eviction caused my body and mind to degenerate into a catatonic-like state so that one afternoon, when my mother was sleeping, I left her alone and wandered outside for several hours until a neighbor brought me home, fed me hot tea, and put me to bed. The next day, after I had a good night's sleep and was well-rested, I came to my senses, and realized that it was I who would provide; there would be no miracles, no God-provided gifts. I was it. We would not be put out on the streets, but we would have to move into the public housing projects and receive welfare checks like all the other welfare people. I could not allow that. We were always able to provide for ourselves, we didn't need the city to take care of us. And with that thought in mind I sat down and compiled a list of every person or business we had ever known who could lend us money. The banks were the first to be crossed off. Without collateral we could not borrow from them. My mother had a savings account of a few dollars and for as long as I could remember, it had never been over a few dollars. As for our neighbors and friends, they were as poor as we were. I would be embarrassed to ask them for anything more than a cup of flour. Then there were all the people we had some business or financial contact with: people we bought from, beginning with the neighborhood stores; sometimes we had to charge our purchases, but we always paid it up within a month or two. I placed their names on a clean sheet of paper. I babysat for people who were well-off financially and who knew me and my mother for my whole four years of high school. I wrote their names down on that list. My mother worked all her life in a bakery, and in her spare time she sewed for others. Their names went down on the second list as well. My college teachers— they were all nuns; my high school teachers—they also were all nuns, and there was no sense in asking any of them for a dime. Then one man came to mind. I couldn't understand why I didn't think of him first.

Father McLaughlin was a family friend. He baptized me. When I was in elementary school, all of us kids were crazy about him. We searched for him every morning after mass when we crossed the alley to the school building. Without warning he would pop out from a recess in the building and in a booming voice, the frost of the winter morning hugging his breath, ask us: "And are we all ready for our swim today?" We would shriek and squeal and rub our arms with our little mittened hands and sing out "It's too cold, Father," as if we believed him. We did. We believed in his every word. He'd take one of us up in his arms and hold us high in the air so everyone could see. The nuns beamed, the child beamed, and the rest of the children in line hoped they'd be next. He was our hero.

Father McLaughlin was not just the children's idol; he was respected by the parish and throughout the city. He championed the poor, helped the sick and the needy, and fought the pornographers. It was only logical that I called upon him for help. I was the poor and needy. He knew my mother and me forever. He would never turn us away; he never turned anyone away. I went to him first.

"Good morning! Good morning, my dear! How are you faring?" Father McLaughlin thumped into the vestibule, his broad shoulders sagging so that his six-foot-plus stature appeared shorter, his smile large and transcending.

He led me to the rectory office, which had a crumpled look, the massive leather armchairs made for men, the shelves filled with books on theology and Christ and biblical histories, the smells of cigars and pipes wafting through the musty air of the room. *If I were a man, would I have to beg?* Although it was a sunny day, his office was dark and lighted by a few lamps.

"Good morning, Father!" I forced my voice to sing out. How else could I sound? I was down so far, it wasn't possible to sink any lower.

"Ah, Rosemary, my dear. Is your mother well today?" He sat opposite me, bent forward, his feet planted in front of him, like an aging boxer. The bottom part of his black rayon cassock parted, showing the meticulous creases in his black trousers.

"About the same," I answered him. I didn't know how I would begin to ask for money, but it was either that or face Mr. Wolochowicz and welfare. "Father, I'm sorry I have to ask, but I can't make the rent this month. Would it be possible for you to lend it to me? I can pay you back as soon as I go to work." I spoke fast as if speed would disguise the shame.

His eyes, which had always appeared normal to me, had taken on a glazed look—I thought of cataracts—before he answered. "Of course, of course. I know you'll pay me back. That's no problem, dear. There's plenty of time for that, but are you eating? Sleeping well?"

"Yes, Father." Anxiety spiraled through my breasts, and I breathed in deep gulps of the smoky air in an effort to calm myself. I longed to be outside in the sunlight, inhaling the fresh air; I wanted the early autumn winds to extinguish my growing wretchedness.

"What did you eat today?" He stood and crossed over to his desk.

I could not remember when I last ate.

"I'm going to give you a check," he said when I did not answer him. He was already writing it out as he spoke to me. "On one condition. I want you to promise me you will take better care of yourself. You have dark circles around your eyes, and you're too thin. I want you to stop at the store before you go home and buy all the food you want. Do you promise me?" His voice was firmer than I had ever heard.

"Yes, Father." His back was toward me, which was just as well; I could not look the man in the eye.

He turned and gave me a check. "Oh, no, Father! This is too much!" I held it out to him hoping he would not take it, but he had already walked me to the door, one hand on my shoulder. His voice softened into a demeanor one hears in confessionals when the penitent is truly remorseful or from a doctor giving a fatal diagnosis; his tone provoked my humiliation, which shimmered inviolably there in the welcoming shade of his home.

"No, it's not. It's the least I can do for you and your mother. But look at you. Look at your clothes. Promise me you'll get someone in for a few hours a day to help you. Tell your mother I'll stop by later this week with Communion. I'll say mass. She'll like that. And eat! Eat a meal today!" He shook his finger at me.

I looked down at my skirt. When had I last cleaned it? I had stains on my blouse. And my shoes! They were filthy and falling apart. And then the reality of my life flew up before me so that my humiliation surged with shame and hopelessness; I had never been that unkempt.

For as long as I could remember, my mother sewed beautiful clothes for me. She sewed for other people as well to make extra money. I'd often watched her late at night as she worked with the miniscule light from the sewing machine guiding her way. I was always well dressed; my friends teased me about being a runway model. But I was no longer a student dressing for dances and parties. I was a caretaker, helping my mother to the toilet, coaxing food into her, cleaning up the puke and the shit, pouring life into her, holding on to that part that gave me life, that part without whom I would die. I had not seen my friends in months. I had not had a date since I was in school. Instead of beer fests, I held rosary fests, and instead of sororities, there were my neighbors attempting to help me with their feeble resources.

When I was a safe enough distance from the rectory, I broke into sobs and I cried the rest of the way home. The fear of welfare, the smell of death, all had receded. I promised myself that I would get through it, my mother would live, and whatever it took, I would control my life so that I would never again feel the disgrace and terror of poverty.

As soon as my mother could be left alone, I went job hunting, and in late October I was hired as a receptionist by a large oil company in Manhattan. I was lucky. When the dean of women at my college learned I was not returning to school and was in the job market, she arranged for my interview. She knew someone who knew someone. I worked for Marge Calloway, the secretary to the chairman of the board in his executive suite.

Marge was more than twice my age, and I adored her. She was easy to work for, and she knew all the ropes of her profession. She also knew all the people in the company. I had seen right away that she was liked and respected and all the top-notch people relied on her. Virtually, she was the top woman in the company.

In the early sixties it was a man's world; there were no women in the professional ranks. The secretaries then enjoyed their heyday. Marge dressed in designer suits and alligator shoes and bags. She had nice jewelry and perfume and her own apartment in Manhattan. Being the right hand "man" to the chairman, everyone kowtowed to her.

Although I would have preferred to be back at school, I loved the luxury of the executive offices. Everything in the chairman's suite was first class, from the thick wall-to-wall carpeting to the mahogany desks and electric typewriters to a fresh thermos of ice water every morning. Pages ran the errands, even mine. I never had to leave my desk. When I had the time, I worked at increasing my typing speed so I could move into a secretarial position, which paid more, and I wanted to be a competent secretary when the opportunity came up.

I registered for evening school at New York University. The company would refund my tuition 100 percent for As; for Bs it was something like 80 percent, and so on down the line. I aimed for As, even though that limited me to two courses. I didn't think I could maintain As taking three courses, and if I didn't have to pay for my tuition, I wouldn't. Frugality had been implanted in me from birth, and even though I was making a nice salary, still I hovered over pennies with a serious parsimony.

It was just before Christmas when I met Samantha Westcott. Her father had an appointment with the chairman at noon.

"The chairman does not want Mr. Westcott's daughter in the meeting, Rosemary, so we both decided that you would be a perfect companion for her." Marge smiled at me.

I leaned back in the soft leather chair in front of Marge's desk, a benefit those at the top received, and ran my hands over its expensive texture. I knew from her smile and the way she looked at me that this would not be pleasant. Even though I had been working for her a couple of months, I could read her well, and I tried to get out of it.

"What am I supposed to do with her?" I affected my little girl lost voice; most times it worked with Marge.

She ignored my attempt at intimidation. "Take her to lunch. She's about the same age as you are. She's just coming back from Paris. The little brat had a year at the Sorbonne. Go anywhere you want. And take your time," she added a bit too quickly. "The chairman and Mr. Westcott have a lot of business to discuss." She flashed me a smile behind which I sensed a subtle derision. "Mr. Westcott has a little fledgling company all his own." She turned away from me and began to type.

"Why would a rich girl just coming back from the Sorbonne want to have lunch with me, a receptionist?" I made a face that suggested Marge's idea was nonsense.

"Because I will tell her she's having lunch with you." She flashed me a smug smile. "She has no choice in the matter."

"Where will I take her?" I asked, my hope for a reprieve fading.

"Oh, you ask too many questions." Marge continued to type without looking at me. I was dismissed, and I returned to my desk and waited for my "important" lunch date.

At noon, Mr. Westcott came roaring through the door. It was as if a tornado had hit without warning. He was huge, overweight by about a hundred pounds, with a face too small for his frame. He had no neck. His voice was loud and potent. His dress was impeccable and rich.

"I haven't met you yet, have I?" he bellowed, thrusting his large hand at me. His hand was warm and comfortable and his large, dark eyes locked into mine, so that I knew underneath all that noise and bluster there was a humane man. Before I had time to say hello, he was in Marge's office, pumping her hand and hollering compliments at her. Marge's easy diplomacy was at work, and even though she appeared to be enjoying the man, she did not spend more than a minute with him before leading him into the chairman's office. I would have heard his voice if I were a mile away. "Hey, you son of a bitch!" I caught a glimpse of him and the chairman in a bear hug as the door shut on them.

I still remember the exhaustion I felt when Marge winked at me with a huge smile on her heart-shaped face and returned to her desk. I plopped down at mine, grateful for the quiet of the executive suite. For a moment I thought his daughter had changed her mind and decided not to come, but when I looked down the long, softly lighted corridor, Samantha Westcott was walking toward me as if in slow motion.

Contrary to her father's entrance, Samantha's was gracious and dignified. I admired her elegance. She was wearing a white silk skirt with a matching blouse;

a salt and pepper overcoat was draped over her shoulders. She wore a necklace of real opals. Her shoes contradicted her otherwise smart and expensive outfit; they looked as if rodents had gnawed away at the heels, and I wondered how she managed to walk on them. She told me later all her shoes looked like that. "Bicycles," she explained. "I rode bicycles just about all the time in Paris." Samantha Westcott used little makeup. She had her father's large black eyes set against her own clear, ivory skin. Her shoulder-length black hair, thick and shiny, made those features even more alluring. She had a long neck, unlike her father, which I envied. Samantha Westcott was beautiful.

Not wasting any time, Marge was at my desk introducing us. "You will be having lunch with Rosemary Beckett." Her instructions to Samantha were firm and unarguable. "The chairman and I know that you'll be more comfortable with Rosemary than sitting in on a business meeting."

"That's really great!" she exclaimed. Her voice emanated a great energy. As we descended in the quiet elevator to the ground floor, she moved closer and whispered in my ear. "I can't stand listening to their sleazy deals anyway."

I had never thought of the chairman as sleazy or doing anything that would be defined as sleazy, but I flashed her a weak smile and let the comment slide. "What would you like to eat?" I asked.

"Pizza. Please. I haven't had really good pizza in a year. Unless you have something else in mind," she added.

"Pizza it is." I had hoped she would leave the choice to me. I wanted to eat in the restaurant in our building that catered to the executives. I had lunched there a couple of times with Marge. Their meals were sumptuous. I always felt smart sitting at a table with a crisp linen cloth and crisp linen napkins and service that was fit for all chairmen. Also, because the temperature outside was below thirty degrees. But pizza would do.

We walked five blocks to a small Italian restaurant that was famous for its pizza and where Marge often ordered lunch for us on rainy days. The weather that day was bitter cold, and the wind was sharp, but Samantha loved it.

"It feels really great to be home," she chirped, her coat hung over her shoulders, her magnificent body opened to the freezing elements as if she were in Miami.

"I'm glad to hear it," I tried to chirp back, my short body in pain from the cold, my three-year-old heavy coat buttoned all the way, with my muffler wrapped tight around my short neck. The winds were hostile. The noon crowds could not diminish the bitter cold weather.

Despite her rich clothing and New York cultivation, Samantha stared up at the downtown skyscrapers, stopping sometimes to take it all in and smiling as if she were seeing a modern world for the first time. The lunch-hour crowds jostled us, and at times I found it necessary to take her arm and guide her.

When we arrived at the restaurant, I breathed in the pungent aroma of Italian cooking and was grateful for the warmth of its ovens that exuded their heat throughout the small rooms. The tables and booths were being taken up by the hungry hordes of office workers, and I looked around to see what was left. One of the waiters who delivered lunches to our office recognized me and led us ahead of the waiting line to the last available booth. I was grateful for Marge's belief in generous tipping.

"This is really great!" Samantha tossed her black-maned head and looked over the working-class scene as she squeezed into the small booth with a grace that matched a fashion model.

I pushed into the other side, facing her. "The food here is very good. I know you'll like it."

"I love pepperoni. How about you?" she asked.

"My favorite." I gave our order to the waiter and sipped on my ice water.

"So tell me everything." She flapped her hands over the carved-up table, her black eyes dancing. "Who do you think killed him?" She lowered her voice and inclined her head toward me so one would have thought the assassination was a secret.

Kennedy had been assassinated just three weeks before, and the country was still in the grips of horror. But for us Irish Catholics, it was far worse. At long last we had placed one of our own in the highest office of the land. Defeat smacked us senseless. The churches were packed, and my mother and I attended prayer services every night. It was as if he were our son and father.

"So what do you think?" she asked when I didn't answer. She had not taken her eyes from me. "Oswald? Or a conspiracy?"

"I don't know," I answered with a shrug and with an obvious reluctance. My response rang empty and obtuse in my ears, and I wished she wouldn't continue the discussion. I was still breaking down and crying for the man; he was my hero, and I could not fathom his death despite the many theories about it.

"What do you mean you don't know? Can't you even speculate?" She challenged me, waving away a cloud of smoke that wafted over her head. "Maybe the government did it," she added, giving me a quizzical look.

She was not going to give up, so I tried. "It's possible. Not probable, though. It could have been Castro or the mafia. Is that all you want? Pizza? They have delicious mussels here." The wooden booth felt hard beneath me, and I shifted in my seat.

"Johnson?" she asked, her large black eyes clinging to me as she sipped at her water in tiny sips.

"Johnson?"

"The President of the United States!" She laughed, her hands hung out in front of her, displaying a desperate need for a manicure. She was beautifully dressed and expensively dressed; I couldn't understand why she wouldn't have a manicure.

"I know who Johnson is, but I don't want to think he did it, do you?" I was shocked at her candor and more than annoyed she would think I didn't know who Lyndon Johnson was. Now both of us spoke in lowered voices.

She watched me with liquid eyes, their blackness glistened with anticipation. Her lips were tight, but I could have sworn she was smiling. The waiter placed a piping hot aluminum tray of pizza in front of us.

"Don't forget our cokes, please?" She ordered with a gentility I envied. "Why not?" she asked me when the waiter left.

"To have the president of the United States a murderer? Ugh!" I extracted a slice of pizza from the tray, hoping she'd eat as well and leave the topic of conversation on hold. I was still going to church and praying every day for the man; it didn't take much for me to burst into tears. I had wanted to be one of his Peace Corps volunteers, I had wanted to do for my country when Kennedy was elected, and I had hoped to join the Peace Corps once I finished school.

"You're kidding. You don't believe those thugs in politics wouldn't kill to get their way, do you?" she persisted.

I couldn't help but be amused by her grin.

I picked at the pepperoni with my fingers; the pizza was piping hot. "You know, I can't be that hard. It's too easy to say all politicians are crooked."

"How about evil?"

Desperate for another topic, I took my time in answering.

She cocked her head and peered at me waiting for an answer.

I gave up. "There are bad people, of course, but evil? I don't think so."

"Murderers? Death row?"

"Sickos. They're people who snap."

"So everyone who kills is sick. Is that what you're saying?"

I would not let her intimidate me. I would have preferred another topic of conversation, but I didn't want to be rude; she was the daughter of the chairman's colleague, after all, so I grinned and satisfied myself by watching the light red oil drip down the arm of her white silk blouse. I waited a few minutes before passing her a bunch of paper napkins. I tore off a second slice of pizza and refused to speak, munching on a big bite of the pizza and pointing to my mouth.

"We're all capable of murder, Rosi," she continued, patting the napkin against the grease on her silk blouse, "if given the right circumstances." She leaned over the table so that I thought our heads would meet. "If the world listened to your ideology, everyone would get away with murder."

She was getting too heady for me, but I responded anyway. "I wouldn't kill, Samantha, because I don't hate, and I would never harm a living thing, human or animal—or insect, for that matter. Under any circumstances. People who kill should be helped, maybe even studied."

"So what are you going to do, become a missionary?" She thrust her chin at me and waved for the waiter. "And don't call me Samantha. I detest that name. Everyone calls me Sam, except for my parents, but they don't count." She flapped her hands above her head as if to wave off something distasteful. "So what are your plans? You're not going to stay in that job forever, are you?"

"No. But I'll most likely move up to a secretarial position. Some of us have to work for a living, Sam, in case you didn't notice." Now I cocked my head and eyed her.

The waiter approached, and she ordered another large coke. I shook my head to a second.

"So? What are you going to do when you're all grown up?" She nibbled on the still warm pizza.

"Well, when I get my degree, I hope in about three years, I want to write a book, a best seller, of course, travel the world—I want to see everything, get married, and have kids." For a moment, I felt as if I were back in school with my old friends.

"Kids!" She said with disgust. "Who wants them?" She picked up the last slice of pizza.

"How was Paris?" I asked to change the subject.

"Great! Really great!" She leaned close to me and whispered so that I just about heard her. "The Frenchmen are the best, Rosi."

I hesitated for a few moments while I thought over her serious and somber statement. All I knew about Frenchmen was that they had black mustaches, black eyes, and they fought in the underground in World War II. I gave up. "The best what?" I asked.

"The best lovers. What do you think I mean?" She looked puzzled.

I tried to hide my ignorance. What did I know? I was the nice Irish-Catholic girl. My religion reinforced my virginity, and I wore them both with modesty and obedience and without complaint.

"So what are you going to do now that you're back?" I asked to change the subject.

"Georgetown. I'm going to study for my PhD." She leaned back against the booth.

"How old are you?" I asked.

"Twenty-one. I finished up in three years at Columbia. Anything to get away from my parents. I'm going to go to school, well, if I can, forever. Why not?" She shrugged. "I've plenty of money, even if it is my parents'. I don't take credit for it either. But I'm fortunate enough not to have to work for a living. And besides, no one expects me to. I'm going to have fun with my life."

"Don't you want to get married? Sometime?" I knew she would say no.

"Nah. Never. I'd probably wind up with the same kind of marriage my parents have. It's not for me. Besides, I want to do something for people, you know, make this world a better place to live in."

"Like what, for instance?" I asked her with a mild curiosity.

"I'm not quite sure. But there's a world out there that exploits people, and I would like to stop it."

I changed the subject to college life, literature, anything that would not touch on the subject of evil or Frenchmen or Kennedy, and two hours later I delivered her back to her father. Even though we had just met, and despite our differences, I felt as if she were my best friend.

"Come visit me in DC, Rosi. We'd get along really great."

I smiled.

"I'll send you my address." She waved both hands in the air and left to begin work toward her PhD, and I returned to my desk, which would help me work toward my bachelor's degree. More than a gap existed between Sam and me; it was a chasm really, but I admired her a lot. To have all that money and think nothing of it was an epiphany for me.

The following March I had almost forgotten about Sam. I was busy with my two courses at NYU and preparing for exams. I was also working on a novel. One of the great parts of my job was that I had plenty of time to create—the office was quiet and conducive to thinking—and the act of creating characters and events was one wonderful feeling, almost meditative, a complete freeing up of the mind from the clutter that inundated it daily. I had few interruptions. I had started my story soon after I was hired. Since I have never been one to sit and do nothing, nor did I enjoy pretending I was busy, I brought my manuscript into the office every day and continued to work on it. I couldn't read my textbooks at my desk—reading was not allowed—but I could type. Typing always made a secretary or receptionist look busy, and Marge preferred to type the chairman's letters herself. As a result, there were times I had whole days when I worked on nothing but my novel, with the exception of answering the phone when it rang and greeting an infrequent appointment. I had finished my outline and was beginning chapter one when I heard from Samantha.

It was a few days before St. Patrick's Day and I had received a card from her; it was the first St. Patrick's Day card I had ever received. She was settling in, she wrote, and getting to know the town. She hoped I would visit her soon. I penned a quick note to thank her for the card and told her since it was the only St. Patrick's Day card I received, it was special. Then she called in April.

"Come on down! I have this tiny, tiny house in Georgetown. You'll love it!"

"I already have a tiny, tiny house, Sam, but I'll come anyway." I could hear her laughing at the other end of the phone.

I didn't feel the least bit guilty telling Sam I'd go, even though it would be the first time away from my mother since college. My mother was able to work a few days a week and was kept busy. She would be fine without me for a couple of days.

I left the following Friday night on a Greyhound bus and arrived with as much excitement as a five year-old at a birthday party. I could see Sam's tall, regal frame over the heads of the scurrying travelers.

"Hey, Rosi! Hurry up! I'm in a no-parking zone!" She grabbed my suitcase and was thirty feet ahead of me before I realized it.

On tiptoe I was able to keep my eye on her as she raced headlong into the weekend crowd. I picked my way through the Greyhound set, clutching my small suitcase under my arm and hard against my ribs. When I caught up with her, I jumped into the shiny black car. I had never been in a Jaguar convertible before.

"Dear God, this is fantastic." I interrupted her babble of conversation. I hadn't heard a word of what she had said.

"I bought it last week," she offered with a carefree indifference.

Sam drove like a madwoman in and out of the heavy weekend traffic. She rode the accelerator most of the time and hit the brakes at the last second. My body rocked until I thought it would explode.

"This is my first time driving. I just got my license yesterday. You need a car in this town, Rosi. The buses take forever. Not like the good old New York subways. Let's see. I need to make a right onto Massachusetts Avenue." We had a green light, and she made a right, which put us directly in front of another car facing us. She had turned too soon, and we were facing north when we should have been facing south on a four-lane highway, on the other side of a concrete island.

"What the hell is this?" she asked over the noise of honking horns.

"I think you made the right turn but into the wrong lane. You're supposed to be on the other side of the island."

"How do I get back?" she asked with a puzzled look on her beautiful face.

"The policeman will tell you." I turned my head away, seeing the furious expression on the cop's face.

He threw his cap on top of her car, placed his hands on his hips, and then finally he walked up to her.

"Do you have a license?" he asked in a loud and gruff voice.

"Yes, officer, I do. I just got it yesterday. See?" She was rummaging through her bag to find the piece of paper that proved she knew how to drive.

"I don't want to see it!" He scolded her in a loud voice. By this time there were no horns honking; it was absolutely post-nuclear shock quiet. "Back up!"

She backed up so that she was about fifty feet straight back, still facing the oncoming traffic.

I couldn't help it. I scrunched down in my seat and laughed until I thought I would pee. I didn't want the policeman to see me. He was furious.

The policeman—very, very carefully—stood to the side and directed her up to the right place so she could back up and move to where she had made her right turn from originally. The light was red. The policeman put his cap back on his head and walked over to her.

"If I ever see you do that again, I will take your license away, do you hear me?"

"Yes, officer," she replied. "I'm sorry."

"And you," he pointed over to me. "Instead of thinking this is funny, you might help her out."

I chewed on my lower lip so I could stop laughing and nodded to him. The light turned green, and he was already walking away. I didn't pee, thank God, but I continued to laugh until I thought I would cry.

"Christ! I hope I can do this," she said almost in a whisper.

"Go straight," I instructed her. "That's it. Now start turning the wheel left. Slowly!" I screamed. "Go straight a little bit. There."

"I got it!" she exclaimed as she straightened the wheel and was correctly in the northbound traffic lane. "That was easy. I don't know why he got so angry. My driving instructor thought I was really great."

"I'm sure he did," I said.

"Are you hungry?" she yelled over at me. Noise from the revving of the Jaguar's motor and the street precluded any normal conversation. "What? What are you laughing at?" she asked, shaking her head as if nothing had happened.

"Nothing. I'm not laughing at anything. Oh, my God! Just take your time, Sam. Think!"

"Are you hungry?" she asked me again with a mother-like tone.

"I'm starving," I yelled back as she continued to rev the motor and push up K Street toward Wisconsin Avenue. "I forgot to have dinner. How long did it take you to learn to drive?"

"Just a couple of hours. Driving's easy. What would you like to eat? You have a choice: pizza, Chinese, or hamburgers. Pick hamburgers. Clyde's has the best. And, besides, it's my favorite hangout. Lots of neat guys." She looked like the happiest person in the world, her smile huge and generous, her eyes sparkling.

"Hamburgers." I felt good being there, with a friend, in a great and exciting city. My emotions yielded to a strange but pleasant sensation I recognized then as freedom. I liked that. I hadn't been away from home since school.

"Great! You'll love Clyde's. It's supposed to be *the* place in Washington. It's really great."

The Key Bridge was just ahead of us. I had read a short history of Washington, DC, including Georgetown before I left New York. I didn't want to seem like an ignoramus. She made a sharp U-turn and then a quick right, and we were down by what I could make out as a small creek lying low below a lot of old historic-looking buildings.

It took almost a half hour to find a parking space near Clyde's. So while Sam cursed and griped, putting the Jaguar in reverse and then drive—she loved using reverse and did it habitually whether she needed to or not, she just didn't know how to turn when she reversed—I drank in the scenes around me, holding onto the dashboard with two hands while my feet pushed into the floor in a simulated gesture at braking. I said my prayers because I knew beyond a reasonable doubt that that night I was going to die. To alleviate my terror, I concentrated on the scenery around me. I tried to see if I could spot a well-known personality. Georgetown was crowded with all types of people: young singles, couples, visitors and tourists, and some army recruits who were recognizable by their shaven heads. It was a beautiful spring evening with a hint of a tropical breeze. I looked for a Kennedy.

"Voila!" Sam pulled into a space that read 'Large cars only' and proceeded to get out.

"Aren't you afraid someone might steal it? At least put the top up," I urged her.

"Nah, it's insured." She ran ahead of me, her long legs stretched in front of her, and I, the short-legged bus rider, strained to keep up.

"*Vite! Vite!*" She called back to me.

"I'm viting! Slow down, for God's sakes! What's your hurry?"

Sam burst out laughing and waited for me. "I love your sense of humor, Rosi. Viting," she mimicked me.

"Well, I'm not altogether ignorant, you know. You think you're the one person in the world who knows French?"

Sam was still laughing when we arrived at Clyde's. The place was packed, and cigarette smoke hung thick and heavy. A Bob Dylan record sent out a ballad that was hard to hear over the noise. Sam pushed her way in, and I followed close on her heels. All heads turned to stare at her. She stood above the crowd, resembling a Vogue model on vacation, but she smiled at every-one as if she were a politician making the rounds. We made our way to the back of the room. The crowd was, as Sam had said, "Really great!" There were more guys than girls and they were all nice looking, very preppy, very collegiate. We stood at the end of the bar, and then I heard a rich, baritone voice say, "Here you go."

The most beautiful man I'd ever seen was smiling at me as if I were the only woman left in a world of men as he offered me his seat at the bar. He was taller than I, but not by much. The contrast between his blue eyes and black hair—cut Madison Avenue style—struck me. He was a definite conservative with an Oxford button-down shirt beneath what looked like an expensive suit; the tie was navy blue with red and white stripes. His look traveled through me, electrifying every organ in my body. I felt my blood heating up and my face flush. I wanted to say something, anything, but the words fused in my throat. I hopped up on the stool and sat facing him. I wanted to speak, to say something to him but I couldn't find the words. I couldn't even say thank you.

"I've never seen it this crowded so early. Anything going on?" Sam asked him.

"Not that I know of," he said, looking at me. At least I was able to face him and smile at him.

Sam and I ordered Clyde's famous bleu cheeseburgers and draft beer. In less than a minute, the bartender slopped down our two icy drafts, the foam spilled over the wet bar, and I turned, picked up my drink, and drank almost half of it at once. It was delicious. I wanted to turn around and strike up a conversation with Mr. Magnificent—I could sense him right behind me—but I couldn't think of anything to say that wouldn't sound dumb. I didn't have to worry.

He leaned toward me and whispered in my ear: "Are you visitors or real, live denizens?"

That broke the ice, and I erupted into a gale of laughter. I swiveled on the stool so that I was facing him; my knees brushed against him, and he tried to step back to give me room. "I'm visiting." I finally had the temerity to speak to him. "Sam lives here." I nodded at Sam, who was lighting some guy's cigarette.

"Where are you from?" he asked. He was standing directly in front of me, almost touching me.

"New Jersey. Jersey City." I noticed he was drinking a scotch or bourbon.

"Really? You don't sound like you come from New Jersey."

"How am I supposed to sound?" I asked somewhat puzzled.

"Sorry. I didn't mean any offense." He leaned in to me.

I was dying. "No problem," I said, trying not to fall for him, although there was a slim chance I'd see him again anyway.

"I did some work up there a few years ago."

"What kind of work?"

"I was a legal aide to a congressman from New Jersey." He looked straight into my eyes when he spoke, indifferent to the noise and everyone hanging over him as they fought to get the bartender's attention. "But that was a long time ago."

"And now?"

He told me his name was Cal Bryant, that he was thirty-seven, a lawyer, had graduated from UVA, and was a legislative aide for a senator.

Sam joined in the conversation, and even though they had a lot to say to each other about the Washington scene, Cal continued to keep his eyes on me. He spoke to Sam, but his smile was mine.

We had just finished our hamburgers and a second beer when Sam said she wanted to leave. "I'm exhausted, and the smoke is making me sick." I could have smacked her. Just when I met "Mr. Magnificent." But what could I have said or done? I was her guest after all.

"Next time you visit, Rosemary, why don't you give me a call at my office? I'll show you the real capital city." Cal winked as he handed me his card.

"Thanks, I will." I winked back, surprising myself. I put his card in my bill fold knowing that in that place – my vault - it would be impossible to get lost or misplaced

Sam's house was an attached house, and the house it was attached to was attached to another and so on. I counted twelve of them, more or less, all in a row, straight, built of brick, one house distinguishable from another by its color. Sam's house was a pale lemony yellow with white trim. They stood upon a crest like so many soldiers on dress parade, with small patches of green lawn stretched down to the sidewalk. Across the street, behind an ivy-covered, red brick wall, was Georgetown University, with its spacious campus and its reputation for being one of the top universities in the country. I thought of at least three more years of night school at NYU.

Sam fiddled in her purse for the house key until, with a controlled impatience, she dumped its contents on the step, and under the weak light that hung over the door, she found it. Upon entering the house, I had the impression it was empty, but when she turned on the lights, I could see a few pieces of furniture, old and eclectic, and lots of unidentifiable things thrown about. I thought of a vacant lot filled with debris. To

the right of the entranceway was a small living room,
and beyond that was a small dining room. "It needs
something." She shrugged her shoulders and looked
around the room. To the left was a small kitchen. It
was too dark to see the backyard, but I took Sam's
word for it that it was "really great."

The second floor boasted two small bedrooms and
a small bath off a small hallway. All of the windows
were bare except for the two in Sam's bedroom. One
large, dirty sheet covered both windows and was fastened by a large nail hammered into the wall at either
end. Sam's bed consisted of an old army-folding cot
that was pushed up against the far wall; a white quilt
lumped in a heap served as bed linen. Shoes—I swear
she had dozens—and clothes were strewn over several suitcases. There was no furniture except for six
small lamps placed around the room on the floor,
giving plenty of light. One thing that was missing in
the house was a TV, but there were ample books and
bookcases.

"I could use a dresser," she sighed as if it were the
most important thing the house needed. "One of
these days…" her voice trailed off.

And that was it, except for a cellar that housed a
lot of dust and some rather large bugs that looked

straight at you with big eyes, the only big things in the whole small house. Sam said they were ancient bugs and had lived there since the houses were built. No one seemed capable of getting rid of them, she told me; they were invincible, but they were harmless and stayed in the cellar. Some people called them dust bugs. Other than that, the cellar contained nothing.

All kinds of boxes, trunks, and assorted pieces of beat-up furniture were scattered about the rooms downstairs. I would have thought that Sam, with all her money, would be living in something a bit more opulent, but it was no different than any other student housing except for the high rent.

"Just step over everything. I don't have time to fix it up. Besides, I'm not good at decorating. One of these days," she repeated. "Want a drink?" All of a sudden Sam was pepped up and raring to go.

"Sure." I moved some boxes and bags to the other side of the sagging old couch and sat down.

"What do you want?" she asked, poised between the dining and living rooms, her hands resting within each other, looking like the elegant hostess amid the clutter. I was tempted to laugh but didn't.

"Whatever you have." Except for a sporadic beer and wine, I was not a drinker.

"What did you think of Cal? Do you think he's nice?" she sang out from the kitchen.

"He's really good-looking," I answered, studying the contents of the room.

The noise from the kitchen was deafening. Glasses were being broken and bottles dropped, but somehow, knowing the size of the kitchen, I didn't think I should go in to help out. Still. "You need any help in there?" I called to her.

"Nah, I'm fine," she said as I heard another bottle drop. "Too good-looking," she continued. "Perfect, really. A few zits wouldn't hurt." She poked her head out. "Don't you think?"

"Who?"

"Cal! That's who we're talking about."

"What's wrong with perfect?" I asked, knowing there was no such thing.

"No scars. He's perfect." She returned from the kitchen holding a large round tray containing two huge tumblers. "Perfect eyes, perfect nose, perfectly shaped face," she said in a mock singsong fashion, wagging her head back and forth. "There's got to be a flaw somewhere. I prefer my men rugged. I want them to look like mountain climbers. Cal looks like a concert pianist. I made us drambuies and coke. Ever had one?" She grinned like a Cheshire cat and placed the tray of drinks on a low-lying coffee table.

I leaned over to pick up my drink and noticed rust covering the tray, which I swear had dozens of dents. I couldn't help but laugh. "You seem to like everything rugged, don't you?"

Sam laughed with me. "It's old. It has character. Don't be smart."

We sat up most of the night drinking drambuies and cokes and talking about ourselves. Sam's parents were rich, I learned, new rich. Their real success came, after many failures on her father's part, when his company succeeded at last. He was fifty-five when he made it, and much to her mother's bitter disappointment, they still weren't accepted in the social circles they coveted. In their lifetime struggle for success, they pushed their daughter aside and left the parenting to nannies.

We discussed sex.

"I love one-night stands," she declared.

"Dear God, Sam." I was shocked at her candor but at the same time I felt pleased she thought enough of me to confide such an intimate piece of sexual behavior. Back then few women would discuss their sexual appetites with just anyone. "Why one night stands?"

She laughed. "Did I shock you 'dear God?' "She laughed even louder. "It's a fast high."

"What happens when you come down from that high? Then how do you feel?"

"Oh, you're too serious, Rosi. You have to have some fun in life, you know."

Her words struck me strange because I didn't think I ever had fun, at least not fun the way Sam did. I didn't have time to go to parties, I was too busy working and studying. But Sam—after she began classes at Georgetown—decided it was boring to study history, and she switched to literature. Sam looked upon fun as if it were the supreme catalyst for eternal happiness, and she constantly grabbed for it as she stretched out her secular soul for it, as a child reaches for the brass ring on the merry-go-round. We were different, Sam and I, but in our differences we weren't that far apart.

I was on my fourth coke and drambuie. Sam was at least one ahead of me.

"Do you like living with your mother?" she asked.

"I never really thought about it. I guess."

"I couldn't stand to live with mine." She seemed angry.

"Why?"

She appeared to be deep in thought for several moments before answering. "You know how you can be in a crowd and still feel lonely?"

"I don't think I've ever experienced that, Sam. I love crowds." She didn't ask me how I felt outside of a crowd. Like Sam, I was a lonely child. My mother worked long hours, leaving me by myself; but when she came home, she made up for it by hugging and kissing me and bringing me whatever cookies they didn't sell in the bakery. Her boss, many times, would give her an éclair and tell her to give this to "my little Rosemary." I used to feel important at those times; someone outside of my little world knew me and liked me.

"I was a late child, you know," she said. "I think my parents thought it would be fun to have a baby. Like a new company. Then, if it's not the right thing, you can sell it to someone else. I guess it wasn't much fun, because they just handed me over to a nanny, and she's all I remember as a child. What a bitch she was. No matter what I said or did, my parents would never get rid of her." Tears dribbled down her face, and she stared straight ahead as if she had just seen a horrible event. "They traveled a lot. I used to scream at the door for them to take me with them. I would throw my whole little body against that door, hitting it with my fists, screaming at the top of my lungs, but they never would. Would you believe that my own parents never took me on one vacation? My vacations were always with my bitch-nanny. They wouldn't even send me to camp with other kids. God forbid I might catch something. Like happiness!" She emptied the remains of her drink and got up to make another.

I thought of my mother bringing me to the beach every summer, where we would spend a few days, and I still wonder about the sacrifices she had to make to afford those vacations. We went by bus, and our meals were restricted to the luncheonette at the far end of the boardwalk. I don't think she had to pay for a room for me until I was older, because when I was very small, I shared her bed. But none of that matters today, because when I think about it, I can still smell the salt air, I still feel the touch of the ocean on my tanned and young body, and I can still see the vividness of the colors of the sunsets. But most of all, I remember that woman to whom I used to cling. The feel of her body, the softness of her tiny belly when she hugged me to her, the skinny but strong arms enveloping me, the smiles she directed at me as I played in the foamy surf, as if I were the one person in her universe, as if I were the long-sought secret of life. I can still feel her hands when she lathered me with sunscreen, when she brushed my hair in the evenings. I remember being lifted into her arms before I fell asleep to be hugged and kissed one last time for that day, and I remember the smell of her—the slightest hint of talcum and crushed lavender permeating everything she touched.

Of course those annual vacations were for my enjoyment. My mother loved the sea, but she detested the heat. She never acclimated herself to American summers. She was Irish. She was used to bundling up in sweaters and raincoats and "practical" shoes. She was used to the wet. I loved the heat of summer. I drank in the sun as if without it, I could not survive. My mother would sit, covered from head to toe, under an enormous umbrella, the only luxury she allowed herself in those days. I would sit or lie about ten feet away, making sure not one part of my body was shaded. I loved my tan, even as a child, and mourned its fading with the end of summer. My mother was white as milk. It wasn't until I was sixteen and began to work that we stopped our annual ritual.

I could not believe any parent would not take a vacation with their child. I visualized Sam in her luxurious Upper East Side apartment alone, except for her nanny. I thought about me in my impoverished small apartment alone while my mother worked. I found it difficult to even think of hating one's parents.

Sam was on her fifth or sixth drink.

"I grew up by myself, Rosi. I didn't have any parents. So screw them! Drink up, pal! Welcome to the capital! Welcome to the most corrupt city in the world!" She developed the hiccups and began to cry.

Poor Sam. Lost in Puccis. Poor me. Lost in poverty.

In the morning both of us had violent hangovers.

"Let me show you how to get rid of these little suckers! Come on."

Sam threw on her clothes, brushed her hair, and was ready in minutes. She didn't even have to wear makeup; she looked the same with or without it. That morning I was just a little jealous of her black, wavy hair, her black eyes, her creamy clear skin. My hair was mousy brown, my eyes were mousy brown. I was the mouse. She was the doe—beautiful, sleek, unique.

The Jaguar lurched forward, my head jerked back. I sat up straight, my eyes closed to the early morning sun. We left the campus and drove away from Georgetown, in and out of the light, morning traffic, in and out as she sped down M Street; I swear she was doing 90 miles an hour. It was dizzying. Constitution Avenue was deserted. It was ten o'clock in the morning. I can remember a near-blinding blur, and then we came to a sudden stop. I opened my eyes again, and an agonizing whiteness struck me. I pulled out my sunglasses and put them on.

"That's the Capitol." Her long, slender fingers slapped the air. "Now we'll go and see the White House."

"Wait a minute!" I cried out as Sam was about to begin her second race down Constitution Avenue. "Can't we even go in and see it?" I laughed a lot with Sam.

She shrieked over the roar of the motor. "We'll come back. I have to show you everything. This city is really beautiful. Corrupt but beautiful."

Sam packed that day and the next in full: a tour of Georgetown, a concert with Leonard Bernstein conducting, a long, soothing visit to the National Gallery of Art, a few special exhibits around town, topped off with a few beers at Clyde's, which was quiet for a late Sunday afternoon. I hated to leave.

"You could come back and get a job. You could share the house with me. We'd get along really great,

She sounded like a child explaining her bad conduct to her mother, and I turned my head so she wouldn't see me smiling. "That's fine, Sam. I'm sorry I have to bring it up, but it would make me nervous having strange men hanging around."

"I understand that and the fact that you have to work for a living, it's OK with me. You know, I'm offended that you would think I'm snobbish. My parents, you know, came up the hard way. My father was very poor, and my mother wasn't too far behind. We're *nouveau riche*. In fact, that's why they're not in New York's Blue Book, which just kills my mother. My father could care less. As for working, my father will recommend you to several congressmen. He knows a lot of people. And you'll get a more substantial position than you have now, with my father recommending you."

"That's terrific, but what about rent? And utilities? What do they cost?"

Sam shook her head and made a face. 'Rent? I don't pay any rent. My father pays for this."

"I'd have to pay something, Sam. It wouldn't be right to live here without paying something."

"Who would you pay it to? Me? I don't want it. Offer it to my father, you'd offend him. He'd be glad that I'd have someone living with me. Don't be crazy." She did her customary hand-pushing-air gesture and that was the end of the conversation.

I considered her offer carefully. Working for a congressman would open more doors for me than working in New York. There were more women in the halls of Congress than in the halls of the American corporation. I would have a higher salary, and rent-free was a bonanza. As for college, even when I would get my degree, what would I do in New York as a woman? A top secretary? I didn't think so.

I thought about it on the way home Sunday night and again Monday at the office.

Marge was happy for me when I presented her with the news. "That's terrific, Rosemary. I'm glad for you, and the chairman will give you a nice recommendation. I'll see to that. But we'll miss you, dear. I trust you so much. Who will I have to gossip to?" She smiled.

"But I haven't said I would, Marge. We're both so different. And I don't like leaving my mother."

"Isn't her cancer in remission? Didn't you tell me she received a clean bill of health not so long ago?"

When I nodded, she continued. "Now, listen here, Rosemary. You're a big girl, and it's your turn to hoe your row. Stay here and you'll be a secretary all your life. Oh, I know, you think it's great working for a top man, and it is. But Washington? That's where the power is for someone like you, Rosemary. You're smart and capable and very pretty. And you have great presence. You go, missy. Make something of yourself."

Midmorning, Mr. Westcott called me. After the preliminaries—that he liked knowing his daughter had a nice friend like me and he wanted to know that she was safe and happy—he asked me point blank if I would move in with her. "I think you would be a perfect roommate for her, honey, and she spoke very highly about you. I worry about her living alone. It might be a nice turn for you. If you're worried about a job, that's no problem. I'll recommend you to some friends on the Hill." He told me I wouldn't have to pay any of the expenses for the townhouse, he would take care of that, and he would see that I was working for a congressman, and so on. I couldn't understand why Sammy disliked her parents. I thanked him and told him I'd think about it and I hoped he'd understand. He did.

The chairman gave me more than a refer-ence. He gave me a letter of introduction to a US senator and two congressmen. All I had to do was name what I wanted to do, and he'd support me. All of this served, of course, to encourage me even more.

That night, after my mother and I had finished eating, I told her. "Sam invited me to come live with her in Washington."

Her mouth opened into a round silent letter. I supposed then it was fear that stiffened her bony frame so that she remained immobile for the longest time.

"Oh, dear. It's so far away. I hope you said no," she said with a steel flatness when she had recovered her composure. She turned to pick up her cup and saucer and carried them to the sink. I didn't answer her right away. I hadn't expected that feeling in my gut.

"I told her I would," I said with as much softness as I could muster. Pity for my mother gathered as bile at the top of my throat.

She kept her back to me and ran hot water in the sink. "But you work for the chairman of the board. How can you leave a job like that? And you're doing so well at school."

I had told her several times I did not work for the chairman, I worked for his secretary, but she could never accept that.

"Mother, I'll have a better job in DC with a lot more money. I can finish school there. And Sam won't take rent from me. She's really stubborn about it. So I thought I would pay your rent instead. This way we'll both have more money in our pockets."

It was as if I had not spoken.

"It's so far away."

"It's not that far."

The steam rose from the gushing hot water—it would soon turn icy cold—as it poured into the soapy sink. She kept her back to me and began to wash the dishes with an uncommon fury.

"You don't mind, Mother, do you?"

It was difficult to hear her over the noise of the running water and the clanking of the dishes, but her protests sifted through.

"You should finish school first before you decide to traipse around the country. You should think about getting married. You should be having children."

"I'm talking about a four-hour trip, three small states away. You crossed the Atlantic." I got up then and wrapped my arms around her. "Mom. Listen. We have no money. We're poor. I have to go. I'll have a fantastic job with a great future, and I'll be making more money. And you'll have more money. It will be easier for both of us. I have to go, Mom." I turned her around and held her by both arms. "I have to," I repeated, looking into her downcast eyes.

When at last she looked at me, she said, "I don't want to lose you, Rosemary. You're all I have." Tears fell down her sunken, work-worn face. I think it was at that moment, looking at this poor, loving woman, codependent upon her one child, that I would do all I could so that I would never find myself in her position. But the guilt began to eat at me.

The following day I received a call from Father McLaughlin asking if I could stop by the rectory on my way home from work. I still owed him the money he had lent me—he would not allow me to pay him back. He had told me to put a little aside each payday, and after a year or two to give him a lump sum. But I knew this visit had nothing to do with money. I did not ask why he wanted to see me. No decent Catholic woman questions a priest. I said I'd be there at six o'clock. I tried not to think about my meeting with him, because I knew in my heart what it was about. I walked from the train station to the rectory, taking my time, wishing I were already in DC. Then I was ringing the bell, and Father McLaughlin stood in the doorway, blocking any light from behind him, shattering the weak, western sun before him.

"And how are you, dear?" he asked, leading me into his office.

"I'm fine, Father. And you?" I sat across from him, still wondering if it were inappropriate to cross my legs in front of a priest. The man was like family.

His whole face tightened, and he looked away from me. He always did that when he was about to pose a serious question. He'd been doing that for as long as I knew him.

"Ah, Rosemary, your mother is very upset about your leaving her."

I froze. I froze because I was furious that the two most important people in my life were attempting to impede my progress. I lowered my eyes away from him and remained silent.

"What about your education, Rosemary? You're not thinking of giving that up now, are you?"

"No. But I can go to school in DC." My anger manifested itself.

"I know you've had a hard time, my dear. This hasn't been easy for you, your mother sick and you having to drop out of school full time. But that's a simple problem. We can arrange for a full-time scholarship for you. Your mother's well now and working a bit. You can pick up where you left off."

I still did not look at him. "I appreciate your offer, I really do, but I want to go to Washington."

He stood up looking hurt, his eyes pleading, his mouth pouting. "You're twenty-one now, aren't you, child?"

I nodded. I was several months short of twenty-one, and I didn't want him to catch me in a fib.

"You're still too young." He leaned toward me. "Living alone is no joy, Rosemary. Your mother has had it hard, God bless her. Don't do this to her. My God, child, you have New York City fifteen minutes away. It's got everything there, more than the capital. And you have a very good job. Why must you go all the way to Washington?

"I don't live in New York City, Father. I live in a cheap, fifth floor walk-up. Sometimes we don't even have heat or hot water. I live in poverty, Father. I live with poverty. All around me is poverty."

"Well, it's not the best place in the world, I know, but we're talking now about your mother, dear." His voice was softer than I'd ever heard, but my chin was still up.

"No, Father. We're talking about me." My finger drummed on my angry chest. "Me. Not my mother. My mother has lived her life, and I have yet to live mine. If she has failed, well, I'm sorry for that. But you can't take away my chance to succeed because my mother failed. That's not fair."

A moment of intense silence hung defiantly in the air, and then he looked at me with clear and wizened eyes. "No, you're right, it's not fair. But you could stay and finish college here. You don't have to go all the way to Washington now. I'll help you get your scholarship back." He looked away from me then and almost to himself muttered, "Something can be done there."

I had always known my scholarship was awarded based on Father McLaughlin's generosity more than anything else, even though my grades were good. How would he arrange another scholarship almost two years after I dropped out? I stood up.

I could not speak, not even to say thank you, because if I did, I knew I would not be able to control my tears. I placed my hand on his arm and walked out.

The day I left home, I tried not to look at my mother. She had been up all night crying. I couldn't hear her, but I knew she had not been in her bed at all, and when I did get up the courage to look at her in the morning, I saw that her eyes were red and puffy. As bad as I felt, I knew I would never return. It was as if when I had made my decision, I had not changed the course of my life, but hers as well. I would always take care of this fragile woman I loved. I would see that she would not be lonely. I would call her every day. I would send her gifts. I was leaving my home, but I would never leave my mother.

She prepared a big breakfast for me, and we ate in silence. I had said all I had to say days before. When I was about to leave, she grabbed me by both arms and shaking me with a ferocity I did not think she had, she said, "Promise me you'll be good. Promise."

"Oh, Mother, I promise," I said, not knowing what she meant.

"Promise me you'll be good." She held me tighter.

I laughed, but it was a nervous laugh. "I'll be good. I promise."

"Promise you'll never fall into sin." Her eyes were wet, and I expected to see tears roll down her face.

"I promise I'll never fall into sin." I almost laughed and tried to pull away, but her little hands and skinny arms were too strong for me. She would not let go.

"So many young girls do terrible things when they're lonely, Rosemary. Promise you'll call me when you feel lonely or sad. I'm your mother. I'll always be here for you. This will always be your home. Promise."

I knew what she meant. She didn't want me sleeping with men. "I promise, Mother. If ever I'm lonely, I'll call you right away. I promise."

"God bless," she said in a whisper, almost to herself.

I picked up my purse and my shoulder bag, and just when I was about to open the door, she smiled at me. To this day I have been grateful to her for that smile. I've carried it with me all these years. With all that was to happen, I've never forgotten that smile. It was a genuine, loving smile, not simulated for show or bravery. It was a mother's smile, giving off a generation worth of pure, unselfish love. And when I walked away from the only home I ever knew and the woman who had loved me more than anyone in my life, the guilt that had been eating at me continued to devour me.

CHAPTER
2

As American Airlines' Flight 45 banked over the Capitol, the ribbon of power that that entity holds emanated skyward, so that my heart flinched with a sensation of patriotism. The excitement it provoked within my soul surprised me. I took a deep breath and sat back in my seat as the plane touched the earth with a soft, short bump. A good landing, I hoped, would be a good omen.

I had mailed most of my clothes before I left, so I carried only a shoulder bag with me. That way it took no time at all to alight from the plane and go straight out to the entrance. Sam was already there, her Jaguar standing out like a moneyed icon from the ranks of taxis.

"Hey, Rosi!" I envied her tall, slender form slung against the Jaguar as if they were one. I reminded myself to lose a few pounds and stand up straight.

The weather was warm and sunny, and I pulled out the extra sunglasses in my purse and put them on. In Washington, especially on the Hill, I always had to wear sunglasses—unlike New York, whose skyscrapers absorbed the sun before it reached the streets.

Throwing my shoulder bag into the space behind the front seats, I hopped in next to Sam, and we sped away.

"So how'd your mother take your leaving? Was she sad?" Sam turned her head toward me, which made me a bit nervous. Her driving had not improved, and she liked to race. Still, I was touched by her thoughtfulness. She had never met my mother, but she always asked about her.

"Oh, no. She's happy for me. Told me to pick the right senator. Thanks for asking. Ah, Sammy, could you look at where you're going?"

"I could if I knew where I was going. I'm not good at directions, but I think this is the way home." She held an eight- by eleven-inch sheet of bond paper in front of her and proceeded to read. "Yup. We're on the right track."

I took a deep breath and settled in for the ride.

"By the way, we're having a party. It's your welcoming party. Tomorrow night at eight." Sam turned and grinned at me.

"Dear God, Sam! Not so soon! I need time to settle in. Keep your eyes on the road." I commanded her, feeling more fear than nervousness.

She looked at her solid gold watch hidden under her long-sleeved, 100 percent dry-clean-only silk blouse. "It is now two o'clock, Friday afternoon. You have thirty hours to 'settle in.' You have to learn, 'dear God,' living with me, you have to move. Don't twaddle. Oh," she added in an attempt at facetiousness, "you'll have plenty of time to settle in. And by the way, my father set you up with an interview on Monday, ten sharp, with a crook from New York. I don't remember his name. I wrote it all down for you. Calls himself a Democrat." She made a face.

I laughed. "You work fast!"

"My father works fast." She frowned.

"Who is he, Sam?" I grinned her grin. "One of the good guys or one of the thugs?"

"Who knows? I have a short bio at the house. I know you will like him." She emphasized the *you*.

"Manhattan?"

"Oh, no, I think it's someplace upstate. I hope it's not part of Albany. You don't ever want to visit that hole."

"Is he liberal? Conservative?"

"I don't know, and I don't care. He's probably conservative, knowing my father. He doesn't have anything to do with liberals. They're all the same, Rosi, whether they're Democrats or Republicans. They all have the same debts."

We arrived in Georgetown in one piece. Miraculously, Sam did not get lost, and miraculously, we did not have an accident. The narrow, lemony-colored house was delightful to see.

We spent the rest of the day putting Sam's clutter away—in suitcases, boxes, whatever was available, and shoved them into the few closets. Sam had bought us two beds and two dressers, so the bedrooms weren't totally bare. Of course, she refused to let me pay for my bed and dresser. "My father paid for it. Don't be crazy."

"The windows are a nightmare, Sam. How can I get undressed for bed—or even lie in bed—with everyone staring in at me?"

"Look out that window," she commanded, turning me around so that I faced two windows framing a couple of trees about twenty feet away. "Unless there's some pervert sitting all day in those trees just waiting for Miss 'Dear God' to come home, you needn't concern yourself. Besides, you can just hang a sheet over them. That's what I did in my room when I moved in."

I couldn't help myself. I fell on the bed laughing. "You mean you purposely hung up that filthy sheet?"

Sam saw the joke and laughed with me. "I'm not good at all that, Rosi. I don't know how to fix windows or buy those things. I've never had to put up a shade. Besides, the sheet works."

I stood up and turned serious. After all that Sam was doing for me, I wanted to pay her back. "I'll do it for you. In fact, I'll make drapes for you, and matching pillows. Maybe a bedspread later on."

"You can do that?"

"Didn't I tell you? I sew. I make all my own clothes. I never buy."

"That?" She pointed to the dress I was wearing, my favorite coatdress.

"This too."

"Wow, you are talented."

"Now let's finish up here," I said, straightening the blanket.

"No one's ever made anything for me." Her face brightened, and her eyes glistened.

We went into the bathroom, and while I sprayed Windex on the mirror above the sink, Louie emptied the rest of the Ajax in the tub. It was really dirty.

"So what time is this shindig?" I asked. "What did you put on the invitations?"

"What invitations?" she asked, scrubbing the tub with a rag.

"You didn't send invitations? How did you invite fifty people?"

"Called them. Passed the word." She stood up. "There. That's done."

"So what time did you tell them?"

"I don't remember. Eight? Hey, it's no big deal."

After the party, when I had time, I'd clean the house. Obviously Sam was useless in that department.

By the end of the evening, the house really looked nice. "Hey, Rosi, we're going to get along really great. I appreciate your help."

That was Sam—useless, but grateful and kind. And she was right. We were going to get along "really great."

"How did you do the party so fast? Who's going to be here?"

"You told me two weeks ago you were coming. Who are they? Let's see. I invited a few of our neighbors, some friends from school, and an odd one here and there. And they'll be some people who work on the Hill. I invited Cal Bryant, by the way. Remember him? Now, listen. The people in this town need about a month's notice for anything, since they're all so important, don't you know? So maybe about half will show up."

Close to a hundred people were packed into the tiny, tiny house. They lined up outside the kitchen, which served as the bar. Of course, it was not a BYOB. I was to learn that Sam was more than generous to everyone. She had put a small card table up against the doorway so no one but the student bartender could get into the kitchen. No one but the student bartender could fit into the kitchen.

Sam had provided enough food to feed half the city. A huge turkey, deliciously roasted to a crisp and beautiful golden brown, its cataleptic limbs sporting white doilies, served as the centerpiece of the dining room table. Next to the turkey was a large roast beef that must have weighed about twenty-five pounds; a paella with enough rice and morsels to serve at least fifty people; a huge cheese board, potato salad, and macaroni salad; another rice dish with beef and sausage in it; tons of spreads and dips; and rolls and assorted breads. Scattered about the living room on top of the small rickety side tables were dishes of peanuts and chips. Even a hundred people couldn't have eaten up all that food. We had taken most of her ratty furniture and moved it to the cellar, leaving a few straight-back chairs and end tables in the living room. Most definitely a stand-up affair.

"Do you know all these people, Sam?" I asked her when I finally got her alone upstairs. "There's more than fifty."

"A word of wisdom. Washington men are the cheapest men in the world. Since this isn't a BYOB party, they brought along all their friends. It's a wonder they didn't bring their grandmothers too. Now, come on down. I saw someone you'd enjoy meeting. Mr. DC himself.

"Hey, Richard," she called out from the bottom step. "I want you to meet my friend and roommate, Rosemary Beckett." She winked at me before disappearing into the crowd, and I could see from the way her back was shaking that she was laughing.

"Hello, Rosemary, I'm Richard Stuart the Third."

I don't think I had ever met anyone who called himself "the third." He extended his hand, and his fingers touched mine. Despite its clamminess I squeezed hard, hoping I could sprain a few ligaments.

I always do that to people who don't know how to shake hands. His Harris Tweed jacket seemed a few sizes too big for his bony frame, and I wondered if maybe he had borrowed it from a friend. The veins in his neck glowed livid under the spacious collar of his button-down Oxford shirt. Richard Stuart the Third was not what any young woman would find appealing.

"What do you do, Rosemary?" Richard the Third asked with a smug grin.

"Right now I'm looking for something on the Hill. What do you do?" I asked him with a gracious smile.

"I am a historian with the State Department." He emphasized the *a* with the same witless grin. "What did you do before you arrived here?"

"I was working as a receptionist." I answered, wishing he'd go away and not liking him. The crowd had us hemmed in too close.

"Is that all you do?" he asked in a rather haughty and rude manner.

"That's all I did." I looked around for someone else I could meet.

"Where are you from?" His skinny head fell back, and his little chin jutted out so that it resembled a large wart.

"New Jersey." I was hopeful someone would save me from this bore.

"Where in New Jersey?" He appeared impatient.

"Jersey City. Why do you want to know?" I wanted to get away from this creature, but it was hard to pull away; the house was jam-packed.

"What does your father do, Rosemary?" I could smell his laundry soap.

"My father's dead, Richard."

"What did he do before he died?" His witless grin had returned, but now it was edged with a sugary smugness.

I stared at him, disbelieving. "You're serious," I said with amazement. He was actually waiting for an answer. I turned without speaking and pushed my way to the door where Sam was letting in another dozen or so people.

"Dear God, Sam. I thought you said I'd like that ass!"

The modern day Pearl Mesta let out a shriek of laughter. "Watch your language 'dear God,' you should be thanking me. Now you've seen a real civil servant in the flesh, GS asses or other. He's their rep."

"What's GS what?" I asked, totally confused.

"GS. Government Service. You'll hear that a lot in this town. Just about everyone is a GS something or other. Now you know what you don't want in this city. See? I saved you a lot of time and energy. Say 'Thank you, Sam.'"

"Thank you, Sam."

Throughout the evening the questions were not as blunt, not as naïve, but it was clear that people in the capital did not have the time for those who came from nowhere. Jersey City is a place one does not come from. A year of college in a small New Jersey town did not make a degree. I was sensitive to their little nuances, to their condescending smiles as they excused themselves to move on, to the tenseness of their facial features whenever I said Jersey City. But I pushed on. If I were to succeed in this town, even if I were destined to be a receptionist all my life, God forbid, and despite its corruption, its power-seeking political climbers, I had to know the players and the game. I had to know how it worked.

Most of the people were dressed well and expensively—the men in suits and ties or sports jackets and the women in some pretty smart outfits. What people in the capital looked at, after power, of course, was a person's schooling, family name, or credentials. Since I lacked the proper credentials, I knew I'd have to work harder.

A small group of four people stood close to the front door. They appeared shy, introverted, as if they had not been invited. They were dressed in jeans and chinos. One wore sneakers that were frayed and almost decomposed. I thought of Sam's shoes with the rotting heels. Two wore blazers over their jeans. None of them wore ties. I guessed—correctly—that they were Sam's university friends, the academicians. I looked again for Sam, but I didn't see a sign of her. I saw Richard the Third filling up his plate, and I watched as the pasta salad dribbled onto the floor, as he stepped on it, and shouldered his way into the living room.

And then, amid the loud cacophony of the room, I heard a voice, rich and warm and familiar.

"Hello, Rosemary."

I turned to see Cal Bryant. God, I can still remember the wonderful feeling I had seeing him again.

"Welcome to Washington. And of course, it's nice to see you." He dipped his magnificent head toward me so that I was tempted to grab it. His smile was gorgeous. The fact that he said 'welcome to Washington' was a nice gesture. No one else had said it to me.

"What made you decide to come to Washington? New York's not that bad."

Because of you, Mr. Magnificent, I thought. But I said, "Well, Sam got me liking this city, and I suppose there's romance or intrigue in distance." I smiled up at him.

"You're a romanticist?"

"Perhaps a touch," I said, knowing I was a lot.

"What are your plans?" he asked.

"I have an interview on the Hill on Monday."

He nodded his head as if he were in deep thought, looked at me, and smiled. "Not bad. You didn't waste any time, did you?"

I shrugged. "I'm one of those people who work for a living, Cal. I can't afford to waste time." Why not be honest up front? I was a working gal.

"You don't look like someone who has to work for a living." He winked as he looked me over.

I wanted to die. He was so handsome.

"Which side of the aisle did you choose?"

"I have an interview with Congressman Barone."

"You're a Democrat?"

"I think I could work for a Republican too. I have to believe in the man."

"Really? His politics are irrelevant?" He seemed surprised. He had such a gentle smile.

"Cal. I just got here. Give me time." I was beginning to feel somewhat naïve, but Cal had a way about him so that I did not feel as naïve as I would have with someone else. Cal presented a gentleness and a warmness I found refreshing in the networking crowd.

"You have to remember it's very important in this town to take a side. Once they get to know you're working for one side of the aisle, then that's the way they perceive you."

"Always?"

"More or less."

"No reprieves?" I asked with a jocular astonishment.

He laughed. "Not in this town, sweetheart." He looked around for a place to put his empty glass.

I took it from him.

He removed a thin, black leather notebook from his inside pocket and handed me his card. "Give me a call, why don't you, and let me know how you're making out. If there's anything I can do for you, Rosemary, I will. I don't promise anything, but give me a call."

"I have your card," I reminded him.

"They're cheap enough. Have another." He laughed and pressed the small white card into my hand.

I trembled as his hand touched mine, and I was aware of a tremendous excitement seizing my very being. At least there was one person in this room I could talk with. Whatever he had, it was something magnetic, and it pulled me toward him so that the excitement it created left me speechless. I visualized him with some sophisticated Vassar graduate whose daddy contributed to the President's Club. I didn't think I had a chance in hell, but he was worth pursuing.

"Sorry I have to leave. Good luck on your interview."

There was no way I would not call him.

One of the group of four people who stood close to the front door had smiled at me when I was speaking to Cal. So, now, while I reluctantly watched Cal walk out the front door, I made my way over to them. The party was so loud by that time, it left any sensible conversation non-sensible. I had to scream when I introduced myself. Still, it was better than standing alone.

"Hi! I'm Rosemary Beckett."

"Hello, Rosemary. I'm Rob Whaitley." He nodded at the other three men. "This is Alan, Ted, and Brad. We're friends of Sam."

Rob was not as handsome or prosperous looking as Cal—not that it mattered—but he was attractive.

And very nice. He was what Sam would call a "mountain climber."

"Where are you from, Rosemary?" Alan asked.

"New Jersey," I answered.

"Oh, Joisey." Alan giggled.

"No. Jersey," I corrected him, holding in my annoyance.

"You have to forgive him," Rob said, seeing me blush. "He doesn't know any better. He's from Brooklyn."

The blue shirt against his tanned skin was masculine. He kept his eyes on me as he sipped beer from the bottle.

"What do you do?" Alan asked, his Adam's apple descending and rising with great momentum.

"Nothing right now." I kept my eyes on Rob.

"Well, what did you do?" Alan's question was defiant. Another Richard the Third.

I shrugged. "Just office work. I was trying to finish school."

"Where?" he asked with a nasty tone.

"I did a year at Caldwell…"

But before I could finish, Alan laughed and bellowed, "Caldwell! Where the hell is that?" His derisive laughter upset mc, and I was about to lecture him on his manners when three policemen appeared at the front door.

"Sorry," they called out over the clamor of the room. "You people are going to have to break it up. We've gotten complaints. Besides, there're too many people in here. Let's break it up, please."

"Hey, senator! Can you come out here?" someone called into the dining room." Will someone get Senator Kennedy?"

The cop's face dropped. "Hey, it's OK. I didn't know." He held both hands up, palms extended. "Just keep it down so they don't call again."

Someone pushed his way from the back of the house and offered his hand to the cop. "Hello, officer. Come on in, please. I'm the senator's aide. Is everything alright?" For a moment I actually believed it myself. Kennedy was here?

The policeman backed away, his hands in the air. "No, no, forget it. We didn't know." He shook his head. "It's OK."

"Thanks, officer. We'll keep it down. And most of these people will be leaving soon, anyway. I'm sorry." He leaned in and whispered something to the man in blue.

"No, no, no problem, believe me. It's OK. No one will know."

"Thanks a lot. The senator will appreciate that." He winked at the cop.

I could not believe what I had just heard. These people were capable of finessing the law, and they did it instantaneously and automatically. They knew how to lie without a grin on their faces and thought no more about it. Perhaps Sam's perspective on Washington was a perspective I should have given more weight. The thing I remember most was how no one laughed, no one patted anyone else's back for a job well done; even when the police left, everyone went back to whatever it was he or she was doing. A matter of course. Part of the job. Part of life. I was the only one shocked.

"Now, my pretty, what were we saying before Alan slipped into his Brooklynese?" Rob put an arm around my waist, and a subtle thrill raced through my spine, not quite as strong as the one with Cal, but a good thrill nonetheless. I fell in love that night, but I wasn't quite sure what kind of love. There was Cal, the wealthy lawyer, and Rob, the poor intellectual, and the capital, the richest power in the world. I wasn't sure which one it would be.

"Wow! Do you look terrific!" Sam looked up from her coffee and morning paper as I came downstairs.

"Thanks, Sam. I hope I get the job." I held up both hands with crossed fingers.

"Of course you'll get the job. They'll love you, kiddo. Not many people around this town look like you. Not many women in this city dress as you do."

"But they have degrees," I said, thinking of all the people who came to our party.

"Are you still worried about that, Rosi?"

I had discussed my concerns with Sam on Sunday. She didn't see it.

"You're as good as anyone at our party, maybe even better. Don't underestimate yourself. So you're not a graduate of Vassar. So what? Few are. Besides, my father is recommending you. They're not going to not hire you. Trust me. Oh, don't worry, it's in the bag." She waved me away with her customary fingers flap.

Her words gave me a little confidence, because I could not shake the stinging snobbism I encountered at my party. All of my life, I had been told how pretty I was, and I seldom was rejected for anything I applied for. I had few clothes, but what I had were smart and classic. I was respected and successful in high school and in the small Catholic college I attended for one year that the rest of the world never heard of. I was painfully aware of my lack of education, and it took a long time before I stopped letting it bother me.

I was wearing the black wool suit my mother made for me before I left home. She had worked on it all summer. It was to be a Christmas present, but she gave it to me as a going-away present so I would have something new to wear on my interviews. I thought it deserved a special blouse, so I splurged and bought a cream-colored silk blouse that cost almost a whole day's' pay, but it was worth it. For someone who was always saving every penny, that was quite a purchase for me, but I wanted to do justice to Mr. Westcott and the chairman; I wanted to look a notch above "just good" on the interviews. I also wanted to wear it because my mother had put a lot of work into it. I had my long straight hair cut short before I left New Jersey; it made me look older, more professional. It pleased me. I felt different.

"I'm not overdressed? I asked, turning around.

"Not at all. Classy, Rosi, *tres chic*. And don't change. Men like that look." She nodded her head with approval.

It was Monday morning, almost three days since I had arrived, and I was getting ready for my interview with Congressman Barone. I had not yet called the chairman's contacts, but I planned to call them either that afternoon or the next morning. I did not want to waste any time; every day not working meant less money in my pocket. Even though I had some money squirreled away, just in case, I did not want to touch it. That was for emergencies.

Sam stood up and walked me to the door. "Listen. If you can think of it as just another part of assholia America, it will be fun." And opening the door wide with one hand and her welcome impish grin, she swept the air with her other long, slender hand, and bowed low. We both laughed, and I was grateful for her humor and her support. I knew then that Sammy and I were going to be the best of friends. She would be the sister I never had. I hoped I would be hers.

Georgetown still kept its post-revolutionary cobblestone streets, which were not made for high heels or pumps. I was wearing my best black pumps, and as I walked, my heels became stuck between the stones, pitting deep holes in them. At that rate I would go through a pair of shoes a day. I guarded them with every step I took as I tiptoed down to Wisconsin Avenue. The bus had just pulled up when I arrived—I hoped it was a good sign—and I hopped on. Having been used to the trains in New Jersey that I rode every morning into New York City and back home again, I wasn't used to the slowness of the bus; it took over an hour to reach my stop at the Hill, but I would have to get used to it. There was no way I could afford a car. Besides, I didn't know the first thing about driving and didn't want to.

One of the advantages to having all that free time on the bus was that it gave me a chance to read the morning's *Washington Post.* I had heard comments about Drew Pearson's column at our party on Saturday night—no true political worker started his day without reading the latest scandal, so I turned to his page first. It was great! He was quite a sleuth to unearth all of that information, and I made his column the first order of my day, every day.

When I arrived at the Longworth Building, which at that time housed all of the congressional representatives, I was impressed. It was huge, and the hallways were wide and long and quiet. A lone Capitol Hill policeman sat at a desk near the entrance and directed me to the congressman's office. First I stopped at the ladies' room, where I checked my makeup and brushed my hair. Looking at myself in the mirror, I couldn't help but agree with Sam. I did look good—

good enough for a job interview, anyway. Still, I was nervous, and I willed myself to relax.

I was to learn, after a few months in Washington, that the women tended to be more casual about their appearance, with the exception of dress-up affairs, as if they believed their schooling would get them through and they didn't require any special look. Like the academicians, they had their intellect, they were above the crowd, and in a way they were right. But I knew that the better dressed one was, the better impression one made. At least at first impression. When they say, "It's what's up front that counts," they couldn't be more exact. I wasn't lacking confidence in getting a job; I just hoped I was able to perform whatever work was required in a congressional office, whatever that might be. My work background was selling shoes after school and later answering phones and some typing. I kept telling myself it didn't matter. I was smart; I could learn anything new. I took a deep breath and made my way to the office of Congressman Barone.

Ann Smythe, as her nameplate stated in bright gold letters, greeted me. "Good morning, may I help you?" Her smile was infectious.

"I'm Rosemary Beckett. I have a ten o'clock appointment with the congressman."

"Oh, yes, one moment. Jim," she called over to an older man who sat behind a desk at the far end of the office. "Rosemary is here."

"Good morning, Rosemary, come on back." Jim Hagen stood up. "Would you like some coffee?"

"No, thank you, Jim."

Aside from Ann and Jim, no other staff members were in the office.

"I'm sorry the congressman is not here. Everyone's back in the home office. But congressman Barone and Bea, she's his secretary, will be here on Wednesday." He sat down at his desk.

Jim Hagen, the congressman's legislative aide, was a man of about sixty, and shared his office space with the rest of the staff. In fact, the congressman's entire suite was composed of two rooms, one for him and one for his staff. Five desks were pushed together, leaving some room for the secretary's desk and Jim's desk, and more room for files that were lined up against the wall.

With his sleeves rolled up, his tie askew, and his white shirt opened at the neck, Hagen looked as if he had been hard at work for some time. I wondered what time the people on the Hill began working. On the wall behind his desk, a good-sized American flag was displayed. To the right the wall was filled with photographs of Jim—Jim and the congressman, Jim with several presidents, including Kennedy, and Jim with other people I did not recognize. I learned later he had been with the congressman for ten years, since his first term.

I sat to the side of his desk and tried to relax. I became even more nervous as he read my resume. I wondered what he was thinking. I had one year of college at a small Catholic college in New Jersey, and three courses at New York University evening school. I had two years experience selling Sue's Shoes during my high school years after school, and a year as a receptionist. At least it was for a top man in New York. Still, it wasn't what they were looking for. But I knew deep down that Sam was right; her father's recommendation and the chairman's letter of introduction carried a good deal of importance and distinction. Other job seekers on the Hill had Vassar and PhDs; I had Mr. Westcott and the chairman. When I think back on it now, I was the one with the right connections. I didn't realize just how powerful those connections were.

"Well, Rosemary, delighted to have you with us." Jim stood up, looking awkward, but with a smile that was genuine and pleasant. Despite his sagging jowls and gray hair, he was an attractive man. "Let me be the first to welcome you to our office. How's your availability?"

I couldn't believe I was hired. Didn't I have to meet with the congressman? And what about benefits and salary?

"And the salary? I asked, keeping my voice level and serious. I meant to ask about the benefits first, but the word *salary* just slipped out. I did not have enough experience with job interviews and had yet to achieve what I liked to call interview sophistication.

Jim cast his eyes on the file before him and remained silent. I noticed Ann was at the desk closest to Jim's arranging the mail. He pushed a paper toward me and pointed at a figure. I couldn't believe it! Salaries were high on the Hill.

"Of course, when Bea returns she'll go over the benefits. She'll explain everything to you."

I knew I would have health benefits, and I learned beforehand that I could include my mother, since I would be contributing to more than fifty percent of her support. That was the all-important issue for me at that time. I made a mental note to write thank you notes to the chairman and Sam's father. Dear God, I'd take them out on the town if they would let me.

"I can start whenever you want," I said with too much alacrity.

"Well," he scratched his head and stretched out his six-foot frame. "I'd like for you to start tomorrow. As you can see, no one's here right now except for Ann. If you don't mind, until Bea and I can explain the workings of casework, you might help Ann with the phones?" He looked down at me and smiled. "But we need someone here. Ann's going crazy just answering phones and getting her work done."

"Great, Jim. I'm looking forward to it." We shook hands and I said good-bye to Ann and thanked her as well.

I was a little disappointed that I hadn't met the congressman and that it had all been so easy. Easy come, easy go? But who was I to complain? I had a job! And at a great salary. I would have no problem paying my mother's rent.

When I reached the policeman's desk in the lobby, he let me use the phone, and I called Cal. If he were in, maybe we could have lunch. I was dying to share my good news with someone.

"He's not in right now." The voice was terse and distant.

"Thank you. Would you tell him Rosemary Beckett called?"

"Regarding?"

"It's personal. He knows me."

"I'll give him your message."

That night Sam and I celebrated by going out to Clyde's.

"What are you going to do about the chairman's references?" she asked me over draft beers. "Don't you want to interview with everyone before you commit yourself?"

Good question. That's what I should have done. But I was grateful someone had offered me a job, especially a congressman. I hadn't considered myself a professional woman. I was offered a job, and I took it. Like the beggar with his tin cup. You take what you can get and be grateful. Today, of course, I would scout out all sides, but back then I was looking for a job, as opposed to a career. Later, women's lib, as it gathered momentum, would teach me a few things. Although I did not have to pay rent to Sam, I still had to pay my mother's rent. I also had to pay Father McLaughlin the money I owed him. Besides, the congressman was a Democrat, and the chairman's references were all Republican senators. I grew up listening to Democrats—I grew up in an immigrant community—the city I grew up in had always been Democratic. At that time I didn't know any other way. I was offered a terrific job with a great salary and benefits, and I wasn't about to refuse. Why go looking for something better?

"I could wait and interview with them," I finally said. "But I see myself as a Democrat first. Then there's the immediate paycheck. No, I think I did the right thing, Sammy, but thanks for your interest."

"Good paycheck?" she asked.

"Great." I answered her.

"How great?" she asked.

I was not used to discussing money with anyone. Sam was different. And I guessed she wanted to be sure it was great, since her father was recommending me. When I told her, she smiled and said, "You have Kennedy to thank for that."

"Not your father?" I finished the rest of my hamburger.

"Nope. Kennedy signed the Equal Pay Act into law as part of his New Frontier Program.

My Irish Catholic aristocratic hero had no idea what he was doing for a poor Irish Catholic working gal before he died. Thank you, Mr. President. We finished our hamburgers and beers and went home to bed. I didn't tell her I knew nothing about the Equal Pay Act.

On Wednesday I met with the congressman in his office. Congressman Barone was a roly-poly man, balding with thick strands of black hair that failed to hide his head. He had a face that manifested true contentment as if happiness were his to own. I was to experience his empathy and passion for people as time evolved, but on first meeting him, I had no regrets about having taken the job as quickly as I did. Congressman Joseph Barone was a personable man.

"Welcome, my dear. Feel free to come into my office at any time. Of course, Bea will be the one you go to first, and she knows just what I want. She'll be very helpful to you."

It was a polite way of saying I needed approval to speak with him, and after a brief introduction to Bea, I knew that approval would not be easy to attain. Bea Close, the congressman's secretary, had short black hair with bangs that reached below her eyebrows. When she was introduced to me, her eyes closed so that it looked like she was squinting, and her mouth tensed so that my hunch told me to keep my distance. She appeared to be one hard woman with no pleasant nature to her at all. Later, I was proved to be correct.

Ann was the receptionist and seemed to be satisfied in doing just that; she couldn't have been more helpful to me. Carol Tyler was the political writer and researcher who spent most of her time in our small office at the Library of Congress, where she had access to any information we needed.

A short corridor led to the congressman's private bathroom and a small pantry. The staff used the restrooms in the outside hallways when the congressman was in; otherwise, we were allowed to use his. The pantry had a sink, small refrigerator, and a coffeepot. I thought of brown-bagging and how much money I would save.

I had spent the previous day opening mail, helping Ann to answer the phones, and simply adjusting myself to the office and my desk. On Wednesday, after Bea had settled herself in and opened her mail, she went over all the benefits I would have and taught me my job.

I did casework: I answered letters from constituents who had complaints that involved the federal government, anything that ran the gamut from constituents not receiving their social security checks, or from patients in VA hospitals who said they were being mistreated, and so forth. I discovered it took a simple inquiry such as a buck slip to the appropriate federal agency to get action. The buck slip was already printed up. All I had to do was attach it to a copy of the constituent's letter and file the original in my follow-up file. If results were not forthcoming, which was rare, I would telephone the agency to find out why. I had results. As soon as a congressman's office called, they jumped. I wrote letters to the constituents explaining the results. Most of the time, the constituents were in the right. I became a short-order PR person for the congressman, and I loved it. It was easy, and I began to experience the first embryonic quivers of power. I did not know if it were a good thing or not. But all of it made me feel more powerful than I had felt in New York, and Sam and I had great jokes over it.

Congressman Barone worked long hours when he was in DC. It was not uncommon for his wife to drop into the office every once in a while, and they would have lunch together alone in his office. Shortly after I began working for him, his wife showed up with a cake and their four children to help celebrate his birthday. We were all invited to join them. The congressman had taken off his congressional hat for that of a parent's hat and I can still recall his face as he watched his kids digging into the whipped cream confection. His look of complete joy when he gazed down on them certainly belied any sleazy power plays.

In the meantime, despite working almost ten hours every day, I enjoyed my life. And my salary was, as Sam would say, really great. For the first time in my life, I had extra money, even after paying my mother's rent. But my frugality was still innate. After all, I had been conditioned to it all my life.

At the end of the day, I was content to take a hot shower, have a quick sandwich, and go to bed. Sam stayed up until two, three, four o'clock in the morning. Sometimes, I swear, she never went to bed at all. She claimed sleep was a waste of time, although she liked to sleep late in the mornings.

As for the staff, they were all helpful and pleasant, and I was indebted to Mr. Westcott for helping me procure that position. I sent him a thank you note immediately. I loved my job. I loved Sam's house and sharing it with her. I loved Washington. I was on a high.

By Saturday, when I did not hear from Cal, Sam got after me.

"Call him again, for God's sakes. Maybe he didn't get the message. Maybe the receptionist has a crush on him. You've got to be assertive, Rosi. Learn to speak up for yourself. Push things. With so many women in this town, you'll never get him by sitting back and waiting for him to call."

"I called him once, Sam. That's assertive enough. I can't be pushy. Maybe he has a girlfriend." I was still in my "inferior" syndrome, i.e., what would someone like Cal Bryant want with someone like me, a *joisey* girl, no college degree, etc., etc., and more etc.

"So, you'll be another. Don't let that stop you."

Sam. The girl with everything. I wished I had just a little of her super-confidence.

That Saturday I measured Sam's bedroom wall and windows for curtains or drapes, as well as the bed for a bedspread. Then I went over to DuPont Circle, where they had a pretty nice fabric shop and picked up supplies. First, I bought several slips of printed material to show her. I wasn't about to go to all that expense to have her say she didn't like it. But I didn't have to worry. Sam was easy to please. The blue with the fleur-de-lis. Somehow I knew she'd pick that one, and I quickly returned to the shop and bought the required yardage. I worked on it that Sunday, a few hours during the week at night, and finished it the following Sunday.

"OK, that's it, Sam," I said with great relief. "All finished. Look's nice, doesn't it?" I stepped back to look at my work. Instead of covering the two windows, I covered the entire wall, and I liked the effect. I wanted to do something for her in return for all she did for me, and actually, I did it for me as well. I loved working with fabric and still do, touching the richness of it—I never bought cheap material—admiring it.

"Now, watch." I pulled the blue rayon silk material aside to show her the lining. "I lined them with black liners so you can sleep late in the morning. You won't be awakened by the light anymore." Sam was a night owl and every morning complained about the light waking her up.

For a minute or two, Sam just shook her head from side to side. Finally, she said. "I don't know how you do that. You are fantastic. It's out of a magazine. We should take a picture of it."

"It's not that difficult. I've been sewing all my life. I told you my mother sews. That's how she supplemented her salary. She sewed for other people." I was comfortable with Sam and although I didn't tell her all my money problems, I did open up to her on some occasions. In a way it was my special education project: She knew there were poor people in the world—she just never experienced it. She was on another plane, and I felt I could never reach her. She sent all of our utility bills immediately to her father. The rental of the townhouse was between her father and the university. She never saw a bill. Anything she wanted was charged to her credit card, and of course, the bills were sent directly to her father's address. Sam never thought about money on a regular basis.

The bedspread matched the drapes. I also covered a few throw pillows for the bed, and their contrasting colors were perfect, giving the room a modern appearance. It took a while—months maybe—when I noticed that her room no longer looked like a Dumpster. And there was a change in her cluttering: It was neater, and she was filling the walls with copies of artwork from the National Gallery.

"Now I can start on mine. That sheet I have hanging over the windows looks more like a dead man's shroud. I also want to run down to the Salvation Army and get us some furniture. Want to join me?"

"You've got to be kidding! The Salvation Army? We're not poor!" She admonished me hugging the pillow to her chest and rubbing her hand over the silky material. "I'll get what we need from a decent place. How about Little Caledonia down there on Wisconsin Avenue. Jackie Kennedy shopped there," she added.

"Sam! That's a fortune," I said, walking out of the room. "Besides, you should see the Salvation Army. No poor people are buying there. It seems to be just us singles living in Georgetown. It's cheap, but it's really good furniture, old and used, donated by the very upper classes of Washington." I had been in there just once and couldn't believe people would give away such great antiques. I loved the old, still do.

"Maybe my father will send me another check."

"What do you mean?"

"After I moved in, he sent me a check so I could get a decorator in and buy some furniture."

"And you didn't?" I could not hide my astonishment.

"Oh, you know how they are. They send me money, and that's about it. There's nothing else. I wanted my mother to come down. I thought we'd go out and shop, help me decorate. What a laugh. When I asked her, she just had a shit load of excuses. I guess mother/ daughter isn't her thing. Never was. So, I threw the check away."

I thought of what I could do with that money, but instead, I said, "I'm sorry, Sam. But if you want, I'll go shopping with you. I could help you decorate."

"No, I'll leave it up to you. I trust your judgment. But I have to pay for it."

The following Saturday I went over to the Salvation Army store on M Street. I hoped it wasn't picked over. It wasn't. I chose a couple of end tables and a magnificent mirror for the downstairs hallway. Sam was thrilled with it. Of course, I would not have her pay for any of it, but she slammed a check down on my bedroom dresser one day and said that was final. What could I say?

I had been on the job only a few weeks when Bea assigned me a new project: answering constituents' letters on why the congressman voted for or against a bill. Jim taught me how to write them, and from him I began to learn politics. "Juggle it so they're excited over the fact that the congressman actually thinks enough of them to have answered their letters. Try to answer them immediately. If the congressman voted the opposite way of the constituent's demand, then temper the reason, but make it sound like he's the only constituent the congressman's thinking about. You'll have to meet with the congressman every time he votes on an issue so you'll be able to write these letters. I'll read them when you're through, and I'll sign for the congressman."

My work instilled in me an awareness of the entire political scene, and I read every book and magazine about politics that I had time to read. I loved writing the letters; I loved the placement of words, the manipulation of sentences so that the constituent would be left with pleasure that the congressman had taken the time to write to them, even though he had not voted in the constituents' interest. I loved politics. My novel was nudged to the side. I'd get to it at some time.

I had only been working on the constituents' letters a week or so when Carol called me from the Library of Congress. "How do I thank you, Rosemary?" she asked.

"For what?"

"Answering constituents' letters had been my job, but I'm swamped. I have so little time. I'm glad it's you on the staff rather than some pretentious incompetent. They tell me you're very good at them. How about lunch tomorrow? Cafeteria, just you and me."

Of course I accepted. I had little opportunity to have lunch with people, and despite being colleagues,

I did not get the chance to know Carol. She seldom visited us in the Longworth Building.

"I'll be writing all of the congressman's speeches, now that I don't have the letters to write," Carol informed me over poached salmon.

"How exciting. I'm happy for you."

"Well, that's what I was supposed to be doing all along, except Bea thought differently."

"What do you mean?"

"Janice was the caseworker. You didn't meet her. She left before you came. We tried to have her do the constituents' letters as well. In the beginning she was quite good at it. But as time went on, I guess it got too much for her, because Bea found some constituents' letters to the congressman stuffed in the wastebasket. Bea said she had to check on Janice because she had complaints from the constituents that the congressman did not answer their letters. So." Here she placed her knife and fork on her plate as she gently pushed the plate away. "Janice had to be let go, but not before a fierce argument with Bea. We all felt sorry for Janice because we liked her a lot." She flashed a look at me and then looked away.

I couldn't help but think that she was sending me a message, but at that time I shrugged it off. I just thought it was a piece of gossip.

"So," she continued. "I had to pitch in and do casework, constituents' letters, plus my own work. I thought I'd have a breakdown." She laughed. "Thank you, Rosemary, for showing up in the nick of time. Now I can get back to what I was hired to do, write and research."

"Great. Good luck, Carol."

"How did you like the cafeteria food?" Ann asked when I had returned.

"Good!" I replied. "We had delicious salmon."

"We?" Bea asked from her desk with a huge smile on her face.

"I had lunch with Carol," I said.

Bea's bangs flew upwards. Whenever she was angry or flustered, she'd let out a breath that blew her stupid bangs straight upwards and away from her forehead. When that happened, I learned we were to avoid her at all costs, but I didn't know it at the time. I had thought everyone got along well in the office. I had always been accustomed to openness and trust with people. Nothing had ever caused me to behave any other way. But in that office, I gradually learned to be otherwise, and in short time I got used to keeping all things to myself, as innocuous as they may have been. Ann turned her back to answer a phone and Bea walked out to the hall. With the conversation over, I sat at my desk and resumed working.

Once I was at my desk, I seldom left the office. The refrigerator allowed me to brown bag, and that allowed me more time for my work, letting me save a few dollars at the same time. I did not leave the office at five o'clock; I stayed until six or later, until I was sure everything had been taken care of. Besides, I loved my work and found it exciting.

Sunday mornings I went to mass and then to the office. I was the only one there, and in the quiet, with my English muffin and coffee and *New York Times*, I felt a great relaxation reading and working alone. I had time to think about my writing. I had not even finished the first chapter of my novel that I had started back in New York. I was much too busy in the office and by the time I arrived home and kicked off my shoes, I was too tired to think about it. I did not have a home typewriter, and it was impossible to type it during office hours, but I had every Sunday to dedicate to my novel.

When Thanksgiving came, I remained in the city because I wanted more time off at Christmas and I planned to go home then. Sam and I joined some of her PhD friends at someone's house—I had not met them before—and along with about a dozen other people, we gorged on turkey, stuffing, all kinds of fall vegetables. It was delicious. I brought my favorite mashed potatoes with cheese, which everyone loved, and it was finished up by the end of dinner. Rob was there, and I spent the entire day sitting next to him, talking politics. Rob's field was American history, but he seldom talked about it, so the day was spent talking about the country politically. It had been years since I had met anyone like Rob. Suddenly, he was no longer just OK-looking. He was the handsomest man I had ever met. At one point he held my hand, and when he let go, I felt as if I had lost something. But I didn't. He asked to see me again, and I said yes.

Christmas came, and I had not heard from Rob. I was hurt. But I kept my mind focused on work, of which there was plenty. Between casework—the follow-up was the most time-consuming—and writing to constituents and explaining why the congressman voted for or against a bill, I had little time to think of anything else. Once again, my novel was pushed aside. On Sundays I worked on my congressional work.

I visited my mother for the Christmas holidays. Because I worked the day after Thanksgiving, I was allowed an extra day at Christmas. I did what most of the other singles in Washington did: I bought presents and went home. I ordered a gallon drum of pretzels from Saks Fifth Avenue in New York to be delivered to Mr. Westcott, which Sam said he'd really love, not just because he could eat them all in one sitting, but because she didn't think anyone other than herself or her mother ever gave him a present. I bought a sweater set for Sam. It was expensive, but I didn't care. Letting me live rent-free was generous on her part, and I tried to repay her with whatever acts of generosity she would allow. On Christmas day my mother and I invited Father McLaughlin for dinner, but he already had an invitation. Still, I could not forget him. I gave him an album of Verdi's *Aida* with the booklet telling the story. I included a check, paid in full, for saving my mother's and my life. I started the New Year with no debts, financial and otherwise, and all of my thank you notes had been sent out on nicely printed stationery.

"Wake up, Rosi; we're going to have a party." Sam plopped down on my bed and peered at me with her usual, cheerful grin I liked so much.

I looked up at her with one eye open. "I'm awake. I was trying to rest. I didn't get in until after ten last night, Sam, and I'm tired. It's my one day to sleep in. Go away." I pulled the blanket over my head.

"Oh, come on. You have the whole day to sleep in." She nudged me.

I sat up, wishing I could have more time to relax, and reached for my manicure kit. I was used to doing my nails in bed. "If you want a party, you better hurry up. You only have three more days to New Years," I instructed her.

"We, kiddo."

"Not me, Sammy, I'm tired. You do it. Besides, have any of those people you invited to my welcoming party ever called us, or invited us to Christmas parties? I'm sure they had some. What do you think?" I asked, holding up ten fingers. "Should I start painting them? Pink?"

"Why now? You've never wanted to paint them before. What's going on? Did you meet someone?"

"No, just to do something different. I'm tired of looking at my little girl nails."

"Everyone goes home for Christmas, I guess," she said, handing me the pink bottle. "There are parties, but not many. We had one at school, but you wouldn't come."

"I was working. Some of us work for a living, you know." I leaned back on my pillow.

"Let's have something smaller, more intimate. Try red, bright red. You're too conservative."

"Our last one couldn't have been any more intimate," I said, putting back the red bottle she handed me, and examining the pink one.

"What do you mean?"

"Sam. We were neck to neck, and that's not over-stating it."

"Oh, yeah. That's not much fun, big parties. Well, we'll keep this one small. Do you have anyone you want to invite?"

I thought for a few minutes. I had been in Washington less than two months. Sam was my one friend. "Can't think of anyone," I answered her.

"How about the 'sages,' as you like to describe my friends?" she asked, thrusting her head toward me.

We laughed. "It's alright with me."

"You want me to invite that creep Cal?"

"I don't think so, unless you want to." I had hoped Cal would call me, but since he didn't, I had almost forgotten about him. "I need some coffee." I decided against painting my nails and got up and put on my robe.

"My father loved the pretzels, Rosi; didn't I tell you he would? He said that was very thoughtful of you." She followed me down the stairs.

"I'm glad. Pretzels for the man who has every-thing."

Sammy was silent for a few moments, as if she were reflecting upon something deep. "We really should get to know people in this town, Rosi."

"We should." I said, making my way into the kitchen and drawing my robe tighter around me. The house was cool, as Sam liked it. Since I was not paying any rent, I dressed warmer and said nothing. "How do people get to know each other in this town?" I asked.

"We'll just have to entertain more," she answered my question as she sat cross-legged on the dining room chair.

"You know what I notice about DC?" I called out to her. "It's exclusively peninsular. There's the Hill crowd, the White House/Executive office crowd, the government agencies crowds. We all tend to be isolated within our own group."

"Exclusively peninsular," she said. "I like that."

"So? Who should we invite?" I asked, as I prepared to make the coffee. "I don't know anyone on the Hill outside of my office."

The people on the Hill were, for the most part, an ambitious lot, and aside from running into colleagues in the cafeteria when I decided to splurge and buy my lunch, there was little chance of meeting anyone. All of us worked too hard. Sometimes there would be sessions in the House that lasted well into the evenings. There were a few bars nearby where some of the Hill crowd went, but since I was new to it all, and since I knew few people outside my office, I went home. I preferred my little house in Georgetown, or Sam's house.

Sam had not cleaned up after her "dinner" the night before, which most times consisted of a Dagwood sandwich, and she prided herself in the creative results. The countertop was piled high with dishes, open jars of condiments, and half-wrapped salamis, liverwurst, cheeses, and other assorted deli products. I put some of it back in the refrigerator, and the rest I discarded in the garbage.

"I can dig up about twelve from school. By the way, Rob asked about you."

"That's the third time this month he asked for me. Or are you just repeating yourself?"

"No, really, Rosi, he asks for you just about every day."

"Listen, I don't want to hear that. At Thanksgiving he asked if he could see me again, and I said yes. So?" I looked around with my hands outstretched. "Where is he? I don't like playing games. When he asks for me again, just tell him to ask me himself."

"OK, OK. Will do. You're so hard on people."

"Are you going to invite him?" I asked her.

"Who?" she asked, thumbing through *Vanity Fair.*

"Rob! Who do you think we're talking about?"

"Of course he's invited. If I didn't invite him, he'd really let me have it. He likes you, Rosi, but don't expect anything from him. He has no money, and he won't get married until he has some and a job with tenure. At least that's what he told me. In about ten years, I would think. Professors don't make much money, and it takes a while before they get tenure. He's very old-fashioned. That guy should have lived in the eighteenth century. He wouldn't think of depending on a wife for any kind of support. Really weird! So be careful. You listening to me?"

"I'm listening," I answered her, without giving much thought to what she said, although I heard what she said. Sometimes Sam talked just to talk, and her dialogue didn't require an answer or comment. I was used to her by then. As I wiped up the counter, I eyed a check, stained with mustard and the faint outline of what might have been the rim of a dripping coffee mug. It was made out to Sam for five hundred dollars. Mr. Westcott's name blared bold and formal from the top left-hand corner.

"Sam!" I rushed into the dining room. "How could you be so careless?" I held the check out to her in both hands.

"What?" She looked up at me.

"Your check. I almost threw it in the trash."

"Oh, that." She waved her hand through the air. "Why don't you?" Her voice was low, placid, her eyes glued to the magazine, her body immobile.

I laughed. "Why? This is yours. Take it."

She turned and stood up, so that she was facing me. "Watch," she said, her long slender fingers wrapped around money I would have loved to have had. She walked into the kitchen, turned on the gas jet, and with the initial burst of blue flame, destroyed the already maimed check.

At first I was speechless. She threw the burning paper into the sink. "You little brat!" I scolded her.

"Oh, to hell with them," she said, returning to the dining room, where she picked up her magazine and began to thumb through it again.

"Why did you do that?" I followed her.

"They could have gotten me a Christmas present. All that check is is their guilt. They're still trying to buy me. Well, I'm not for sale, baby!"

"Oh, Sam, your parents are so nice. How could you be so nasty?"

She turned then and faced me, and I don't think I had ever seen her look so hateful. "Every year I send my parents a list of the things I want for Christmas. At their request, mind you. And every year they send me a check. Not at my request. They could lie even. He could send his secretary out for something. But the point is, they don't even think about me until I show up at their doorstep once a year. And even then I'm in their way. That check is their guilt, and I have no intention to relieve them of it. You have to understand one thing about me, Rosi. I don't have a family. You have a mother who thinks about you all the time. You come from a loving background. I don't." She went into the living room and sat on the sagging couch.

I thought of my monthly check to my mother. My guilt or my love? I went over to the couch, and nudging her over, I sat down next to her.

"Listen to me, Sammy." I kept my voice soft. "My father died when I was an infant. Even though I believed my mother, even though she told me some things about my father in bits and pieces, there were times when I wondered if she had ever been married at all. I hated it when the other girls talked about their fathers taking them out shopping, to dinner. I wanted a father so bad. When I was fifteen, I got my mother to tell me where his grave was. Would you believe my father's grave lay less than a half-mile from our home, a fifteen-minute walk down the street to the cemetery? I couldn't believe it! I remember being so happy the day I ran down with a bouquet of flowers to place on his grave. I know it sounds sadistic to be happy seeing my father's name on a tombstone, but it validated my life. It brought closure. I had a father, even if he was lying in his grave."

"Wow, how sad that is. How did your mother do it?"

"This isn't about my mother or me. It's about you. Forgive him, Sammy. Please forgive him."

"Go to hell."

CHAPTER
3

Ten of us were at Sammy's New Year's party. Some of them I had met on Thanksgiving, and Rob was there. He seemed glad to see me, and to be truthful, I was glad to see him. He arrived in cowboy boots and a ten-gallon Stetson.

"Sam said it was to be a Western theme," he complained with some embarrassment upon seeing everyone else in ordinary clothes.

"I was going to have a Western theme at first, but then I changed my mind. I forgot to tell you. That's OK. Your boots look fine." Sam was removing noisemakers and hats from paper bags. "We're having pizzas and beers, OK?"

"OK with me," Rob said, taking his hat off. *I wished he'd have left it on; he looked like one of those handsome heroic cowboys from the old western movies I used to watch as a little girl.* Then he turned to me. "How's everything, Rosemary? Still enjoying the Hill?"

"I just love it, Rob. Thank you for asking." I handed him a bottled beer and left to answer the door.

Someone had put on the Rolling Stones. I couldn't see the deliveryman's face for the stack of pizzas. One for everyone, I guessed. I led the man into the kitchen.

"What do you think, Sam? That everyone in the world is malnourished?" I teased her as she paid for the pizza.

We sat around on the floor or on the old, used chairs in the living room and ate the pizza and drank the beer. I found myself sitting across the room from Rob, and every time I looked his way, I caught him looking at me. I remember thinking how handsome he was, and what great vibes he sent me. Sammy and her friends talked about academic issues, and I could add little to the conversations. But the pizza was delicious, and the beer was nice and icy, so I was content to just listen. I always found their conversations interesting. The sages, with the exception of Rob, were dissecting the music of the Beatles. I couldn't understand any of it, but it was still enjoyable.

One by one we began to dance, first Sam with Rob, then Rob with me, and soon we were all dancing. I danced most of the time with Rob. Later, after some people left and both Rob and I had had too much to drink, we danced our way through the kitchen and sat at the top of the cellar stairs, where we necked passionately and hotly. Necked as I had never necked before. Then we sat for a long time and held onto each other. Finally, without speaking, we danced back into the living room as if nothing had happened. But something did happen. Something inside of me had awakened. And that something was tremendously satisfying. I had fallen for Rob, and I knew he had fallen for me.

"He can't afford to take you anyplace, he's poor as a church mouse," Sam said to me when I wondered why I didn't hear from him.

"Then I'll call him." It was early on a dark Saturday afternoon in late January.

"Hi, it's me."

"Hi, yourself. I was just thinking about you."

"You were?" I asked. "Nice things?"

"Always." Rob was a man of few words, and that was one of the qualities that drew me to him.

"I'm in the mood for omelets," I offered. "That's what I cook best. Want to come over?"

"I'll bring the wine. What time?"

"Seven OK?" I asked.

I raced out and picked up a dozen eggs, canned asparagus, cheese, and a few mushrooms. We had nothing in the fridge; Sammy and I always bought as needed. We never seemed to have the time to shop for food or plan meals. Nor was it our thing. We were big on takeout or sandwiches we made ourselves, unless we went out to dinner, which was unusual since Sam seldom was around.

Rob arrived at seven. Sammy decided to join us "just to eat." She brought the dessert, a chocolate cake from the bakery, which we consumed after dinner without mercy.

"Great cooking, Rosemary," Rob said as we began to eat. "This omelet is good."

"Is that all you can say, it's just good?" I reprimanded him with a smile.

"It's delicious," Sam said. "Are you a Beatles' fan, Rob?" Sam asked.

"Not particularly. I'm a jazz man myself. You like that kind of music?" Rob asked Sam.

"I like all kinds of music." She grinned at him.

True to her beliefs, Sammy experimented with everything, including music. She would listen to a new style as if she were studying it, absorbing every iota of pitch and tone, before she would announce whether she liked it or not. It amused me to witness these periods of her musical education because I was still playing my Nat King Cole records.

"So, Rosemary, how was the inauguration?" Rob turned to me.

"Great, Rob. Cold but great." Our entire office had been given tickets to President Johnson's inauguration, and attending a presidential inauguration transcended the excitement of living in the nation's capital and working for a congressman. For my first several months in the District, I was on a constant high, and I threw myself into my work and politics.

"See a lot of celebrities?"

"Well, we were relegated to the back, but yes, I saw a lot of dignitaries. It was thrilling. We were given grand stand seats for the parade in front of the White House."

"I'm happy for you." He leaned over and placed his hand on mine.

When we finished dinner, Sammy went to the library, and Rob and I were alone. We watched TV and necked during the commercials, and then he left. I finished off the rest of the wine by myself. I hoped he'd call me. My calling him once was pushy enough.

Jim approached me the first week in February to teach me about private bills and how to research the background of every person seeking US citizenship. I learned there were lawyers charging high fees to people who wanted US citizenship or residency. I could do it for nothing. I was learning a lot, more than I ever learned in school. Of course, Jim supervised everything I did. I was not yet ready to fly on my own.

Rob did call me soon after my omelet dinner, and he continued to call me. Our dates were confined to beers at Clyde's or long walks in Georgetown. If something exciting or interesting was happening at school, like an especially good lecture or concert, we'd go there. At first, we were content with cheese omelets and hot necking sessions at my house when Sam was away or popcorn and beer and hot necking sessions at his house when his roommate was away. But as we spent more time together, we found more of a need for each other. We were close, so close to making it, but I would always pull away. "Let's not, Rob," I'd say. And he would hang his head, shake it from side to side, and say with great patience, "I can't hold out much longer, my pretty." And the guilt would get to me. I gave it a lot of thought. Why couldn't I? What was wrong with me? Sam had had sex hundreds of times, and she seemed to be the better for it. I had always been taught that girls who went all the way were the fast girls. Nice, decent girls did not sleep with men. And girls who went all the way didn't get taken home to mother. But I didn't want to sleep with men; I didn't want to get taken home to mother. All I wanted was to love the man I loved. What was wrong with that?

So it happened one night when Sam was away, and the house was ours, and we went up to my room. The warm, sensuous spring air hinted of summer as it drifted through the open window of my bedroom. I still remember every moment of that first night with Rob. He undressed me slowly, kissed me slowly. I had always thought that lovemaking consisted of a man and woman kissing, petting, and then doing it. I had no idea there was so much before consummation. No man had ever kissed me on that part of my body, and experiencing that unprecedented thrill, I did the same to him. I had heard of it and always thought it was a terrible act, but I was doing it and saw nothing wrong in it. It was a part of lovemaking, part of intimacy, and I wanted to make Rob happy. I loved him. I would do anything for him. That night I learned everything I needed to make him happy, and my world was complete.

"Rosemary, I'd like you to accompany Jim to a reception at the Vietnamese Embassy." The congressman's face emanated a large smile seeing my surprise.

"Great, congressman, thank you!" I had been with the congressman less than six months, and already I was attending diplomatic functions. When Jim and I came out from the congressman's office, Bea's eyes were on me. I had learned not to speak until spoken to, and Bea was the last person I would offer any information to, so I went to my desk and resumed working.

"What's going on?" Bea asked.

"Rosemary's going with me to the Vietnam Embassy next week," Jim answered her.

Again, her bangs flew up and outward. None of us ever learned if she was aware of her own alarm signal. Nothing more was said. I resumed working.

It was not a formal reception, but I did get dressed up. I wore a dress I hadn't worn in over a year, but it was stunning for its shocking pink color and Sabrina neckline. Pink used to be my color, and I always looked best in a Sabrina neckline, which made my neck seem longer. Attending a diplomatic function was incredible; except for seeing the Vietnamese on TV news, I had never met a Vietnamese in person, and I looked forward to it with unbridled anticipation.

The night of the reception Jim instructed me, "Whatever happens, no matter who says what, do not discuss the war or politics. Stay away from the war," he warned me. "Not a good topic. The congressman wants us out of it. It's a dirty war. That's why he's not here tonight."

I hoped Jim would stay by my side and do the talking while I remained mute, but it wasn't necessary. The evening was polite and diplomatic. People wanted to know how I liked DC, what school I had graduated from, and how pretty and young I was. Since I had no personal experience with Vietnamese people, I had no expectations or prejudices. I had wanted the United States to stay out of Vietnam. The body bags were beginning to arrive home, and I resented the fact that virile young American males were being sacrificed for people we didn't know, for a country so far away. I even hated to read about it. But I kept my thoughts to myself. Besides, no one was interested in which side I was on. To my horror, that night I learned that the sons of the higher-ups in South Vietnam were in schools in Germany, England, and France. Why were our men fighting their war? So there, in the Embassy of the Republic of South Vietnam, despite being awed and impressed by the guests and their diplomatic demeanors, I was even more convinced the United States should stay out.

"So what do you think?" Jim asked with a smirk as he drove me home. "Diplomatic receptions are exciting?"

"In a way, yes. But no one says anything interesting, Jim. They can be very boring, but very nice. I'm glad to have had the experience of being at one, though. Wouldn't mind another one." I was comfortable with Jim.

"Oh, there'll be more. The congressman will see to that."

"I didn't say anything wrong, did I?" I asked.

"Why do you ask that? Of course not. You were fine." He leaned his head toward me, keeping his eyes on the road. "You were quite diplomatic, I may even add."

"Specifically?"

"When that bastard gook told you his three sons were in school in Germany, you never flinched. Three in college, not one fighting for his country. Why the hell should we?"

"Oh, Jim, I couldn't agree with you more. Is that what the hierarchy does in Vietnam? Send their draft-age kids off to another country?"

"That's what it looks like."

Although there would be no prince searching for me, I felt like Cinderella at the ball. I loved my new life, or what was just the beginning of a new life. And I prayed that it would last forever.

I continued to attend mass every Sunday morning. When Communion was given and I was relegated to watching everyone else receive, I said the Act of Contrition. I was not in a state of grace. If I stopped making love to Rob, confessed my "sins" in confession, and promised never to sin again, I would be forgiven and I would be allowed to receive Communion. But I would never stop making love to Rob. And I couldn't be hypocritical and go to confession, "sin" all over again, and consider myself absolved. If I were to die then and there, would I go to hell? Would God do that to me? All I did was love my man. What could be evil in lovemaking? Despite my religious guilt, I had no guilt with Rob at all. I would do anything for him in love, even going against every principle of the Church. And what was I to do at Easter? If I did not make my Easter duty—a complete confession of all my sins with the firm commitment never to do them again—I would be ex-communicated. That penalty was an unendurable and agonizing abhorrence. Of course, I would commit my "sins" again. So in all consciousness, I could not confess my sins and receive Communion. I was no longer accepted by the Roman Catholic Church.

My love for God was spiritual, and my love for Rob was secular. My secular love was overpowering. I prayed for God's guidance, for his complete absolution. I prayed every day for absolution. In my heart I knew he forgave me. I knew my God understood me. My God would forgive me.

When the weather warmed and spring was near, we would often walk over to the D&C Canal and hike over its pathway. Sometimes we rented bikes and pedaled alongside it. The canal fascinated me, with its well-kempt condition, its cobblestone walls, its locks. Its history alone awed me, and many times we spent the entire day walking a part of its path, returning at dusk. I had come from a city founded by the Dutch and where history abounded, but you had to search it out. In DC it was there, in front of you, staring at you. I found that thrilling. I thought of returning to college if I could find the time. If I did, I would study history, American history, most likely. But I put it off whenever I thought of all the work I had to do in the office. After all, I had been in Washington only a year. There was plenty of time to think about getting my degree. Besides, I also had a novel I wanted to finish.

When it turned even warmer and the weather allowed, we would find a spot near a tree at the entrance to the canal and spread a blanket down. At those times I would fix a picnic lunch with chicken sandwiches and cold Chablis; or we took long walks around Georgetown. I never gave any thought to Rob's lack of money, to our simple pleasures that cost nothing. Just being with him satisfied me, filled me with happiness. Nor did I give any thought to his moving out of the area. Rob loved Washington and had confided to me that he had contacted a few people at Catholic University and George Washington University about teaching positions once he received his doctorate. I remembered

Sam's words that he would never get married unless he had enough money. I never thought of losing him; it just never became a part of my thoughts.

Rob defended his dissertation in May, and a group of us celebrated at El Tio Pepe's, a Spanish restaurant in Georgetown that Sam loved; of course, Sam paid for all of it. Sam later confided to me that Rob's dissertation defense was received with praise from all the leading academicians at Georgetown. I was so proud of him and so in love.

And then it happened. It was a beautiful warm evening in June, and a soft, soothing breeze made me feel dreamy. We sat on the steps of my house, our bodies touching, facing the university with its ivied wall.

"Let's go in, Rob," I said, kissing him on his face. His movement was jerky as if something had hit him. I was holding his hand, but he pulled away and pushed both his hands into his pockets.

"We have to talk," he said with an evenness that was flat and firm. I had never seen him so tense. He took my arm and steered me into the house. He began to circle the living room, rubbing his chin all the while, not looking at me. I remained standing at the doorway.

"What is it?" I asked.

He was quiet for a few minutes before he answered me, and then he looked straight at me. "I have an offer from Michigan. I accepted. I have to be there in August." He was still rubbing his chin.

"Oh, Rob! That's wonderful! I'm so happy for you." I was smiling, so happy for him, hoping he wouldn't accept.

"Will you go with me?"

"What?"

"We'll get married." He wasn't on his knees, but he was staring hard into my eyes.

"Oh, Rob. Married?" Then the hammer fell. Realization set in. I said something, like "Oh, gosh," something dumb like that. I was stunned. Married? What exactly did that mean? What had I been thinking? I thought he'd stay in DC. Sammy had told me he'd never think of marrying until he could afford to support a wife. I did not expect a proposal. He loved Washington; he loved its history.

As if he were reading my mind, he said. "There's not much money in it, Rosi. We'll have to put off a family for a while."

I had told him I wanted lots of babies. I had too many remembrances of being by myself. But then he said the bad word.

"We'll be eating a lot of franks." He shrugged his shoulders and grimaced.

He was telling me I would eat franks when I already went through my frank and beans and water era? I would eat franks when I could afford lobster now? I had lived on franks for too long to do it again. But I couldn't give him up.

"It's not much money," he continued when I didn't say anything. He would make enough of a living, he tried to assure me, but I would not dress the way I dressed, and we would not have children right away. I moved closer to him and put my arms around him, needing to feel his confidence, his strength.

"It's a lot to think about, Rob. Let me think on it. Where would we live?"

"Michigan."

"Michigan? Cold Michigan?" I tried to smile.

"Don't say no, Rosi. Please don't say no." He held me so close to him that I thought he would suffocate me.

"Where would I work?" I asked.

"The university. They'd hire you in an instant."

"But, Rob, I would never make the money I make on the Hill. And no university would even recognize me without a degree. I'll be typing and answering phones. I would have no real responsibility. And what about my writing? They'd never give me a writing job. That's for the PhDs, Rob."

"No, but we'll be together," he said. "Please, Rosemary, say yes."

I thought of beans and hunger and death. I thought of my mother counting out her pennies to the storekeeper as I, a child, reddened in embarrassment. I thought of our shabby three-room walk-up, and I left him there so I could think about it, so I could think about my own life. I walked down M Street, over Wisconsin Avenue, and then back again. It was as if my brain had turned to steel, unmoving, unable to function, like it had when my mother was sick and we were heading for welfare and the projects. Could I live with Rob on his and my meager salary? Could I accept a menial job after I had worked so hard to move up? Could I do without children until Rob made it as an associate professor? And what about my mother? How would she live on her meager paycheck? We would never be able to pay her rent on our income. I remembered the terror of being poor, the humiliation of being evicted, signing up for welfare. I thought of the vulnerability of poverty. No, I couldn't, I told myself. As much as I loved Rob—he was my whole life—I couldn't go back to poverty and everything that came with it. I had worked too hard to pull myself out of it. I couldn't allow myself to walk knowingly into it. I walked home and sat in a hot bath, and cried until I could cry no more. Then I poured myself a drink and drank it in one gulp. I poured another, because I knew what I had to do.

I had worked on a couple of private bills that did not prove difficult. My first complex bill concerned an adoption for a constituent and we got that passed, followed by a few others from people asking for citizenship. But my big one concerned a man in the Philippines who had fought with our forces against the Japanese during World War II. I had letters from the American soldiers he fought with, some of them high-ranking officers, vowing to the accuracy of his testimony, and urging US citizenship. It was a heartfelt case, I thought at the time, and I wrote up the bill to have him declared a US citizen.

"Do you understand the ramifications of this, Rosemary?" Jim asked me one day.

"Yes, that America rewards its friends. Besides, Jim, he's about eighty or so. I would think it's a nice thing to do before he dies."

"How do you know that he doesn't have thirteen children, forty-eight grandchildren, a hundred and ten great-grandchildren? We make him a citizen, he can bring in his entire family, and maybe that's what he wants to do before he dies."

"I don't think so, Jim. According to the immigration law only he's entitled. Let me call Carol and see what she can find out for us."

"No need. Celler himself has been working on a new immigration bill that will allow family so he won't pass this now. He'll want to wait for his bill. And Mr. Barone won't approve it under the new law.

"New bill?" I asked looking up at him.

"They've been working on it for a long time, Rosemary. We expect it to be law this year. Anyway, scrap this one." He returned to his desk.

"You should have known that, Rosemary." Bea said with a sneer on her face. I noticed her bangs didn't move. "Isn't that part of your job?"

I ignored her sarcasm. and turned back to my work. I loved my office and the people in it with one exception: everyone could hear everyone. There were no secrets. At least during the day. I couldn't help but feel embarrassed. That was my first reprimand and from someone I admired so it bothered me. I should have known about Senator Celler's bill. Immediately I asked Carol for all information about the old bill and the new one that would be pertinent to my work. She also promised to keep me apprised of any new developments.

It hurt to send that man a rejection letter after he had done so much for America and our soldiers. What was wrong with making him a citizen? So what if his entire clan could immigrate? Who would care? He fought for us and I had all the documentation in my files. As a backup I copied all of it and kept it at home. Just in case.

He came to see me for the last time, and the picture in my mind to this day is a precise and clear image. I did not forget anything about those few minutes. He was wearing chinos and brown loafers without socks, a blue and white Oxford striped shirt, the sleeves rolled up, and his blond hair curled thick against the strong, muscular arms. The freckles on his arms lay flat and shapeless. His shirt was open at the collar. He was not wearing a tie. His hair was tousled as it always was, except that it was longer, and he was smiling a sad smile. He had a tiny box wrapped in white tissue with a blue—my favorite color—ribbon around it.

"Come in," I said, feeling numb all over.

I unraveled the ribbon and peeled off the white tissue paper. My hands were steady as I opened it. I did not take it out of the box. I could only stare at the gold heart-shaped locket. "Thank you Rob." I moved to put my arms around him, but he held up a hand. He was going to say something, but then he didn't. He was gone in an instant, and I was left looking at the thick ivy growing on the brick wall of the university, the grief on Rob's face etched in my heart. Had he been crying? My guilt once again devoured me.

CHAPTER
4

I knew Rob hurt. It was the first time in my life I had hurt someone I loved, and had he rejected me, I don't think I would have hurt as much as I was hurting. At times my own pain was unbearable, and I thought of hopping a plane and joining him, eating franks and making love. But I couldn't do that. It would take me away from my profession that I loved; it would be leaving my mother all over again, and how would the three of us live? I worked extra hours to forget. I focused on my job.

I returned to my novel, which I had neglected for too long, and I began to question my ambition to be a novelist. After all, writers write. Although I was writing and enjoying what I wrote, I hadn't been writing fiction. I missed the creativity of it, the pleasure of molding characters with words and coming up with a spectacular protagonist. It was hard work, but it was fun and immensely satisfying. It was what I wanted to do, had to do.

Despite working almost ten hours every day, I forced myself to enjoy my life. I would not complain. I had too much to be grateful for. And although I still carried with me the guilt of hurting Rob, I was no longer guilty concerning my religion. I was back in the grace of the Church and free to receive Communion. But it did not make me feel as good as I thought it would, perhaps because I knew in my heart and soul that I had never committed a mortal sin.

Every other weekend, I took a quick train trip to see my mother, who seemed to be enjoying her little bit of luxury, since she didn't have to pay rent and her health was good. I took her out to eat, which she loved. Other than visiting with my mother, there was not much else to do. All of my old friends had steady boyfriends, were engaged, or married and had gone off to live in the suburbs. A few of the boys I knew had gone off to Vietnam. I tried not to sit around the old apartment with nothing to do and too much time to think. I stayed overnight and returned to DC the next day.

When I remained in the District, Sam and I would find things to do on Saturdays. I continued my Sunday mornings at the office, where I prepared my work for the week and edited my fiction. I don't know how I managed to do it, but I completed my synopsis and two chapters by Labor Day, so I joined Sam and her friends for a long weekend at Rehoboth Beach in Delaware.

Her driving had improved and I was able to enjoy the drive. The ocean was beautiful after a hectic week on the Hill, and I vowed one day I would have a house right on the beach and spend the rest of my life looking out over nature's greatest accomplishment and contemplate life.

Sitting on the beach with Rob's friends, for they all knew Rob, doing absolutely nothing but basking in the sun and swimming I thought too much about Rob, which was not good for my psyche. I needed disruption, I needed work. Although I love the ocean, the sand, and the sun, and I enjoyed being with Sam and her friends, I looked forward to returning to DC.

In October, when I had been in my job for a year, I was given a pretty substantial raise, so I took Sam out to dinner to celebrate. We went to El Tio Pepe's, which had become my favorite restaurant as well, and we filled up on paella and Spanish wine.

"Congratulations, Rosi." She held her glass up to me. "Many more raises."

"Thanks. It feels good. Jim's going to let me write some of his speeches."

"Not bad. Just one year, huh? But you do put a lot of hours in, more than you used to. Everything OK?" She sipped on the light Chablis.

"Are you going to start on that again?"

Sam knew I hurt from missing Rob, but I never let her know how much I hurt. She would check on me every now and then—"Hey, friend, how's it going? You OK?" I convinced her I was. "If you'd stop bringing it up all the time, friend, I might be." Then we'd laugh and I'd say, "Sam, I'm OK, stop asking."

"That's because you're a survivor," she'd say.

"Aren't we all?" And that was the end of it. She never again brought the subject up until that night at El Tio Pepe's.

"We should go out, Rosi. Meet some men. We live like nuns, you know?"

"You? You live like a nun?"

"Yeah, haven't you noticed? I'm home every night. I'm insulted." She pouted.

"Well, now's a bad time to go anywhere. I'm over my head with work, and I signed up for some tennis lessons. You want to join me?"

"Nah. You know I'm not the sports type. Who can get turned on by some red-faced sweating breather whose body is as wet as a day-old dead fish?"

"Why do you have to equate everything with sex?" She was still able to make me laugh.

"I thought the tennis season was over anyway," she said.

"We play indoors. Pour us some wine." I held my glass out.

She had raised Rob from the dead, or almost dead.

I began to help out with the congressman's speeches. Carol was getting ready for her wedding, so she was just as glad I was there to lighten her workload. Her soon-to-be-husband was at risk to be drafted, and she was a nervous wreck. She was sure he would be killed in Vietnam. No one spoke of it, but all of us knew the congressman was working on getting him deployed to Germany should he be drafted.

I thought of the possibility of Rob being drafted and I felt faint. I hoped they wouldn't take him. The body bags were increasing. Two hundred thousand troops were already in Vietnam. Teach-ins had begun in colleges throughout the United States. Protests against the war were building. It was not a good time to be an American.

I took work home with me and bought a desk and typewriter for my room. I worked on one of the congressman's speeches every weekend when I wasn't visiting my mother or playing tennis. Most evenings Sam and I went out to eat. Whenever Sam wanted to give a party, I volunteered to help but would not attend. I'd make excuses until she stopped entertaining. I took a few days off during Thanksgiving week and spent it in New Jersey with my mother. When Christmas came, I took a full week of vacation and stayed in New Jersey. I could afford to take my mother to nice restaurants, to buy her gifts, and she was delighted with all the attention I gave her. I was delighted to be able to spend a bit more freely. It was definitely a good feeling. My mother was proud of my success and finally glad that I had taken the big step in moving away. Working part-time, she was able to spend her extra time making clothes for me. I more than appreciated it. My mother could have sewn for Dior; she was that good. I returned to Washington with a new suit, a blue tweed with a navy blue blouse to go with it. It received a lot of compliments when I wore it.

By January when I had finished my tennis lessons a group of us who had taken the lessons got together and reserved a court once a week. It felt good to hit something hard, right dead center of the racquet. And as winter turned to spring, we began to play outdoors. Tennis filled the meager gaps between work and sleep. I played every Saturday afternoon for several hours. Sunday, after mass, instead of going to the office, I played another few hours of tennis. At home I worked on sample letters and speeches. I threw myself even more strenuously into the work I loved. I became a workaholic.

One day in late March, when I had been working for the congressman less than two years, Jim and I were called into the congressman's office.

"Sit down, Rosemary, Jim." The congressman spoke to us from behind the desk, his plump hands clasped on his ever-burgeoning stomach. His face glowed with what I would describe as joy.

"Well, Rosemary, do you have any idea why you're here?"

"Since you're smiling, I know I'm not being fired." All three of us laughed together.

"Jim, as you know, is retiring. As you don't know, he's retiring next month. He decided to push up his date. I want an orderly transition." He pushed back from his desk but remained seated. "Jim has a few people we're going to interview, but I'll be changing the duties around. And you have proven to be one smart lady, my dear. In plain words, we are promoting you. I want you to hire a caseworker to replace you and have her do the casework as well as the constituents' letters. You've been doing that without any problems, so the new caseworker should be able to pick up those responsibilities. You will still do the private bills, run them through me, but present them yourself to Mr. Celler."

I started to groan. Up until then Jim had presented all private bills to Mr. Celler.

"I know," he said, putting his hand up to quiet me. "He makes you nervous. He makes everyone nervous. He makes me nervous, but he has passed all your bills. So don't tell me you're not ready for this. I also want you to take full responsibility for my newsletter with the exception of the monthly column. I'll do the first draft and you can polish it up for printing. You'll supervise the printers—make sure the home office has enough for distribution and be one hundred percent responsible for it, including the feature story. We'll meet, when you think it's necessary, to go over anything you may have questions about. But I trust you one hundred percent. If the work gets to be too much come in and see me and we can discuss it. Now, I've saved the best for last. You'll be writing all my speeches. Carol is getting ready to join her husband. He's being sent to Germany, and I hope he'll stay there until this so-called 'police action' is over." He shook his head and grimaced as he used the phrase for the Vietnam War. Everyone knew it was more than "police action." She's supposed to have chosen someone to replace her, but since we don't know how competent the new person will be, we'll put her on just the research that you and Jim's replacement might need for now. Let's see how she does. She's going to be here at three to meet with me. We'll have to see how she performs and then rearrange everything again, if necessary. So, Jim's replacement's first priority will be on the house bills and anything legal. He will not be your supervisor, but you'll work, I expect, as a team. How does that sound?"

"Great!" I almost stood up. "Thank you, Mr. Barone. I really can't thank you enough. I'm thrilled." I looked over at Jim, whose look told me just who was responsible for this promotion. "Thank you, Jim."

"Oh, I made one mistake," the congressman interrupted me. "That wasn't the best. The best is, we're raising your salary by twenty percent. How does that sound?"

"Twenty?" I couldn't believe what he had said.

"Well, you're no longer a caseworker. You're in a completely new position now, and that's the salary you should be making." He stood to dismiss us. "You certainly have worked hard enough for it, Rosemary, and you've earned it. Congratulations."

Outside of the congressman's office, I hugged Jim. "Thank you, Jim. Thank you so much."

"For what?" he asked, smiling.

"Yes, for what?" almost in unison Bea and Anne called out. I told them the good news, but not before Jim announced to them that he would be retiring. Bea's bangs blew over her eyebrows, and she puffed on a cigarette.

"Nobody told me you were retiring, Jim," I could hear her whispering to him when we had returned to our desks. "When did all this happen?"

I had a lot of work to do and did not want to listen to her. I knew Bea would be angry that she would not be able to hire the new caseworker herself so I kept my distance, and I did not want to be around when the congressman would inform her she was no longer responsible for the newsletter. That job had been her pride and joy.

Carol's replacement, Sidney Whitmore, was approved by the congressman a few hours later and introduced to the staff. Since she would be doing most, if not all, of my research I wanted to get to know her, so I walked out with her and Carol when all the introductions were over. Carol, being the chatterer that she was, did not give me an opportunity to get to know Sidney as I had wanted to, so I invited Sidney to have lunch with me the next day.

That night I worked past my usual seven o'clock and stayed until nine. Then, as I did every night, I took a cab to Georgetown. The house was in its usual darkened state when Sam was not home, and I was disappointed; I wanted so much to share my promotion with someone. I remember wondering why there wasn't anyone to call. Why I didn't have any friends. But then, that's why I was successful, I told myself; I had turned myself into a workaholic. I thought about calling my mother and sharing the good news with her, but I knew she would have gone to bed. Aside from a few acquaintances to whom I wasn't close enough to brag, Sam was my best friend. Our friendship allowed each of us to brag.

Even though I was never much of a drinker and seldom had a drink alone, I poured myself a drink to celebrate. Someone had told me that once I acquired a taste for scotch, I would be a permanent scotch drinker, so I decided to try it. It was good. I didn't understand why I had to "acquire" a taste for it. Sitting alone in the quiet house, waiting for Sam, I thought about my rise to success. In less than two years, I had moved up from low income and a receptionist job to congressional aide/speechwriter with a terrific salary. Focus saved my life—a complete, disciplined focus on my work. Things were changing for me, and the reality of my workload struck me. I had been so flattered that the congressman was promoting me, so thrilled with being a speechwriter—people would kill for that job—I hadn't realized just how much work he was giving me.

I adored my congressman, but did I revere him so much that I would become the office slave? Casework and constituents' letters had been easy. The private bills did not come up that often, so they didn't interfere with my other work. But now I had responsibility for work that required more thought, more time. I had someone to do my research for me, but how would that work? At first I thought it would be awkward, but I did not dwell on it. I would deal with it as I did with everything else. I was a good problem solver. The newsletter was a once-a-month event. A lot that went into it did not take time, but the feature article and the congressman's column did. The printers did the layout, but I had to approve it. Except for one or two addresses, the distribution was the same every month. Bea had me work on it with her a few times; it wasn't difficult, but it was time consuming.

On a day-to-day-basis, I would be working on speeches, finding ideas for the feature story, and at least starting it. No, I could do it, I told myself. It seemed like a lot of work, but I knew I could accomplish it all. I finished my scotch and poured another one to sip in bed. I undressed and placed my bracelets in my jewelry case. I took out the heart-shaped locket Rob had given me and held it in my hand. I had never worn it. I had never touched it. It felt light. I remembered his face as he was about to speak when he presented it to me—how instead of saying anything, he had held up a hand and walked away from me. I turned it over and saw that there were two *R*s intertwined on the back. I finished my drink as I fingered the golden memory, cool and silky under my touch. Then I turned off the lights and went to sleep. When I awoke in the morning, I was clutching the locket.

Sidney Whitmore was a tall woman with legs so straight, I don't think they had knees; she was not a pretty woman. She reminded me of those intellectuals I had met at NYU who spent all their time indoors—their skin as white as alabaster, without a mark, and wearing thick glasses. Although Sidney did not wear glasses she probably wore lenses. She seemed to have no idea of style. The day we met, she was wearing a rayon dress with large black and white flowers. It was a bit too loud, I thought, for office work, a bit too loud for anyone with taste, but I did not want to be unfair just because she lacked taste. Sidney did not speak. She was one of those mute people who are capable of sound but prefer to let others do the talking. I attributed her silence to the fact that she had told me she wanted to be an editor, and I thought that editors tended to be non-talkative people. But it was difficult to get any information from her, however trivial. She was a graduate of Vassar, had been a writer for a small paper somewhere in New York State, and had a string of accolades I knew I couldn't match. Carol had told me she was a great writer. She had seen her portfolio. In view of that would she be satisfied doing my research? Helping out? I was impressed by her background, but not by her personality, and I wondered how she would get along with everyone, most of all Bea. I welcomed her to the office and offered her my help, but she did not seem to need it. She went to Bea and Don when she had questions, and I seldom saw her. When I sent requests to her for research for the congressman's speeches, her response was swift and accurate. I had no complaints. I had hunches though, and I knew to watch my step.

The problems started about a month after I was promoted. Bea was not happy with the new caseworker and complained to me. I ignored it. No one was that bad, and if she were, I would have noticed. Besides, I had heard through Ann that Bea was jealous of anyone who had more than she had. She couldn't stand to see others being promoted or receiving raises, even though she was higher on the office pyramid and had a big salary. I told Maryann to come to me should she encounter any problems. She proved to be a capable, literate, and competent worker, so I couldn't understand Bea's complaints.

"She's late every day," Bea complained to me one evening when we were alone in the office.

"I told her she could come in later because she has a babysitter problem. She has an excellent sitter, but she can't arrive before eight thirty, and she doesn't want to let her go. It takes her a good thirty-five minutes to get here, and by the time she parks and gets into the office, she's only about twenty minutes late. She works during her lunch hour, Bea, and she leaves a half hour later in the evening. So, we're making out. We owe her time."

"You don't tell anyone when to come in. I do that. That's my responsibility. You may be climbing the ladder here, Rosemary, but I'm in charge of the staff, please remember that."

"I'm sorry you think that of me, Bea. I love my work, and if that's climbing the ladder, so be it. I know you're in charge of the staff, and I would never interfere in your job, but Maryann's work is excellent. I can't find any fault with it. She's not a worker we want to lose."

"You'll never be a manager, Rosemary. It's important that people stick to the schedule." She blew up her bangs and went out to the rest room.

I could have told her I did not want to be a manager; I wanted to be a novelist if I could find the time to do it. One day, I had promised myself, one day I would do it.

We held Jim's farewell party at the congressman's house. There was an abundance of delicious food, which the congressman and his wife insisted we take with us when it was over, including the lobster and caviar. We drank champagne and sang ditties to Jim. The congressman played the piano, which surprised all of us, except his wife. The new legislative aide, Don Kelty, was there. Don was tall, attractive, and smart looking. He was thirty, a graduate of Georgetown Law School, and had clerked for a state Supreme Court judge for a year. I did not get to see his resume, but he appeared to have an outstanding background, and he seemed nice enough, although he was not at all talkative. Of course we were all sad to see Jim leave. He was wonderful to the staff, and his generosity went beyond the office. He was always there to help out, despite his enormous workload. The party was fun, and I realized I hadn't had fun in a long time. It was great to leave my work behind for an evening, and I vowed I would have to change.

At first the office continued to operate as it always had. Bea no longer complained about the case-worker. That should have told me something—she was cooking up someone else, and that someone was me.

I had just finished the August newsletter with the printer and saw that it was ready to be mailed to the New York office. It was late when I finished with it and decided against returning to my office. I felt exhausted. I went straight home and went to bed, which was unusual for me, but I needed the rest. I had thought I was catching a cold, because I was never tired. I had left the congressman's speech that he was to deliver to the union officials that night on his desk, where it was easily visible. That was not unusual for me to do. The congressman and I did not always have access to each other, and many times I would leave my notes or work he had to see in the middle of his uncluttered desk.

The next day when the congressman came in, he wasted no time. "Rosemary!" His voice was powerful.

I shut the door behind me as I followed him into his office and made sure the door to the corridor and to his bathroom was also closed. Although Bea didn't know it, Anne and I knew she eavesdropped on the congressman's conversations from his door in the back corridor. I had hoped Ann was still my friend and would watch out for that.

"What happened?" He looked sinister in his anger.

"What?" I asked, not knowing what he wanted.

"The speech I was to give last night. What happened to it?" His jaw was working, and his eyes were no longer open and ready to receive the world.

A scary feeling came over me. "I left it on your desk as I always do."

"It wasn't there last night. What happened to it?" He got up and paced back and forth behind his desk and glanced angrily at me every so often. I was not about to defend myself. I didn't need defending, and I was not quite ready to go on the offensive.

"Mr. Barone. I'm telling you. I left it right there." I leaned over, half standing, and tapped my finger on the middle of his desk. "So, what did you do? Did you attend the meeting?"

"Don gave me a great speech at the last minute," he said, and looked at me as if it was nothing to write a speech.

So that was it, I thought. I couldn't help it. I said too quickly. "Maybe it was a replica of mine?" Immediately, I was sorry I said it.

"Are you saying he stole your speech?" Without waiting for an answer, he called both Don and Bea into his office and slapped a thin sheaf of papers in my hand.

"Don't sit," he spoke gruffly to Bea as she began to lower herself in a chair. "This will only take a minute. What happened to my speech that Rosemary left on my desk?" His anger was visible. His face reddened, his hands boldly placed on his hips. He stood behind his desk, without moving, glaring at all of us. His jaw was moving, and his mouth was tight.

"I have no idea, Mr. Barone," Bea replied.

"Why?" I cut in. "Remember the caseworker before me? Didn't you do that to her? So she would look incompetent? Are you trying to do the same to me?"

"Now wait a minute," the congressman said, holding out his two hands. "You keep quiet, Rosemary."

Then, turning to Bea, he continued. "I believe Rosemary. She has yet to fail me. But I will not tolerate anyone in this office playing dirty tricks. Is that clear?" He looked from Bea to Don. When no one answered him, he bellowed at all of us. "Is that clear?"

We answered him in unison.

"Now get back to work, all of you. This better not happen again!"

He resumed sitting at his desk, and we departed quickly.

A dirty trick had been played on me, and I had better watch my step. Bea was not a smart woman; she was a dirty woman, tough and without morals. But what was Don? Was he that ambitious to fall to her level? Didn't he have enough prestige in his job? Did he have to be dirty as well?

I made a note to myself never to leave anything in the office, although Bea had access to everything. All speeches would be carried on my person; in fact, anything I wrote would be carried on my person. I poured myself a cup of coffee and nibbled at the English muffin I had carried with me from home. The rest of the day continued in absolute quiet. No one spoke. I didn't know how we would ever get back on a friendly basis, but I was too irate to care. It took all

I could muster not to burst into tears from anger. By the end of the day I felt better; at least I didn't feel like crying. Bea and I sat each other out. When she finally left somewhere around seven o'clock—she had never stayed that late that I could remember—she gave me the sweetest smile, but one that I saw was filled with venom. "Good night, Rosemary." And as if she were laughing, she left the office. I noticed her bangs were perfectly smoothed over her forehead.

CHAPTER 5

It was September, and the day was warm and sunny. After calling a tennis friend, I took my racquet and headed for the park. I still played only on the weekends and only after I had worked several hours in the office. The outdoor season was about over for tennis, but I had signed on with a group for indoor doubles over the winter. I loved the game and played fairly well. I played until I was exhausted. Although work and tennis had served to help me forget Rob, he still cropped up in my mind too often; but time had tempered the pain, and complete focus helped me to succeed in my work. I was also more in control with Don and Bea, and even though there were no more dirty tricks—I continued to bring my work home with me—I had bad vibes every day. Also, Ann informed me that Sidney and Don were the best of friends, and she thought that they were working to oust me and put Sidney in my place. So, at the end of the week, when I slammed that racquet precisely where it was needed, my stress lessened, and by Monday I was alert and cognizant. I was ready to do battle.

We were just finishing up our second set; we had been playing over two hours. I wasn't about to let my opponent win, even though she had the advantage. She was long-legged and had been playing for five years. Her strokes were not any better than mine, but she covered the court well. She returned all my volleys. My strokes were not yet perfected. I still needed a lot of practice, but I managed to upset her whenever she tried to put the ball away. I had to rely on power rather than strategy. With my eye on the ball and my body perfectly poised, I sliced most of the returns so that the ball died on her racquet. I was ahead but not by much. I served into the "T," and she returned it to my backhand. My return was swift, low; it skimmed the net, hitting the base line, and disappeared into the green beyond my opponent.

Applause.

I turned, smiling, smug inside. My best shot of the day. My game was improving.

Cal Bryant!

"Hello, Rosemary. You play very well."

He was still as handsome as ever. "Thank you. My goodness, I haven't seen you in ages. Two years, no?"

"About that." His summer tan hadn't faded.

"How have you been?" I asked.

"I can tell you better over a cold drink... How about it?" He smiled, showing perfect white teeth.

"Love to," I answered, knowing I had no place to go after my game anyway.

"When you're finished."

I continued to play and won the set. The day had been warm, and even though the sun was going down, a cold drink sounded inviting. I gathered my belongings and joined Cal, who was waiting by his car.

"Who won?" he asked.

"Me. Who else?" I smiled, glad to see him once again.

We went to Mr. Smith's, another hamburger and beer hangout, but not as popular as Clyde's. It was not yet five o'clock, and there were only a half dozen people in the place. It was quiet for a Sunday afternoon. He placed his hand over mine, and I quickly moved my hand away. It had been a long time since anyone had touched me—not since Rob had touched me. The smooth richness of Cal's voice still impressed me. I told him about my new job.

"I'm the speechwriter. How about that, Cal Bryant?" I laughed. It felt good to laugh. It felt good to be with Cal. I realized I had more confidence than when I had first met him.

"Congratulations! I'm glad for your success. But is it what you really want to do?"

"Oh, yes. Hill life is exciting!"

"Socially or work-wise?"

"Too busy to socialize. That's why I'm a speech-writer. And you? Do you get to socialize in your job?"

He nodded and took a sip of his scotch. "I socialize very little. Work hard. Getting old, I guess." His grin brought me back to when we first met, and a little of that old feeling returned.

"Oh, Cal, how old are you now?" I reprimanded him. "Thirty-nine?"

He nodded.

"So? That's not old." I liked the way he never took his eyes from me.

"Sometimes I feel it."

I thought thirty-nine was old too, but not in the elderly sense. I thought it was sophistication for some-one of my age to date an "older" man.

Our conversation was saturated with small talk. Occasionally we touched on politics, but I knew what legislative assistants did anyway, and it would not be appropriate to ask him anything specific about his work. I enjoyed getting to know him. Cal was quick to turn the conversation away from the Hill and politics. He worked for a conservative senator who believed in the war; my congressman did not, so we avoided war talk. His senator was not too strong on civil rights, as my congressman was, and so we avoided any mention of minorities. I wouldn't dare bring up women's lib. I thought then, correctly, that Cal was as conservative as his senator, but none of that bothered me. Cal was handsome, personable, and easy-going. And I liked him.

He seemed different than when we first met. After our second drink, I looked at my watch. It was getting late. I was still in tennis clothes and feeling grimy. I needed a shower. He put his hand over my watch, and I did not pull away, I felt a tiny thrill.

"Are you in a hurry?" he asked.

"No."

"Any plans for tonight?"

I shook my head.

"How about dinner? Come on," he urged, seeing my hesitancy. He tilted his head so that his features were angulated, one eyebrow raised.

It was strange being asked out on a date. What was wrong with me? I asked myself why I didn't date, why

I didn't have friends. I had always, and still do, liked people a lot, so why did I closet myself up with my work?

He drove me home and waited while I showered and changed. We had dinner in a small, exquisite restaurant in Alexandria. I had the poached salmon while he had steak. Cal knew his wines and after a lengthy discussion with the steward, he ordered a Chablis. It was different than anything I had ever tasted. Later, we returned to Georgetown to dance. I danced. Cal, more or less, stood and sometimes moved stiffly in a circle that made it even more fun. I laughed a lot. I was happy. I felt alive and vital and feminine. I didn't want the evening to end. We didn't get to my place until after midnight.

Cal kissed me good night on the forehead, and I was disappointed. I wanted to feel his arms around me, to know how he kissed. I wanted something a little more passionate.

I watched him drive away. I wondered why he didn't kiss me, I mean really kiss me, like a date would, but I put it to the back of my mind. I had had a wonderful evening, he had treated me like a princess, and I wasn't about to complain.

I saw him again. And again.

Cal and I were busy in our careers; we both brought work home. Most times, during the week, we would grab a quick supper at one of the places on the Hill, and he would drive me home. Every Saturday night he wined and dined me. He would always take me to an upscale restaurant, and I dined like royalty. I learned a lot about wines. When we finished our dinners, we would linger a long time over dessert and coffee, and then we usually went off to a discotheque, where we danced until early in the morning.

It was such a good feeling to be out and dating again. I liked him so much. At first I was in love with his looks and the way he looked at me. He put me on a pedestal, always directing his eyes upon me with adoration. He made me feel beautiful, and believe me, I had no objections to that. Although we had many hot, passionate, necking sessions, we never went all the way.

"You just aren't cut out for that, princess," Cal said to me one night after a rather long necking session. I had found a need for his arms around me. I had found a need for him.

"I'm not cut out for love? With you?" I asked, a bit put off.

"You know what I mean, Rosemary. I don't want a casual affair with you; you're too good for that. When it happens, it's got to be permanent. It's got to mean something. And I think that's what you want too. Besides, I think too much of you to do anything that would displease you." And with that last remark, he took me in his arms and drew me to him. I fell madly in love with Cal Bryant that evening and thought of no one else.

Is he a good lover?" Sam asked me one morning.

"We haven't yet," I sang out, rushing for the front door.

"What! What's wrong with him?" She raced into the hallway after me.

"Nothing!" I said, irritated by her question and halfway out the door.

"Maybe he's homo," she called out after me. "Be careful."

I had thought about him being a homosexual. Back then it wasn't unusual for a gay man to date a girl and go halfway with her, and therefore the girl would think him normal. Many girls did not want to go all the way with their boyfriends, especially Catholic girls. In those days no man wanted to be seen as homosexual. He would not be able to get a job of his choosing. He would always have a question mark hanging over him.

Men would look at him with suspicion. It was the sixties and the run over from the fifties was still in place. All men had to be married, and then they had to have children. I remember the day I met a neighbor on the bus commuting to New York, and during the course of our conversation, he asked if I had a boyfriend. I said no. "What's the problem?" he asked me, not in a conversational way, but as a psychologist would ask a deranged patient. "What's the problem?" All of us were hung up sexually. Men and women had to be careful.

Although I wanted to go all the way with Cal, I was glad he felt the way he did. I also didn't want an affair. I was ready for permanency. Cal expected nothing from me. He wouldn't let me do anything for him. He was always doing for me. Besides wining and dining me, he brought me gifts—flowers and candy. At Christmas he gave me my favorite perfume with a box of truffles. He never forgot what I liked or what gave me pleasure. And there were no religious conflicts. I was still in the state of grace, receiving Communion; there was a glorious absence of guilt that allowed me a freer, less cluttered conscience. I loved my life, I loved being with Cal, and I loved Cal.

"Nothing's wrong with him, Sam," I stuck my head back inside. "He cares about me!" I slammed the door on her, angry at my own words, angry at the memories they evoked, angry at myself for speaking to my best friend in such a nasty way.

I thought about it on the way to the office. I had given it thought that Cal did not want to make love. He had already told me his reason; he wanted permanency. But I pushed it to the furthest regions of my mind. I suppose I didn't want anything to be wrong with him. Cal lived with his mother and brother and sister. I thought that was wonderful despite the fact that most bachelors lived on their own. After all, his father was dead and I presumed he was the caretaker for his family. His sister did not make much of a salary as a government secretary and he had told me his brother did not work. His mother had never worked. Apparently there were some problems. But Cal was intelligent and carried an authoritative air which I liked and trusted. He was gentle, and when he touched me, it was a wonderful feeling. He was passionate too. No man who necked and kissed as passionately as Cal could have anything wrong with him. So, once more, I pushed it from my mind. Even though women's lib was working its way through the American woman's life, there were those of us who did not want to be sexually free. I had had enough sexual freedom. And what did it do for me? It gave me pain to last a lifetime and an invitation to a lifetime of poverty if I accepted. No. I was on a high when I dated Cal, happy and satisfied.

Cal proposed to me on Valentine's Day. The one-carat diamond shone brilliantly, and for the first time in my life, I didn't care about being pretentious. I showed off my ring to everyone. I was, at long last, or it seemed then, ecstatic. I never wanted that feeling to stop. I finally had everything I wanted.

Shortly after we were engaged, Cal brought me to meet his family.

"Will you stop fussing with yourself in that mirror?" Sam laughed. "You look really great!" Sam lay across my unmade bed with her shoes on.

At the last minute I decided to wear my black wool suit with the beige blouse. Although it was getting old, it still made a good impression, and I hoped it would do the same that night.

"Maybe I should wear a dress. The suit's too stuffy. What do you think?" I twirled so she could see the back of the suit. Just then the doorbell rang. "I guess it's the suit. It's OK?" I bit my lower lip in a plea.

"You look *magnifique*! Go answer the door."

When I saw Cal's approving glance, my spirits lifted. How could I be nervous? Cal would never put me in an uncomfortable situation. I knew I would love his family.

He brought me flowers—a spring bouquet—and after placing them in tepid water, I called goodnight to Sam and left to met his family, my future family. We were halfway to his house when Cal broke the news.

"I think I should warn you about my brother."

I smiled. "Is he dangerous?"

Cal kept his eyes on the road. His jaw was clenched; cold steel anger laced his answer.

"He's retarded. It's not something we brag about, but we don't hide it either. Nor do we show him off." He reached over and took my hand in his. "I'm sorry if I should have told you this before."

My heart broke for him and I scrunched over so that we were touching. "Cal, I'm sorry. How old is he?"

"Thirty-one."

"How did it happen?"

"Don't ask." He let go of my hand. "Please don't ask anyone that question."

I didn't ask again, but I wanted to know. Was his brother born that way? Was it a kind of retardation that runs in families? What were the chances of our own children being born retarded? Was it some kind of accident? I knew nothing about retardation. What would I say to him when I met him? Should I try to hold a conversation with him? Dozens of questions ran through my mind, and I was about to ask one of Cal, but then thought better of it. Tonight was obviously not the right time to discuss his brother. I would wait. Another time. But soon, I told myself. I would have to know.

Cal's home was a two-story white-brick colonial, with thick vines of ivy covering one wall. It was set far back from the street, its landscaping of holly and evergreens perfectly manicured. The house was dark, and I wondered if they hadn't left, but once we were inside, Cal turned on a light, illuminating the front hallway.

"I think everyone's in the kitchen. I'll get them." He hung my coat in the hall closet and showed me into the living room. A slight haze of light shined from the back of the house, but otherwise the living room was also dark. Cal turned on a lamp next to the couch, lighting up only that specific area, and I had to laugh to myself: I thought I was frugal, but I loved lights, and many nights I went to sleep with the lights on. Despite the darkness it was possible to make out the furnishings.

They appeared to be old, yet fine and rich looking. I remember thinking that they must have had a lot of money at one time although his father had been an administrator in a government agency.

He went out, leaving me alone in the large, dimly lighted room and did not return for at least ten minutes. I wasn't quite sure what I should be doing, so I simply sat at the far end of the sofa, next to the lamp, the only light turned on, and waited. Despite the volume of furniture and paintings on the walls, the room seemed empty. Finally, when my discomfort began to grow, Cal returned with his mother, sister and brother.

"Rosemary, I want to introduce my mother, Barbara." He reached over and turned on a ceiling light so that the room came alive with people and furniture and things, and I relaxed more.

From a distance, Barbara was a beautiful woman. She had black hair and black eyes, and her large smile never faded. Her teeth were perfect and brilliantly white. But up close, her face was unpleasant. It was only when one came near could one see that it was too big for her body, and a chiseled meanness was clearly visible. She was perfectly groomed—like her landscaping—and she wore just the right amount of makeup. Her face was young, although the lines it housed were plentiful—fine and thin, like so many paper cuts. Despite her graciousness—she could have been a diplomat—I couldn't warm up to her. Indeed, I was afraid of her. She spoke her words as if they were lines in a play, as if she were rehearsing for a role. She was a short woman, but by holding her head slightly back and with her chin thrust forward, she gave the appearance of being taller than she was. She wore a rich brown and red tweed suit with a light red cashmere sweater. Her shoes were chosen for comfort. She looked expensive.

"I am so very pleased to meet you finally, my dear. Callie has told me so much about you." She held out her five fingers, and I reached for them. They were dry and hard.

"And this is Francine," Cal introduced his sister.

The name did not suit her. Cal had already told me Francine's age, but she seemed far older than twenty-one. She was mousy looking, I thought, too quiet. She did not speak to me when Cal introduced us; she only smiled insipidly and nodded. Her skin was white beyond what white should be on a human being, and I thought for a moment that perhaps she had been ill and kept indoors all of her life. Her face was filled with red freckles, blatant and gross. She was the antithesis of her mother. Barbara was strong, the ground that held the living, but Francine was weak, like a thin, weather-beaten reed.

"And this is Warren. Say hello, Warren. This is Rosemary."

His brother stood, or bent over, his six-foot frame and wide girth blocking the little light in the room so that I had to squint to see his face. He grinned an imbecile's grin, and I expected him to salivate at any moment. He wore an ill-fitting suit that hung from his unshapely figure, and he too was milky white in complexion. His mother gripped him tightly by the arm as she introduced us.

I spoke softly to him, feeling a great pity for this poor retarded man who could only gurgle unintelligible sounds. He began to move and squirm about, his gurgles fading.

"Warren will watch some television while we have dinner. He's already had his supper. He's not comfortable around strangers. Callie, dear, take your sister and Rosemary into the dining room. We will eat immediately."

As Barbara led Warren into another room, Cal, Francine, and I went into the dining room. Cal held my chair, and I sucked in my breath and willed myself to relax. It would have been nicer to have sat and talked before dinner, to get to know one another. Although Barbara was gracious and pleasant, I had a bad feeling with her, a feeling that told me to always watch my back. I observed Cal as he seated Francine at the table. It was clear that he was the strong one in the family, the one they leaned on, the one that I leaned on.

The dining room was lit by a chandelier that appeared to be crystal and very old. Candles in silver candlesticks glimmered on the cherry wood table, their light casting a homey sheen over the table setting. I touched the top of the table and leaned slightly over so that I saw my face in it—a blur in the family possessions. Black and red roses dominated the old wallpaper and accentuated the thick, heavy moldings around the ceiling. Everything in that room was old and tasteful.

I attempted a conversation with Francine.

"Cal tells me you're working at the department of commerce, Francine. That must be interesting."

She looked at Cal, and her mouth moved, I guessed to simulate a smile.

I looked at Cal and smiled a pleasant smile.

After a pause of about ten seconds, Cal spoke.

"Francine would prefer to work closer to home. She finds the District a bit frightening at times."

"Especially at night, Callie." Barbara had taken her place at the opposite end of the table, to my right. I sat at Cal's left. "I worry so much about her." She turned to me then and passed a platter of roast beef, cooked medium rare. It looked delicious, but I was not very hungry. "She works a lot of overtime. Do you do much overtime on the Hill, Rosemary?"

"Quite a bit, actually," I said, helping myself to the roast.

"Then how do you travel home? Isn't it danger-ous?" She put her knife and fork down as if she had finished eating.

"No. I take a taxi. There's always a guard to escort us and wait with us. It's really safe." I passed the roast beef over to Cal.

Barbara smiled a larger smile. "That can become expensive in time. Do you take a cab every night?" She reached to the side and removed bowls and platters of food from a glass and chrome cart and proceeded to pass them to us.

I did not like the suspicious nuance, as if I were doing something wrong or hiding something. "Cabs in the District are inexpensive, Barbara. In fact, it's cheaper than owning a car, factoring in the cost of the car, insurance, maintenance, gas, and so forth. And I don't have the problems of a car." I tried to smile her smile.

"We'll have to change that, Rosemary," Cal said. "We'll have to get you a car."

I relaxed when he spoke to me as if words were abstract massages, as if they could heal the growing stress within me. "But I don't know how to drive. And I don't want to learn," I added with a tenuous defiance. I helped myself to a mysterious conglomeration which turned out to be potatoes au gratin.

"I'll teach you. You'll love driving."

"How do you like it on the Hill, dear? Is it exciting?" Barbara changed the subject.

"I love it." I smiled back at her, feeling the tenseness of my mouth.

"Oh, Cal does too. He's dedicated to his senator. Callie, what's happening to that bill you're pushing on the senator?" Barbara asked.

Cal's face darkened. "Let's not talk business or politics, Mother. This is not the night for it."

"Well, don't you think Rosemary would want to know too?" Suddenly Barbara seemed unsure of herself.

She fidgeted, casting her eyes from Francine back to Cal. Then she turned to me, and her smile returned. "Cal's working on a rezoning project. The senator isn't in favor of it, but Cal thinks it would be terrific for his district."

"Mother! Enough!" It was the first time I heard Cal raise his voice.

"What kind of rezoning, Cal?" I asked.

Cal turned to Francine. "Go in there and see if he's alright. Make sure he's not making a mess." His tone was militaristic.

Without the slightest hesitation, Francine left the table.

"Well?" I looked at Cal.

"Well, what?" he asked quietly.

"You can't discuss your work with your family?" I teased him.

He said nothing.

"I'm sorry, dear." Barbara turned to me. "I just love talking politics. It's so interesting."

I found it difficult to relax with Barbara, watching her stiff smile plastered on her face, moving only to grow larger and then to recede to normalcy. She never stopped smiling. Her eyes clutched at me. Francine avoided looking at any of us. I thought she was terribly introverted, and decided that I would have to get to know her. I would do her up, fix her hair, put some makeup on her. Francine wasn't ugly, she was just horrendously plain.

"And when will we be meeting your mother, Rosemary?"

I lowered my eyes. I hadn't given any thought to that at all. My mother would not be up to meeting Cal's family. Barbara would consume her. It was a situation to be avoided. I smiled her smile. "Soon. Cal told me you were born in this house, Barbara."

"Yes. My grandparents moved in the day they were married. And my parents lived with them soon after they married. I was born in the bedroom I sleep in now. And I married here. I never left." Her large smile insinuated pride. "You see," she said, spreading her delicate hands outwardly, "we're still here." She remained fixated upon me for too long a time, and I wondered if she were giving me a message. Were Cal and I expected to move in? Another situation to be avoided.

The roast beef was delicious and tender. Barbara also served creamed onions and a green salad. She was an excellent cook. Dessert was a blueberry pie she baked herself. She promised to give me the recipe, but I don't know if I ever received it.

Looking back to that evening now, I remember not liking Barbara. Despite her plastered smile, her genteel graciousness, her glibness, I felt malice within her and longed to retreat. Francine didn't speak, so I only suffered a slight awkwardness with her. But every time I looked at Cal, I relaxed, and any uneasiness I previously felt had disappeared.

That night, long after I left Barbara and Francine and Warren, after I had kissed Cal good night and gone to my room, I wondered if I should proceed with my engagement and marriage plans. The strangeness of his family unnerved me. But Cal wasn't weird. He was an intelligent, kind individual who loved me, and I loved him, and we were very compatible. My love ran deep, and I was finished thinking about Rob. Then why did I have doubts? Had I expected Cal's family to rush toward me with open arms? So they weren't going to be my best friends. They weren't people one would like immediately. They were still Cal's family. My thoughts made it difficult for me to settle down. I was used to reading before going to sleep, but that night I couldn't read through a page. Something was brushing against me. Perhaps I should have a longer engagement, I remember thinking.

I did not sleep well that night. I dreamed of my mother. I was looking out a window, and I could see her small, dark, and bent figure, silhouetted by a neon light from the boulevard behind her. Her shoulders were hunched as if they could no longer manage the heaviness of the shopping bags she carried in each hand. I was a child, and I was crying. I didn't know why I cried because I was excited to see my mother coming home. I ran down the stairs to greet her, and then she was sitting in an armchair, and I was kneeling on the floor in our living room, taking off her black-laced shoes that she wore at work. "Don't look at my veins, Rosemary. Don't look at my veins," she scolded me softly as she patted the top of my head. My eyes had been shut, but I opened them in disobedience. I saw that the ugly varicose veins, knotted and thick from the years of standing and working, were now greenish-black, and they were bulging, growing, turning into snakes and crawly things, and I ran into the bathroom and threw up.

In April we bought a two-story house in Arlington, Virginia. It was the first and only one I saw. Cal had found the real estate agent. He called me at the office the day he found it.

"I told her what we were looking for, the location we wanted, the price we could afford, and when she found it to let us know. House hunting shouldn't be a problem. That's what those agents get paid for. So, when do you want to see it before we make our offer?"

It was a relief to know that I would have my own house; in the back of my mind I had expected him to want me to move into his mother's house. I was thrilled at the thought of my very own home. I didn't care that I didn't have the chance to see it first or to house hunt as other people do; my relief overcame all my worries. I was, however, surprised by the authority of his tone, but I attributed it to the act of purchasing a house. There's so much to think about. When I mentioned to people that my fiancé and I were going to buy a house, I learned just what it takes to find what you want. I heard horror stories about working with a real estate agent and horror stories about not working with a real estate agent. I received a lot of tips on what to look for, names of the best lawyer for closing. But what was the use? I had absolutely nothing to do with the choice of my future home, except to approve it. I wonder now what he would have done if I had said I didn't like it.

It was a beautiful spring day when I saw it. The weather was warm, the sky a magnificent blue with only a few wispy clouds. The sun waxed light and hinted of summer. I had caught up with all of my work, and I was feeling free and unrestrained. The agent was waiting for us as we drove up. True to Cal's words, it was precisely what we wanted: red brick, ivied on one side, a large backyard where I planned to have my garden, an old-fashioned colonial garden, and an herb bed close to the back door. A neglected strawberry patch wound its way around one side of the house, close to the foundation. In the back, beyond a black oak tree, a blackberry patch had been growing for several years. It too had been neglected, but a lifetime in a city apartment made me crazy for anything green, and I could barely wait to get my hands in it.

"Come on, darling. Let's see the inside first. The yard is secondary." Cal was in a hurry, and I pulled myself away from my future garden and joined him in the living room.

On the first floor was a living room, dining room, and an eat-in kitchen. They were big and spacious rooms, and I could visualize a high chair in the middle of the kitchen. Behind the kitchen was a glassed-in porch. I'd paint the inside walls a sunny yellow and furnish it with white wicker furniture with yellow cushions. It faced south.

Upstairs was a master bedroom with its own bath, two smaller bedrooms, and a hall bath. We both decided that one bedroom would be our office, and the other would be a guest room. The house had a full basement, which had not been used for anything but storage of junk.

"This will be great as a recreation room, Rosemary. I'm going to panel it in walnut—not the cheap crap that everyone uses in their basements, but the better kind. It will look good. Warren can do that. You know, he's simple, but he's good with his hands. He's a great house painter, and he has done a lot of repairs for us. If you need anything done at all, let him help you."

"Oh, Cal," I sang out. "It's magnificent. How much?" I looked up at him.

He took me in his arms and hugged me. "You don't worry about money, sweetheart. I'll take care of all that." Then he kissed me and I felt so good I did not wait for the answer I would have liked to have heard.

"I'm going to fill it with children. We'll have huge family dinners. Christmas trees, and Easter egg hunts." I spun around the kitchen.

Cal laughed at me. "Whoa! Not so soon, sweetheart. All in good time."

I immersed myself in my dreams, my fantasy. I would cook my first turkey here. I would teach my children to cook, to sew. I would read the great children's classics to them: *Jane Eyre, Little Women, Aesop's Fables.* Oh, when I think back on it, I was drunk with my plans, the blueprint for our lives. My happiness, my pure and flawless happiness, blinded me toward everything else.

"And guess what, Roseheart?" he asked, putting his arm around me.

"What?" I put my arm around his waist.

"We're in walking distance to my mother's." His face radiated a great happiness.

It was a Saturday afternoon, and Sam and I were eating hamburgers at home. I fixed mine with sautéed onions and mushrooms, and just before I ate it, I melted a thick slab of cheddar cheese on it. It was raining a heavy rain, and I felt high, knowing I would be a bride in a few months. Suddenly, in the middle of whatever I was saying—I was probably talking about my wedding—Sam asked me to shut up.

"Don't do this, sweetie. Why don't you have a longer engagement? What's the big hurry?"

Her questions startled me. I knew she didn't care much for Cal, not that she would ever tell me, but she seemed not to be around whenever he was there; and when she was home, she would have a paper that was due, or she would be on the phone the minute he showed up, or someone would be waiting for her somewhere. I was so involved with Cal, I didn't get it right away.

"Cal wants to get married in June. Why do you ask?"

"Cal wants to get married in June," she mimicked me. "Do you hear yourself? What about you?" She sat across from me on the couch, leaning toward me. "It's too soon, Rosi. Don't do this. I think you should sit on it a bit longer." Her voice was soft and maternal.

Sam and I shared our most intimate thoughts and prejudices. We depended on each other when friendship was needed; we lent each other space and privacy when it was needed. I have always admired her keen perception, envied her acuity. But I was perturbed with her then for her interference. I resented her unauthorized intrusion into my life.

"Oh, Sam, it's OK," I said, hoping to change the subject. "Don't worry about it."

"If it's OK, then why don't you have a longer engagement?" she challenged me.

"I already told you. We want to get married in June. I've been dating him since September, for heaven's sake. I know him like a book."

"Have a trial marriage. Here. Right here. I'll move out. I have to go up to New York anyway after exams."

"You mean live in sin?" I asked her, my irritation growing. "Really, Sam," I said, "it's OK."

"Will you stop saying it's OK like it's some kind of a zit problem? We're talking about your life. Don't you care?"

"Of course I care. What's gotten into you?" My voice was louder.

Suddenly Sam laughed. "What, are you trying for the Miss America Contest? You know, the parade of virgins?"

I didn't think she was funny at all. "The trouble with you, Sam, is that you have no sense of propriety. No sense of responsibility. You think nothing of sleeping around. I can't do that. I believe in the sanctity of marriage. You obviously don't. I don't impose my values on you. Why should you impose yours on me? There isn't a thought in my head of having a trial marriage. And Cal wouldn't hear of it either." Sam threw up her long, slender hands and hid her face in them. Sam, the cynic. No sentiment. No romance. Just cynicism on cynicism.

I had never driven a car before I met Cal. I had never needed to drive a car before I met Cal. Back home in New Jersey, buses were plentiful, and I rode the train into New York. In the District I took the bus; and since taxis were cheap, I took taxis home from the Hill just about every night. I had no thought to driving. Cal didn't understand my aversion to driving, and shortly after we were engaged, he insisted on giving me driving lessons.

I was eating breakfast standing up in the kitchen when Sam yelled down to me. "There he is, Rosi! Your Prince Charming. Hooting his horn for you. Does he have to hoot so early?" she grumbled.

I had just returned from early mass and was finishing up a breakfast of toast and half an apple. "I'm sorry, Sam. I'll tell him not to next time. Have a bad night?" I grinned up at her and raced out the front door. He was, indeed, my Prince Charming. The driver's door was open, and he was half hanging over it, handsome, smiling, ready to teach me the impossible, or so I thought. I never met anyone with so much energy.

I hopped into the passenger side, and we drove off to the Pentagon parking lot. On Sunday mornings the huge lot was nearly empty, a perfect place for soon-to-be licensed drivers. That day we had the lot to ourselves, and I breathed easier.

"I'm terrified, Cal, I really am." I said, gritting my teeth in the driver's seat and holding onto the steering wheel.

He took one of my hands and kissed it. "Would I put you in any kind of danger, sweetheart? I promise, when this is over you will wonder why you never wanted to drive before. Now," he said as he moved closer to me from the passenger seat. "You're just starting up. See? The keys are in the ignition..."

And so every Sunday morning, sitting next to me, he watched as I slowly drove around the Pentagon parking lot. But it was a nuisance, and despite my love for him, I wanted to scream. They say no one should be taught to drive by anyone close to them. And it's true. Cal was impatient with me. Under his exacting tutelage, I grew nervous and made lots of mistakes. He wouldn't let me take the exam until he was sure I would pass. But it was taking an interminable time. He stretched the Sunday lessons into the evenings after work. I couldn't bear it. So, without his knowing it, to get it done with once and for all, I secretly took a series of lessons from a driving school. Cal was thrilled that I had progressed as I did, and I got my license. I didn't even tell Sam what I had done. She would have insisted on teaching me herself. Cal received great pleasure from my little triumph, or lie, I should say. He was a little boy bringing home all *A*s, and I felt terribly guilty for having deceived him. But it was done. I learned to drive, and he thought he had taught me. I remembered my mother saying, "There's more than one way to skin a cat," and I never paid any attention to her. Then I learned.

"Hey, Rosi! Wake up! Today's the day you get fitted for your chastity dress."

I awoke to see Sam leaning against the doorframe, holding her stomach and laughing silently. I threw a pillow at her, but I had to laugh too.

After she went downstairs to make her breakfast, I lay awake taking in the comfort of a late sleep, breathing in the spring air from the open window. I had been extremely busy the previous weeks, Cal always having things for me to do, plus extra work in the office. A late morning sleep-in did the trick. I got up feeling energized and looked forward to picking out my gown at Garfinckel's. I had wanted to make my own gown, but Cal would not hear of it. "There's so much we have to do, Rosemary. Why add more work to it? And besides, I think you deserve something a bit nicer than a homemade wedding dress."

"You mean handmade," I corrected him. "Cal, nothing I make looks 'homemade.' My handmade clothes are perfect; all of my clothes are beautifully finished. You don't understand. I love to sew, always have. I love fiddling with materials and prints and coordinating them, I love making something out of nothing. You'll see, it'll be beautiful."

"Please, Rosi, buy your gown. We have so much ahead of us and so little time."

The next day Barbara called. "Rosemary, dear. Callie tells me you want to make your gown yourself. Now if it's a matter of money, dear, I would love to buy your dress for you. That'll be my wedding gift to you."

"Thank you, Barbara, but I have decided to buy my dress after all. Cal's right. We both have a lot of work to do, so why create more? Thank you for your gracious offer."

It was nice of her to offer, although I had an underlying feeling that if I did let her buy the gown, I would have a heavy price to pay for it one day. I tried—and not just for Cal's sake—to establish a bond between Barbara and me, to feel something for the woman. We were, after all, family, or soon would be, and I was the one who was big on family, so I tried hard to look at Barbara's good side.

I wanted Sam with me when I picked out my gown. Even though Sam didn't care much for clothes, she had taste, and I trusted her judgment completely. Of course, she was my maid of honor. Cal wanted Francine in that role but I put my foot down on that suggestion. I gave in to Cal a lot because most times it didn't matter to me and it always mattered more to him. But Sam was my best friend, indeed, my only friend. We were as close as sisters. She would be my maid of honor, and that was that. I asked Francine to be my bridesmaid. Cal was hurt and showed it; he even sulked for several days, but I didn't care.

We arrived at Garfinckels about ten o'clock and decided that the saleslady would bring out the gowns and show them to us first. I pretty much knew what type of neckline looked best on me, and between Sam and me we could save a lot of time. After seeing some nine or ten gowns, I decided to try on the Victorian. Looking into the mirror, after the two ladies and Sam had buttoned me in, I asked the price.

"Mr. Bryant called before you arrived, Miss Beckett, and forbade us to tell you any prices."

Everyone laughed, including me. Cal knew me too well. I dare not economize on my wedding dress. So be it. I was too happy to care. I twirled so everyone could see.

"Oh, Rosi! That's really great!" Sam exclaimed.

The gown was magnificent. I felt beautiful in it. I looked radiant. And why not? I was marrying a man I adored, who loved me. I was starting a whole new life. How could Sam think I wasn't ready for this? I hoped that my feelings would show. I chose the Victorian and ordered the saleslady to send the bill to me and not to Mr. Bryant. By God, Cal was right. Certain things in life, you don't put a price on.

Sam wanted to go to a bar in Georgetown for lunch, but I insisted on Garfinckels. We sat across from each other at a table covered with crisp and snowy white linen. Sam spoke first.

"I met Rob yesterday."

"I thought he was in Michigan."

"He'll be teaching at Catholic U in the fall. He didn't like Michigan. He told me he'd rather be living in the District."

"How is he?" I felt a vague feeling in my breast as if my heart had stopped a few beats.

"He asked about you. He wants to know if you're happy. "

A numbing sensation enveloped me.

"What shall I tell him, Rosi?" she asked when I didn't answer. Her voice was gentle and soft.

"Sammy. I am very happy. Please, why are you doing this?"

She leaned forward and in a low, desperate voice said: "Rosi, listen to me. Go see him, please. Please. Do me this favor. You know, Rosi, have I ever asked anything from you? Have I? No, I have never asked anything from you. But I am now. I love you, Rosi. You're my best friend, and I won't have you ruin your life. It's Rob you're in love with. Don't do this, for God's sakes!" she pleaded, her voice diminished and weakened.

"No." I said. I think that was the first time I ever got truly angry with Sam. "No, Sam. What the heck is this? You two conniving behind my back? Planning my life for me? You've got to be kidding! I'm in love with Cal. We're getting married. That's it, Sam. That's final."

"Have you given thought to what we discussed the other day, Rosi?" Cal placed his strong, warm hand over mine as we waited for our salads. It was another night that we had both worked late, and we were having supper at a small restaurant on the Hill.

I didn't say anything immediately but he was waiting for an answer. "Oh, Cal. I don't know what to do. I love my work, I love working for the congressman. It's so difficult for me to quit."

"Will you be able to do it all?" he asked me. "There's a lot to do, Rosi."

"Why don't we try it for a while and see how it goes?" I suggested, knowing he would not be amenable to it.

"Rosi. You know it won't work. And do you really want to work with someone like Bea? Don doesn't sound too ethical either. Why not leave now before they do something else to you, make you look bad? Leave when the going's good. Don't you want to be in your own home, decorating it and planning a family? You love to cook too. And what about your novel? At home you can get back to it. At home you can be your own boss. And what about me, sweetheart? I don't want a wife who is too tired for me at night and maybe has to work on Saturday or Sunday." He picked up my hand and kissed it. He did not let go.

"I know, Cal." He was right. I didn't think I could hold down what I did for the congressman, run a house, and still have time for my husband. Especially a husband who did not want me to work. "I'll give my notice. You're right."

Several days later Cal closed on the house. I had expected to be there. It was a workday, and the closing wasn't until three o'clock. At two I was about to clean up my desk and leave when Cal called.

"Hi, sweetheart! Guess what? We closed."

"What?"

"We closed. I talked them into closing early. You don't mind you weren't there, do you? I know how busy you are."

"Well, yes, Cal," I answered a bit reluctantly and with more than a bit of anger. I didn't know whether I cared or not. I eyed my in-box and knew I shouldn't complain. "It's my house, too, you know. You could have called and asked me." I read the note Don had just put before me. *Reminder: Congressman wants you to attend reception at the Nigerian Embassy tonight. Reception starts at 7.* "How did it go?" I asked with a tired resignation.

"No problem. It only took about a half hour. The owners were not out to nickel and dime us to death. And you know there wasn't much to squabble about. It was a beautiful, neat closing. As I said, no problems. I did put an addendum in it that they were to clean out all the rubbish in the cellar. That way we get it broom clean. We'll just have to paint and fix the floors. I can do that myself."

"I should have been there, Cal. I've never been to a closing. I would have liked to see what it's all about, and it is going to be my home." I crumbled Don's note in my hand and dropped it in the wastebasket next to my desk. I would have to attend. Don had attended a builders' reception for me over a week ago as a favor, and I owed him one.

"I'm sorry, Rosi, I didn't know you felt so strongly about it. Anyway, I can tell you that closings are boring as hell. I'm sorry. Forgive me?"

"Of course. I've just been told I have to attend a reception at the Nigerian Embassy, so tonight's off." We had planned to look at living room furniture.

"Can't you get out of it?"

"No. I can't get out of it." I could see Ann motioning for me to pick up an extension. I signaled for a minute.

"We'll have to do something about that. We have a lot ahead of us, you know."

"What would you have me do?" I doodled on a blank sheet of paper to keep myself busy. I was anxious to dig into the pile of work waiting for me.

"Get his legislative assistant to go. What about that secretary of his? Can't she go?" His voice was testy. "What the hell does she do anyway, Rosemary? You're the one who does all the work!" He was becoming angrier, but I couldn't blame him. I did work long hours.

"It's my job to go." I crumbled the sheet of doodles I had made and threw them in the basket. Then I reached for my in-box. Everything in my in-box would be taken home that evening. Suddenly, I felt exhausted. I was tired of watching out for dirty tricks, tired of pushing myself on deadlines, tired of watching my back.

"Did you give your notice?" he asked after a slight pause.

"Yes," I lied.

"What did he say?" he asked.

I poured myself a glass of ice water from the thermos I kept on my desk, a habit I developed when I worked for the chairman in New York, and sipped at it. My throat felt parched.

"He's disappointed, of course. He has to start all over with a new person. Well, anyway, honey, I'll see you tomorrow night, OK?"

"OK. Have a good day."

Immediately, I reached for a request for a private bill and hit the extension that was blinking.

I had a late appointment with the congressman to go over his column in the newsletter. I'd talk to him then. I knew if I told Cal I hadn't, he'd just get angry and pout. That day, with my disappointment at not witnessing the closing, with my work piling up, and another evening working, I wasn't up to arguing with Cal or anyone. I did what I always did when I became upset; I focused on my work, one piece at a time.

At four the congressman ushered me into his office.

At two minutes after, I took a deep breath and announced my resignation. If I didn't do it then, I would not be able to do it at all.

"I know I should be happy for you, Rosemary, and I am, truly I am!" The congressman twirled in his chair so that I could not see him. "What are you going to do home all day?"

Get pregnant, I wanted to say. Instead, "Cal prefers I stay home. We want a family right away, congressman. And there's so much work to do on the house."

"I understand," he muttered, twirling back to face me. "How long can you stay with us?"

"As long as you need me. We have to find my replacement, and I have to break her or him in." I shrugged. "My wedding is the end of June. That gives us enough time to break someone in. How does that sound?"

"How about part-time? From home?" He stared straight at me.

I gulped. I hadn't expected it. "Oh, maybe. What did you have in mind?"

"For starters, the newsletter. Since you've been working on it, there hasn't been one mistake. Always on time." He smiled his huge smile.

"Oh, Mr. Barone, I'd love that. Work from home? I can do that."

"And maybe just for the first few months, be on hand for consultation, let's call it, if the new person needs help with the speeches?"

"Absolutely." Now I was the one with the huge smile. I just hoped Cal would smile as well, but I didn't think so.

"What about us?" Cal asked me when I told him. It was Saturday, and we were looking for a living room couch.

"Cal. It's part time."

"And what about your novel? I'd hate to see you give that up, and I know you haven't been working on it much lately."

"I'll get back to it. I'm not worried about it. You know, Cal, Congressman Barone has been very generous to me with raises and promotions."

He cut me off. "You earned it. He's not giving you anything, Rosi. Haven't you been generous to him? Working overtime every night, weekends, attending receptions? Well, haven't you?"

"Yes, you're right, but I like working for the congressman, Cal, and this is a good way to end my career, going out slowly. Besides, I'll be earning a nice salary still, not as much, but nice anyway. We can use the money, no?"

"We don't need the money. I am well able to support us both."

"I still have to support my mother, Cal."

"No, you don't. I make enough of an income to take care of that incidental."

"Really?" I gave him a big grin. "I had no idea. You know, Cal, I have no idea how much we have. You have never told me your salary—I told you mine—nor have you mentioned if you have a savings account. We have to sit down and talk finance."

A long silence.

"Well? Can we talk money?"

"You're right. But let's sit down one night, Rosi, and see what we have, where we're going, what we want. OK? But we don't need you to work."

"I can't take it back now. Do you want me to go in there and say my fiancé won't let me work? Anyway, I won't be doing the speeches and I'll just consult on the column and feature story. I'll only be coordinating, consulting with the printer, proofing the distribution list, that kind of thing. Sydney's dying for my job. There's no way she'd let me do it. Bea and Don have lined her up already to replace me. At least that's what Ann and Maryann are telling me, and they're usually right in their assumptions. Ann has been there for so long, she gets all the vibes. Happy?" I asked with a smile.

Then there was silence, and we never spoke of it again.

The house needed a lot of cosmetic changes. I was grateful that was all it needed, because Cal wanted us to do everything ourselves. When he became obsessed with something, nothing could stop him—his obsession was imperious, and everyone around him suffered because of it. But I attributed his faults at that time to the fact that he was as busy in his office as I was in mine. An upcoming wedding was enough to make both of us nervous, a mortgage added to it, and he was planning the honeymoon. He had a lot to deal with all at once, and I was more than willing to forgive him for any minor sulking. After we were married, things would settle down, and he would once again be his old self. I would see to that.

"It will take too long to do it the way we want, Rosemary so let's just paint it so it's clean. Then we can think about the wallpaper and moldings later on when we have more time."

"We only need to do the kitchen and the bedroom right away. That shouldn't take long."

He gave me a long and exasperated look, which annoyed me. "The whole place has to be cleaned and painted," he said. "The rec room is the only room that can be finished later on."

We had less than a month to get the house ready for move-in condition. I was tired just thinking about it. Immediately after work, Cal and I would drive over to his house to pick up Warren. We usually stopped on the way to get pizzas and ate them while we painted. Cal wanted all the rooms painted off-white, a creamy color, which was fine with me.

Warren proved to be a great house painter. We gave him the hallway to paint, and he was ecstatic. Cal took the living room, and I had the dining room. I wanted all of us to paint one room together, but Cal estimated that we could have all three rooms painted by the end of the night if we did it his way. What he didn't figure on was my five-foot-three-inch frame. I had a hard time reaching the ceiling.

"I figured you'd have a problem," he laughed at me good-naturedly. "That's why I brought along an extension for you." He attached a long, slender pole onto the handle of the roller. It was great. I didn't have to use the step ladder. I could paint from floor level.

The first night, after we had been working for a few hours, I felt a cold draft. "Where is that cold coming from?" I asked.

"Doesn't it feel great?" He flashed me a big smile.

"No. It's cold," I complained. "Where's it coming from?" I looked around the room.

"It's air conditioning. I had it installed yesterday."

"Cal. Why didn't you talk to me about it? That's a fortune! How can we afford that?"

"We can," he answered blandly and matter-of-factly.

"We can?" I asked with more than a little annoyance.

"Hey, Rosi, let's get this place finished, OK?"

"Wait a minute. Wait a cotton-pickin' minute, Cal. First of all, this is my house too, you know. I have to be in on decisions around here. We couldn't have discussed this together? How much did it cost?"

"Rosi, I'm not up to this!" His voice was a roar that stunned me.

Warren had peeked into the room appearing frightened and I felt bad for him but I continued my discussion anyway. "I am." I followed him into the room, carefully walking on the drop cloths.

He saw that I was not about to go away. It was the first time I had seen his face red and he spoke with an uncontrolled rage. "This is going to be our home for some time, and I want my comfort. You know how hot it gets! I'm not spending my summers sweating like a pig!"

"What's wrong with a few window units?" At that time his anger did not frighten me. Cal did not frighten me. I continued. "Why do we have to do the whole house? That's a lot of money, Cal."

"Knock it off!" I had never heard him so violent.

"I will for now," I said in a low voice keeping my control. "But I want to be consulted in all decisions concerning my home." I left him and went back to my painting. We would have a talk when he calmed down.

The dining room was spacious, and it took me almost two hours nonstop to finish the ceiling. My pride in my work was dampened, however, when I realized Cal expected me to give it another coat and to paint the walls as well. I quickly and sloppily did a second coat over the ceiling, which only needed one, but when he expected me to finish two coats on the walls, I burst into tears.

"Two coats! No way, Cal, that's it!" It was midnight, and I was exhausted. "We've been painting since seven o'clock. I'm tired."

"OK, sweetheart, OK. You rest. I'll do it."

"No. No one's going to do it, Cal. We're finished now for the night. We're all going home." I looked at him and Warren. They appeared to be just starting. They didn't look tired at all. Neither had a speck of paint on them. My face dripped with water-base off-white whatever the hell tint it was, I didn't even care. I felt as if someone had dipped me into a paint vat. The air conditioner did not keep me cool. I couldn't stop crying. I didn't realize tears could move him. It was the first time he had ever seen me cry. By the time he dropped me off at my house, it was after one o'clock. I made it up the stairs without falling, stripped my clothes off, let them fall where they may, and dropped into bed. The hard mattress was therapeutic, the sheets cool and relaxing. Sleep came easily and quickly.

Cal drove Warren and me without compassion. Once he started, there was no stopping him. By Sunday night we had painted the entire inside of the house. Two coats! I was so exhausted, I could barely move or think. I fell asleep that night forgetting about my mother. I had promised her I would call about the wedding arrangements.

The house was beginning to take shape. One club chair had arrived, along with a side table and two bedside tables. The four-poster bed arrived the day before our wedding, along with various chests and dressers. Cal and I and Warren had picked up the kitchen table and chairs ourselves. Barbara had given us a very old but beautiful Queen Anne dining table and chairs she had stored in the cellar of her home but there was still so much more to get. I needed end tables, lamps, occasional pieces, and a coffee table in the living room. It would mean more days of shopping and browsing. I wanted to mix contemporary and modern with antiques. I wanted a country kitchen. I wanted a lot of things. I couldn't wait to get started.

CHAPTER
6

Father McLaughlin married us at Holy Trinity Church in Georgetown where I had attended mass. It was a beautiful wedding. Although I had no one other than my mother for family I felt that it was a true family wedding. Father had baptized me, had known me all my life. I had attended mass at Holy Trinity for several years. And, of course, Sammy was my maid of honor.

Cal did not object to a Catholic wedding in a Catholic church, but he was adamant about not having a mass, and I understood his feelings. His mother and sister had never been inside a Catholic church, and Cal did not want to spend all that time on a ceremony they would not understand. We had discussed our religious differences long before we were married: he believed in God, but he did not belong to any organized religion, and that was not important to me. What was important to me was that I be allowed my religion, and our children had to be Catholic, but Cal had no objections: "You take care of their spiritual needs, and

I'll take care of their material needs." We both wanted children right away.

The guests filed out after us, throwing Uncle Ben's converted rice and pink confetti. The day was sunny, and the milky essence of the freshly mowed grass wafted through the summer's air. Thinking back on it now, my wedding was a storybook wedding. Not so long before, I had been enveloped in poverty, facing welfare, and I was able to turn it around. Failure retreated into obscurity. I found my own strength. I also found Cal. With him I would have the world—a home, children, security. And should anything happen to him, well, I had myself with all my capabilities; I was strong and intelligent. I would never face poverty again.

A few weeks before the wedding, after the house had its two coats of paint in every room—Sam and I had worked in the backyard in an effort to make it into a garden. Sidney had taken over most of my responsibilities and she proved to be smart and competent. I had every evening and weekend free. It was great to have someone else doing my work, or what had been my work. The year before, in between tennis sets, I had tried to garden by myself, planting a few rosebushes and herbs, but at that time it proved to be an interruption in my life, when I was trying to forget Rob. Then, gardening was dangerous—too meditative. But before the wedding, I was back with bags of white gravel, which together Sam and I poured around the miniature beds of roses and flowers, constructing even more miniature pathways. We had bought flowers already in bloom and in their pots. The roses struggled for life, and I helped by blitzing them with all kinds of fertilizers and chemicals, anything that would save the blossoms for my wedding day. I remember Sam and me, dripping from the humidity, dirtied from hours of work on our hands and knees, hurting from the weight of the bags of gravel, but loving it, laughing and celebrating with ham sandwiches and ice cold Chablis. I had rented a half-dozen white wrought-iron garden chairs and a small bench and placed them around the tiny yard. I hired a cleaning crew for the inside of the house. Although we had a woman clean it once a week, it needed heavy-duty scrubbing. The house sparkled the day of the wedding. Sam and her friends decorated the inside with dozens of white flowers in baby's breath—all roses, large and budding and beautiful.

The caterer's did a sumptuous job with the buffet. Dozens of trays of the most exquisite-looking hors d'oeuvres started us off, followed by small cups of a deliciously cold avocado soup; bite-sized chicken in a lemon sauce with rice; a green salad; and a dessert of orange mousse with whipped cream. No knives were necessary. Of course, champagne, wine, and whatever the guests wanted to drink were served. It was a stand-up luncheon, but I had arranged for enough chairs that people could sit and rest.

The house was just the right size for the number of people we had invited—just under twenty-five. Neither Cal nor I had extended families, and we both preferred small groups in any situation. The thought of planning a wedding for a hundred or more people, which seemed to be the norm for wedding parties, was frightening. And, to be truthful, I did not have a large group of friends in Washington. I had lost contact with my old friends in New Jersey and New York after I left for DC, and distance had severed any lingering ties; my mother was my only relative. On Cal's side, besides his immediate family, he invited two cousins whom I had not yet met, with their spouses. That made up our entire families. We invited most of the people in our offices, and of course I invited Mr. and Mrs. West-cott. The only one missing was Warren. They left him home. Surprisingly, I missed him. I think he would have loved to have seen me in my wedding gown; he was such a little boy and I had come to care for him.

My mother arrived two days before the wedding. She had made herself an ice-blue silk dress and bought a hat that matched it perfectly, and for which she paid a handsome price. "You only get married once, dear," she told me.

It was a homogenous group of people, and everyone had a good time, except for Francine. She seemed terribly unhappy the whole day and, as was her nature, did not speak to anyone. Some of the guests spilled out into the little garden, finishing off the champagne and food. The music that Sam and her friends had taped earlier in the week was just perfect. Cal never left my side. My mother sat in a chair looking like a wealthy *grande dame*. Sam never left her side. Barbara played the role of the Washington hostess, loving every minute of it, savoring it, her smile plastered for eternity. I had never seen her look so happy.

My family and friends were generous to us: silver candlesticks, silver teaspoons, crystal vases and glasses, pewter, china. As much as I savored that day, as happy as I was, I wanted my reception to be over; I wanted to be alone with my husband. I wanted the beginnings of my family to begin. I felt so rich, so luxurious, and

I was so in love. My life was only just about to start, and I knew that even though my wedding day would be over, it would never end: we would have children and they, in turn, would have children, and we would always continue on. That day was the most exciting day of my life.

My mother took me aside as I was dressing for my departure. "Sit down, dear," she commanded me with an authority I was not used to. I sat down. "When young women marry, they have dreams of what should be. They idealize their lives. Life is not like that. You take what you have and mold it *to* your liking." She emphasized the word *to*. "You have a magnificent husband. He's handsome, intelligent, and loves you. If things happen that aren't to your liking, Rosemary, then make them to your liking. Don't sulk and cry about it. You have a lot to be thankful for. You're such a lucky little girl." She hugged me then and cried a little before letting me go. Now when I think back on it, my mother never knew the pains I went through to get where I was. Of course, I made things to my liking; did she not know? But she was attempting a mother-daughter talk, which I had denied her the past few years. I suppose she was trying to make up for all that time. And I loved her even more for it.

❦

We had just checked in and been in our room less than an hour when I discovered one of Cal's many flaws. I had placed my perfume and cosmetics on the dresser, and then, with one hand he swept all of my things into a wastebasket. I had deliberately put them to one side so he could have the other side for his things.

"What are you doing?" I asked him. "That's my makeup, my perfume!" I jumped up and retrieved them from the basket. "Why did you do that?" I asked.

He looked a little surprised, and then he laughed. "Oh, I'm sorry, sweetheart. That's a fault of mine. I have an aversion to anything not put away. It looks like clutter to me. You'll have to remember that. I'm compulsive about it. I'll leave emptying the wastebaskets to you." He laughed again. It was very funny to him. I pushed it to the back of my mind.

Cal was a great lover. He was extremely gentle and loving the first night. I couldn't have been happier, or more satisfied. I would give Sam a good scolding when I got home for all her warnings that there must be something wrong with him. But somewhere during the first few days—time has diminished the exact details of when—he became sulky, almost angry. After about five days, I knew there was something wrong. So, then and there, I finessed him into having room service instead of going down to dinner. I put on my prettiest peignoir and sprayed on the perfume he liked best on me. Cal had been quiet most of the day, and I hoped his mood was just a result of all the work we did before the wedding, the wedding itself, and all he had to do for his senator before we left. We did a lot of walking and swimming, and sightseeing and sitting in the hot sun every day proved to be exhausting. I hoped his silence was due to fatigue. But at dinner he wasn't speaking at all.

"Is something wrong, Cal?" I had been standing behind him, and I leaned over and kissed him on his cheek.

"No." He shook his head in an effort to free himself from my arms.

"Oh, come on, Cal." I said, keeping my voice sweet and flirtatious. "Something's bothering you."

And, then, after a few moments of silence, he erupted. He stood up, the back of his knees tossing the chair into me so that I jumped back. He spun around, and I saw his face. He was seething. He pointed his finger at me, and said in a loud voice, "You're not a virgin." I couldn't believe what I was hearing. I was speechless. I didn't know what to say. I stood there like a dumb clumsy calf and stared at him. I was intimate with only one man in my whole life, and now this?

"You're not a virgin," he repeated when I didn't say anything.

"No, I'm not." I finally spoke up.

"You told me you were."

"Cal, I never said such a thing. You never asked such a thing."

"You led me to believe it."

"What difference does it make?" I asked him.

"You misled me," he said.

"I never misled you," I answered, feeling my anger growing inside me. "I've always been honest with you. But you're not being honest with me. What is this really about?"

"I have to know I can trust you."

"This is crazy. This is absolute nonsense. Of course you can trust me. I had an affair a long time ago. It had nothing to do with us." But as the words tumbled from my lips, I knew indeed that my affair with Rob had to do with us. I pushed him to the back of my mind. Rob was history.

"Who did you have an affair with?"

My confusion and dismay was gone, and in its place was an anger I did not like. I was not used to anger and it bothered me. How dare he question me like this? On our honeymoon? He should be seducing me, not interrogating me. I didn't answer him right away, and when I did, I spoke quietly and composed, my anger controlled. "That's none of your business, Cal. Are you a virgin?"

He stared at me without speaking and then he stormed out of the room, slamming the door, and he didn't come back until late that night. I was crazy. I didn't know what to do. He made me feel horribly cheap and low. Cal was not a one-track-minded person. He had sophistication, maturity, understanding. At least that's the side of him I saw until that night. I had a sudden urge to throw in the towel, get on a plane right then and there. But I couldn't. I had always been good at solving crises. Sam used to tell me how absolutely useless I was when little things upset me; but when something drastic happened, and all the "chicken littles" were shouting, "The sky is falling," I would be the only one using my head. I wasn't about to let my marriage go down the drain over this. My marriage was my life. And Cal could be such a little kid at times. Most times he was wonderful. So I decided to treat him just the way he behaved. If he wanted to sulk, he wasn't getting any attention from me. He could sulk until he tired of it. Of course, I didn't sleep at all. I heard him come in later, and I turned the light on and sat up in bed. I didn't say a word, just stared at him with an angry look. And then he was kneeling at the side of the bed, his arms over my legs, and he was practically crying.

"Oh, my darling, I'm sorry, please forgive me, I'm so sorry."

I pushed his arms away and got up on the other side of the bed. "I do forgive you, Cal, but why was that so important? This is our honeymoon!" My voice broke, and I held back my sobs.

"I don't deserve you, Rosemary. You're the best thing that has ever happened to me. Please, please, don't be angry with me. I need you."

What could I do? I forgave him. On one condition. "My affair was over a long time ago, Cal, and you're just bringing it all up again. I'll forgive you, but only if you never do that to me again. My past romances are over, they have nothing to do with us." I couldn't believe what I was saying. I only had one.

He threw his arms around me, hugged me, and said he was sorry. Then all of a sudden he was his old self, the man I fell in love with. He wanted to make love, but I wasn't up to it. I was still angry. In the morning my anger was gone. Cal reached over to me. I was no longer anxious or afraid or angry. *No one's perfect,* I thought at the time. *I married an old-fashioned man and that's not altogether bad.* Besides being in love with Cal, I really liked him, too. We had a great honeymoon.

I had thought about it on the plane back to Washington: how I would fix the wall behind the couch. The painting *Ballerinas* would be just perfect. I had decided to buy the painting that I had seen at a sidewalk exhibit on the Hill. It was of ballerinas with a backdrop of smooth blackness. I knew it would be perfect for our living room, but I wanted Cal's approval, since he had to look at it too. Just about every artist in the world does at least one painting of ballerinas, but this particular one was about the loveliest I had ever seen. The grace and softness of the dancers came through so powerfully that one could almost feel their movements, see them dance their pirouettes, hear the music. I planned to run down and buy it the next day if it hadn't already been sold. Cal had put up chair rails in the living room, and I wasn't sure whether

I should wallpaper above the chair rails and paint below, or paper the whole wall. At our reception, after I had opened all the gifts, Barbara sweetly informed me that her gift was on its way. It was going to be a surprise, she said. I hoped she wouldn't make the same mistake so many in-laws make. I hoped she wouldn't buy us furniture. I didn't have to worry. It was there when we arrived home, with her, Francine, and Warren waiting for us.

"Surprise!" They called out in unison. The look on Cal's face was one of great enjoyment. My look was one of astonishment. What were they doing in my home? How did they get in? I tried to smile, but my shock at anyone having access to my home was pervasive. Barbara hugged Cal. You would have thought she hadn't seen him in years.

"Callie, I knew you'd love this painting when I saw it. It's perfect for this wall." She stepped aside, and there above the place where my couch would be, where my ballerinas were supposed to be, was a modern abstract that screeched of red and orange colors. It was supposed to be the universe. Smiling still, my face muscles hurting from twitching, I thought of how I would get rid of it, where I would put it. My couch would be coming soon, and its cool light green with subtle touches of blue was not going to work with *The Universe.*

Cal nodded at the painting. "It's nice," he said.

I could have died, but I caught myself right away. I knew it wasn't his taste. He was being polite.

"Look at what Francine made for you."

A small work of macramé hung on another wall. Despite the fact that I have never cared much for macramé, it was pretty and artistic, but still unwanted nevertheless.

"It looked so empty," she informed him sweetly. "It needed color, Callie."

Did she think I had finished?

A bowl of silk, multi-colored flowers sat arrogantly on a side table. I said nothing. My face still ached. Patches of their love for Cal hung, stood, or sat in the dining room, kitchen, and hallway. They had even taken it upon themselves to hammer nails into the walls, which had been freshly painted. I seethed with an inner, almost uncontrollable rage at that violation of my home. I directed that anger toward myself, because I had never in my life felt such anger at anyone, including Cal when he had accused me of not being a virgin. So, I told myself it didn't matter. I would get rid of it all in due course, in time, somehow, without hurting anyone's feelings. I loved my new house, but I was sorry it had to be in walking distance to theirs, and the thought flew through my mind that this visit of theirs might just be a daily occurrence.

No one cared what I thought anyway. They hugged Cal and kissed him. My presence was unrecognized. It was as if I was not even there. His mother took his arm and led him into the kitchen, where they had coffee brewing and a cake.

"I thought you might be hungry, dear."

When I first walked in the door, Barbara acknowledged me by a stiff hug and by placing her cheek next to mine. Once done, she did not look at me again. But Francine never took her bovine eyes from me.

Warren stole glances at me, grinning his usual, fatuous grin. Oversized and bulky he appeared to have no teeth at all, his mouth a black, empty slit on his puffy sheet-white face. Small droplets of saliva hung motionlessly at the corners of his thin lips. That was the first day I felt something resembling love toward him, the kind of love you'd have for a neglected child.

I sat down with them and listened to the casual, familial chatter, nibbling on the homemade coffee cake that was delicious, but wishing they'd all go home. I wanted to make love to my husband. I wanted to make dinner for him. I wanted to finish the finishing touches in my home; theirs would go. Finally, when I could see that the four of them were firmly ensconced and their party was going to continue for a while at least, I stood up and with some awkwardness, tried to shift the mood of the afternoon tea party. I said I had to go to the supermarket.

"Oh, but you have!" Barbara gaily announced. "We already got everything for you. Look!" She opened the refrigerator door, and I could see that it was crammed full with food—milk, eggs, bacon, butter, jams and jellies, lots of fruit. She had thought of everything. "Bread too," she added, opening the cupboards. I could see there was a box of saltines, Cal's favorite. "Cookies?" She looked at me sheepishly, holding the package of Oreos up for me to see.

"Well," I stammered rather feebly and with a certain amount of embarrassment. "That was very nice of you, Barbara. Thanks so much! But I do need to get some meat for supper tonight."

"Why? I thought you were eating with us." She looked disappointingly at Cal.

"We'll eat with the family tonight," Cal stated.

And with that final edict, without a care or a thought to me, they resumed their conversation, and I resumed sitting next to Warren, across from Cal and Francine and Barbara.

That night was the first night he hadn't made love to me.

"Oh, please, Roseheart, I'm exhausted. Tomorrow, OK?"

I believed him. I didn't realize the honeymoon was over.

The next morning I busied myself in the kitchen making breakfast. I knew exactly how Cal preferred his eggs, once over lightly, toast dark, bacon crisp. The coffee that Barbara had bought for us dripped obediently, its pungent aroma mixing with the hickory-smoked bacon.

I was already dressed and made up. One of the promises I made to myself before we were married was that I would always be dressed and made up at all times. My husband would never see me without makeup or in curlers. I would treat every day as a housewife as I did when I was a working woman.

"Morning." Cal was dressed in a blue and white striped summer suit, a navy blue tie. He looked smart, brilliant in fact, his briefcase on the floor next to him.

"Morning, honey. Hungry?"

He shook his head disdainfully. "I never eat breakfast, Rosemary. Bye."

"What do you mean?" I asked, following him to the front door. "What about all those gargantuan meals you were eating in Florida? You love breakfast."

"Only on vacation. Not when I have to work. I always take an early lunch. Bye. Have fun."

Staring at the closed door, puzzled and a little disappointed, I returned to the kitchen to salvage some of the meal. I swore he ate breakfast. I thought he told me he did when we were dating. I thought of that night on our honeymoon and his anger at my not being a virgin. I shook my head in an effort to clear out the negatives. I had a lot to learn about this man I was about to share my life with.

I poured myself a cup of coffee, emptied the rest into a glass decanter, and put it away in the refrigerator. Later in the day when I wanted something cold to drink, I would have it over ice cubes. I laid the bacon on paper towels to absorb the grease and put two slices on my plate next to an egg, sunny-side up. I would grind up the remaining bacon for salad toppings. The years of living with my mother and watching her save every bit of food, storing it in jelly jars—just a teaspoon was royal enough to be saved—made me think about the extra two eggs. I threw them out. I was not poor, I told myself. No need to save everything. Then I sat down and ate my breakfast and sipped on the hot, steamy coffee, listening to the sounds of the empty house. I heard a creak from somewhere upstairs and a short, rough hiss escaped from, I guessed, a pipe. I could hear a slight tapping sound coming from the cellar, and with coffee in hand I went down to find its source.

"Warren!"

He turned awkwardly, looking frightened.

"What are you doing here? How did you get in?" I tried to keep the surprise in my voice to a minimum, for I immediately saw I had frightened him.

He looked about to cry and then realizing his limited intelligence, I smiled and said it was all right. "Let me see what you're doing."

He raced to the opposite wall and smoothed his hands over the paneling, his mouth stretched wide into a black slit that was his smile. He had paneled one whole side of the cellar. He must have begun work while we were away.

"That's very nice, Warren. You've done a beautiful job." I noticed that the paneling was not all the way in. It was more or less basted as in sewing a dress, preparing it for the final stitch, the final nail. The pieces seemed to fit, but they were not in tight. So that was the timid tapping that I heard. I decided to teach him how to do it. "Here, Warren. Watch me and then you do, OK?" I pulled the ladder over and stood on the top step and slammed the tool hard against the iron nail. "See? Like that." I slammed it down again.

Warren jumped up and down on his two chunky legs, gurgling while he laughed.

I laughed with him. "OK? See how easy it is?" I climbed down and handed him the hammer. He took it from me and, with a visible and bulky clumsiness, he ascended the ladder. I watched as he took a nail from the apron-like belt he had tied around his huge stomach and, laughing like a mad man, his chunky arm flailing through the air as he pounded the steel bit into the paneling, I knew I had gone too far. I noticed his clumsiness and wondered how he was able to do all the work he did without falling or hurting himself. He took a nail from the apron-like belt he had tied around his huge stomach and began to hammer. He hammered wildly, laughing like a mad man, his huge, fat arm flailing through the air as he hit the nail on its head. I knew then I had gone too far. I should have let Cal take care of this task. I called up to him. "Warren!" I pulled at his pants leg. "Warren. Come down. Stop that hammering." But he was lost in some fantasy, and I left as fast as I could, feeling uncomfortable and sorry that I excited him. I returned to the kitchen and tidied up, still hearing the noise of the hammer as it hit its mark every instant.

Hoping I hadn't created a monster, I began my tour through the house, beginning with the front hallway. Thank God they didn't touch that. I started a list, making notes of everything I could think of. A thick, yellow-ruled, legal–size pad absorbed it all. The list on the first page was now stretched onto page two.

I decided on a small wall table in the hall with a vertical mirror and a round rug. I would have to talk to Cal about carpeting. The floors were a beautiful hardwood; Cal did a great job cleaning and polishing them, but he still wanted to put in wall-to-wall carpeting. I couldn't see the sense of covering them up. We were buying expensive furniture and I was frustrated using a charge card whose limit was a mystery. Maybe I could talk him out of that idea, but I doubted it. Cal could be stubborn at times.

I moved on into the living room and there loom-
ing before me, red and orange and hideous, was *The
Universe*. I knew it would take time, but I would get
rid of Barbara's gift, if I had to work all day, every day,
scheming and plotting, I would get rid of it. For the
moment I threw a white bed sheet over it—I couldn't
think having it there before me—and continued on
with my work. I would have to remember to take it
down before Cal got home. It was, after all, his mother's gift to us, and I wouldn't hurt him for the world.
Nor would I hurt Barbara.

I removed the bowl of fake flowers from the coffee
table and brought it into the dining room. It would
stay on the table there. With the lights out. Then I
took Francine's macramé and hung it in the hallway,
where it was more appropriate. I couldn't imagine
Barbara having such things in her home; she had such
good taste.

I scribbled a few notes to myself and then went
into the dining room, the kitchen, and into my future
sunroom. I did not hear the sounds of hammering, so
I risked a visit to the basement, where Warren sat in
a corner on a pile of drop cloths staring into space.
He stood up when he saw me, smiling and appearing
calmer. I let him know he would be alone, and I would

be home in a few hours, and then I left for the first round of errands.

The car I was to use during the day, while Cal drove the Volvo to work, was his sister's old '58 Plymouth. It smelled of gasoline; I counted sixteen dents on one side and didn't bother to count how many were on the back, front, and other side. It bucked and shook in the middle of a ride, and it had no air conditioning. Cal assured me it was in excellent condition. I doubted it but said nothing. "Run it to the ground, Rosemary. When it stops on us, we'll get you a new one."

So there I was in his sister's old '58 Plymouth in excellent condition driving to the supermarket. It was the first time in my life I drove alone. I was petrified. But I vowed to do it. The streets were almost deserted, and if I went slow, I shouldn't have any problems. Besides, I had always believed I could do anything I set out to do, but halfway to the supermarket, Francine's 1958 Plymouth with sixteen-plus dents in excellent condition stopped on me. In the middle of the road. On a sweltering hot, June morning. The stinky, dirty smell of the old machine spewing forth its gaseous fumes almost made me ill. It had only been five minutes or so—it felt like five hours—when a carload of young teenage boys came by, six of them all told. They pushed my car to the side of the road and offered me a ride to the supermarket, which was a short distance away. They were sweet, and I felt they were reliable, so I got in. I refused to sit on anyone's lap, so one boy sat on another boy's lap, and I sat in front between the driver and his friend. The boy next to me was wearing shorts, navy blue with a white stripe up the sides, and his legs were muscular and beautifully hairy. We were cramped for space, and his leg rested against mine. I didn't have stockings on, and I could feel the slow trickle of sweat roll down the leg that was touching the boy's leg. The young man smiled at me and I smiled at him. He rubbed his leg up and down mine. "Stop that," I chided him, and all of us laughed. He stopped his teenage lascivious prank but continued to smile at me.

When we arrived at the supermarket, I fumbled in my bag and handed the driver a ten-dollar bill and told them to have some beers on me. It was later when I wondered if they were old enough to drink.

I hurried into the supermarket and found a telephone just inside the doors. Cal had given me the name and telephone number of his garage man, which I had remembered to insert in my pocket address book, and I called him. He answered immediately, and after I told him who I was, I gave him the address and place where I left the car. Then I pushed the empty cart ahead of me and began to shop for my food.

I didn't have much shopping to do. Just some meat and fresh vegetables. Barbara had stocked us up with frozen vegetables in all kinds of awful sauces. I'd never eaten a frozen vegetable in my life, and I didn't intend to start. I picked through the asparagus, the green beans, the lettuce, and thought about the garden I would have the next summer. I planned to grow all my own food. I would freeze and can it. Sometimes my mother and I lived on foods she had canned. In the late summer, when I was a little girl, I would find her in the kitchen canning tomatoes and other good things. She'd get the vegetables from her customers who had gardens. Sometimes she'd can for them, too, her way of saying thank you. When winter came, when it was dark and cold outside, she'd take some of the canned goods from the cupboard and cook them. They smelled different, better. I can remember the big bowls of succotash with lots of sweet butter and salt. We'd also get fish from our neighbors. A lot of the men in our neighborhood went fishing during the summers, but their wives did not want to clean or cook the fish, so they'd give them to us. My mother did not mind cleaning and gutting the fish, although it would take days to get the fish smell out of the house. She would poach the fish and make a delicious white sauce to go over them. Those were the foods I savored when I was a child, and I can still taste them to this day.

When I finished my shopping, I called for a taxi and went home.

Cal's favorite meal was filet mignon, baked potato, and a simple green salad with blue cheese dressing. Although I had seen him eat enormous portions of lasagna, mousaka, and all kinds of international dishes, he always insisted that steak and potato was his favorite meal.

I prepared two steaks for broiling and made up a salad and scrubbed two potatoes. I laid a snowy white linen tablecloth over the dining room table and put out the two sterling silver candlesticks we had received as a wedding gift. I inserted white tapered candles in them that I had bought in Miami. I set out the two crystal glasses his senator had given us and fixed the lights so that the room sparkled and gleamed. At six o'clock the doorbell rang.

Francine.

I hoped she hadn't planned to stay. I had only two steaks. There was plenty of salad, but only two potatoes. And I wanted candlelight, not Francine. Finally, after we had stared at each other for several awkward minutes, I invited her in.

She moved sadly. Her thin body with the brown, dateless dress looked out of place in the modern world. She stopped, hesitating, in the middle of the living room.

"Sit down, Francine." I tried to sound pleasant.

She remained standing.

"Well," I smiled brightly. By God, she was not about to intimidate me. "What occasions this visit?"

She looked at me for a few seconds, and eventually her eyes returned to the place where the painting hung. *The Universe* in a shroud. I had forgotten all about it, and the humor of it made me laugh. I couldn't help myself despite the look on her too-white face. I pulled the bed sheet down and folded it up in my arms. What could I say?

Francine sat down on the one chair in the living room and pointed a bony finger at the coffee table in front of her and—blessed be to all the saints in heaven—she spoke.

"What happened to the flowers?" Her voice squeaked, emitting a high pitch.

"They looked nicer in the dining room," I said in my "Let's be sisters" voice.

"They looked very nice here." She shrugged her bony shoulders and shook her head.

"Well," I said, trying to keep my voice bright and gracious. "Cal isn't home yet, Francine. Can I do something for you?" The words fell out, disconnected, unhinged.

She shook her head and actually smiled. "I see you put my macramé outside."

"Yes," I said. "It's a very pretty piece. It deserves more space. Everyone can see it there."

"Everyone can see it in here too," she pouted.

I focused my eyes directly upon her and kept my voice firm but pleasant.

"This is my house, Francine."

As if on cue, Cal walked in the front door.

"You needn't be so rude about it." She spoke loud.

"What's the trouble?" Cal asked from the hallway. He had the slightest edge of nastiness in his voice. He shot an accusing look at me.

"There's no trouble, Cal," I answered firmly. This snippet was not going to cause trouble between my husband and me.

Francine stood up but did not move away from the chair. "We try to be nice, and look what we get."

"Alright. What's the problem?" Cal walked into the room, his hands planted authoritatively on his hips. I had never heard him so arrogant, and his arrogance was directed at me.

"There is no problem, Cal." I tried to hide my irritability.

"You could have taken the sheet down before I got here, Rosemary. That was offensive. And cruel." She turned to Cal. "She covered our painting with a sheet!"

"Why?" His mouth stiffened, and his brown eyes narrowed into slits.

In an effort to alter the hostility that Francine created, I said, "I made you some martinis, Cal. We're having steak and salad for dinner, your favorite." Then I turned and faced Francine, and smiling at her so that my anger was somewhat lessened, I asked if she would join us. But at the same time as I was extending the invitation, I realized that that was the purpose of her visit.

"Of course she's staying for dinner. This is Mother's night out for shopping."

Two things caught my attention that evening. One was that Francine's insipid smile never faded throughout the rest of the evening. The other was that in her eyes I saw an intense fear that did not manifest itself until Cal showed up. I was so upset over Francine's unexpected arrival and the subsequent ruination of my romantic dinner for two that I put that observation aside and didn't think about it for several months.

"That was nice of you to give your steak to Francine, sweetheart," Cal called to me from the bathroom later that night.

"I didn't mind. I ate tons of salad." In addition to my steak, Francine also got my potato. "By the way, Cal, Warren was here today."

"I know. He's working in the basement. I told you I want a billiards room down there."

"You told me that, but you didn't tell me Warren was in the house this morning."

"So?"

'So, I'd like to know when he's here. I got scared. I heard something in the cellar and went down. That's how I found out he was here. Do you think you could tell me when he's coming?"

"He's coming."

"What?"

246

"He's coming. Every day. He's working in the basement."

I didn't know if I wanted Warren in the house with me, but I had a feeling I shouldn't say anything. Yet, that is. "Why is he leaving the paneling just hanging? I tried to show him how to hammer it in, but he got a little bit too excited."

I could feel the silence, and then I looked up from my newspaper to see Cal in the doorframe of the bathroom. His anger was penetrating.

"Stay away from him."

"What?"

"I said stay away from him!"

"Why?"

"What the hell were you bothering him for?"

"I didn't mean to bother him. I meant to be helpful."

"Well, stay away." He turned and went back to the bathroom.

"Why are you speaking to me like that?" I got up and walked over to the door. He tried to shut it but I blocked it with my body. "What is the matter with you?"

"Just don't bother with him, that's all." His voice was smoother, mellower. "I'm sorry, Roseheart; it's just that he gets us all down at times. I'm sorry. And thanks for being so nice to Francine. That was nice of you to give your dinner to her. You're very good, you know. I don't deserve you."

Click—he's on. Click—he's off.

"That's alright, Cal, I didn't mind." I did mind, though, and I was feeling hungry, so I went down to the kitchen for a sandwich. I spread a huge mound of peanut butter on white bread and poured myself a glass of milk and brought it back to bed.

"Roseheart! What are you eating?"

"Peanut butter. I'm hungry."

"You ate up a storm in Florida."

"So?"

"You're getting bottom heavy." He patted my can and got into bed.

"You think I'm fat?" I sat up. "Everyone tells me I'm slim."

"Of course not. You just look a little heavier than before. That's all.

I immediately began planning how I would lose a few pounds. First I would buy a scale. I had heard that after twenty-five, it was harder to lose weight, and I would soon be there. I would start the next day.

"Cal?"

"Yes?" he asked, turning out the lamp on his side.

"You don't really like that painting your mother gave us, do you?" I snuggled up close to him.

"Not really. What should I say to her?"

"Can we move it someplace else? Please? It won't go with the couch."

"We will. In time. I don't want to hurt her feelings. In fact, after the couch arrives we can move it. We'll have a good reason to then. How's that?"

"Thank you darling." I reached up and kissed him on his cheek. He turned on his side.

"Was there some reason why you didn't tell me Francine was coming for dinner?" I asked.

After a long pause, he answered me.

"I did tell you she was coming."

I was aware of an unfamiliar flatness to his voice.

"When did you tell me?"

Another pause.

He sat up but did not turn to look at me. "You know we're a very close family, Rosemary. It wouldn't hurt to keep extra food around. That way you won't have to sacrifice."

"Suppose I did have three steaks out, or four even, just in case, and no one showed up. What would I do with all that leftover meat?"

"Throw it out, for Christ's sake," he yelled hotly at me. "Have it the next day. Why worry about it? We're not poor."

"Why must you yell?"

There was no answer. He fell back onto his pillows and pulled the sheet over him.

"Cal?" I spoke softly. My romantic dinner was ruined, but this night might still be mine.

"What?"

"Make love to me?"

"Rosemary, I'm tired. Let me rest. Please."

I thought of the way Rob used to tell me to "…get your pretty little ass over here, baby," when I would be undressing and taking too long. That really did something to me.

"We didn't make love last night." When he didn't say anything, I added, "I need to make love."

"What are you telling me?"

"I'm horny, Cal." I put my arm over his chest.

He jumped so fast out of the bed, I thought something had happened to him, some communicable, horrible disease had descended upon him. "You sound like a slut!" He stood rigid, staring at me, without even a blink.

"I'm not a slut!" I yelled back at him. I jumped out of my side of the bed and stood there, the two of us, staring at each other. Finally, I burst into tears and fell back into bed. When I had stopped crying, I looked up to see that he was gone. I went out into the hall and saw that the door to "our" den was shut. My instincts told me not to go in. I went back to bed, hurt, insulted, angry. I did not sleep until much later on. When I awoke in the morning and thought over the night's events, I became even angrier. Cal wasn't just old-fashioned. He was screwed up somehow. And I intended to find out what the problem was.

I had showered and dressed by the time he returned to our bedroom the next morning. The morning sun lit up the room, but I didn't feel any better.

"Where were you, Cal? Where did you sleep?"

"In the den. Listen, Rosemary. I'm sorry about what I said last night. He gave a grumpy laugh. "When you used that word *horny*, well, it blew me over. That's a man's word, honey, please don't use it. And again, I'm sorry." He wrapped his arms around me, hugging me, and I was relieved, but I wasn't about to let him off with that slut remark.

"You're forgiven. I won't use that word since it bothers you, but you have to know I enjoy sex, and that doesn't make me a slut. And I don't like sleeping alone."

"I know, Roseheart. I know. But you have to remember I'm older. I'm not the same as when I was twenty. You're still a little chicken, honey. Be patient." He hugged me closer.

"Did you sleep on the floor?" I asked him, pulling away. We did not put any furniture in that room except for his father's roll-top desk and a chair.

"On the floor. I took some pillows from the linen closet. Actually, it's not bad sleeping on the floor. It's nice and hard. I slept well."

"I'm glad you did. I didn't."

With his arms around me we sat on the bed and he buried his face in my breast and we stayed that way for several minutes. Then he stood up and went into the bathroom. I soon heard the shower running. When he was dressed for the day and ready to leave, he asked—as if nothing had transpired between us, as if nothing happened—"Rosemary, we don't have any scotch. Pick up a bottle of Glenlivets, and would you try to find this book for me today?" He handed me a scrap of paper with the author and title. "Try Brentano's. Someone told me they have a large stock in. And don't forget a receipt."

"Why do you need the receipt?"

He looked at me with a condescending look on his face and laughed.

"Did I say something funny?"

"Roseheart. Please. Don't give me a hard time. Just get the goddamned book, OK?"

"OK. I'm sorry."

"And call my mother if you get the book. It's for her. You can drive it over to her, OK?"

"If I have time."

"Oh, excuse me. 'If I have time.' What the fuck are you doing with the whole day?"

"Hey, Cal. I work too, you know. I have to stop at the office and pick up some supplies. Then I want to get a lead on next month's story. I have your scotch and your mother's book to get. I also have housework to do, and I have to shop for furniture. No. I may not have time to drop the book off at your mother's. In fact, I know I won't have the time. And I don't appreciate your using vulgar language at me. In fact, I don't appreciate you using that word, period.

He sighed with irritation and turned away from me.

"By the way, Cal, and don't be mad, but with Francine here last night I forgot to tell you. I had to have the car towed." I related the previous day's incident to him.

"You mean the car broke down yesterday morning, and you waited until now to tell me about it? Where is it?"

"At Nick's."

I still remember the nastiness of his voice, the pauses between words, the anger in his eyes, the madness of it.

"The...next... time...that...happens...see...that... you...tell...me...immediately. Do...you understand?"

Was this Cal talking to me? Or a madman? I heard myself say, "Yes, of course. I'm sorry, Cal. I'm really sorry." I sounded like a child. How else should I have sounded? How does one confront a crazy? One says, "Yes, dear. Of course, dear. Whatever you wish, dear."

"Well, you can drive me to work, since you don't have a car. Let's go."

I followed him out the door. Thank God I had made that promise to myself to always be dressed. Cal was not about to wait a second. We drove in silence. I was numb. I had never heard Cal like that. I had never seen that behavior in him. It scared me. We were halfway to the Capitol when Cal broke the silence.

"Do you have enough money on you?"

I fished through my purse. "Oh! I left my wallet back at the house. Oh, God, Cal, all my credit cards, and checkbook too. I'll have to make two trips."

"Yes, you're going to have to drive back, and back again, all because you didn't concentrate on what you were doing. We can't keep filling this car up with gas. It costs money, you know. Rosemary, get with it, OK?"

"OK. I just hadn't planned on going into the District so fast. You're always rushing me, Cal, you know that?"

"I work faster. Does that bother you?"

"What?"

"That I'm swift and organized?"

"No." I laughed awkwardly. "I just hadn't thought about it. Don't worry. I'll get it together."

He pulled up to the Senate side of the Capitol, put the car into neutral, and got out. I slid over to the driver's seat.

"Have a good day, Cal." I tried to smile at him.

He leaned over and kissed me on the cheek. And then he did that thing that always melted me; he brushed my face with his finger as he kissed me on the lips.

"Don't use up too much gas, Rosemary. I'm budgeting this week." And he was gone.

Budgeting? I was about to remind him that we weren't poor but he had already gone too far up the Capitol steps to hear me. As I turned to drive over to the Longworth Building I suddenly remembered: I didn't remove my wallet from my purse. I never did. It was a fool-proof method not to forget it. I kept all my money and cards in it as well as anything really important. Where would I have put it? I knew I did not take it out.

I was welcomed enthusiastically at my office by Ann and Maryann. Bea was polite but cold. Don remained at his desk and appeared to be occupied by papers and telephone. After they heard about Miami and the weather, and told me how great I looked, I packed up in one big box the supplies that would last for a month or two. Since I was doing only the newsletter, I didn't need much, but just enough so I would not have to return for a couple of months at least, and that would save me time. Time: I was always trying to save on time.

When I arrived home, I searched the house for my wallet finally finding it on the kitchen table. Then I immediately made the bed, tidied the bathroom, and threw a dozen of Cal's shirts into the washing machine—he was adamant about not sending them to the laundry. I was just about to leave the house to finish up my errands when Cal called.

"Hi, sweetheart. How's it going?"

"Good. I was just about to leave."

"What for?"

"The book, Cal, and the scotch. Remember?"

"Now, Rosemary, don't be angry. You're nicer the other way."

I was so grateful he was in a pleasant mood, I would be any way he wanted.

Twenty minutes later I was driving over the bridge into Georgetown. I would have loved to have browsed through some of the shops and get ideas for my decorating, but I didn't have the time. I found the book his mother wanted and walked to the liquor store to get the scotch. I had to laugh. Cal tells me to watch the gas and at the same time is drinking a scotch that's really not necessary. Surely there was a cheaper brand, and I went back to the store and picked up a price list. About a half dozen brands cheaper than the Glenlivets. I tucked the price list into my purse and drove over to Sam's, but she was not home. Since I had a zillion things to do, including the newsletter, I turned away and drove home. The phone was ringing when I opened the front door.

"Cal."

"Hi, sweetheart. How's it going?"

"Good. I got your scotch and your mother's book."

"Great. Would you have time to drop it off to her, sweetheart? Please?"

I didn't have time, but I said I did. I thought about his shirts that needed to be put in the dryer. I thought of the frozen meat that needed to be thawed for dinner. I thought of the newsletter. And what would we have for dinner? I had no sooner hung up from Cal than the phone rang again.

"How are you, dear?" Barbara asked.

"Fine, Barbara. Thanks. I have your book by the way. Will you be home so I can drop it off?"

"What book?"

"Cal asked me to pick up a book for you *The Death of a President* by Manchester."

"He didn't say anything to me about it, but don't bother today. What I'm calling about is to invite you and Callie over for dinner on Sunday. Can you come?"

"Oh, I'd love to. I'll mention it to Cal."

There was a short pause. And then Barbara spoke. "I understand Francine joined you for dinner last night."

"Yes." Now the pause was with me.

"That was nice of you to invite her. I appreciate that." Again, the pause. "I usually shop on Monday nights, dear, but Francine should be sitting with Warren. That's her job. Warren is not to be alone. So next time you just shoo her away, hear?"

"Perhaps she could bring Warren," I said with some reluctance.

"No, dear. That would not work. Besides, you'll tire of all of us very soon. I want the both of you here every Sunday, that is, if you and Callie don't have more important things to do than family. But Monday night is out of the question. I put my foot down there. Hear?"

I felt I was the one who did wrong.

"Well, what do I say to Cal, Barbara? He said Francine's to come every Monday night."

"Absolutely not!" she shot back. No pause there. "Tell Callie I said no."

I was surprised by her adamancy. Was there some previous hostility I had not perceived? But at the same time, I was relieved. I was free of Francine at least for Monday nights. Our Sundays would be family days. I refused to whine. We were family and how many times when I was younger did I wish for family? I threw Cal's shirts in the dryer, took out five lamb chops to thaw for dinner that night, knowing the two of us would not eat five, and hoping there would be only two of us who would not eat five. I carried the stationery supplies up to the den. Originally, it was supposed to be Cal's study, but since I was still working, we decided to share it. The desk was locked. I searched for a key, to no avail. I laid out the Scotch tape, stapler, a Rolodex, and an assortment of files. Then the phone rang.

"Sam. I called you, but you were out. I even stopped by, but you weren't home."

"Come by tomorrow. For lunch. I'll have time then. Right now I have to run. OK?"

"OK. See you around twelve."

The next time the phone rang, no more than five minutes, it was Cal.

"Hello, sweetheart. How's it going?"

"Fine. Cal, where's the key to the desk?"

A long pause.

I waited, but I was anxious to get set up in the den and begin work.

"What desk?"

"Cal. The desk in the study, our study." The desk was a roll top and had belonged to his father. "It's locked."

"Oh, my desk. Why?"

"I need to get into it. I'm working."

"I didn't know you were going to start so soon."

"Well, I am. Where's the key?"

"I don't know. I don't think we have a key."

"That doesn't do me much good, does it?"

"Well, do you need to get into it? What do you need?"

"I wanted to put my supplies away."

"Supplies?"

"Supplies. You know. Files, papers, pencils, pens. Supplies."

"Oh, well, we'll set you up somehow. No problem. Listen, Rosemary, did you get the book to my mother's?"

"She said not to go over today. And by the way, your mother said Francine was not to have dinner with us on Monday nights. She's to sit Warren."

There was the longest pause.

"Cal, did you hear me?"

"Yes, I did!" His voice rose to a roar. I knew everyone in his office heard him, but the violence it carried was worse. It scared the living daylights out of me.

"What's the matter?" I asked, keeping my voice low and timid.

Another of his long pauses.

"Nothing. Thanks for doing all that work for me. Did you get to my shirts yet? I'm low."

How did he do that, I thought. Go from high to low. "You won't reconsider about sending them out?" I asked with some trepidation but more out of desperateness. Ironing his shirts took hours and it was not an easy task getting the wrinkles out of them.

"Rosemary, is it such a big chore? Am I really asking too much? Just a little spray starch and a quick iron. Can you at least get to one or two of them today?" The Cal I fell in love with returned. He was annoyed but there was no violence.

I spent the rest of the afternoon spraying and ironing Cal's shirts and watching *Hawaii Five-O*. I would have the rest of the week with uninterrupted time to work on the newsletter. But the hostility I heard earlier, from both Barbara and Cal, stayed with me. Scared me.

I was just about to get up. Cal was in the bathroom and had just finished his shower. I turned in time to see Warren standing in the doorway grinning.

"Warren! What are you doing here?" I pulled the covers up over me.

He turned and raced down the stairs. I got up and locked the door.

"Cal, what was Warren doing up here? He was just standing there in the doorway looking at me. In fact, what is he doing in our house?"

Cal shrugged his shoulders and smiled. "I don't see him. What are you talking about?"

"He was here. Your brother. Just standing there in the doorway grinning." Cal's grin did not please me either.

"Was he in the bedroom or in the doorway? He's not allowed in bedrooms." He chuckled.

"It isn't funny, Cal." I didn't like him teasing me. "Why was he grinning at me?"

"He's always grinning," Cal exclaimed. "You know his problem. What the hell do you want me to do about it?" he yelled, taking one of his shirts out of the closet.

"What's he doing in the house?" I asked, keeping my voice low, sorry that I upset him.

"He's working in the basement. That's why he's in the house."

"I thought he was finished. And why didn't you tell me that? Who let him in? He doesn't have a key, does he?"

He grabbed me by an arm with his two hands and twisted as children do when they're giving a playmate an "Indian burn." I tried to pull away.

"Don't you ever question me again, do you hear?" He released me and pushed me onto the bed. "I will be responsible for my brother coming in and out of my house, do you understand?" I heard an audible hatred in his voice. I cringed. "What the hell is wrong with these shirts? Don't you know how to iron? What are all these wrinkles?" He gave a precursory glance at the shirt and threw it on the floor and took another one off the hanger.

It is irrelevant now to say how I should have handled that scene. What I did was to sit down on the bed and speak, just to speak, because that was the only way I knew how to respond to a fear I was not used to, a fear I could not diagnose. I talked as if in talking, words would weaken the fear.

"I'm having lunch with Sam today," I told him. "I'll be gone for a few hours."

He came over and put his arms around me. "I'm sorry, Roseheart." He pulled my head to his chest. "I love you, you know. You're good, my love, too good for me." He kissed me with passion; I would have preferred that same emotion at another time. Sometimes Cal knew how to touch me, how to get to me. He just didn't always do it. He moaned, holding me close, his after-shave smelling masculine, his body warm and dry next to mine. "Listen sweetheart. I have an idea. Meet me for lunch. We'll go into the District, someplace nice. And you won't have to cook dinner tonight. We'll see a movie instead. We'll order large popcorn. How's that?" He kissed me again. Long, sexual. I wanted to make love, but he turned away from me.

I put Sam off for another day.

It was another week before Sam and I could get together. Cal could find dozens of odd jobs for me to do, and with my furniture shopping and newsletter, I found little time for visiting. But it didn't matter. Cal was generous to me with presents—inexpensive but pretty things—and I was learning to accept this crazy life of mine. However, I did not tell Cal when I was having lunch with Sam. I did not tell Sam I did not tell Cal. Some things, I was learning, were better left unsaid.

"Hey, friend, welcome back!" Sam's reception was warm and enthusiastic, and it was good to see her again, to be with her.

"Hey, friend yourself. It's good to be back."

We hugged.

"Listen, shorty, we're going to eat in OK? Because I want to hear all of the uh, intimate details. Yahoo!" She raised a fist in the air and, laughing, rushed into the kitchen.

I smelled something burning.

"Oh, shit! Hey, Rosi! How do you cook rice? I just can't cook rice. I try so hard, but it burns all the time." She laughed again and dumped the blackened pot, rice and all, into the garbage.

The extravagance of that act, for some inexplicable reason, left an indelible mark on my stranded psyche. I would be reprimanded by Cal for doing what she did and yet he continued to tell me we had plenty of money. The next day we would be budgeting.

I took over and prepared the rice, stirred the delightful amalgamation of beef and sour cream and onions that Sam, miraculously, had melded together, and uncorked the wine.

"This is an unusual corkscrew. Where did you get it?" I asked, the wine bottle between my thighs, the stubborn cork unmoving and heavy.

"It's Brad's." She answered me with a cool indifference.

"Who's Brad?"

"My new roommate." She grinned, her indifference took on a new look.

"What?" I exclaimed.

"You heard me," she said, carrying the steaming bowl of rice to the table.

"I'm gone three weeks, and you replace me? How long has this been going on?" I laughed.

"Since yesterday," she said.

"I take it you're serious?" I asked with a puerility I didn't know I had.

"Hell, no!" She cried out. "He just needs a place to stay. It's convenient for both of us."

I still loved this friend I thought decadent and beautiful, and I could not help but feel some jealousy toward that unseen intruder who had taken my place. But what did I expect? Her request for my permission? And somehow, her freedom, her complete and uncomplicated freedom, only heightened my jealousy. What was wrong with me?

"How long have you known him?" I asked.

"A week."

"A week? Dear God, Sam, he could be a lunatic."

"Oh, no. He's not a loonie. He's a playwright. You know, down on his luck, that sort of thing. I'm helping him out. He doesn't have anything. And he's a good writer."

"Where is he now? Am I going to get to meet him?"

"Naw. I told him I was having company." She helped herself to the stroganoff.

"That's nice of him. Does he leave every time you entertain?"

"Yeah. I told you. He's a nice guy. We get along fairly well. Enough about him. What about you?" She was looking at me eagerly, her grin lascivious and amusing, her eyes gleaming, her head thrust forward. "Still going to make the Miss America contest? Huh?"

I laughed. "You are hysterical, Sam, for God's sake." I helped myself to a tiny portion of the stroganoff.

"How many positions?"

I screamed with laughter. "One! Just one, Sam. Will you stop? I don't want to discuss my sex life with anybody. Have a heart."

"My God, you're still blushing!" She pointed a pedantic finger at me. "Will wonders never cease."

I couldn't help but laugh with her. Those mischievous eyes were always ready to receive battle. I wondered if she had heard from Rob, about him. But I didn't think it would be right for me to ask. I was a married woman now. Adultery comes in many forms; it doesn't have to be physical. I would not betray Cal.

The stroganoff devoured, the wine drunk, our attempts to solve the world's problems dealt with, we parted. I suppose Sam knew me better than I've ever given her credit for, because as I was walking down the steps, she asked, "You still have a key?"

"Oh, I forgot. Here." I opened my purse to return it to her.

"No. You keep it, Rosi. This is still your home. Whether I'm here or not. Use it when you need. Bye, friend." She shut the door on my smiling but puzzled face.

The car started up but with multiple tries. Cal had taught me the proper way to start up Francine's still-good-1958-Pontiac-with-sixteen-plus-dents, with one exception.

"Just step on the accelerator lightly," he told me in his usual paternalistic way. "All the way down. See? Three times. Now turn the key. See how easy it is?" For him it was. It usually took seven steps on the accelerator for me, and then I would turn the key. It never started when I stepped on it three times. I drove away after having stepped on the accelerator eleven times.

I was on the Key Bridge when it died again. Black fumes spewed from the motor, and licks of flames attempted to escape through the hood. Immediately I put the car in Park, turned the ignition off, and ran back some ten feet. I thought it would explode. A kind motorist moved it to the side and graciously offered me a lift, but I declined, thanked him, and walked back to the stores just below the bridge to look for a phone.

I called Nick, who was becoming my good friend, and then I called a cab. The five o'clock traffic was just beginning, and of course, the huge, ugly antiquity that blocked the lane only made the daily traffic jam doubly worse. I had put a notice on the windshield for the police should they come by, but Nick promised to be there within a half hour, so I didn't worry about it. I wished someone would steal it.

I had no sooner arrived home when Cal called.

"Hello, sweetheart!"

"Hi, Cal. Sorry to have to tell you, but it broke down again," I said in a rush. I was not about to forget to tell him.

"Did you step on the accelerator three times like I taught you?" my "father" asked me.

"Yes."

"And you turned the key after stepping on the accelerator?"

"Cal, I stepped on it eleven times. It just wouldn't start."

"You flooded it! You idiot! Oh, fuck it! You can't do anything right." He hung up.

My hands were shaking. I went upstairs and removed my clothes, which were wet from the day's heat. Cal and I would talk. I would not allow him to speak to me with such violence. This would not happen again. We would have a serious talk. I took a cold shower and dressed in a flimsy robe. Although I was not a drinker, I poured myself one of Cal's Glenlivets to calm me down; the smoothness, the mellowness, allowed me to relax. I felt cooler and bit calmer when Barbara called me.

"Have you seen Francine, dear?"

"No, Barbara. Why?"

"Oh, she just upped and left an hour ago. I thought maybe she was there. Well, no worry. She'll show. She always does."

I had to laugh. If Barbara were my mother, I'd have to run away too. I finished my scotch and concentrated on my talk to the "master," but the thought did lurk in my subconscious: why would Francine be here?

Cal came home at eight and I steeled myself for my wifely speech.

"Well, Roseheart. It looks like you get yourself a new car." He flopped on a kitchen chair and placed both feet on the table as he worked to unloosen his tie. He did not look pleasant. In fact, he looked angry. I delayed my wifely speech for another time.

"I'm not surprised." I sat opposite him, hoping he would not be violent.

"I am. That old Plymouth could have lasted another twenty-five thousand miles if you knew how to drive it."

"What did Nick say about it?"

"It needs a little work. Not worth the money. Cheaper to buy a new one."

"How about a used car? You know, a demo model. People tell me they're good cars."

"Absolutely not. You'll get a new car. A good one. That will last."

"Can we afford it?"

"Of course," he said. "Pour me a scotch with a little water, please. I'm exhausted."

I got up to make his drink. "How much can we spend?"

"Don't worry about it. I'll take care of it."

"I have to know. Listen, Cal, I'm buying a lot of furniture and things. Our money isn't limitless, is it?"

He turned then and gave me a brief but blank look and said, "We can afford it."

"I still need to know our income. I know the outgo with the exception of the mortgage."

He got up and began to walk out of the room. I followed him.

"Don't run away. What is our mortgage?"

"We'll go over it tomorrow." He said as he continued to walk up the stairs.

Satisfied with my little victory I added simply for something to say. "Well, we don't have to furnish the whole house right away."

"Yes, we do," he called down from the hall. "I want a home. That's your job, Rosemary. Don't worry about the money. I'll take care of that end."

"Our home is where we live together, Cal, where we love together. Furniture doesn't make a home."

"Oh, for Christ's sake, don't get poetic on me, will you? Just get it furnished. And right away. I can't stand living like this anymore." I heard him enter his den and shut the door.

It would have been nice to have taken all the time in the world to decorate my home. I loved the planning, the decorating, the shopping, I enjoyed every moment of it. But I would do as Cal wanted. After all, I was one lucky girl.

I was happy, or at least I thought I was. Despite Cal's moody ways, and although it was uneasy living with him, I still believed I loved him. After all, there are solutions to problems. I would learn what they were, and I would deal with them. One problem at a time.

He bought me a new car. I didn't have a say in picking it out, but it was nice. I never cared much for cars and I still don't. They get people places. It's a neat way of commuting. So I didn't mind not having a say in choosing it. I wouldn't know what to choose anyway. He bought a station wagon, just what I would not buy—little too big for me—but it was pretty, and it was my favorite color, maroon. I guessed he was thinking in terms of family and kids when he picked it out. I was so glad to be rid of Francine's heap of junk and so grateful for air conditioning, I didn't care what kind of car it was. I was thrilled.

"Let's go." He looked so handsome, standing there waving the keys in the air. "Let's take a drive."

"Just around the block, Cal. It's so big." I was nervous driving a brand new car without dents, shiny and smelling like leather. I got into the driver's seat and started it up. I can still remember the newness of it, the coolness of the air conditioner—it was lovely.

"Take a left," he told me.

"Where else?" I asked him facetiously. Had I taken a right, I would wind up in the cul-de-sac a hundred yards away.

"Don't get fresh. Drive up to the corner."

"I'm not getting fresh. You can't tell when I'm joking, can you?" I suddenly realized he was not even focused on me.

"Rosemary," he said wearily. "Just drive."

"How much?" I asked. He had removed the sticker before he brought it home.

"All my love, Roseheart."

What could I say? It gave him pleasure in presenting it to me, and I was not about to take that away from him. I was fortunate to have a "normal" husband for however long it was going to last. I took what I could get when I got it.

"Thank you my love. Thank you." I leaned over and kissed him.

"By the way, I have to go to the home office next week. Just for a few days. Think you can do it alone?"

"Of course," I replied a bit too enthusiastically. "What's going on?"

"Nothing you want to know. Just to see a few people for the senator."

"About what?"

"Turn back, Rosi, I'm hungry. What's for dinner?"

"You asked me to try a pork roast. So. Pork roast it is."

"Thank you, Rosi. Baked potatoes?" He gave me an imploring look, boyish look.

"Everything you asked for, darling."

It was a wonderful evening. I did not insist he tell me what was going on in the home office. Considering his wonderful and normal mood that was unimportant. I had a new car and I didn't mind receiving a gift I had no choice in. I didn't mind that it was so big. I didn't mind I hadn't been able to pick it out. It was one lovely automobile. And it had air conditioning.

Sam and I continued our once-a-week luncheons. Sitting there with her in her "tiny, tiny" house, it seemed as if I had never left. We drank Chablis in the backyard. Sam loved the wrought-iron garden furniture and decided to buy it, although she neglected the plants and rosebushes, and they died a little bit with each visit. But we enjoyed the summer and the Chablis.

The monthly newsletter was easy except for the column. Although the congressman wanted to come up with the subject, he was most times too busy to catch, so I would just write it once it came to me. He did little, if any, editing. The column was his pet even though I was the one writing it. I became the great manipulator of time, juggling my household duties with my office duties. When Cal was home, it was difficult to do, but when Cal had to work late or work on weekends, I was able to make the time. I was thankful I had left full-time work. I don't know how I would have accomplished all of it.

I gardened whenever I could snatch an hour in the morning or in the later part of the day. I planted rosebushes soon after we had returned from our honeymoon, an herb bed, and lots of perennials. The next year, by God, I would have my own vegetable garden.

Warren was a great help to me. He dug all the holes I needed for the half dozen rosebushes and turned over the earth where I wanted my herb bed. He loved doing things for me, and I was beginning to feel comfortable around him.

On Sundays we had dinner with Barbara. Those days were unpleasant for me. Although dinner was never served before six in the evening, Cal insisted on getting there just after lunch. I dreaded Sundays. Once, when I suggested doing something else, Cal said that "...my mother would be crushed if she weren't allowed these little family get-togethers." And so, I considered every Sunday visit mandatory. Actually, I couldn't blame Barbara for wanting everyone together; isn't that what families are for? And didn't I want family? But Francine and I just couldn't get together on anything, and she remained placid and quiet, a little too placid and quiet. Barbara, when she wasn't speaking with Cal, did speak with me, but always in a short manner. She gave me recipes and loved to talk about her ancestors to me—no shortness there—but I still kept my distance. I could not allow myself to trust her. Every Sunday morning I psyched myself up for the day and managed to suppress my dread.

We sat in the living room—Cal and I and Barbara and Francine and Warren. After a while, Warren would traipse off into the den to watch television. Francine was fond of one-syllable words when she chose to speak. I continued to tolerate her with a gracious indifference. What else could I do? I learned to accept her smug sneers. I told myself it was her pathetic attempt to be pleasant. And she was Cal's sister, my family now. I had to be kinder. Her one good quality was that she was a good listener. Barbara never stopped talking about current events and politics, which she knew a lot about. Barbara, I soon learned, was highly intelligent. But mostly, Barbara monopolized the conversation, and spoke only to Cal. In the beginning I would sit and listen to her attentively. My second sermon of the day. No wonder Francine did not speak. One day Barbara asked if I had read the Sunday papers. I hadn't. She handed me the *Washington Post.* Grateful for her permission—Cal never wanted me to read when I was there—and for the opportunity, I would absorb myself in the myriad of national and international events, only to look up and find I had been abandoned. The living room was always dark and cold, and I could hear all of them in the kitchen talking, that is, Barbara and Cal. That was the first of many times I felt unwanted and out of place. My polite and genuine offers to help with dinner were never accepted, and I used every pore and gland in my body not to get angry or feel sorry for myself. For such was their way, I told myself. I decided to offer up my Sundays. They would be my penance, an offering. Just as I was taught as a child when I had to do something I didn't like—I would be told to offer it up as penance. After all, I had six days of the week when I was happy. I was not about to ruin those six days by concerning myself with one.

It was a day in August, hot and muggy, but I didn't care. As soon as Cal would leave for the office, I would work in the garden. He was nowhere upstairs, and as I came down, I saw him standing in the living room to the side of the bay window, peering out through the opening of the blinds.

"I thought I'd invite my mother for a few days, Cal." I had not seen my mother since the wedding.

He did not answer me.

"Cal," I called over to him.

"Shh!" He held a hand up to quiet me.

I went over and looked out too, curious to see what he found so interesting.

"Stay back!" he hissed at me.

"What is it?" I asked, staying back.

"John Wagner. He jogs about five miles a day."

"Who's John Wagner?"

"Our neighbor, dummy. His wife's name is Phyllis."

"Don't call me a dummy. How do you know he jogs five miles?"

"I can tell. He started out at six twenty this morning. At twelve minutes a mile—anyone can do that—five miles would be one hour, and it's seven twenty now." He tapped his watch. "And I call you a dummy because you never pay attention, you're in another world."

"Excuse me, God, but I do pay attention. Believe me, I'm not in another world."

His look emanated such violence, I trembled.

"Don't...you...ever...speak...to...me...like...that...again."

"How about my mother?" I asked, wanting him to leave me, wanting to be by myself, wanting not to feel this fear.

"What about her?" Another man spoke to me. I could not get used to his ups and downs.

"Do you think we could have her come for a visit?"

"Sure, invite her. It'll be nice to see her again. You know, Rosi, instead of spending all your time with that ditz, Sam, you should be cultivating people like the Wagners. Why don't you invite them over for dinner?"

I was still thinking about the way he spoke to me.

"See what I mean?" he sneered, as he picked up his briefcase and left for the office.

My emotions ran from hurt to anger and back again to hurt. He knew Sam and I were best friends. And what was that hostility in his voice? What happened to that great guy I dated?

Except for a few errands and my morning housework, I was free. It was the day before I turned in the monthly newsletter, and I would not have to think about the next one for another two weeks. I made the bed and tidied up the bathroom. I was beginning to be grateful for Cal's obsession against clutter. Our house had little of it. I was forced to put everything away after use, otherwise, I had to check the wastebaskets. But I was learning to get used to his ways.

I no sooner had donned my jeans and sneakers and pulled my garden equipment together, when the phone rang. I knew it was Cal. He could call me twenty times a day and not think it was too much. I was afraid he'd have an errand for me to do. I turned the phone to a low tone, and then I went out into my garden, shutting the door behind me.

It was wonderful! I was alone with me. No errands, no chores, just me and my garden. Every twenty minutes I could hear the faint ringing of the telephone through the kitchen window which was closed tight. With the air conditioning on I was not allowed to open a window.

I had already planted little pots of just about everything in my herb garden, to the right of the kitchen door. I had chives, rosemary, sage, basil, lemon thyme, thyme. The lemon thyme was my favorite. I would pinch a bit every so often and sniff. I wanted tons of it! It was a small plot, but I intended it to be about ten feet by eight feet later on. My flowerbed, which was over by the side of the fence, to the right of the house, had daisies, mums for the fall, lilies of the valley, and a few other unidentifiables that had been planted long ago and neglected. I would straighten them out later on. In the middle of the yard, I began my favorite project—my rose garden. The six bushes that Warren and I had planted earlier were blooming prolifically. We would have long-stemmed roses in September or October.

I weeded the herb bed and raked around it. Then I worked on the flowerbed, weeding and raking. I left the roses alone, since they seemed to be doing fine by themselves, and went back down toward what was going to be my vegetable patch. Cal hated that patch of garden, calling it the cabbage patch. "Why do we have to grow vegetables?" he asked me several times. "We can afford to buy them, you know." I told him to wait until he tasted them fresh from the garden. He'd soon change his tune.

"What the hell are you doing?" Cal was standing at the back door, both hands on his hips, legs splayed, looking furious. "I've been calling you all morning, Rosemary. What the hell have you been doing?"

I knew it was he who was calling, but I never expected he would leave his office to come home. I was jolted from my beautiful world back to reality. "You have, darling?" I asked in my truest alto voice. "I've been out here all morning. What are you doing home?"

"Just to see if you're alright. I really wish you'd pick up that phone."

"I didn't hear it."

"How could you not have heard it? I have it switched to high. How can you stand there and tell me you can't hear that phone?"

"Would you like some lunch, honey? I'll make some tuna salad." He loved tuna sandwiches.

"Yeah. OK. But next time answer the phone." He knew I was lying.

And then he did what I hoped he wouldn't. He went over to the phone and turned it up.

"You turned that phone down, didn't you?"

"No, I didn't," I lied.

"Sure you did. Well, it's up now and leave it that way."

My gardening was over. It was almost one o'clock. Cal didn't leave until after two. I showered, changed my clothes, and went to the cleaners for his suit, to the shoemakers for his loafers, to the store for his favorite hot fudge topping. I bought him two more white shirts, which he didn't need but would cut down my ironing to once every two weeks. I arrived home at five thirty in time to get supper ready. Cal would be home by six, and if dinner wasn't on the table, he would be grumpy.

I could hear Warren hammering in the cellar. I knew Cal had given him a key, even though he denied it. But I dropped the subject. Cal's moods were mercurial, to put it modestly, and I learned to roll with them. I was learning what I should say and when, and what

I shouldn't say and when. I know I should have spoken to him about his outbursts, but every time I tried, he was in such good humor I'd put it off for another time.

Warren was a great worker. Before he could begin the paneling, he had to clean up the cellar. It was a mess before we moved in, and it was worse after we moved in. Despite the fact that Cal had insisted it be cleaned out before we closed on it, no one did anything about it. But Warren loved to clean and putter, and he had it completely emptied in a short time. By the sounds of his hammering, I knew he was still working on the paneling. Cal must have spoken to him because Warren was no longer hammering as I had taught him. He had reverted back to his old way, just tapping at each nail so that it would only be halfway in. Cal had picked out the wood: thick, rich paneling of stained walnut. It was beautiful. *Too good for a cellar*, I thought at the time. It belonged in a library. Cal had just left for the office, and I poured my first cup of coffee for the day. I would go down later to say hello to Warren. But I had no sooner sat down than I heard a grunt, and I looked up to see him in the doorway.

Warren never came into a room without being invited. He hung out in doorways. I discovered also that no one spoke to him. Except to give him an order or an instruction, no one ever engaged him in conversation. I thought this unfortunate and so I had taken to having small, brief conversations with him when I had the time. I made him speak slowly. I taught him to pronounce each word correctly. He was quite good, although it was only possible for him to achieve a few words or one complete short sentence at a time. Day by day there was a progressive improvement. He appeared to enjoy our little talks, and I could tell he looked forward to them. That morning, though, he seemed really sad.

"Hello, Warren. Come in."

His head was down, his eyes riveted to the floor.

"What is it, Warren?" I asked. "What's wrong?'

He walked up close to Cal's photo, encased in a gold frame on an end table. Pointing to the photograph, he rubbed his index fingers together and pouted.

"Oh, no, Warren," I said. "Cal is very nice. You mustn't do that."

But Warren insisted, and he was very agitated, jumping up and down and rubbing his fingers together.

"Alright, Warren. Come over here and sit down. Sit by me." I patted the place on the couch next to where I was sitting. "Tell me about your work."

He did not sit, but ran toward the doorway and signaled for me to follow. I got up and went after him.

The cellar was really shaping up. The ceiling had been spackled so that there were no longer any visible cracks or holes. It had been painted a bright white. Cal had an electrician put in track lighting, and it created strong but soft lights. Most of the paneling was up. When Warren would finish, we planned on putting in wall-to-wall carpeting, a billiards table, and perhaps a full or half bath. Cal wanted a big game room, and it looked like he was going to have it sooner than he expected.

"Warren, this is lovely. A very good job, Warren. I'm very proud of you."

He was laughing, making rasping noises from his throat, gurgling. He raced over to one corner, and under some dirty blankets and sheets he had been using for drop cloths, he picked up a wooden figure. He raced back to me and held it out for my acceptance. "F…f…f…fer u!" he yelled out, his smile black and wide.

"Why, thank you, Warren. Where did you get this?"

He went back to the drop cloths and threw them aside. On the floor small blocks of wood were scattered about amid mountains of shavings. He picked up a knife. I could see it was a carving knife. He held it in one hand, the block of wood in the other, and pretended to be carving.

"You did this?" I asked, pleasantly astounded.

Laughing, rasping, breathing hard, he nodded his empty and shapeless head rapidly up and down.

"This is beautiful." I spoke slowly, enunciating every letter. "And I'm going to put it in the living room so everyone can see it."

He began to jump up and down, crying, "No...o... o...noo!"

"Alright, Warren." I placed my hand gently on his shoulder in an effort to compose him. "I'll keep it just for me. No one will see it. Is that what you want?"

He was shedding tears, but I couldn't hear him crying. He nodded yes without looking at me.

"Then that is what I will do. This will be our secret, Warren. Yours and mine. Alright?"

His fat face brightened, and I felt him relax as I removed my hand from his shoulder. "Now. Come here and talk to me. I want to know if you're happy."

He sat beside me, smiling, stealing glances at me. Warren could talk, though he seldom did. The only times I heard him speak were those infrequent times he spent with me. I asked him how he did the paneling, and he answered as a child would, but articulated and pronounced so that even Barbara, I'm sure, would not have known it was her son. We had our usual short and brief conversation, and then Warren stood up and returned to his work. I never told Cal about our speech lessons. He never mentioned Warren to me, and I thought it best that I follow suit.

I had planned to visit my mother that week, but did not get around to discussing it with Cal. She did not want to come down to my place, even though we had plenty of room and I was eager for her to see my new home. When Cal came home that evening, I mentioned it to him.

"Tomorrow we're going out. Remember?" He reminded me.

"Oh, I forgot. Well, I'll go up Thursday then and be back on Saturday afternoon."

"Good idea." He turned away from me and took his drink upstairs with him. I heard him go into the den and close the door. It always bothered me when he closed doors on me. And I had forgotten to ask him about the key to the desk again.

I went to bed with thoughts of my mother on my mind. Cal remained in his den. I never heard him come to bed. Our sex life was like his personality—on again, off again. We'd have satisfactory sex for a few days straight and then nothing for a week or two. I discovered that I was a sexual woman in a semi-sexual marriage.

The next day I worked in the garden. Although I had planted my herbs late, they were already sprouting. I weeded out the bed, taking great satisfaction in having an orderly garden like so many clean and tidy children. Next year I would enlarge it. I would add anise and dill and maybe some Italian parsley. I was deep in thought when Phyllis Wagner stopped by.

"Rosemary? Hi. I'm Phyllis Wagner. Sorry we haven't met before this, but it seems I'm always working. I live right across from you in the white house—the one with the overgrown lawn. My apologies for not coming over sooner." She shrugged.

Phyllis appeared to be in her late twenties or early thirties. She had a face full of freckles, but unlike Francine they only added character to her finely chiseled features, features that exuded strength and firmness.

She was a pretty woman with a pretty demeanor. She wore a smart-looking dress made for business. It looked expensive. "No apologies are necessary, Phyllis. It's nice to meet you. Can I get you something to drink?"

"No, thank you. I'm on my way to work. Another twelve-hour day. I get more work done at home than I do at the office. Oh, well, mustn't complain. My husband and I were wondering if you and your husband could join us for dinner on Saturday. I know its late notice, but that's the way we are. I'm totally disorganized."

"We'd love to. What time and how should we dress?"

"Sevenish and dress casual. Very casual. I wish I could have some of the neighbors in to meet you, but I have to say it's just the four of us. Is that alright?"

"Why, of course, look forward to it."

"Me too. Well, I'm off to work, so I apologize for my abruptness. See you on Saturday." She waved goodbye, and I watched her walk out through the side yard.

Cal would be happy. For weeks he had been insisting that I invite them over. Just about every day he would remind me to have them in for a drink or for dinner, but we were the newcomers, and I thought it best to wait until we were invited. After Phyllis left, I went into the house and showered and changed. The soft, tepid water felt sensual against my skin, and I allowed myself the lacy freedom of it for a long while. Then I put on my white linen slacks and cotton blouse and left the house.

I drove to the stationer's to pick up stationery I had ordered for Cal a week before. He wanted the best stationery with our initials embossed on it, and it took about four trips and numerous samples before he finally chose one. He could spend more time making to-dos about things when I could have had it all done in a short time. But I was growing accustomed to Cal's ways and with each passing day, they bothered me less.

Cal drove up to the house at six o'clock sharp and blew his horn. I raced upstairs to grab my purse and was out in a few minutes. We were going to have a romantic dinner together in my favorite restaurant, El Tio Pepe's in Georgetown.

He looked impatient when I opened the door and got in.

"Hi, darling!" I edged over to him and kissed him on the cheek.

"I wish you wouldn't leave me waiting, Rosemary."

"But I'm on time. It's just six. On the dot," I added, checking my watch. "And you weren't waiting," I reprimanded him softly. "You just pulled up."

"Ten after."

I would not argue with him. Just the slightest contradiction could blow our whole evening.

We drove to El Tio Pepe's in almost total silence, broken only by my short, tenuous clips of conversation. I was so bent on cheering him up, I forgot about Phyllis' invitation for Saturday night dinner.

The restaurant was quiet that evening, matching our moods, and Cal ordered a scotch and water for himself and a martini for me.

"Since when do I drink martinis?" I asked with a smile.

"Now," he replied. "Why not?"

"They make my head spin. You know that."

"Well, God forbid we should do anything that would make your head spin." He reached over and placed both his hands over mine. It used to be his touch was always warm and comforting but then his hands felt rough. I pulled mine away. "Roseheart," he began in the way I hated to hear him begin anything. It usually ended by being sarcastic and condescending. "I know now. I just didn't think. I'll change it." He called the waiter over to our table. "My wife changed her mind."

"I'll have a scotch and water too, please. Did everything go alright today, Cal?" I asked after the waiter left.

He jerked his head and gave me a strange look. "Yes, why?"

I tried to smile, but couldn't. Most times I could contend with his moods, but that night I would have thought he'd want our dinner to be, if not romantic, at least civilized. "I was just trying to make conversation. I'm interested in what you do. You know, Cal, our communication needs improvement."

"Does…that…bother…you?" Again, that awful way he had of pausing between words. I felt my nerves twitch. His small, rigid eyes shrank even smaller, fastened on me, studied me, as if they had never seen me before.

The waiter brought our favorite—paella—and when we had eaten, Cal suggested we have our dessert and coffee at home. The evening was a complete flop, and I gave up all attempts at saving it.

Driving over the bridge into Arlington, I spoke if for nothing else but to break the dreadful, strained silence that always seemed to scare me.

"By the way, Cal, I'm going up to my mother's tomorrow. You didn't forget, did you?

He took a deep breath, shook his head, and looked away.

"Cal. What's the matter? Please. Why do you get like this?" I felt like crying.

"Maybe if you weren't out in la-la land so often, I wouldn't get like this, whatever the fuck I'm supposed to be!"

The black mood coming.

I also took a deep breath.

"How long do you plan to stay? Or shouldn't I ask?" He asked me with a veneer of civility.

"No, you should ask. Overnight. Two days. I'll be back on Saturday. Oh, Cal. I almost forgot. Phyllis Wagner invited us for dinner on Saturday night." *My God*, I thought, *he's right. I'm always forgetting.*

"Yes?" he asked, looking down at me.

"Phyllis came over to introduce herself and invited us." The edge in my voice was blunt, a rusted piece of metal.

There was the longest pause. "And you forgot to tell me. See what I mean?"

Finally, I got up enough courage to look at him. He had the crispest bit of a smile on his beautiful, mean face. I burst into tears.

I decided to take the train into Manhattan and then change to the Pathway to Jersey City. The thought of driving alone for almost four hours on the New Jersey Turnpike made me a bit nervous. Although I was beginning to love driving I was not yet ready for a long drive by myself. The train would prove therapeutic; I needed that time to think about my marriage. It would give me time to de-stress. The thought of leaving Cal occupied that space in my head that I tried to leave open. I wanted to be fair to him and to me. The thought of divorce was abhorrent, and whenever the thought occurred, I dismissed it immediately. I knew I had to sit down with Cal and discuss everything that bothered me. I had to discuss with him his blatant flaws that frightened me at times and other times frustrated me. We both needed to adjust to each other and to a brand-new life. Cal's moods were beginning to depress me. It was difficult to get him to open up and talk, and he was just plain hostile too much of the time. Did I want to continue with that for the rest of my life? Indeed, did I want to continue with that for another day or week? What went on in the brilliant head of his? I did not know this man I married. But divorce? I couldn't. At that time I just couldn't think of divorce.

I was taking my mother to dinner and had previously told her to meet me at the restaurant, so I walked over; it was less than a half mile from the train, and the walk felt good after so many hours of sitting. I arrived at the restaurant before my mother and made myself comfortable at a table for two and ordered a scotch and water. The scotch relaxed me and I felt a sense of freedom, complete and quiet freedom. A magnificent detachment. Even the arrival of my mother did not diminish the feeling of detachment.

It was wonderful to see her, and I made a promise I would not let as much time go by again.

"I'm sorry I haven't been up sooner, Mother, but there's so much to do."

"And Cal? How is he?" she asked, looking me square in the eyes.

I looked away from her. I had never in my life lied to my mother, nor was I ever successful in fooling her. She knew me well. And aside from Sam who else could I talk to freely. "He's so hard to understand…" and it all came out, how I was trying to be a good wife, a good housekeeper, but it didn't seem to work. Nothing pleased him.

"Not to worry, Rosemary. Your husband comes first, remember now. Things will work out. Just keep loving him, make him feel like a man. He'll come round. You're such a lucky little girl, dear. You've done so well for yourself. Why not in marriage? It's only been a couple of months. Give it time." She looked at me and smiled. "I'm proud of you. Keep working at it. You'll see. It will be worth it. These problems most likely will prove to be nothing. Years from now you may even laugh at yourself." She squeezed my hand, but her grip was weak.

"Are you taking good care of yourself, Mom? Seeing the doctor? You're still going every six months for your checkup, aren't you?" I realized I hadn't asked her those questions since I was married. It was important that I keep after her.

"I am. Don't worry. Now, let's eat." She commanded me in her motherly tone. The waiter placed our dinners before us, but I discovered my appetite had disappeared. I ordered another scotch.

I stayed overnight and slept in the same bed I had slept in all my life. The room was close, almost musty, and I realized that my mother must have lost her fervor for cleanliness and organization. She was always good at that. Everything seemed to need cleaning.

I got up and went into the kitchen to make tea. I opened the cupboard to retrieve the tea bags, and my hand touched something sticky, gooey. I stood on tip-toe to see that it was a half gallon of ice cream congealed over the shelves. I cleaned it up and threw away the box. In the morning, after she had had her breakfast, I told her about it.

She laughed. "I'm getting old, dear."

"You have to be careful, Mother, and focus more on what you do."

"Everyone makes mistakes dear, it's not a big thing. Getting old is not a sin. Some things you must learn to laugh at. We're not all perfect, you know."

Was that what was wrong with me? Was I expecting perfection from Cal? No one had ever accused me of being a perfectionist. Was I taking everything too seriously? Maybe my mother was right. Maybe I wanted something else from Cal. Maybe I should laugh at his craziness, his idiosyncrasies.

"Would you like to come down in a few weeks, Mom? I'd love you to see my home. We have a guest room."

I will, dear. That sounds nice. I want to see your wedding album when I come."

I realized I had forgotten to bring the small album I had made up special for her.

❦

Saturday night. Phyllis and John. Cal rushing me.

"Hurry up, Rosemary! We don't want to be late for the attorney general!"

"What are you talking about? What attorney general?"

"John. Who do you think I'm talking about? Hey, Rosemary," he teased me. "Tonight. Remember? In five minutes? We're due at the Wagner's'? That's why you're getting all dressed up. Remember?"

"Yes, I remember, Cal. But John is not the attorney general." My voice was tense, tight.

"He will be one day. Stand up straight. Don't do that." He grimaced.

"Don't do what?" I smothered my anger.

"That. You'll get a hump on your back if you do. Stand up straight," he commanded.

I squared my already-squared shoulders. I would not let him get to me. The place between my breasts hurt, the sensation rising in great waves so that I felt faint. I sat down, breathing easy, willing myself to relax.

"Why are you dressed like that?"he asked.

I was wearing Bermuda shorts with a casual blouse and sandals. "Phyllis said to dress *very* casual, Cal. You're too dressed." He wore a suit and tie and a

301

white shirt that I had ironed. "I told you. Now who never listens?"

"Hurry up, goddamn it! What the fuck are you waiting for?"

My anger and indignation allowed me to only look at him without speaking.

"Rosemary! Let's go!" he yelled at me as he raced from the bedroom.

I followed him out, my shoulders squared, my breathing easy, my chest pains gone. The air outside was a lingering and welcomed summer air.

We crossed the street. The Wagner's house was imposing, and I wondered how the two of them lived in it without losing themselves in it. Cal rang the doorbell. I could hear John calling to his wife. And then, Cal, in his black mood, leaning toward me, voice low. "My future rests with these people, Rosemary. Don't fuck it up."

My initial reaction was shock—as the door was beginning to open—instantaneously followed by angry frustration. I sputtered "What?" or something stupid, just as the door opened wide, and Cal was smiling his lawyer's smile, the perfect gentleman of twentieth-century Washington society, while I couldn't control the awful twitching in my face, and

I found it hard to smile at my new, friendly neighbor, but I did. I smiled crookedly as I shook John Wagner's hand for the first time. I knew he felt my hand trembling.

John was dressed in jeans and a wrinkled, what seemed to be a very old, cotton pull-over top.

"Don't sit!" Phyllis called out from one of her cavernous rooms as John was escorting us into the house. "First a toast!" She came into the living room carrying a tray. She, too, was dressed in jeans and an old top. Black sneakers without socks made up her outfit. "Hello, Cal. Nice to see you again, Rosemary. Welcome to our home." The large living room was set up for family. No fancy living there.

"John! Haven't you got that thing uncorked yet?" she scolded him.

"I'm trying, baby, I'm trying." He smiled at us.

"Well, everyone take a glass, and John will do the honors. She offered the silver tray, which held four paper-thin French crystal champagne glasses. "John, sweet! Hurry!"

A loud pop.

"There it goes!" Phyllis laughed.

"The little woman likes to nag." John smiled, pouring the champagne into our glasses.

My discomfort—or my fear—showed. I can remember how my hand still trembled as I held my glass out for John to fill. He touched it with a gentleness I was not used to, and said, "You're with friends, Rosemary. Welcome." I shall always be grateful to him for that smile.

We toasted each other and then sat down in chairs that were so overstuffed and comfortable, I was tempted to curl up and fall asleep. But the Wagners were not people one would fall asleep on. They were exciting and fun. They filled us in on the neighborhood news. Unfortunately, we had moved into a staid and conservative part of town, but Phyllis humorized it so that we were laughing so hard, we were crying. And I had forgotten I was married to a crazy man.

"Oh, Virginians!" Phyllis cried. "They're so, so, what do I want to say, John? So…blue-blooded…"

"That's good, Phyllis. Blue-blooded. Write it down."

I took a peek at my Virginian husband, but he was smiling, not minding Phyllis' facetious jeering of his background. Or did he?

Phyllis and John laughed at each other, with each other. I envied them their love, their humor, their natural rapport. There was no way on God's earth that I could speak to Cal without great reverence and solemnity. He would not accept any other manner in me, which only added to my slow but deepening depression, and which kept me so far down the rabbit hole I had lost my way up. I couldn't be any other way but solemn.

After an appetizer of cold lobster with mayonnaise followed by steak and salad, Phyllis served a strawberry mousse tart for dessert.

"This is delicious, Phyllis," I said, scooping up a small mound of the pink softness.

"Thank you, I made it myself," she proclaimed with a great but facetious modesty.

"Aggh!" John threw his two hands up across his throat and mockingly gagged.

"Stop that, you lunatic!" She laughed, admonishing him. "Fill up Rosemary's wine glass. It's empty. Make yourself useful, John!"

We were all high. We had finished off a magnum of champagne and three bottles of white wine. John was uncorking a fourth.

"Rosemary." Cal nodded his head back and forth.

"What?" I asked, wondering what the heck he was driving at.

"No more for her, John. You don't look well, Rosemary. Are you feeling alright?" He gave a knowing look at Phyllis. I glanced at our hostess; she looked down at her empty plate. *What is going on,* I wondered.

"She looks fine to me!" John declared in a full baritone, sloshing the dry Chablis into and over my glass.

"Thank you, John," I said. My! My! I had disobeyed. I looked over at Cal. He was without expression. I had no idea what was on his foul mind.

"You've had enough, Rosemary," he said with an unfamiliar gentleness.

"No, I haven't!" Enough had given me a boldness I had never experienced with my father/husband. I loved being bold. I could tell my husband off being bold. I drank that liquid that made me bold, my eyes resting defiantly on Cal. When I finished, with my eyes still resting defiantly on Cal, I held my glass sideways, toward John. "I'll have some more, please," I said in my best Oliver Twist voice.

Through my drunkenness, which at the time was just beginning to develop, I could not help but feel a sense of power. My, but it was nice. It was strange and nice and pleasurable, and when I had sipped my last sip, I looked over at John, and we both laughed. Our eyes locked. Partners in crime. Finally, I had relaxed.

Cal was speaking to Phyllis about a *Law Review* article in direct opposition to her request earlier in the evening that we would have "no work talk tonight."

I could feel the wine ever so softly spinning circular webs in my head, shaping its potency, building its momentum. I was drunk!

"We should go, Cal." I stood up, embarrassed. I had never gotten drunk before in my life.

Cal looked at Phyllis as if relieved. And then I froze. Oh, my God! I fucked it up. Whatever it was I did, I fucked it up.

We crossed the street in silence.

Cal opened the door with his key. I would make light of a situation that was serious to him. I could tell he was not happy.

"Ooo! I had too much to drink, Cal." I waited for a response. When I didn't get one, I asked. "Did you enjoy the evening, darling?"

He was furious. He pushed past me so that I fell against the open door and without a word he sprinted up the stairs. I heard the door to the den slam with such force the house shook.

Alone, without him, I felt an enormous relief. I was convinced I was not as drunk as I had feared. I went to bed, and for the first time in a long time, I slept through the night, without awakening. When I awoke in the morning, Cal was gone.

I took two aspirins to relieve my headache which pounded non-stop. I vowed I would never drink that much again. Cal had not come to bed, and his whereabouts were as mysterious to me as the life cycle of a fish is to a dining cat. I didn't care. If I hurried, I could make the eleven o'clock mass.

After mass and a quick trip to the bakery for Barbara's favorite bread, which I picked up for her every Sunday, I made my way home. Still no Cal. As I waited, the phone rang, its sharpness banged metallically in my head and forced me to pick it up with an abrupt quickness so that my head continued to hurt but less painfully. I knew it was Cal. Now what would he be? Apologetic or bullying?

"Is Francine there, dear?" Barbara asked in her genteel voice.

"No, Barbara. Why?"

"Oh, the silly ran out of here a couple of hours ago, and I haven't seen hair or hide."

"Well, she's not here."

"Is Cal there?" Her voice was no longer genteel. I never could understand that lady.

"No."

"Where is he?"

I lied. "He's just on an errand, Barbara. He should be home momentarily. Shall I have him call you?"

"When did he leave?"

"Just a short while ago. Why?"

"I just want to talk to my son. Is that a problem?" she asked returning to her sweet way.

I laughed. "Barbara, of course not. I'll have him call you when he returns."

"No, don't bother. We'll see you at one. Bye."

Click.

I waited until one thirty and when Cal didn't show, I called Barbara.

"How are you feeling?" She still found it hard to use my name.

"Fine," I answered, wondering if I should be sick. "Is Cal there?"

"He just got here a few minutes ago. You stay in bed and take care of that flu, hear?"

And then Cal was speaking to me. "You don't have to join us. Stay in bed."

"You could have waited for me." Not wanting Barbara to know of our differences, I added, "Let's talk when you get home. OK?"

"Go back to bed."

I held the dead phone in my hand and suppressed my anger. It would have been better if I broke a few dishes than to hide my emotions, but that was unthinkable at the time. I was fighting to hold it all together. I was fighting to hold me all together.

I worked in the garden. I cut a few rosebuds and clipped more basil. I placed the basil on a cookie sheet and put it in the oven. I filled the bud vases with roses. I weeded the beds and trimmed a forsythia bush that grew in the back. I mowed the patches of grass in the backyard. I worked feverishly. I'd let Cal mow the front lawn. I did not want to see the Wagners. I preferred to hide my embarrassment. My drinking was gross, my drunkenness even grosser. Everyone else was able to hold his liquor. Why not me?

Did I behave badly? What did Cal mean by telling me not to "fuck" things up? He also knows I hate that word. I had gotten drunk. Even Phyllis, fun-loving, democratic Phyllis, had seemed disgusted with me. But John didn't. Maybe that was the answer. Maybe I had paid too much attention to John. What did Cal mean? Was I not smart enough? Or nice enough? What did he mean? I was going crazy with my paranoid thoughts. My God, what was wrong with me? I felt ill, and the sun didn't help, but I could not pull myself away from the garden. I decided I would put another rosebush in the next day, and I proceeded to dig up the turf to make an area or circle of about three feet around. I don't remember how long I dug, but I do remember feeling faint and practically crawling toward the chaise lounge chair I kept under the big tree. When I opened my eyes, my body felt as if it had been run over by a truck, and my skin was clammy. When I opened my eyes again, the sun had gone down.

I sat up; my body reacted in pain to the simple movement. It took a while before I was able to stand and walk back to the house, and by that time it was dark. I dressed for bed. The fear of fainting in the shower was greater than my dread of going to bed dirty. I made myself sit on the toilet and sponged myself down, letting the warm, soapy water drip onto the towels at my feet. When I had dried and powdered myself, I felt somewhat better, but still felt sick and woozy. Leaving the damp towels on the floor and forgetting to drain the water from the sink, I made my slow, halting way to bed holding on to whatever piece of furniture or wall I could grab. It was nine o'clock when I slid between the inviting sheets, and it was nine in the morning when I awoke. I could hear Warren hammering in the basement. Did he let himself in? Was he up here again? Maybe Cal let him in. It didn't matter. Warren had become my little pet. I trusted him; I believed I had his complete adoration.

I drew on a long, terry cloth robe and went down to the kitchen. Although I didn't feel sick, I didn't feel strong, and I told myself I was coming down with a bug. My strength was gone and an ennui had settled over me. The sadness, the loneliness, was excruciating, and I lay my head on the kitchen table and cried. Warren came to me and patted my head as a child would pet a kitten for the first time, soft enough to feel, not hard enough to break. When I didn't stop crying, he put his arms around me, and dear God! I needed some loving arms around me, even if they did belong to Warren. I could have laughed through my tears. The two family idiots. Are they doing to me what they did to him?

I didn't see Cal until that evening. He did not call even once during the day, when it was his usual habit to call up to a half-dozen times. I stayed in bed and read. Before Warren left at noon, he made me a cheese and tomato sandwich and carried it up to me on my favorite tray with a glass of milk. Half the milk was on the tray, but it didn't matter; he had placed a newly cut rose on the tray and smiled a fat, dark, slitty smile. I was grateful for him, for his presence, for his caring. I thought about my mother. I would go up again in a few days when I would be feeling better.

I thought about the Wagners and realized I had done nothing wrong. I was being too hard on myself. I had not been drunk. Just a little tipsy. What the heck was wrong with that?

Lying in bed all day, without chores, without Cal bugging me, I let my thoughts roam, and I was able to think clearly. That awful heaviness that had stopped my brain from functioning was gone. Thank God. Tonight Cal and I would have a chat. A good, long one. He had a lot of explaining to do.

My head was clear, but the rest of me was still weak, so I made up a bed on the couch. I was tired of lying in bed, and I waited for Cal. At five fifteen, earlier than usual, he stormed into the house. The black mood had arrived!

The door slammed with a thunderous report, and *The Universe* tipped.

He stood over me, holding his briefcase, looking crazed.

"So! You weren't satisfied with leaving your dirt upstairs, you have to bring it down here too!"

Maybe I should have apologized for whatever I had done wrong, maybe I should have had something cooking in the oven, the aroma of a roast. But "maybe" is a useless word because this is what happened.

He screamed at me. "You fucking slob!"

It's a wonder I didn't faint there, lying down on the couch.

"You fat pig!" He ripped the afghan from me. "Get up and go to bed if you're sick! I had to clean that goddamned bathroom after you last night, you cunt!" He stood over me screaming words I had never heard before, his face so close, I could see the spittle lined over the inside of his mouth. I thought of a mad dog foaming at the mouth, ready to shred his prey. I was powerless, really, my head pressed down into the pillows. I remember holding up my hands in a semi-defense motion, but he never touched me. When he was through screaming his dirty words at me, he stepped aside and screamed at me to go to bed.

As I crossed the room, the stairway moved farther and farther away from me. When I awoke, I was in bed, and Cal was on the phone. His voice normal. Normal. It was the voice of an intelligent, cultivated, concerned husband, not the crazed madman I had witnessed downstairs. He was the loving husband.

"She hasn't been well, doctor. If I brought her in now, could you look her over?"

The heaviness in my brain was back. The sound of his voice was a symphony.

He wrapped me in a light blanket and carried me to the car. I did not have much clarity. Sleepiness was taking me over. I still remember my head on his shoulder, like a baby. His voice was soothing, comforting. Click, he's off. I didn't care anymore. I was so tired. Let him do with me what he wants. I was so tired. Somehow I got through the physical exam with my doctor. Somehow I allowed Cal to carry me once again in his arms to the car and place me gently in the front seat, and somehow I arrived home, settled into bed, and fell into a deep sleep.

CHAPTER
7

"Congratulations! You're going to have a baby!"

Until you hear those words, you can't imagine how beautiful life is. Those words erased all the bad. We had returned to the doctor's office two days later. I was deliriously happy. Cal was deliriously happy. He hugged me. Kissed my face. Rubbed his hands, those hands I had not felt in quite a while, over my face, my neck, my shoulders, down my bare arm. I should have a baby every day. He kissed me repeatedly. The doctor smiled, wrote instructions. I was in heaven. I was two months pregnant. I forgot everything else. Even the fact that I had never missed a period.

The doctor gave me a diet to follow. "And no drinking," he admonished me. "Understand?"

No drinking? Why did he say that? As if I were an alcoholic. Did Cal tell him I was a drinker? That I drank too much at the Wagners? I let myself be led home by Cal, the other guy, the man I met when I first arrived in Washington, the man who loved me and cared about me. What was going on? Somehow I was not meeting his needs. And that was due to my pregnancy. Well, it would all change. I would concentrate on Cal now, on my baby. All was well. I would try not to be Miss Perfect. I would try to laugh at it.

For the next month Cal could not have been a better husband or a better person. After a few days of vitamins and tonics and the right foods and rest, my strength had returned, and I was feeling well. I was so pleased not to have any morning sickness either. But I would have tolerated that for all the good things that were happening in my life.

I finished my last newsletter for the congressman and handed in my resignation with a flowery letter. It was bittersweet. I had worked long and hard to achieve my position, and even though I was elated with the news that I would be a mother, I felt sad. I loved my congressman and aside from a few people I had to tolerate, there were others I loved working with. I would miss them all and my work, especially. The congressman gave me a generous bonus and thanked me and said should I be needing a job in the future, he had to be the first person I would call.

My mother was ecstatic when she heard she was to become a grandmother. She began to sew baby things. She was making a quilt. Even Barbara who up till then would not even use my name, was now coo-ing over me. Sweet Mary! I was suddenly a Thanks-giving Day turkey warm and plump and all dressed up for show.

We had the Wagners over for dinner and drinks. I drank ginger ale. Cal was his old normal self again, no slip-ups, no on and off again. He was changed. It was incredulous. Cal had stopped assigning me errands; Francine was doing them. And I spent my time with such simple housewifery chores that cropped up— nothing strenuous, nothing hard. We hired a woman to come in twice a week to clean up. It was relaxing, but I still did not get back to my novel.

Sam and I continued our luncheons, but now they were every two weeks. Cal did not want me "running around too much."

I spent most of my time sitting in a garden chair, soaking in the sunny, early fall weather. I read and sewed baby things.

Cal did not think sex was a good idea. "It might hurt the baby, Roseheart." When I think now about it, I wonder how I could have accepted his rejection of me. But I was good at compartmentalizing. That's how I survived. Section it off. A piece at a time. Besides, I was so happy with him being in what seemed to be a permanent good mood, and beginning my family, I refused to see the negative in anything. I made myself fall in love with him all over again.

I decided to take advantage of Cal's good nature while I had it. It was after dinner on a Friday night when I pinned him down. "We have to talk, Cal."

He had a drink in his hand and was heading for his den. "What is it?" He didn't look at me.

"Warren."

"What about Warren?" He took a deep breath and turned to face me.

"I have to know. Was he born that way?"

"Oh, for God's sakes, Rosemary! No."

"We are having a baby, Cal. I have to know everything about Warren's condition."

"We'll talk tomorrow." He continued up the stairs.

"No. Now." I followed him.

"Tomorrow." When he reached his den, he opened the door, went in, and locked the door after him.

"Cal!" I yelled. "Now! Open the door!"

There was complete silence, and I was defeated again. But no matter. I would talk to Barbara in the morning. I didn't need Cal's answers.

✿

"Hi, Barbara. How are you?" I kept my voice friendly but daughter-like as Barbara opened the door. I knew she was alone. Francine seldom took a day off from work, and Warren was at my house in the basement.

"What brings this pleasant visit?" Barbara gave me one of her usual wide smiles.

"We have to talk."

"My, it sounds serious."

"It is, Barbara," I said, sitting down on my favorite chair, an old wing chair with carved footings. I guessed it had been in her family for a few generations, along with everything else.

Barbara said nothing; she continued to smile, and sat opposite me on the sofa.

"As you know, there's a baby on the way, and I would like to know some of the family history. Cal is very quiet on that topic."

She still said nothing but her smile was fixed.

"Can you tell me anything I should know?"

"Like what?"

"Warren. How did his condition happen? Was he born that way?"

Suddenly her frozen smile disappeared, and she looked worried, which made me worry. I waited for her to say something. It took a few minutes, but then she did say, "Warren was a rambunctious little boy, Rosemary, and he fell down the stairs. It was awful. I have never forgiven myself. I should have been watching him more carefully. He has never matured. But he was born normal, with no defects, and you have nothing to worry about there."

"How old was he when it happened?"

She thought before she spoke. I thought she may have forgotten. "Three. Three and a half."

"He seems to have an intellect more than three."

"Oh, we had special training for him. He progressed marvelously. We are so proud of him, really. He learned a great deal." She continued to inform me of his education until he was in his early teens. She went on to tell me that aside from old-age infirmities, there was nothing for me to be concerned about. "Unless, dear, it comes from your side." Her freak smile returned.

That night the black cloud returned. The front door slammed and the drapes shuddered. Cal strode into the kitchen where I had just taken a chicken from the oven.

"How dare you talk to my mother about Warren?" His face was dark, and his eyes bulged. Froth showed at the corners of his mouth.

I was petrified, but I would not be beaten down anymore. "Cal, stop. Calm down. Warren is her child. I had every right to speak to her."

"You upset her. She's been calling me all day in tears. You brought up that horrible accident to her, and she's been reliving it all day. How dare you!" He threw his briefcase on the kitchen table and went into the living room, but immediately returned. "I am the one you speak to about family affairs. Me!" He continued to pace from one room to the other.

"I tried to, but you refused to speak to me. What were you doing in your den that I couldn't go in?"

And then what happened next chilled my blood. He raced over to me and grabbed me by the arms and squeezed me so hard I thought he would break my arms.

"Cal," I cried out. "Please, I'm pregnant." He let go of me then and left me there speechless. He went up into his den and later, when I had put everything back in the refrigerator I went up to my bedroom and tried to sleep. I didn't see him again until the next night, when he came home after ten o'clock.

About six weeks later I miscarried. I was in my fourth month. It happened in the middle of the night when I was sound asleep. I awakened Cal, and there he was again: protective, loving, and caring. I knew I was losing my child, but I couldn't bring myself to accept it. Nor could I tell Cal. I would let the doctor do that. They kept me overnight at the hospital and then released me.

Cal did not bring me home. Sam picked me up.

"Thanks, Sam," I said as we pulled up in front of my house.

"No thanks. What are friends for?"

Through the pain—the meds had not kicked in yet—and my grief, I managed a smile. I wanted my baby desperately. "I asked the nurses what I had, a boy or a girl, but no one could tell me. I know it was a girl."

She reached out and squeezed my hand. "I'll see you in," she said.

"I'll be OK. Thanks anyway."

"I'll see you in." She took command. "Want to stay up, Rosemary, or go back to bed?" she asked when we had walked into the living room.

"No. I'm so tired of bed, Sam. I'm ready now to go back to work. In fact, full time." And I burst into tears.

Sam held me, her arms wrapped around me, holding me together. And then I realized, feeling those arms of support, of friendship, I had not felt Cal's arms around me in a long time. I became hysterical. My cries hurt, but I couldn't stop crying. I thought of Rob. Sam's arms became warmer, firmer, and then she put me to bed. She gave me a sleeping pill the doctor had prescribed, and I slept for a very long time.

Cal at least had the decency to leave me alone for the next few days. He seldom spoke to me. Did he think it was my fault? The silence was deafening, penetrating. My nerves screamed silently in the silence of my home. My home. What good was having a home when life was miserable in it? I continued to take my pills and drank my scotch. Other than that I did not eat or drink or bathe. I went from the bed to the couch and back to the bed. I switched from reading to watching television. And then, on the third or fourth or maybe it was even the fifth day after I returned home, I pulled myself together and prepared dinner for Cal. I felt guilty for not feeding him all that time. I called his office at three in the afternoon but he was "...busy, Mrs. Bryant. He's not taking calls."

I left a message with the receptionist that we were eating at six—steak and salad. Bring wine if you can."

"Oh, sounds romantic!"

"I hope it will be. Thanks for giving him the message."

I made it romantic.

Again, the formal white linen tablecloth, the silver candlesticks, the long, white tapered candles, crystal glasses, flowers. I made a beautiful centerpiece. I kept myself occupied and then he came home. At six. With a pizza.

"Oh, Cal. I left a message. Didn't you get it?"

"Sure. I got it. But I wasn't going to count on it. You've been out for five days." He threw the box of pizza on the table, knocking down the candlesticks.

"Cal," I pleaded. That's not fair. I lost my baby."

"Our baby. Did you forget me?" He pointed his finger at me. His voice was low, terse. "And... you... killed... it."

"Cal! What in the name of God are you saying?"

He took a slice of pizza from the box and sat at the table. His voice was so low, I barely heard him. "You...killed...it...by...all...that...drinking. You did. Ask...the doctor. You killed ...our baby...and that's... something...I can't...forgive...you...for."

He was mad. Insanely mad! And so was I! Could that be true? I killed my little baby?

I made my way up to my room. I didn't want to hear anymore from him. I didn't want to look at him. I went to bed. I had two sleeping pills left. I took both of them. And then, what the hell. I poured myself a scotch. What did anything matter now? It was all over.

It was the first week in November when I visited Sam. The weather that day was warm and sunny, with no hint of winter except for the trees that were shedding their summer leaves. Seeing their advancing barrenness I wanted to cry so very much. Since my miscarriage sadness had pervaded everything I did. I could not accept the loss of my baby and I retired into myself. Sam had been calling me daily to do things with her but I refused. I knew I should snap out of it but it was futile. I took all of the baby things I had sewn and knitted and brought them to the Salvation Army. Cal began to speak to me but with a frugality I welcomed. I did not want anything more to do with him. I wanted to be back with Sam, in her house, having pizza parties, making omelets, working on the Hill. I thought about Rob more than I should have. I became a robot. I stayed in bed in the mornings pretending to be asleep until Cal had left. Then I got up, threw on slacks and a top and went off to church and prayed for my baby. I drove a lot. I don't remember where I went but I drove, endlessly, for hours. Shortly before Cal was due home I would return to the house and prepare a meal. I roasted chicken one night, another night a roast beef; I picked up a dozen steaks, five pound bags of potatoes, salad fixings. Sometimes I had no idea what I was doing, I just did. I spoke to him and pretended it was a play and I was a great actress: *Hello, darling. How was your day?* If I could I even walked up to him and kissed him on the cheek. *I made your favorite, dear. Steak and baked potato.* We ate usually in silence; when we spoke it was the actress reciting her lines followed by a grunt from Cal. When we had finished eating he went to his den and shut the door. On Sundays I feigned illness and remained home alone. My brain still screamed silently. So, one cool day I visited Sam for lunch.

I waited a while before Sam answered the doorbell. "Come on in, Rosi. Let me finish up this page, and I'll be right with you. Pour yourself something to drink."

I took a coke from the refrigerator, listening to the clacking of her typewriter. I wondered why she wouldn't get a quieter one. It was the same one she always used, but when I lived with her, I was not aware of the sharp sound it made. That day the sound of heavy metal striking out its message against the worn-out roller vibrated through my pores so that I was tempted to shriek.

I went out to the garden to wait. It was overgrown with weeds and grass; hints of color could be seen from dead roses, resembling aged and drying polyps waiting to fall. I thought of my wedding day. When I couldn't hear the noise of the typewriter anymore, I returned to the house and poured myself another diet soda. Sam had made us corned beef sandwiches.

"Do you want your coleslaw on the sandwich or on the plate?" She held a platter in one hand and a cardboard dish of slaw in the other. "If you have it on the sandwich, I don't have to wash the plate," she suggested, seeing my hesitation.

"The sandwich." I would help her out. Sam detested housework.

"Good girl."

"What's up?" I asked, trying to hold in the anger I felt at her happiness.

"I'm changing fields for one. I'm going into anthropology."

"Oh, Sam," I exclaimed with a tentative disappointment. "Why's that?" The coleslaw felt cold on my teeth.

"Literature was getting dull. I'm going to study a tribe in the Amazon. A shitload of excitement that should be!" She smiled her usual devilish smile, looking up at me, but I noticed her expression change. "And you? How are you feeling now?" she asked with a transparent solemnity.

"Fine," I answered bluntly.

"Hey. This is Sam. Remember? Your friend? Come on. Out with it."

What could I say to her? How does a murderess look anyone in the eyes? Is that what women do who don't want their babies? They drink things to miscarry. What was wrong with me? I was married to a handsome and brilliant lawyer. So he had a bad temper. If that was all that was wrong with him, I was lucky. It was time for me to grow up, to be a woman. I wasn't about to whine or complain. I had everything.

"Nothing's wrong." I tried to smile. "This is delicious, Sam. By the way, your house is so clean. Did you get a cleaning lady?" She had fired the one we had used.

"You don't think I did it, do you?" She looked askance.

Sam was clean and neat about her person, but her house and car always looked as if a cyclone had hit them.

"You might say I had that man washed right out of my house!" She laughed uproariously.

"What happened?"

"What a twit he turned out to be!"

"Tell me what happened!" I pleaded, enjoying her humor and realizing how much I had missed it.

"The guy was crazy, Rosi. He was on drugs, you know? That scared me. I don't trust drugs."

"Drugs? Like LSD? Like the California type?"

"No. Marijuana. He puffed it all the time and acted weird. I never thought he'd get that goddamned play written. It's good, by the way. The twit can really write."

"Will you for God's sakes tell me!"

She laughed at my impatience and waved a hand in the air.

"I meet him, right? He's nice. I bring him home. Just like bringing in a kitten from the rain. I feed him. And maybe I shouldn't have, don't yell at me, but I gave him money." She lowered her voice.

"Sam!" I scolded her. "That could be dangerous!"

"I know, I know, but only once. I felt so bad for him. In the beginning, anyway. So I brought him in, fattened him up, had his clothes deloused." Here she laughed so hard, I thought she'd fall off the chair. "Just kidding. Anyway," she continued, wiping the tears from her eyes, "I threw him out. But he's in New York. He was going there anyway, to peddle his play. Do you know he had the unmitigated gall to bring another girl into my house? Can you imagine? And I'm supporting him? Feeding him? And guess what he said when I walked in on them? 'You wanna do a *menage a trois*?' Jesus Christ! I mean, I'm no lollipop, Rosi, but that guy was kinky. So I kicked him out. Right then and there." She grinned, sat back, and rested her bare feet on the table.

I laughed at her impudence to all social mores. Still, there were things she wouldn't do. Sam was her own person.

"Your old room is free, in case you're interested."

I did not comment.

"You look so sad, Rosi."

I said nothing.

"What's he doing to you, sweetie?"

I put my face in my hands. "I'm so depressed, Sam."

"About what?"

"My baby. I want my baby." I began to cry.

"Oh, Rosi, I'm sorry. I wish I could help you. And maybe this isn't what you want to hear, but you'll have lots of babies."

"It isn't what I want to hear. And I know I'll have lots of babies, but this one, I wonder where she is. I can't stop thinking about her. Is there really a limbo? Would God put my baby in a limbo?"

"Nonsense! Your baby's in heaven."

"You don't even believe in heaven, Sam. Oh, I'm sorry. I'm sorry to lay all this on you, but I believe in heaven, and I'm going to work very hard to get there. I want to hold my baby someday in my arms, even if it is after this life." I could not stop crying.

"Is Cal helping you through this?" She moved over to me and rubbed my back.

Again, I shook my head. "He said I killed her with all my drinking."

"Oh, to hell with him! Is that all he's saying to you?"

"Sometimes, Sam, he doesn't say very much at all." I stopped crying.

"Is he a good lover?"

I shook my head a lot that afternoon.

"That's your problem, Rosi. Does he make love to you or is he just bad at it?"

"No. He's a great lover. When he makes love to me. It's just that, well, before the baby we didn't make love very often, once a week, if that. Then when I became pregnant he didn't think it was a good idea." He said it might hurt the baby. And he still hasn't touched me, not a hug, nothing, although I will say, Sam, I don't invite him to, either."

"Maybe he's getting it from someone else. Maybe he's got someone somewhere."

"No, I'm sure he doesn't." I reached for a Kleenex from the box on the coffee table.

"I think he does, Rosi. If he's good at sex, he must enjoy it. I don't think he'd be happy having it once in a while. He's a man, you know. Would you think of leaving him?"

"Oh, no. I want our marriage to work." I knew my decadent friend would not agree with me.

"Why?"

"For decency's sake, Sam! I can't take marriage lightly. You know me."

"No one does anything for decency, Rosi."

"I do. I have to try. I can't just give up. I'll get over this depression I'm in, get a grip on myself, maybe go into counseling. Maybe that will help. I'll give this marriage a year, then, if things don't change, I will leave."

"That's really decent of you, Rosi, but decency today gets you nowhere. Decency's out of date. You have to think of yourself. Look what he's doing to you in just a few short months. He's driving you crazy, you know? Leave him. If you care about yourself, leave him!"

"I'm staying with him because I do care about myself. He's my husband, not just a passing fancy. He's my life." I reached for another Kleenex.

"Have an affair," she exclaimed, standing up. "That will at least get rid of your depression, and, of course, counseling."

"Honestly, Sam. You should hear yourself. As if all I had was a cold. Take a big bowl of chicken soup."

"Chicken soup," she repeated. "That's an appropriate analogy. That's what most women do, you know, when they're stuck with a husband they don't want or can't get rid of, or can't stand. They have affairs," she said resuming her place next to me. Some even come to agreements with their husbands. You've got to have an affair. Now, let's see. Who do I know?" She stood up again and paced the room.

"Oh, Sam. I wouldn't know what to do." I was beginning to be annoyed with her.

"I'll tell you what to do," she said, her mind on her newly found project, her hands slapping out at me to shut up. "How about Rob? You want to see him?" She gave me a huge smile.

"God, no, Sammy. I'm not ready for Rob, please." I did not want Rob to see me crazed. I did not want him to know how unhappy I was.

She sat next to me and looked straight at me. "He always asks about you."

I shook my head in futility.

"Are you practicing birth control, Rosi?" She asked.

"No. That's something we never really discussed. We wanted to start a family right away so we just didn't even talk about. It wasn't an issue. Now," I shook my head. "I think I should go on the pill."

"That's an excellent idea, Rosi, because you don't know where you're at with Cal. Maybe you will leave him. What would you do if you become pregnant? Of course, this will always be your home, you can come live with me anytime."

"Thank you, Sam. I can always rely on you. Thanks." I wiped my nose and stood up.

We made plans to have lunch in a week. Then I went home to prepare dinner for Cal.

The fall had come in quietly so that the warm, summer smells grew crisp and fresh without much notice. The more fragile, daintier flowers in my garden were replaced by giant, golden mums. Lots of flowers were left and I began to cut them with an abrasive ambition. I hated to see them die. I filled the house with them. There were not enough vases to hold them all. I cut my garden back and bought cones for the roses. The aroma of burning leaves replaced the fragrance of freshly cut grass. I put away my feathery sandals and brought out my leather boots and wool skirts.

Sam was to leave December 10 for a trip to the Amazon with a group of anthropologists. They were studying a specific tribe that was dying out. She would be gone through Christmas and maybe New Year's. They did not expect to go into the Indians' camps—it would be too dangerous—but with armed guards they hoped to meet up with some. I went to see her in late November.

She was visibly concerned about me. I was visibly concerned about her.

"Rose, do you know how much money you have?"

"God, no."

"Why don't you know?"

"Cal won't talk about money with me."

"That's crazy. You make him talk money with you. You've got to know what you're worth. And what if something happens to him?"

"I've tried to speak to him about money a thousand times. He's good at putting me off when it comes to money."

"Rosi, you and Cal should sit down and talk about your problems. Either leave him or come to some sort of agreement. And an affair will make you happy. Trust me."

"I try but he's so difficult. He's always evasive, and I'm afraid of him when he's in his moods."

"Has he ever struck you?" She moved closer to me.

I thought of the times I thought he would. "Oh, no." She let me think for a few seconds. "Although, sometimes, I think he comes close, Sam." I looked up at her. "Actually, now he's somewhat better, not a lot, but I see an improvement."

"What do you think that's from?"

"I just keep telling him how great he is; I'm always there for him, and of course not having any work but housework, it's easier to give him that attention."

"That's good, Rosi, I hope it gets even better. But I can't come up with anyone worth going to bed with. Everyone I know is all yucky, so you're stuck with Cal." She laughed sarcastically. "Do you guys make love at all?"

"The other night. He took me by surprise. I didn't feel anything though, sad to say."

"Are you on the pill?"

I shook my head. "I'm seeing the doctor next week. I'll ask for a prescription."

"Buy some condoms today. I don't trust Cal. He'd love to see you pregnant and dependent."

I laughed. "I'd be too embarrassed. Men buy those things." I really didn't want Cal to use them anyway. The thought of condoms disgusted me. The thought of a birth control pill didn't.

"You are too much. No, too Catholic. Think big, Rosi, excuse the pun. But get those condoms today. You need to be protected."

I helped her with her packing, made her promise she would obey all the rules of the group, not to do anything dangerous. I promised with one hand on her unread encyclopedia of houseplants to water the already dead plants, and then we said our good-byes.

After my visit with Sam I began to visit my mother every other week. I took to long-distance driving, liking the sense of detachment it gave me, my escape from my unhappy home, the home I wanted to fill with children and books and happy holidays. They say that distance makes the heart grow fonder. Perhaps in my case in did, in that distance helped to de-stress me; and foolish as it seems now, distance precluded all the bad in Cal. I was able to be kinder toward him.

Other than sporadic lapses of memory, my mother seemed well enough. She worked a few hours during the day, and she sewed at night. She had made friends with a new neighbor who lived on the other side of the hall. My visits lasted two days, and I always felt guilty leaving her. Even though Cal didn't care how many days I was gone, I did not want to be away from my home for too long. I worked hard at keeping the peace. I fought my frustrations with a discipline that was all consuming; a soldier would have received a medal.

Warren continued to make me Madonnas, and I continued to hide them. His love was wrapped in wooden secrets. My love was wrapped in smiles and comforting talks.

Phyllis and I had become good friends. I met her in the District every so often for lunch. Cal encouraged our friendship. "She's the kind of people you should be cultivating, Rosemary. She can do a lot for you. Let the Sams of the world keep with their own kind." I didn't ask what Phyllis could do for me. I learned when not to question. I learned not to defend Sam. She didn't need defending. We were best of friends and always would be. It irked him if I stuck up for her. He'd stomp off to his den and stay there for a while. He loved closing doors on me. I found I was no longer trying to open them.

I was downtown in the District the day after Sam left for the Amazon, enjoying the Christmas colors and music, the shoppers scurrying about. Cal needed a special tool to fix the lock on the garage door, and no other hardware store carried it except the one in the District. I had already been to three stores who had told me over the telephone that they had it, but upon arriving they did not have it. I had called five who said they didn't carry it. I spent one whole day trying to buy his damned tool. I couldn't wait to return to work. Then he could hire someone to run his errands. Or Francine could do them.

I parked in an outdoor lot, went into the store and saw him again: the teenage boy I thought attractive the day after my honeymoon, the one with the navy-blue shorts with a white stripe up the sides, whose legs were muscular and hairy, the boy who rubbed his leg against mine. I felt an electricity seeing him there, smiling at me. I thought of Sam's advice about having an affair. Perhaps I walked right into it.

"Hello," he said. "How's your car?"

"The one you pushed for me died." I smiled back at him. "I bought a station wagon."

His face was soft and boyish. He was tall and blond and muscular. He waited by the door with an awkwardness peculiar to young men, pretending to look until I had made my purchase. He walked with me to my car. I don't know how it happened, but we were in the car, and he was kissing me, and I took his warm, strong hands and placed them where I ached. And there in the car, in broad daylight, with his hands he eased my pain, and I held onto him for a long time while I cried with pleasure.

I did not feel the shame right away. I felt wonderful, and the glow lasted for almost a week. Sam was right. By God, she was right about everything. But then the guilt soon descended upon me, ripping through me, hurling me into such wretchedness that simple, everyday tasks were difficult. I became dysfunctional. Even Cal noticed it.

"What's the matter with you?" he asked one day. "Who are you looking for?"

I was peeking out the side of the living room drapes wondering if my man/boy was anywhere in sight.

At the sound of Cal's voice, I jumped. "What? No one. No one. Why are you asking me that?"

He gave me one of his smirks and walked away. But it gave me reason to worry. What if my lover should come when Cal was home? What if Cal walked in on us? He'd kill us both. I became more nervous with each day. I dropped dishes, could not focus on whatever I was doing. I jumped when the phone rang, and it was always Cal. My guilt was overwhelming. I prayed for forgiveness every day. I thought of my baby in limbo. I ran to confession and received forgiveness and said my penance. I promised the priest I would at least consider seeing a marriage counselor, but the answer was clear. I either had to accept Cal and my life as it was, or leave him. I was a Catholic, married in the Catholic Church by a Catholic priest; I had to try to make it better. After all, Cal did have a good side— sometimes—and I was determined to bring it to the fore. No. There would be no divorce. I had to hang in. And I had forgotten about my birth control pills.

A few days later, he came to my house. His name was Bill. I didn't want to know his last name. We consummated our burning lust, our bodily appetites. I thought I still loved Cal, and that knowledge stayed with me even when I released my sexual energies into the magnificent body of a Boy Bill.

"I love you!" he cried, looking deep into my eyes as I lay on my back. "You're beautiful!"

It was his first time with a woman, and I felt comforted knowing that at long last I had made at least one man happy in my life.

Christmas was too close. I still did not know what to get Cal for Christmas. My mother would be spending the Christmas holidays with us. I knew Cal wasn't too happy about it, but that was too bad. I had neglected her long enough, and nothing I did for him made him happy anyway. I was making up our Christmas card list when Father McLaughlin called.

"Your mother isn't well, Rosemary. We had to put her in the hospital this morning."

"What happened?"

A long pause—so many pauses in my life. I don't remember his exact words, but I knew what he was saying. My mother's cancer had returned.

"I'm leaving now."

There was no time for driving. I flew into Newark Airport and rented a car there and drove to the hospital.

My mother looked old and frail. Her thin, lean wrists were translucent, the blue veins like pacific rivulets against the white, wrinkled arms. She did not see me when I entered the hospital room. She was staring into space, her mouth open, the saliva finding rest in the crevices of the avicular mouth.

"Mother." I held back my tears. Crying would not help her. I needed to be strong. I had to find out how to save her life.

"You didn't have to come, dear."

"Of course, I did. Do you think I'd leave you alone?" I asked, knowing I already had.

The doctor interrupted our reunion. I could tell by the way he came into the room that it was not good. His large face was dark, too serious. He fussed with my mother, listening to her heart, her pulse. "How are you feeling today?" he asked her.

"I'm fine, doctor."

Then he turned to me, and as he spoke his eyes met mine. "It's stage three."

I collapsed into the chair. I don't know what I had expected to hear: "It's all out," or "We got it." But the words "stage three" forced my body to contract, and the blood raced to my feet.

"You need another mastectomy," he said to my mother. "We'll do an axillary dissection tomorrow, and when we go in, we'll know more. It's been there a long time. You know that, don't you?"

My mother answered with a slight nod of her head and an almost imperceptible smile.

"What are my chances, doctor?" She was holding my hand.

"We'll know tomorrow after we do the mastectomy. You still have a chance for a good life. It doesn't have to be fatal."

"Going to God is not fatal, doctor." I never saw my mother smile with such joy.

I followed him out into the hallway. "Is it hopeless?" I asked.

"Not necessarily. If we get it all, she may have a chance."

"A chance? At what? Five years? Twenty?" Could he not tell me more specifically?

"I'm sorry." He patted my arm in a reassuring way.

It would start all over again. Surgery and more radiation. My first thought was that she would never withstand major surgery. I couldn't even begin to think about the radiation. Still, there was hope; she had a chance, and where there was life, there was hope.

"I think I'll let it be," my mother said when I returned to her side. Her voice was strong and round.

"What do you mean?"

"It's no use. I've lived my life, Rosemary. I'm ready to go. I'm ready to see God. I don't want to go through that again. I want to go home to my own bed."

I burst into tears. "Mom! Don't do this! Don't leave me. I need you." I threw my arms around her and buried my head in her blanket and sobbed. I needed my mother more than I ever needed her as a child. My whole world was dying. I couldn't let her die. "You have to do it!" I felt her frail bony hand on my head, and I knew she would do it for me. For me she would suffer the agony of modern medicine. For me she would suffer.

That night I called Cal.

My mother would come home with me. We had a guest room, and I'd take care of her. I'd leave him if he gave me a hard time. I'd go back to work and take care of my mother, but then who would take care of her while I worked? I couldn't leave him. I thought of moving back with Sam, but how could I bring a sick person into her home? That would not be fair. I couldn't do that to Sam. Better to stay with Cal and visit with my mother.

"Absolutely not. What's wrong with a good nursing home?"

"Because I don't want to put my mother in a good nursing home. And besides, she doesn't have the money for a good nursing home, Cal. What about our health plan? Does it include nursing homes?"

He didn't answer me right away, and I became nervous.

"Is she even on our plan?" I was angry.

"Of course she is." He spoke using his reassuring voice, the one I liked.

"Why can't I bring her back with me?"

"Let me look into this. I'll call you tomorrow."

"What are you going to look into?"

"I'll call you tonight."

"No. Tell me now. What's it going to cost for me to bring her home?"

"I'll call you tonight."

"I'm not putting my mother in a nursing home when I can take care of her."

"You?" He laughed. "Sweetheart, you can't handle what you have now. Your mother needs medical care. Good nursing care. I'll call you tomorrow."

"No, Cal, tell me now. What are you going to look into?"

"I do not want a dying person in my home!" he bellowed into the phone.

No, I am the dying person Cal.

I heard a click, and he was gone. He did not call me back.

The next day on the way to the hospital, I stopped to visit Father McLaughlin.

"How long has she known this, Father?"

I think she's known for a few months. That's when she began to forget things. She's had the cancer on her mind."

"For example?"

"One day she left the gas on. Fortunately, her neighbor went over to say hello, and she smelled the gas. And in conversations I've had with her, she was generally forgetful. So now what?" he asked, changing the subject. "She'll be going back with you?"

"Cal says she should be in a nursing home with good medical care. But I prefer to bring her home with me. I took care of her before."

He thought for a minute or two, staring straight ahead without speaking, as if he had seen something unusual. And then, "Maybe Cal's right. Maybe she'll be better off in a nursing home."

"I can take care of her."

"But if Cal doesn't want her, she will be better off in a nursing home."

"Oh, it's not that he doesn't want her. He really thinks she needs care that I can't give. Nursing care," I added defensively.

He stood up, his whole being massive in that room made for massive men. I was overshadowed. He walked to a file cabinet, returned, and resumed sitting. The squeaking of the ancient, cracked leather unnerved me so that I wanted to scream, race away, race away from my religion, my marriage, my mother, death. He handed me a check.

He knows. He knows there's a problem with Cal, and he thinks it might be money

"Father, thank you, but we have my mother on our health plan. We have money. I don't need this, but thank you anyway.

"Hold on to it, dear. This will get her into St. Michael's Home. They'll take good care of her there, and I'll look in on her. She gave this parish many hours of her time as a volunteer. This is the least we can do." His eyes were wet.

Thank you, blessed father, for not making me say I cannot take my mother in.

We sat there for a long time, and then I left him in his leather chair and his hickory smells and his memories. I left him understanding. I knew, and Father knew, that Cal would not take my mother into his home. I was not sure if my mother was on our health plan, if indeed we had a health plan. I had lost all faith in Cal. I had lost faith in myself. My brain was rapidly deteriorating.

My mother survived her surgery, and I stayed with her until the early evening. When she had fallen asleep again, I went back to the apartment and waited for Cal to call. When he did, I let the phone ring several times before I picked it up.

"What the hell are you doing? That place isn't so big that it takes you half an hour to answer the phone."

"Father McLaughlin gave me a check. It's for my mother and the nursing home."

He didn't answer right away.

"Cal. Did you hear me?"

"Yes. I heard you. I can give you a check too. How's that?"

"Really? Where's it coming from?"

"My savings."

"Your savings? You mean ours, don't you? And where would that be, Cal? I've never seen a savings account book."

"Don't get smart!" he snarled. "When are you coming home?"

"When I'm ready." I couldn't believe that it was me speaking.

"There's a cocktail party Saturday night. I want you to be there with me."

"Where?"

"At the German embassy."

"Well, I don't see how I can make it now, Cal. My mother's had a mastectomy today. She's pretty weak. She'll be in the hospital for at least five days. I can't leave her. I don't want to leave her."

The famous pause.

It was as if I had said nothing.

"I guess you'll just have to go it alone for a few more days, Cal. I can't do it."

"You have to."

"No."

It felt good saying no. I was his yes girl for so long, the word *no* rolled magically off my tongue, massaging, healing.

He hung up on me, and for a change instead of feeling guilty, I felt relief. I was rid of him, even if it were only for a short time. I liked not having him around. I liked it very much. And it was then that I knew our marriage was over. No matter how much I tried, or would try, our marriage was not salvageable.

Not two minutes elapsed before he called me back. "Roseheart, I'm sorry. You must be going through hell, and here I am complaining about being alone. I'm really sorry."

Cal was an expert in changing the tone of his voice. From a raging madman one minute to a soft whining little boy the next.

"Thank you, Cal." I was not to be moved.

"How about if you fly down Saturday, go to the reception with me, and then we'll fly you back on Sunday? How's that? Please? Your mother will be OK for a day, and I miss you, Roseheart."

He was being reasonable. And civil. I said, "OK."

Except for occasional shouts from the neighbors, the apartment was quiet. To avoid the silence I turned on the TV, but I couldn't concentrate. I went to bed but I couldn't sleep. I moved over to my mother's bed. Her fragrance was there, a faint, delicate scent of soap and talcum steeped forever in her temporal crypt. I can still remember being wrapped in my mother's arms on a thunderous, rainy night, the lightning electrifying the whole room and my mother hugging me tighter each time it appeared. I fell asleep then in her bed on the sheets that bore her imprint.

Saturday morning, after seeing my mother, I drove to the airport, where I parked the rental car and hopped the shuttle, enjoying the luxury of its expediency. I had told Cal I would take a cab from the airport, he didn't have to pick me up. I wanted even more time by myself. But as soon as I arrived home, the panic set in. There was no way of telling when Cal could be in one of his foul moods, and I wasn't up to it that night. He should watch his mother fight for her life; he should have to put his mother in a nursing home. One bad word from him, and I was ready to hit back full blast.

Cal wasn't home and I took a quick shower and changed my clothes and waited. At seven I was curled carefully in a chair so as not to wrinkle my dress. I awoke at nine feeling cold but strangely alert. I knew we had missed the reception. I had to leave my mother to fall asleep in a chair. I was furious. I dialed Barbara.

"He just left, dear. How is your mother?"

"Did he get to the embassy reception?" I asked ignoring her false sympathy.

"Which embassy?" She sounded uncomfortable.

"Never mind. I'll talk to him when he gets home. G'night."

I knew he had not made it to the embassy.

It was midnight when he arrived home.

"Cal. Where have you been?" I was sitting up in bed, trying with great difficulty not to show my anger.

He looked worn-out as he stood by the door with a scotch and water in one hand and a pretzel stick in the other.

When he didn't answer me, I asked, "Are you alright?"

"I'm alright."

"Did you get to the party?"

Again those shrinking eyes, tiny and mean.

"I am no longer Senator Smith's legislative assistant."

"What? What happened?" I got out of bed and rushed over to him. His whole look was one of great stress.

"I quit."

"Why?" I asked incredulous.

He turned his back to me and walked away. Suddenly everything opened up to me. I could not take this treatment any longer.

"Don't walk away from me, Cal. I'm your wife, if that means anything to you. Why did you quit?"

"Don't dictate to me," he called over his shoulders.

"I have a right to know."

"You have no rights." His voice was hoarse, scratchy. He turned and faced me. His eyes were bloodshot, still shrinking. His face looked older, the once beginning lines had grown deeper. He was about to say something, but then turned away from me and went downstairs.

"Don't tell me I have no rights. I demand to know," I called after him. "This is my life too." My voice was firm, and for the first time since we were married, I felt as if I were in control. My pleading days were over. Barefooted, feeling the wood floor cold under my feet, I followed him down to the kitchen.

Silence.

I waited.

He poured a drink. I poured myself a drink.

"Roseheart," he said indifferently. "We had words. I got hotheaded and quit."

"What kind of words?" Again I was looking at his back. "Well, apologize, Cal," I said without waiting for an answer. "Was it that bad that you had to quit? A lot of people have problems with their bosses. Intelligent people work it out. You'll be months, years even, before you find anything as good."

"I have prospects."

"Prospects? Were you planning this?" I knew he was lying, and when he didn't answer me, I let it go. I made myself another drink and in disgust left him in the darkened living room and retired to my bed. Another place I could find detachment.

Sunday morning when I awoke, I did not see or hear a sign of Cal, and I did not care. I got up, dressed, threw a few things in an overnight bag, and called for a cab. Two hours later, when I arrived at Newark Airport, I drove the rental car away from the parking lot and went straight to the hospital. I went to my mother's room and sat on the bed and held her hands. She was sitting up, and I detected some color in her cheeks—not much, but there was a hint of good health.

"How are you, Mother? I know this is very hard on you. How do you feel about a nursing home until you're well? You'll have people waiting on you there."

"It's alright, dear," she said.

"Well, it's not really, Mother. I'd rather take care of you myself. But Cal is not pleasant to live with, and it will only be for a few months."

"Don't leave him," she interrupted me. "Work it out."

"That's what I'm doing now, Mother. That's why it's going to be difficult for you to come down and stay with us, at least for now. Up here, you have your friends who can drop in and see you. And Mom, I'll come every week for three or four days, or however many days you want. And we'll keep the apartment so it will be ready for you when you're well again."

"Nursing homes are so expensive, Rosemary. Can't I go home and do all this?"

"How are you going to take care of yourself at home, alone? I can't be with you every day. You won't have anyone to help you. At the nursing home you'll have all of the nurses and aides doing for you, taking care of you. You can stay in bed whenever you want, all day if you want. Your meals will be prepared and served to you. It will be better, Mom. Think of it as hotel living." I tried to lighten it with a laugh but couldn't. "And the money is there. Cal, I have to tell you, has been very generous. Father gave me a nice check. He said it was a reward for all the volunteerism you did for the church. We have the money." I held her tiny face in my hands and kissed her. Then I held her in my arms, carefully, easy. "Hey," I said, "a lady who crossed an ocean isn't afraid of a nursing home, now, is she?"

We both laughed, erasing some of the stress.

I had so much to do, and I wasn't up to it. Mentally, I was exhausted; physically, I was just tired, but I had to prove to myself that even if Cal thought I wasn't capable of nursing my mother, I could still take the initiative; I could still take care of her life while she was incapacitated. I could do it.

That night, back at the apartment, I packed some housedresses, underwear, stockings, socks, and slippers. I made up a separate toilet bag of deodorant, talcum, makeup, and cologne. I had no idea what one took to a nursing home, but if I forgot anything I would bring it to her the next day. And besides, she wasn't going to be there forever.

As soon as the hospital's administration office opened, I was there. But Father McLaughlin had already alerted them, and a place was available. She had to remain in the hospital for several days; she was still too weak to travel, even by ambulance. I stayed with her that day and the next, and on the third day we transferred her to the nursing home.

A nurse's aide met us at the door and accompanied us to her room. It was a semi-private room, small and neat; narrow and long, like a nunnery. The one window looked out upon a courtyard, which appeared to be neglected. More than ever I wanted her home with me, in the guest bedroom. I wanted to be able to wait upon her, feed her when she didn't want to eat, nurse her. I did not want my mother in a home. But dutifully I unpacked her bag and made a note to bring another pillow for her bed and chair pillows. An armchair sat next to her bed, but it was hard and bare. It needed softening; it needed a big, billowy pillow. I made another note to bring her radio. Most times she would be content to listen to music.

"Now I'll be fine here, dear. Don't you worry about me. I'm more concerned about you and Cal than I am about myself. You must work that out, dear. Your marriage comes before anyone or anything else. Don't let me get in the way. I'll be fine."

With those words something loathsome began to eat at my heart, my soul, my very being. I held back the tears and the bitterness, the burning acid forming a lump in the depth of my throat. I should be bringing my mother home with me. I thought about his mother. I would not want even Barbara to go into a nursing home. I would take care of her as well if she were ill. I shook the vile hatred from my thoughts and answered my mother.

"Cal is OK with my coming up here for half a week, or even more if you need me. He's very good about it, Mom. Right now, you're our priority. Cal said to get well," I lied. "And I'll be back tomorrow with a few more things for you."

I saved my grief so that I could take proper care of her. My effectiveness would not be measured by tears. This was not a time for ineffectual grieving. I had grown, matured, since my mother first had cancer, and I knew this disease had to be fought every day and had to be destroyed. I would fight my best fight to keep my mother alive as long as was possible, but deep down I knew a nursing home was not the place to heal. Her own home would save her life.

That night I began my cleaning. I started with the refrigerator. Everything had to go. I put it all in a box for her friend down the hall. When I had disposed of all the food, I cleaned out the refrigerator with baking soda. Then I began with the cabinets.

I threw out most of what was there, and when the food cabinets were emptied, I washed them out with warm water and mild soap. When my mother would return home, I wanted to start her out with everything fresh, boxed or canned. It was almost ten when I deposited the box with Mrs. Polanski. It was obvious she could use every ounce of food I had. I refused her invitation to take tea with her and went back to the apartment to finish up my work.

I took the empty suitcase I had brought back with me and began to pack it again. I packed a few cardigan sweaters, some pullovers, and two wool skirts. I took her jewelry case and put it with my things. Nursing homes had a reputation for patients missing anything pretty or valuable. I would bring that home with me. I packed the only four framed photos she kept in her house. One of me as an infant, a little girl, and a teenager; the latest one was me as a bride. Then I closed up the suitcase and placed it by the front door.

I disposed of everything in the bathroom medicine cabinet. I packed hand cream and fingertip towels, then I scrubbed the cabinet with Mr. Clean. I couldn't stop. I scrubbed the tub, toilet, and the old ceramic tiles that had surrendered its satiny luster a generation ago. It was four in the morning when I lay back in my old bed, not bothering to undress, just shutting my eyes. When I opened them again, it was eight o'clock in the morning.

After changing my clothes, I left the house and had breakfast in a nearby coffee shop. I arrived at St. Michael's by eleven.

I arranged for a TV. The nurse's aide would get the TV man to fix the reception. I placed her small radio by the bed. Over the plain, gray blanket on her bed, I placed her favorite quilt from her bed at home. Then

I hung her clothes in the closet and set up her toilet articles in the medicine cabinet over the sink. I had bought her perfumed soaps, shaped into seashells. I explained the procedures that awaited her.

"Your treatments will begin next week, Mom. I'll be here to take you. It may make you sick or it may not, but it will work, it will work. And you'll be home in your own place when it's all over. I'll take you to all your treatments and bring you back."

I turned on her radio to her favorite classical station. The sadness of her figure stayed with me. I spent the rest of the day with her, walking through the corridors so she would become familiar with her new surroundings. "Make sure you walk every day, Mother. Don't just sit in your room." I pointed out the game room where many of the other patients were sitting quietly. At the end of the day I left her, had dinner at the same coffee shop I had breakfast. It was almost seven o'clock when I arrived at her apartment, and I went to bed right away, I was exhausted.

I could hardly move to turn off the alarm, which was blaring inconsistently in my ear, but I soon realized in my semi-conscious state I didn't have an alarm. I grabbed for the phone next to my mother's bed.

"Roseheart!" His voice was impatient, annoying. "I have been ringing and ringing. Where the hell have you been, darling?"

"Oh, Cal," I answered groggily. "What time is it?

"Nine o'clock. Time for all good girls to be in bed." He laughed. "What are you up to?"

"I was sleeping. I didn't back from the nursing home until seven. I'll be home tomorrow night."

When I think back now on those days, I don't think he understood or felt the reality of my situation.

I visited Father. He had the seven o'clock mass, and I attended but didn't receive Communion. We had breakfast together in the rectory.

"You must remember, Rosemary, that should you need anything, I am here for you. Promise? You promise to call me?"

"I promise, Father. Thank you so much."

"And try to be happy. You're too young and pretty to be sad. You can't bottle it up inside, you know. That's not good. God be with you, my child." He placed one hand on my head and with the other gave me a blessing.

"Thank you, Father." I genuflected and made the sign of the cross and went on my way.

I drove back to Virginia with the same rental car. It would cost a bit more since I was not returning it to the same place, but I didn't care. Let Cal pay for it. I needed the drive. I was beginning to like driving; perhaps one day I could drive cross-country. I thought that would be fun. It took me close to six hours when it should have taken me no more than four. I drove in the right-hand lane all the way; I would have to get use to using the middle and left lane, but I wasn't concerned. My driving habits would improve in time.

The next day I shopped. The Wagners were stopping over for drinks after dinner, and I needed to buy some snacks and cocktail napkins. We were out of food. I needed Christmas presents. Thank God the house was in order. Although Cal's hostility toward clutter of any size still bothered me—indeed, it sometimes maddened me—it meant our house was always neat if not clean. He would not let me have someone in to help me clean it. The one exception was when I was pregnant. And as soon as I miscarried, he cancelled the cleaning woman. So it was always neater than it was clean.

I left after Cal in the morning. He was off to see some people about a new position and would be home for supper late. Could we have stew for supper? Just when I didn't have the time to prepare it. I said yes anyway. What good would it do to say no? He'd only argue, say a few bad words, and push me down some more. It was easier to yes him. I wanted both of us to be in a good mood for the Wagners. They were always peppy and seemed so happy with each other. I pushed his unemployment to the back of my mind. I wasn't ready to deal with it. And if I were, well, I just couldn't.

My mother would be getting powerful doses of radiation. I circled the dates of her treatments on my calendar; I would be with her for all of them. To function, I had to compartmentalize again. Although I refused to admit it at the time, it was there, lurking in my subconscious: I had lost my baby, my marriage was dying, my mother was dying. The lack of control freaked me out. And there seemed to be nothing I could do about it. I was there for the ride. I took everything a day or half day at a time. Something had happened in Cal's office that he was either embarrassed or hurt about. I would get him to open up to me but slowly. In the meantime I was going to be nice and loving to him as I had never been—no matter how rotten he was I would smile through it. I would treat him as I would treat a toddler with his tantrums.

I went to Woody's in the District and bought cologne for Francine, a small crystal bud vase for Barbara, three blue shirts for Cal, a leather belt, aftershave, and for my buddy, Warren, I bought a red plaid tie. He had shown me something similar in a magazine, and he pointed it out to me with his pudgy fingers. I promised I would buy it for him.

By noon I was finished with my shopping list. I would buy my mother something pretty later on. Sam could not receive packages, but I would buy her something when she came back. Then I drove to the supermarket, stocked up on as much food as I could fit in one cart, and made it home by five o'clock.

Cal was already there. "I changed my mind, Roseheart. Could I have a steak?"

"Of course, sweetheart. How was your day?"

He didn't answer me. I didn't mind. I made a quick salad, his favorite Rice-a-Roni, and grilled two small Delmonico steaks. When I had finished, I had just enough time to clean up and get ready for the Wagners. I was no longer tired, I was numb. And although I was ready to call it a day, I looked forward to seeing Phyllis and John. They knew how to add lightness to a person's life.

"You're not wearing those pants, are you?" Cal asked with a look that told me they were too tight.

"Don't they look alright?"

He shook his head from side to side and sneered.

"And please, Rosemary, don't drink a lot tonight. You know when you drink, you tend to laugh kind of raucously. It sounds awful. Be nice."

The doorbell rang, and as usual Phyllis and John saw Cal's beaming, friendly face and next to it my soured, distorted, and pained expression. A thousand thoughts raced through my head as Phyllis and John came into our home. With an enormous discipline, I pulled myself together, remembering how much better I felt if I smiled, if I allowed myself a laugh. So I smiled, albeit late.

"Good evening, everyone!" Phyllis was her usual happy self. "And is it a good evening. I just love winters!" Phyllis was wearing jeans and an oversized sweater.

"Oh, don't say that," I cried. "We barely saw the fall."

"To heck with fall. Winter's my favorite season."

"Hello, John. Come in." I ushered them into the living room. "Summer is mine," I continued. "Hot, hot, summer. I love it. When everything's alive and breathing."

Phyllis sat on the couch under *The Universe*. Thank God she didn't have to look at it. I sat across from her.

We still hadn't been able to move that painting and I had given up on it.

Cal left to mix the drinks in the kitchen.

"How's your mother, Rosemary?" Phyllis asked.

"Not good, Phyllis. Let's talk about it some other time, OK? But thank you for your concern."

"Yes, please," Cal called out from the kitchen. "Not tonight, Roseheart." He returned with a tray holding three drinks.

"You're not drinking with us, Rosemary?" John asked.

"Later. I just had a coke," I lied, wondering why Cal left me out.

"We're sorry we couldn't take you up on your dinner invitation, Cal," John apologized.

When did Cal invite them for dinner? We had both agreed on drinks and nibbles. Thank God they couldn't make it. I didn't know how I would have done it.

"I have some things in the kitchen," I said, and I left Cal with our guests. I had prepared a dozen scallops wrapped in bacon that I had slipped under the broiler to cook for five minutes. It was quick and easy. I turned off the oven and slipped the plate out from under the broiler. Then I made up a dish of celery sticks that I had already quartered, and filled them with cream cheese. I added a bowl of cashews. I poured a glass of ginger ale for myself.

"Wow!" John got up and took the large tray from my hands and placed it on the coffee table. "Rosemary, this looks scrumptious!" He sat down and began to eat.

"Come on, you two. Get over here," I called to Cal and Phyllis, who were looking out the front window. "What are you looking at?"

"Rosemary. Come here, please." His paternalism edged coldly against a loathing I could only feel.

"Is that the car you rented?"

I looked out to see the rented blue Buick parked in front of the house. I looked at Cal, staring. I forgot! My God! I forgot to return the car. My brain spun crazily. How could I have forgotten?

"Please, Roseheart," he leaned over and whispered, "Don't get kooky on me, will you?"

Then it all piled up on me, and I burst into tears. My knees buckled, and Cal was picking me up, carrying me away. Once more I was in his arms. Only when I cracked or fell apart did he put his arms around me. He carried me upstairs and put me on the bed and shut the door, leaving me alone in the dark, uncluttered, quiet, safe room.

I lay there, sobbing, fearing the loss of my world, my sanity. My memory was shot. Tomorrow I would see a doctor. I would have a checkup, and then I, we, would get counseling. I would save my marriage.

"Rosemary?" Cal came back into the room. "Get undressed." He had no emotion in his voice, no rage, no threat, no fear. There was no kindness either.

I stood up and undressed. I put on a long, flannel nightgown and opened the window. It was cold, but I needed the clean air it carried. I got back into bed and pulled the covers up over me. Like a child with my father watching.

He handed me a glass of water and a pill. "Here. Take this."

"What is it?"

Again the deep breath, the shaking of his head, the tight lips.

"What does it matter? It will help you sleep. Take it."

"But what is it?" I asked again.

"The same goddamned pills the doctor gave you when you miscarried!" he roared.

I quickly put it in my mouth; my hand shook, and I swallowed the pill down with the water. Those pills had long ago been finished off. I had taken every last one of them. That I didn't forget. I have always been cautious with pills. So what did he give me?

"Cal?"

"Yes?" He was subdued, like me, sitting in the chair across the room, his head bowed as if in prayer. I felt sorry for him.

"Tomorrow I'm going to see the doctor."

"Why?" he asked as if nothing had happened.

"Something's wrong with me. Something's wrong with us. We need help."

"There's nothing wrong with you or me, Rose-mary." He stated it with such dogmatism, I was jarred. "Go to sleep now." He walked over to the window, shut it, and locked it. Then he left me.

But I couldn't sleep. I thought of my mother. Could she really fight this dreadful disease again? I thought about Sam. Was this trip to the Amazon dangerous? I wanted her near me. She always knew what to do in a crisis. I tried hard to synthesize my fragmented thoughts that spun crazily in my head. I willed myself to think. The dark was soothing.

You look so sad, Rosi.

You're too young and pretty to be sad.

Congratulations, Mrs. Bryant! You're going to have a baby!"

You lost your baby, Mrs. Bryant.

You're always forgetting.

You killed our baby.

I reached over and picked up the phone. The line was dead. It couldn't be. I sat up and switched on the lamp and tried again. The phone was dead. I went out into the hallway.

"Cal!" I called down to him, but here was no answer. "Cal!" I went down but he was not there. My fear heightened, and once again I tried to pull myself together. But a myriad of questions raced through my brain, splintering it so that the black funnel came back, whirling the questions around with no space for an answer.

Why was the phone dead? What kind of pill did he give me? Where did he get it? Neither of us took medication of any sort. Was it possible I had forgotten that I finished up the pills?

I went into the living room and looked out the window—at the Wagners. Cal must be with them. But their house was dark. I circled the living room. The panic began to build. I looked out the window again. The rented car was gone! Oh, my God! What was I thinking? Cal had left to return the car I had forgotten to return. To return the car I never even told him about. He had the phones disconnected so I wouldn't be disturbed. So I could sleep. So I could rest. And I was beginning to think...oh, my God! I went back to my bed then, and lay there with the door open, waiting for him, listening for him.

The twelve hours sleep restored me back to sanity, at least for a time, and I was able to confront Cal. I had no idea how he would react or respond. I never knew. He always took me by surprise, but I didn't care anymore. I was fighting for my mother's life. *I was fighting for my life.* I had done it once before, and I knew I could do it again. The next day I managed to get his attention, and I confronted him. I kept my voice controlled and firm and, hopefully, affectionate.

"This is not going to be easy for me, Cal, least of all for my mother, but this is an emergency. I'm going to spend half my time with you and half with my mother. That's it." I shrugged my shoulders. "She's in a nursing home in New Jersey, and she'll be getting radiation treatments. You'll have to put up with a lot of inconveniences, but so will I. We'll both have to go over our finances. I have to know how much we have. I want to see the bank statements. All of it," I raised my voice in a warning. "But I'm not up to it now. I have too much on my mind. You keep telling me we have money, so I'm trusting you. I hope you won't disappoint me. We'll go over our income and expenses later."

Again, his awful pause, but I waited and then finally, he said. "Look. Here's what we're going to do. Today I'm going out to get us a tree. Warren will help me with it. You don't have to do anything. We don't have to send any Christmas cards this year. We have a whole lifetime for that, Roseheart. And tomorrow, if you're up to it, you and I will go out and get some tree decorations. You always said you love shopping for those things. We'll spend the whole day doing it. But only if you're up to it. OK? And we'll eat out. No cooking! I don't want you to cook until you absolutely want to. How does that sound? And no Christmas shopping. I'm unemployed anyway. No presents this year. My family will understand. You're to rest, do whatever you like, when you like. We'll have Christmas at my mother's. How's that?"

He was kneeling in front of me. I reached out and put my arms around him, and then he did something he hadn't done in a long time. He put his arms around me and held me to him, and despite everything it still felt wonderful. I knew then that I had to give my marriage time. I had to help him. I had to help me.

Christmas Eve!

Cal had done what he promised. Our tree was magnificent! And it was Cal who shopped for it and for the Christmas decorations. I followed him around like a puppy dog, holding on to the good part of him. We laughed together, and I held onto the hope that the worst was over. Francine and Cal decorated the tree. I cooked a simple Christmas Eve dinner for just the two of us. I had hoped my mother would be well enough to visit for Christmas, but the radiation had weakened her, and she was not up to any travel.

Cal and I had planned to drive up the day after Christmas, and she was looking forward to the visit. "Don't worry about me, dear. I've had a lot of Christmases." Barbara and Francine were busy preparing our Christmas Day dinner; the Wagners had gone to John's family in Oregon; Sam, I hoped, still had her head on in the jungle. So it was just Cal and me.

Cal had been wonderful to me—no errands, no chores—I wanted to do everything for him. I tell you, that day was wonderful. Cal gave me a great Christmas. He even went to midnight mass with me. He had never gone to church with me before, not that I ever asked him or expected it of him. I didn't ask him then either. It was his idea. Looking back on that holiday, it was the most serene time of my whole life with Cal.

We spent Christmas day with Barbara, Francine, and Warren. Even that was nice. True to her word, Barbara cooked a great banquet: roast beef Wellington, roasted potatoes, brussels sprouts with white sauce, glazed carrots, the works. Cal bought the wine, which I knew was expensive but I didn't care. Barbara gave us a magnificent cut glass vase. And Francine, thank God, did not make us a gift, but gave us a lovely white damask tablecloth. I gave Warren his red plaid tie, and everyone laughed to witness his enjoyment. He gurgled and squiggled. I helped him put it on, and he wore it all day. We all had gifts to give but Cal. He even managed to laugh at himself because of it. I didn't mind. Cal was his old self, the man I knew before I married someone else. That was the greatest gift he could give me. He was changing. Our marriage would change. Everything was working out. Or, at least, I told myself so.

The day after Christmas I drove up alone in my station wagon. I drove all the way without stopping. I sang half the way, until my voice became hoarse, and then I turned the radio on to full volume. Cal had complained of a stomachache, and with all he ate and drank, he may well have not been feeling up to it. But I doubted that. A visit to an old aged home was not one of Cal's priorities. And besides, he had been kind to me. He had come back. And he hadn't asked anything of me, keeping his previous promise; he was jovial, happy, and giving. He also left me alone. And that was a vacation in itself. I had time to think for myself, to unclutter my scattered brain, or what was left of it. So I accepted his excuse and drove up to my mother early.

I found her sitting in the TV room, the room all the patients sat in during the day. They sat in a semi-circle, the TV placed like an altar at the end of room. No one watched it. Lost in their vacant worlds, it went unattended, only the colors in the commercials influencing perhaps a molecule of energy or intelligence, the voices reminding them they still lived, they were still part of the world. A huge poster on one wall read: "Today is Wednesday. The month is December. It is raining outside."

My mother did not look well. "Hi, Mom! Merry Christmas!" I hugged her, happy to be with her, comfortable with her, her body close to mine invoking images of past comforts.

She hugged me too and smiled, but she did not say much.

"Are you feeling well today, Mother?"

"I'm fine now, dear. Just fine. "

I had bought a light-blue sweater set for her and filled her Christmas stocking—the one I had filled for the last fifteen years of my life—with lipsticks, nail polishes, candies, and other pretty stocking stuffers. It brought back memories of all our Christmases together. I could even smell the roasts she would prepare and the special way she cooked the potatoes. And the pudding. I couldn't help but wish we were both back in that tiny apartment with just each other, closing out the rest of the world. We were poor, but I was never aware of it until I was in my teens. Sometimes, when my mother was especially low on money, she would turn off the lamps and light candles. The shadows of the yellowing flicker of the wicks would dance against the windowpane, and with the snow beating down in great, big flakes and the wind making its loud noises, I always felt safe and secure. The world looked beautiful there in that room with my mother.

I sat next to her in the unbusy room watching what once were vital human beings, now reduced to senility or simple old age. An old lady hummed without stopping, cradling something in her arms every so often. Another cried. But most of them slept or smiled away the minutes. Perhaps it was catching as I looked at my mother who was entranced by the colorful TV picture.

With my help she was able to sit up gradually, then stand for a minute or a half. She seemed to be weaker than when she first had cancer. I tried to get her to walk, but it was impossible. I put her in a wheelchair and wheeled her up and down the corridor. She never complained, barely spoke, and there were moments when I wished I had let her do what she had wanted to.

"Come on, Mother, let's go out." I helped her up, dressed her in sweaters, long johns, her warm winter coat, and a knitted hat with a thick muffler. Gloves on, I wheeled her out the door and over to the car. We would go for a drive and to a restaurant. I knew she loved tuna salad sandwiches, and a deli at the Square had thick, luscious tuna sandwiches.

"Could I just have an iced tea, Rosemary?" she asked sheepishly as she sat back in the wide leather booth.

"You can have anything you'd like, Mother."

I had the tuna salad sandwich and coffee, and we ate in almost total silence. We took a drive in the same quiet, and then I took her back, settled her into her bed, and drove over to the apartment. Everything was clean, but the air was musty. I opened a window and ran the taps. It would not surprise me if they froze up, but the cold and hot water ran freely. After a few days, I returned to my husband and a marriage that I prayed could be salvaged.

My mother died in late January. I have never forgiven myself, nor have I freed myself of the guilt for not giving her the death she requested. She had wanted to go back to her home, to die peacefully in her own bed, and I had denied her that. She died in a strange bed, with strangers around her, all moribund. I couldn't even have given her a decent death. Maybe Cal was right, I couldn't be a caregiver. I wasn't capable.

Aside from my mother's neighbors and friends I attended the funeral by myself. Cal was busy with "lots of important interviews." I had not even heard from Barbara, and I didn't expect anything from Francine or Warren. I had sworn then they were all on the same mental level, but I did receive a magnificent wreath of flowers from them. After the funeral I returned to the apartment, packed a few of my mother's personal belongings to take with me, and gave the rest to the neighbors. Then, after a few days, I whispered good-bye to my mother's spirit, thanked her for her love and caring, and left my beautiful home forever.

"I'm joining the law firm of 'Weeks, Maughan, Letterman, and Foley,' in Arlington," Cal announced with great brightness on a sunny winter afternoon in early February.

I couldn't believe it. How did he do it so fast? I was exuberant. "Cal, congratulations! How did this happen so soon?"

"Knowing the right people."

"Who?"

He sneered at me.

"Well, who?" I insisted.

"Roseheart. I'm a born and bred Virginian. I know people in this state."

"Oh, Cal. I'm so happy for you. Are you pleased with it?"

"Well, of course, stupid. What the hell do you think I took it for?" He laughed at me. "You think I'd take something that didn't please me?"

"Cal." My voice was steady. My eyes met his. "Never call me stupid."

"Rosemary." His voice was steady. His eyes met mine. "Fuck you."

Click. He's off.

I gritted my teeth. I had expected it. We had not made love since Christmas night, when we had returned from his mother's and put our presents under the tree. I had started on birth control pills and I hoped I started them on time. I prayed I started them on time.

"Would you like a drink, Cal?" I asked, ignoring his black mood. I turned to find him looking at me in a way I had never seen him look before. "What is it?"

He walked over to me and ran his hands over my body with a welcomed gentleness. When I tried to speak, he kissed me undressed me slowly, expertly, there in the darkened living room, and we had sex.

We did not make love. It was sex. Two weeks later, I was hot and horny, with no idea how to satisfy myself without him. It just wasn't fair, I remember thinking.

He was standing in the hall doing his last-minute primping in the mirror that had replaced Francine's macramé. It was to be his first day in his new position. We were both excited. I went into the living room to retrieve his briefcase. I don't know why, perhaps intuition, but I walked over to the window and looked out to see my Boy Bill peering up into the house. Without thinking, I closed the drapes, as if hiding him from my view, I could also hide him from everyone else's view, shutting out my sin.

"Want me to pick up a pizza tonight?" Cal asked, stopping at the front door. "Or do you have something else planned?"

Oh, I don't know. Maybe a love affair with that handsome young man out there. Maybe I'll drive up to the cemetery and put flowers on my mother's grave. Or maybe I'll just sit home and drink my scotch. "Nothing," I said.

Again, that patient smile and a sound from somewhere in his throat. "I'll pick up a pizza. Pepperoni.

Your favorite. How's that?" he asked, just like a daddy to his little girl.

I was dying. What was Bill doing out there? "That's fine." I tried to smile. "Sounds good, Cal."

Suddenly the doorbell rang. Cal glanced out through the small window in the door.

"Get that, will you, Rosemary?" He sneered. "It's some kid. Probably collecting for something. Don't give him anything. I can't stand kids collecting." He picked up his briefcase, and with one more brush of his lapels, he was ready to go. "Well? Are you going to answer it or not?"

It took every pore in my stunned body to move toward the door. I opened it wide so Bill could see Cal. *Please don't give me away, please,* I prayed. But Cal, unperceiving, actually helped me out with my young lover.

"See my wife," he muttered and walked right by him, not even glancing at him.

"Yes, sir," Boy Bill chimed. "Excuse me, ma'am. But my name is Roland Santanini. I live just down the street…" his head followed Cal to the curb, "and I was wondering if…" Cal got in the car. "…you had any handiwork that had…" Cal drove away. He stepped inside, shutting the door behind him.

"Are we alone?" he whispered.

"Yes," I whispered helplessly. I didn't want him there, but I needed him there before I died.

He put his arms around me and kissed me just as Rob had kissed me; it seemed like decades ago. He took my head in his strong, lean hands, kissing me all over my face, not leaving an inch. "I love you, Rosemary, I love you," he groaned. He moved his hands down to my buttocks and pushed me against him, and I let him. I let him take me there on the floor in front of the mirror that replaced Francine's macramé. I let Boy Bill take me as Rob had never taken me, as Cal never had, and I didn't care about sin or adultery or Cal or decency. This human beauty was innocent and kind and loved me torridly, and I hurt so bad I didn't care. This time he cried on my breast when he had come, and we repeated our lust until we were both spent, and he went away then to have lunch with his father and mother. It was his nineteenth birthday.

The house was quiet except for a radio morning show Cal liked to listen to every day. Warren did not come that day. I had gotten used to him and could tell if he was in the house or not; I could detect his presence.

A mourning dove cooed from her winterized perch, reminding me it would soon be spring, and I would be able to garden again.

I would have a big breakfast. I took out eggs, ham, bread, and milk and began to create a quick version of eggs Benedict. As I pulled a chair away from the table, my hand fell on Francine's scarf. I picked it up and folded it and left it on the countertop and continued to make breakfast. I would return it when I had the chance, or she could pick it up herself. She must have come by when I wasn't here. It bothered me that she did that. I knew she had dropped in several times before, and I was sure she came deliberately when I wasn't home. It bothered me that I felt that way. After all, she was a part of Cal's family—she had every right to drop over for a visit—but it still left me with an uneasy feeling.

"Well, you seem to be feeling a lot better these days, Roseheart." Cal came into the kitchen. I noticed that twitch just under his left eye. It came and it went, according to his stress level. He had it when we first met, but it was always subtle; one had to be up close to see it. Today it was noticeable from across the room.

"I feel good, Cal. Join me. I'm cooking a big breakfast."

"No, I'll grab a bun and coffee at the office."

"Why don't you let me make you some toast at least?"

"No. That's no fun. I'd rather a bun. A sticky bun. You know the kind that sticks to your fingers?"

I gave him an exasperated look. I tried to instill in him healthy eating habits, but he refused to pay attention to me.

"By the way, Roseheart, if it's not too much of a problem, could you pick up some bulbs for my mother?"

"Bulbs? Light bulbs?"

"Don't be smart. Tulip bulbs," he answered in his usual nasty way.

"Don't get testy! I'm just asking. You want me to pick up tulip bulbs in February? It's freezing outside! Why are you always so nasty?" My voice was raised. He had just ruined what was going to be a good day for me.

"Oh, I'm so sorry, Roseheart. I didn't know I was nasty," he sneered.

I took a deep breath. I was always taking deep breaths. "Where am I going to find garden bulbs in February?"

"Call my mother. She knows where to get them." And before I had a chance to remind him that his mother also did not work and she had more time than I did, he was gone. But I enjoyed seeing him leave for the day, and I forced myself to enjoy my badly pre-pared eggs. Then I called Barbara.

"Yes. Garden bulbs, dear. I'm going to put them in lots of bowls in sunny windows. You've seen that done, haven't you?"

"I have, Barbara. But where would I get the bulbs? I thought they stopped selling them in November."

"At the hardware store in Georgetown. Near P Street. You know where that is, don't you?"

"Yes, I know. What kind?"

"Oh, any kind. Whatever they have. You're the gar-dener. You pick them out. I need them today, dear."

Did she think I was her hired servant?

Before I went into Georgetown, I called Mr. West-cott. Since Sam had left on her Amazon trip, I hadn't heard a word from her, not a card or a call. In fact, no one heard from her. I thought her father might know something.

"He's in a meeting now," his secretary informed me. "Do you want to leave a message?" She always said that, even when he was putting golf balls in his office.

"This is his daughter's friend, Rosemary Bryant. He's expecting my call."

In seconds he was on the other end. "Hello, sweetheart! How nice to hear from you." His voice matched his body—voluminous. We chatted. I couldn't understand Sam's hostility toward him.

"I'm worried about Sam. Haven't heard anything. Have you?"

"No, darling." Mr. Westcott never called me by my name. It was always a pet name. "I haven't heard anything either. But the school is keeping tabs on them. I don't know what possessed her to go there, honey. What do you think?"

"Oh, you know Sam. Always looking for an adventure." I thought of her childhood alone, without birthday parties.

"I'm sure she's safe, honey. I'm trusting in the school. No one else is worried. They're not lost. Just camping in a safe spot with guards."

The typical businessman. Never let anyone know your true feelings. I knew he was worried. "How is Mrs. Westcott?"

"Hasn't slept a night since Samantha left, dear. Otherwise, she's fine. Give her a call. She'd love to talk to you."

"I'll call her." We said our good-byes and hung up.

I called Mrs. Westcott, but she was out. I left a message I would call again, and then I went to Georgetown to pick up Barbara's bulbs.

I bought two dozen multi-colored bulbs and drove on to Barbara's. I remembered to bring Francine's scarf with me. My God, I must have been feeling better. I remembered.

Barbara's house was in complete disarray. Clouds of material covered the heavy and cumbersome furniture that had been moved around the rooms. The curtains in the dining room and living room had been removed.

"New drapes?" I asked. I couldn't help but notice the yards of different fabrics hung over the chairs and sofas. "Are these samples?"

"Kind of. They only give us a teensy bit of cloth. Now how can anyone tell by a few inches? I need at least a yard or two."

"This must have cost a fortune, Barbara," I said, fingering the expensive material.

"Well, I can afford it, dear."

Did I detect a note of Cal in her tone?

"Give me a hand, won't you?" She stood up, carrying yards of chiffon in her arms.

I don't know where my courage came from. Maybe it came from all the errands I did for her. Maybe it came from all the condescending smiles I accepted from her, but it came nevertheless.

"Sorry, Barbara, but I'm in a rush. See you tomorrow. Sorry I can't help you out. Why don't you get Warren to give you a hand? He's so good at helping out. Oh, and by the way, Francine must have left this at my house." I placed the folded-up scarf on the end table and turned and walked out. I looked forward to the day I would not have to be in Barbara's house again. I wondered at her extravagance. She had dozens of pieces of material, each a yard or two in length. Drapery material is expensive. I thought of Cal and my finances. Why was everything such a big secret? And where did Barbara's money come from? Her husband had been dead for over twenty years.

"Rosemary, did you tell my mother that Francine was here?"

I was in the kitchen preparing dinner.

"You mean yesterday? Uh, yes, I guess so. I was in a rush. Why?" I answered absently, turning the beater to high.

"She wasn't here." His tone was flat and dogmatic.

"Alright, Cal. If you say so."

"Not if I say so!"

The black rage was back.

"How dare you?" he screamed at me.

"But, Cal," I replied. "What's the big deal? I'm sorry."

"Why do you always think you know everything? Well, you don't!" His face was in mine. "You can't get anything right, ever." Tiny spots of spittle formed at the corners of his mouth.

I did not speak. You didn't speak to the Black Rage. He was not to be spoken to. You let the black, twisting funnel blow until he went away and another man showed up in his place.

"I'm fed up with this shit! You can't even remember what the fuck you're doing. You'll wind up in that home where your mother was, you sicko!" His face was touching mine, his familiar breath in with mine, his spittle lining his tight-lipped mouth.

"Please, Cal," I murmured. I murmured because I was incapable of speaking up. I thought—*if he hits me! Don't let him hit me, God! I've never been hit in my life!* The blood drained to my toes, my head spun, and his hands were around my neck squeezing and my knees went out from under me, and a cloud of blackness reached up to envelop me.

When I came to, I was in bed. Cal was sitting next to me, holding my hand, patting it, caressing it, kissing it, his voice gentle, caring—the loving, contrite husband.

"Roseheart, darling! I'm sorry. Please wake up, please!"

His face was a blur at first. My mind was...well, it just did not exist. I knew my name and the man next to me was my husband, but I did not recognize the room I was in, nor could I remember why I was in it. I had no idea what had happened. I couldn't remember anything. I threw my arms around him. I had never been that frightened in my life.

"What happened to me?" I cried into his neck, holding on for dear life.

"Oh, Roseheart, I'm sorry." He kissed my face several times. "Thank God you're alright. Thank God! I'm sorry! I'm very sorry!"

"What happened to me?" I repeated, the uncomfortable fear subsiding. The room was slowly becoming familiar, but I still couldn't remember what had happened.

"I lost my temper again, Rosemary, and you fainted. Oh, I'm sorry. Do you forgive me? Please forgive me! Please, Roseheart!"

He was panicked, more panicked than I. He held me close to him; his touch was reassuring, comforting.

"It's alright, Cal. It's alright." Then I was the comfort giver. We went downstairs, where I finished making dinner, and we ate at the kitchen table just like any other normal married couple.

On Monday, when there were still blanks, I called the doctor and insisted that he see me as soon as possible. I was really scared. I did not tell Cal I was seeing the doctor.

"How are you, Rosemary?" Doctor Woodward looked at me carefully.

"Fine," I answered.

"Well, then, what are you doing here, huh?"

I loved his kindness, his gentleness. I loved him so much.

"I think…" I saw Cal's angry, mad eyes, and I collapsed in the doctor's arms sobbing. He held me for just a minute or two, and then I heard the nurse's quiet cough behind me. She laid her hands on my shoulders, but I would not let go of the doctor—my lifeline. He would make me well. He had to.

Finally, I allowed myself to be pulled away and followed the nurse outside. I gave them my urine, my blood. The nurse took my pulse and blood pressure. She weighed me.

"You lost five pounds. Congratulations!"

I would have to remember to tell Cal that. He was always telling me I was gaining weight.

Voices rang out from other places in the office—cheerful voices.

"Who lost five pounds?"

"Ask her how she did it."

"When you're that young and beautiful, it's easy."

The doctor examined me and then we were in his office alone.

"What's happening, Rosemary?"

"I'm forgetting things, whole parts of my life, I can't remember." I was more relaxed, in control.

"Like what?"

I recited all the times I had forgotten things that Cal had told me. I mentioned the rental car, the night I fainted.

"We all forget things, Rosemary. When we're under stress or pressure, we're even more likely to forget things."

"But I've never forgotten things before. I've always been very sharp." I pointed a finger to my head.

He smiled at me. "I'm not concerned about your forgetting. What I'm concerned with is your sadness. That concerns me. What are those marks on your neck?"

I touched my neck. "What marks?"

"These." He held a mirror in front of me.

I saw large welts, purple and black, the colors muted but obvious. I looked up at him. "I don't know." I did not remember Cal choking me at that time.

"You haven't looked in the mirror? I can't believe a pretty woman like you hasn't looked in the mirror." He kept his eyes on me, watchful. "Also, you may be pregnant. Are you aware of that?"

I stared at him. *Not now, God,* I thought. *Not now.*

"How are you and your husband getting along?" He had not moved, nor had his eyes.

"Fine. Fine. We're fine, doctor." I was not saying those words; a voice inside me said them.

"Do you know where you got those marks?"

When I didn't answer, he asked, "Would Cal know? Should I call him?"

"I'd rather you didn't." My voice was my voice, and I was once more in control.

"I want you to go home and get bed rest. Go right to bed. Buy yourself a big box of chocolates and a good book. And stay there until I call you tomorrow with the results of the test. Spend the rest of the day telephoning your friends and yakking. OK?" His eyes were still on me, reassuring.

Just being there and having a good cry made me feel better. I needed to see a psychiatrist. I needed help. If the tests showed I wasn't pregnant, I would go back to work part-time. Cal would just have to accept the fact that someone else would clean our home. Cal was the one who would have to adjust, and I would tell him. I was fed up with adjusting. His shirts would be sent to the laundry. I would shop for food and cook our meals. It was time to start saving my life. I left the doctor's office and drove home with all the windows open. The freezing air felt good.

After parking in front of the house, I walked up the street. I took long, purposeful steps, and after some ten minutes, I turned around and walked back. I would do this every day, maybe twice a day. I would take vitamins and deep breaths. I would get well.

I did what the doctor ordered and surprised even Cal when he saw me propped up in bed with tons of pillows, magazines, and comfort food strewn about like so much junk in an abandoned city lot. I didn't care if he yelled or screamed or beat me. I had stopped caring.

"What's up? What are you doing in bed?" He stood by the door.

I looked him in the face. I was getting better. "I went to the doctor today. I'm forgetting a lot of things. I'm worried. I'd like to go back to work. This life is not working for me." I couldn't believe that was me speaking. "And I don't want to become pregnant. You know what I mean?"

"Oh, baby," he almost rushed into the room, throwing his arms around me, arms I no longer felt loving or caring, arms I no longer needed. "I'm sorry, I'm so sorry."

"Yes, you're sorry now, Cal. What is it about you?" I got out of bed and stood looking down on him. "You seem to enjoy apologizing. You're always apologizing to me. Why? What the hell is happening here?"

"Give me a chance, Rosi. We have to get to know each other. Please let's give ourselves some time."

"What's this, Cal?" I held my hands up to my throat. "Did you try to strangle me? Is that how bad your temper is? Do I need a bodyguard? Do I have to lock this bedroom door?" Memories of his last temper tantrum were returning, and I was frightened.

He got up from the bed and stood on the other side facing me but not looking at me. "Rosemary, you're my life. You're more important to me than anyone or anything. Stay with me, I beg you. I'll do better. I promise you." He came to where I stood and knelt before me, his arms around my legs. He began to cry. "Don't ever leave me, Rosemary. I love you so much."

He was so pitiful. I had to help him. If he were physically sick, I would drag him to the doctors, but he was mentally sick. I couldn't leave him. I had to stay and help him. We made love that night. I was the caregiver. He had a problem, and I didn't want to be the source of that problem, so I would nurse him back to health. I would not leave him. Things would get better. I would make it better. I would. I was grateful I had been taking my birth control pills.

CHAPTER
8

The doctor called late the next day. I had almost forgotten about him. Alone in my pillowed, soft bed I luxuriated, sleeping most of the time, resting my crazed brain.

"Congratulations, Rosemary! You're pregnant!"

I was sick. My husband was sick. I wanted a divorce. I couldn't have a baby. I didn't want a baby. My thoughts were incoherent, jumbled. I didn't know what I wanted. I knew what I didn't want.

"I guess I'm not ready now. I didn't expect this." No happiness emanated from my voice.

"Are you alright? Are things alright at home, Rosemary?"

"What?" I had lost my focus.

"I want to see you tomorrow. You and Cal both, together." His voice was firm, serious, and emphatic.

"How far along am I?" I asked, sitting up in my cave. How long had I been on the pill?

"About nine weeks."

Again my mind ceased to function. I couldn't add or multiply, I didn't know how many weeks were in a month. "And delivery?"

"September. Early. A good month to have a baby."

"Thank you, doctor. I'll see you tomorrow. Cal's going to be out of town for a week. What time?"

He called out to his nurse and after a few minutes, he came back on the line. "I'll see you at 9:00 a.m."

"Thank you, doctor, I'll see you then.

I did not tell Cal, or anyone for that matter, since I was just two months along. What if I miscarried again? I would wait until I passed my first trimester, until I had seen the doctor again, until I was sure I could carry. I wondered about the Black Rage, wondered if I could carry to full term. I wondered what would happen to my baby when I went insane. I wondered about the Black Rage taking care of my baby when I was finally insane. I wondered if Sam's head was still intact. I prayed for a miscarriage, and that night, as I lay down to sleep, I asked God to forgive me my sins and never let me wake up again. I prayed he would let my baby and me go to heaven, and I prayed he would remove my first baby from limbo and bring her to heaven as well.

I did not get up in the mornings to see Cal off. In fact, I slept through most of the mornings. But at night I prepared his dinner, left it simmering on the stove or warming in the oven, and I returned to bed, where I read without stopping. It was wonderful to have a whole day uninterrupted. Cal didn't seem to mind.

I ate green salads and fruit and took my vitamins. In the afternoons I took long walks. Once or twice I let Cal make love to me, and although my heart was not into it, I tried to love him back. But what was needed in the intimate act of lovemaking to bind two people together was not there. I tried nonetheless. We had sex. We did not make love.

When I had marked my calendar three months, I finally told Cal. His reaction was just what I had expected—the loving husband who couldn't do more for me. Once again he did not want me to do anything. He hired a woman to come in and clean for us twice a week. She was to do all the scrubbing. Francine would do any errands we had. (We?) And Cal would do the supermarket shopping. "Not a thing, Roseheart. Stay in bed and rest. And no drinking."

"I know that," I said without any emotion.

"Yeah, but can you do that?"

I had no idea what he was talking about. "Do what? What do you mean?"

He pulled the father bit again. Like I was a ten year old. "Can you stop drinking, just like that?"

He was so ridiculous, he carried no credibility. I went up to my room without answering him.

He brought me flowers almost every day, coming straight to our room after work. He was always in good form, even laughing, feeding me bits of information from his office. And then, being a good boy, he'd leave me to eat his supper alone in the kitchen. Sometimes I wouldn't see him again until the next evening.

Bill came to see me. "You must never come here again," I said. "My husband found out about us. If he sees you, he will kill you." I had come to my senses, and I knew what I had to do.

It seemed I was always lying about something. I wanted honesty, openness, and candor, and I swore it would change. I went to confession and confessed my adultery. The priest advised me to see a marriage counselor, and I said I would, even though I knew I wouldn't. I prayed for God's forgiveness. Because I am a believer and trust in God, I knew he had forgiven me, because

I was sincerely sorry for all my sins and I would not sin again. That's what Catholics are taught. If we are sincerely sorry for our sins, God will forgive us. I was cleansed, I told myself, I was well. I went to bed every night at nine o'clock and read. Cal went out every night. I had no idea where he went, and I did not care. I wanted my privacy more than anything. The quiet of the house was calming, and I was able to relax more without him around. I moved a small TV into the room and watched the news when I tired of reading. I did not get up until nine or ten in the mornings. I went for long walks, despite the cold. With layers of sweaters and socks, I walked a mile every day, sometimes twice a day. In the afternoons I soaked in hot, scented baths and drank hot teas.

At the end of February, Sam came home with her head intact. I went to see her. It was bitter cold, but I didn't notice. I felt my baby growing inside me. This one would live. I knew that. It would be a girl, and I would call her Katie.

Sam answered the doorbell. She was wearing an arrow through her head, the kind kids play with all the time. When we had stopped laughing, we hugged each other.

"Welcome home, you devil. We were all so worried."

"I told you I'd be OK, for God's sakes. Those poor Indians, Rosi. We're doing the same thing to them that we did to the American Indians. It's revolting. I think I'll write a book about it. People should know what they're doing down there. I'm going back in the summer."

"Not alone, I hope?"

"No. I'm not that brave anymore."

"Was it scary?"

She made a face. "Not really. We had a lot of armed guards. Some of them spoke the language. The Indians didn't bother us. Having armed guards around us scared the shit out of me."

We ate deli sandwiches and exchanged gossip.

"So! How are things, Rosi?" She looked at me with the same look Dr. Woodward gave me.

I did not want to tell her of my troubles. It was her second day home, and she seemed happy and carefree. I preferred talking about anything other than my problems. I felt better not even thinking about them. Besides, everything was fine with me at the time.

"Good," I answered her.

"I mean with Cal. Do you guys talk to each other?"

"It's a little better, Sam. Not much, but it's better."

"And then tomorrow? And the day after that? Will it still be better?"

I shrugged. She was right. Things would never get to a point where I would want to live my life with him. And I did not want to tell her I was pregnant. I wanted to give it another month. I wanted to be sure I could carry before announcing it to anyone, even to my best friend.

The doorbell rang, and Sam got up and put on her coat and boots, not taking her gaze from me.

"Where are you going?" I asked, bewildered.

"There's someone out there I want you to speak to. Who wants to speak to you." She came over to me, looking closely into my face. "You look so sad, Rosi. You're not happy. You haven't been in a long time." She turned then and opened the door and walked out. The cold air rushed into the room, and Rob stepped inside and closed the door behind him.

Time stopped. The man I loved, had never stopped loving, stood before me. The man I still could not have because I was carrying another man's baby. I think I gasped. I knew I still loved him. I don't remember saying hello. I stood or jumped up.

He came close to me. "Hello, Rosemary."

I felt faint for a moment, then recovered myself. I smiled up at him, willing myself not to fall into the arms I needed so much. He stood in front of me, close. We were almost touching.

"I'm fine. And you?"

He shook his head. Sadly. He smiled sadly. "For what it's worth," he said. I almost didn't hear him. "I'm sorry to walk in on you this way, but Sam said you didn't want to see me. I had to see you. Rosemary, I've never stopped thinking about you."

How could he? How could he walk in on me now? See me half-witted, dysfunctional? Where was he before? I fell into those magnificent arms and sobbed. I had forgotten the warmth of human contact. How necessary it is. How really holy it is. When I had calmed down, we talked. I told him of my poverty growing up, how it scared the hell out of me when he mentioned we'd be living on franks. I never wanted to be poor again. He moved closer and placed both hands on my shoulder. I looked up at him. "I have lots of money now, Rob, but it's not doing me much good."

"That shit doesn't hit you, does he?" His voice rose, and he pulled me toward him, but I turned away and walked over to a bookcase, as if anything in those books could explain the meaning of what I was living through.

"No. No. He doesn't hit me, Rob." I thought of my near strangulation.

"I'm sorry you lost the baby, Rosemary." He came over to me then and turned me around facing him.

"Thank you," I said.

This couldn't continue. It had to end. "Rob, I'm pregnant again. I didn't tell Sam. I'm only three months along. I didn't want to tell anyone too soon. Bad luck, you know." I tried to smile.

"I don't care. I love you, Rose." His hands tightened on my arms.

"It won't work, Rob. Jesus, I can't make any life decisions right now. My marriage is over. I lost a baby, I lost my mother, I'm having another baby. I'm just holding on. Please help me. Go away. Let me take care of my life. Maybe later. I have to put my life together."

"No." He shook his head. "It's not too late, Rose. I made a big mistake leaving the way I did. I should have stayed and fought for you."

"I have to put my life together. I can't leave Cal now," I said. I knew I'd leave him sometime. I had said "now." An enormous lump closed up in my throat, and the pain made it difficult to speak.

"No. You won't give up without a fight. I know you won't. But one day you will. You'll have to leave him. And I'll be here for you." His voice echoed a soft tremor. "Remember that, Rosemary. I'm waiting for you. When the time is right, you come to me. Don't let him hurt you. I'll be here."

We didn't say anything for the longest time. And then I spoke.

"Rob. I love you, I have always loved you, but I am married. And I'm carrying Cal's child." The last time I saw him, his face manifested grief so sad, I never forgot it. It has stayed with me to this day. Then, in Sam's house, the place we met, the place we shared our love, it was I who was stricken. I don't know how I did it, but I lifted my head, reached up on my toes, and kissed him on the cheek. I put on my coat and hat and turned from him and left my only chance for happiness in Sam's house.

Spring came and with it the garden catalogues. I spent the rest of March planning my garden. In April Warren tilled it for me. It was magnificent to see everything come alive. All was green and new, and I couldn't wait for my baby. Although there were times when I felt true happiness about my child, my depression still flourished, and it seemed that nothing could destroy it. Just when I thought it was gone, it returned so that I became quite used to it, like a live-in roommate who doesn't speak. I thought if I ignored it, it would go away.

And then an awful incident happened. I think I felt sorrier for Warren than I did for myself.

It was June, and all our seedlings had come up. Warren had put up the poles for the string beans and the racks for the tomatoes. We spread blood meal to keep the rabbits away, even though they were disappearing. He erected a little trellis that would serve as an arbor for grapes. I pictured myself sitting under the shade of the huge grape leaves with my baby in my arms, soaking in the coolness of the autumn. It was so nice to dream about it.

"What the hell is this?"

I had not expected Cal to come home for lunch, but it didn't matter. I always had food prepared so he wouldn't be too foul.

"Hi, Cal! This is our garden. Wait 'til you see it when it's all up. It's going to be great. And look, Warren made me an arbor."

Before I could finish speaking, he was pulling down the poles and the racks and the arbor, trampling on the seedlings like a crazy man. "Didn't I tell you I wanted grass with a patio?" He turned to Warren, who looked as if he would burst into tears. "Now you clean this up. Get rid of this junk." He kicked the tomato racks toward him. "You till this whole fucking mess and plant grass, you hear me?" He was yelling louder, and I turned and went into the house. What else could I do?

When he had eaten—I refused to make him lunch—and left, I went out to the yard.

"Warren. Come inside for a few minutes."

He walked alongside me, still sobbing, his fat body trembling. I rubbed his arm in a futile comforting gesture, and we sat down at the kitchen table. I poured him chocolate milk and sliced a huge piece of peach pie and place them both before him, but he didn't seem hungry. Another time he would have wolfed it down.

I began to speak to him in a soothing, comforting way. "We know Cal isn't bad, Warren. I think he just had a bad day today at the office. Don't you?"

He stared at me for the longest time, absorbing my words, and I let him. He stood up and gestured for me to follow him and led me to the staircase. He made hand and foot gestures and pretended he was falling down the stairs. He raced over to Cal's picture and rubbing his two fingers together, he jumped up and down and raced back to the staircase, repeating what he had just shown me, and racing back to Cal's picture.

I had to take a deep breath. "Cal threw you down the stairs?" I stopped him from showing me a third time.

He nodded his head violently. "When? When did he do that to you?"

He held his hand to the side of his body and lowered it to the level of his hip.

"When you were a little boy?" My horror was growing, and I hoped I wouldn't be sick.

Again, he nodded his head up and down violently and jumped up and down.

He was telling me how tall he was when it happened. He had to be older than three, seven maybe, eight. Why would Barbara not know? Why would she lie? I put my arms around him to calm him, and he followed suit. The two family idiots, taking care of each other while we waited for Cal.

Sam told me Rob was writing a book on eighteenth-century American politicians and was closeted up someplace in Pennsylvania. I was glad for him, and I recalled our earlier conversations about how we would write a book together one day. "Hey, pretty, you write about the people, and I'll write about the facts." We laughed over the idea that with both of us doing it, we were bound to have a blockbuster. We made plans on how we would spend our millions, both of us always wanting the same things—no debts, fine wine, a pretty house lost amidst gardens of roses and oak trees.

I tried to write, but found it difficult; focusing was not possible. When I was further along in my pregnancy and feeling physically strong, that I could carry full term, I bought a lot of children's books, with pretty colors, hoping it would change my mood. Still, my brain refused to move. I took to arts and crafts. I made a quilt for the baby's crib that I had not yet bought, still not trusting my womb. I made a quilt for her carriage to come, a quilt to hang on the wall. I knitted booties by the dozens and gave every other pair to the Salvation Army. And then, without any forethought, driven by what had been in the far crevices of my mind for so long, I called the locksmith. I became angry not being allowed to use a piece of furniture that was in my home. Who the hell did he think he was? It wasn't his father's desk. His father was dead. It was ours.

"What kind of desk is it, Mrs. Bryant?" The locksmith's voice was quick and short.

"A very old one, that's about all I know. I lost the key. It came with the desk."

"I'm real busy, but I think I can stop by this afternoon."

I gave him my address, hung up, and waited. I was terrified that Cal would come home early. I prayed to God that would not happen, and then I asked God for his forgiveness for asking another favor.

The locksmith arrived just after three. It took him all but two minutes to open it, and it took me less than a minute to pay him and see him out the door. Then I went back upstairs to discover what secrets my husband was hiding or not hiding.

I opened the middle drawer and to my relief found nothing but a yellow legal pad, two pens and a pencil, sharpened to an extra-fine point. The right-hand top drawer contained shoe polishes in a small, clean cardboard box—blacks, browns, saddle soap, a brush that seemed not to have been used often, and some small rags that were also clean. So far, so good, I remember thinking. Perhaps I was too hard on him. But he had told me he couldn't find the key. He had. Why didn't he want me to use it? I opened the lower drawer, which was the file drawer, and I found the papers from the closing and the mortgage. At first I thought it was the mortgage for Barbara's house, but I checked the address. I couldn't believe it. I looked at it again, studied each line, and confirmed what I had seen right away. My home was in my mother-in-law's name.

And then I remembered that Cal had the closing planned ahead of time. He tricked me. Deceived me. He didn't want me at the closing because Barbara was buying the house! My heart began to thump. Quickly I went through the other papers. I found an insurance policy in the event of his death; all went to Barbara—$500,000! I couldn't believe what I was reading. I checked the date of the policy. It was taken out after we were married. Why would it go to his mother? I found another insurance policy in the event of my death. Double indemnity. For $200,000. My hands began to shake. It was dated a few months after we were married. I picked through the files until I came to the last one. There was a box behind the last file folder. I took it out and opened it. Money! Lots of money! I counted up to $100,000, but there was much more. I had to stop. Where did it come from? Did he steal from someone?

I was sick and remembered my baby. I had to protect her. But it was not that easy to put aside. Was this why he left his job? Was he fired from his job? I slammed the drawer shut, not wanting to see anymore, to know anymore. Just a few more months. If God would give me a few more months to see my baby born, all this would be over. I would leave him, return to the Hill, and make a new life for myself. I prayed to God to give me time. But I had to know where the money came from.

I went into my bedroom and lay down. I pulled the blinds so that the darkness of the afternoon was soothing, and I allowed myself to think back on it all, but I couldn't come up with even a nuance of how he got that money. I had to know. Cal would be home soon. I would start tomorrow when he would be gone for the day.

The next morning, one minute after Cal had left the house, I called Congressman Barone's home. His wife answered.

"Rosemary! How nice to hear from you. Hope this call is what I hope it is." Her voice was as friendly and warm as I remembered, and I realized how much I missed her.

"Hi, Helen, but no, unfortunately. I just have to talk to Mr. Barone."

"Hold on, he's walking out the door."

I could hear her call out to him and the footsteps clear and loud on their wood floors.

"Hello, Rosemary! How are you?"

It was then I realized how much I missed him. "Fine, Mr. Barone. I'm calling you at home because I want to keep our conversation confidential. Could I come and see you at your home? I hope you'll understand, but I can't come to the office, and it's difficult for me to come in the evening."

"No problem, Rosemary. Can you tell me what it's about?"

"I'd rather not discuss it on the phone."

His voice turned grave. "Tomorrow at twelve. Come for lunch."

I couldn't imagine myself having lunch with what I had on my mind. I couldn't sit through a friendly meal. "Thank you," I breathed out, feeling better as I did, "but I won't have the time, although I would love to taste some of Helen's cooking again. I'm…" I groped for the right words, "…tight on time." I knew he'd know I was lying. "I'd like to just stop by really quickly. Is that alright?"

He hesitated before answering. "I look forward to seeing you, Rosemary. Til then."

I would find out tomorrow where Cal's money came from.

My stomach was huge as I waddled up the path toward his front door.

Helen stayed long enough to say hello, hear my good news of motherhood, and then she left us alone. I could hear the children screeching in the background against the high volume of a television.

"So, my lovely mother-to-be, what is it that turns you so serious, so sad? Are you alright?"

It took a minute or two before I was able to speak. It was important to say just the right words.

"I'm fine, congressman, but I have to know why Cal stopped working for the senator."

He nodded; there was a tightening of his mouth that was noticeable because I had studied his every expression during my tenure with him.

"Why do you want to know? What I mean, Rosemary, this is somewhat old news. Why are you asking now?"

"I'm his wife. I have to know."

421

This time he took a minute or two before responding. "It may not be news you want to hear."

"I have to know. It's important." I leaned forward. My voice cracked. "For my child's sake, for me. We must know." I never took my eyes from him.

He was quiet for a moment and then he spoke. "I'll be in touch." He placed his pudgy hand on top of mine and patted it. "I promise."

It was a week before he called.

Again we met in his living room. This time there was no Helen greeting me. The quiet of his usual noisy home was ominous. I can still remember the nubby feel of the armchair he directed me to.

I noticed the beginning of a smile upon his face, which had been closed and dark when he greeted me. But it turned into a grimace, a tight spreading of his lips that manifested firmness rather than conviviality. This time it was Congressman Barone who took a minute or two before he spoke.

"He was accused of taking bribes. Big money, Rosemary."

Just for a few seconds I couldn't speak. Couldn't I have guessed that? Why was it so shocking?

"How much?" I asked.

"They don't know." He leaned back in the leather La-Z-Boy.

"From whom? How did it happen?"

"Do you mean how was he discovered? He was the senator's right-hand man. The senator relied upon him for everything, for years—twelve, I believe. The senator blames himself, Rosemary. He left too much in Cal's hands. Cal would tell him how to vote. In the beginning it was the senator who made out. Cal was brilliant. He proved himself admirably. It happened that the senator left too much up to Cal. Sometimes it would be just a nod from Cal standing off the floor that would prompt the senator to do or say or even vote on something. But then things began to go bad. Something was changing, and the senator had a suspicion. Of course, he wasn't aware of anything wrong until about a year ago. So when a bill came up that Cal was strong on, and when the senator had the opportunity to do so, he voted the opposite way. He watched Cal and knew something was screwy. He went to his home office that night and waited; and sure enough, they were gunning for him. Just a phrase, just a phrase." His hands went up and stopped in midair. "The ones who paid the money to Cal thought it was going to the senator. They paid a visit to the home office too. That's how Cal was found out. Well, he had to pay it all back, and the senator fired him. It's generally believed that Cal took bribes from others. It just can't be proved or traced. I suppose this was a classic case of power corrupting. But it was Cal who was the corrupter. No one knows how many bribes he took before that, but it's thought that Cal had been taking bribes for the last couple of years." He leaned forward in his chair. "He'll never get a job on the Hill again or near us. That's for sure."

"A law firm hired him."

"Yes. I know. They owe him."

"What?"

"I don't know anything about it personally, but that's how the scuttlebutt has it. That law firm owes Cal."

I was sick. And speechless. I knew there would be dozens of questions floating through my mind that evening, but at that moment I couldn't think, couldn't speak. I stared straight ahead.

"Are you alright?" Congressman Barone asked me.

"What?" I looked at him.

"Is everything alright with you? And Cal?"

I shook my head and bit my lip.

"Rosemary. Are you in any kind of danger?" He leaned toward me, and I heard the squeak of the La-Z-Boy as it came upright.

"Oh no! No! Not at all." I tried to smile, but my face would not obey. I thought of the insurance money. I thought of all the cash in the drawer. "I'm not in any danger." How could I tell him what I had discovered? I felt shame knowing I was married to a crook.

"You seem very unhappy, my dear. I'm worried about you."

"Oh, you needn't be, Mr. Barone. I've never felt better. At least physically. I take good care of myself now." I patted my belly and forced another smile. "But you're right. Cal has disappointed me before and now this." I stood up abruptly. "I have to go," I said. I leaned over and hugged him. "Thanks so much. I appreciate all this, Mr. Barone. And don't worry about me, I'm not in any danger." I hoped I wasn't.

He walked me to the door, took me by my shoulders, and looked directly into my eyes. "You are to call me or Helen if you need anything. Understand? My home is always open to you"

So I knew. Strangely enough I felt better, relieved, knowing it at last. I knew what my future plans would be. After the baby was born, I would leave him. He would come home one day, and I'd be gone. But I would be prepared just in case. And once again I prayed to God to give me time, time enough for my baby to be born.

By the first of July, my roses were blooming. I was able to cut several bouquets. I sent some over to Phyllis and put the rest in a vase in my living room. I was getting bigger, and the weather was getting hotter, I wasn't up to traveling or going far from home. Sam came to my house for our luncheons and sometimes Phyllis joined us. I served cold tuna with black olives and supermarket potato salad. I could not cook nor would I. Some days I varied my menu with cold lunchmeats and pickles, which I didn't touch. Some days I wanted iced tea and ice cream, but I forced myself to eat lots of salad, dry, and lots of fruit.

"My God, Rosi, if you have these many roses now, think of what you'll have when the baby comes!"

Sam was always making big splashes over my gardening.

"Just keep sending them over," Phyllis joined in. "I put those white ones in a deep crystal vase in the living room. It looks like something out of *Better Homes and Gardens.*"

It was a Thursday in late July, and they were about to leave. I was wrapping flowers for them.

"You need a haircut, Rosi," Sam informed me.

"I do?" I asked.

"And your nails, Rosi. You could use a manicure." She reminded me of a loving mother.

"Oh, yeah. I never get the time to do them."

"Why don't you go into the District and get a beauty treatment at Liz Arden?" Phyllis suggested with some hesitancy. We still weren't close enough yet to tell each other what to do as Sammy and I often did.

"Great idea, Phyllis. Why not, Rosi? You'll feel a lot better."

She was right and I told her so. I would go that week, as soon as I made an appointment.

Sam knew me well. I had not made an appointment at Liz Arden.

She called me a few days later. "Rosi? You're on! Next week, Tuesday, one o'clock. Red Door. You're having a manicure, pedicure, haircut, and a blow dry. They give good blow jobs, kiddo. Yuk, yuk! Anything else you want, you're going to have to call them today."

"Now why does that not surprise me?" I asked with mock exasperation.

"Well, I knew you weren't going to do it. You're welcome! See you!"

My friends always made me feel good, but Sam brought me up to another level.

"Is today the day they make you beautiful, Rose-heart?" Cal called to me from the bathroom.

"Yes."

"What time are you due there?"

"One."

I swung my legs over the bed and waited a minute before standing. I always waited for him to leave the house before I'd get up, but that day I needed more time to prepare myself for Liz Arden. I needed a long, perfumed bath, but a shower would do. Despite the fact that I was going to have a shampoo—my hair had not been washed in over a week—I had to wash it before leaving the house.

"How long does it take?" He poked his head out the door, half his face soaped for shaving.

"What?"

"All that stuff. You know. To do you." His fatuous grin bothered me.

"Oh, I don't know, Cal. Why?"

He came into the bedroom with that hateful rage on his face. "Why? Do you mind if I ask? Is that too much? Fuck you!" He went back into the bathroom.

I felt my stomach and could feel the baby move just a bit. It made me happy. It erased all the ugly. My baby would be in my arms soon, and then I would be a working mother, away from that house, from him.

"What time will you be home? That's all I'm asking." His voice softened.

I had gotten bolder with Cal through my pregnancy. I took chances and got away with all of it, but I didn't want to push my luck. Although I couldn't remember him ever striking me or even strangling me, I still remembered the welts around my neck and my temporary amnesia.

"Around five. Maybe later. What do you want for supper?"

"How about one of your famous omelets? You know, the kind you stick the asparagus and cheese inside?"

"OK. Today's going to be a scorcher. And thunderstorms later, so take your umbrella."

"I know." He left the bathroom, and I went in to shower to make myself as presentable as possible so the Red Door people could make me even more presentable.

I was bumped. My first visit in more than a year, and they bumped me. Just when my need for pampering had reached the desperate mark. But it happens a lot in Washington. The politicians' wives always get immediate service. I wondered who I got bumped for—a Kennedy? The power of the Capitol somehow seeped down into the lowest part of the pyramid. Since the day did turn out to be a scorcher—ninety-seven degrees—I decided to go straight home and turn up the air, lie on my cool, cotton sheets, and sip iced tea.

I drove up to the house, and as I did, I saw Cal's car in the driveway. What was he doing home? I hoped he hadn't been fired again. But at the same time something in me surged, and I continued on to the cul-de-sac and returned to the street above ours. There it was. Francine's car. Why was it there? And everything flew up into my calcified brain. The telephone calls, Barbara always looking for her in my house, Cal not wanting any sex from me, Sammy telling me he had to have some-one else. I continued back to my house, parked the car and closed the car door without making a sound. An alarm of some kind went off in my head as I turned the key in the front door. I heard nothing but silence. I could see only a darkened hallway. I felt the coolness of the dark. I looked toward the top of the stairs—I could hear a slight noise, faint. I crept up the stairs to my bed-room, and there it was—Francine and Cal. Naked. In my room. In my bed. They hadn't seen me.

I don't know how long I stood there. I remember my legs would not move. But somehow I managed to turn around, walk down the hall toward the stairs, and quietly, one step at a time, descended them, the heav-iness of my baby weighing on me. When I reached my car, I shut the door and drove away.

I drove south. I did not think to call Sam or Phyllis. I did not think of my friends. I drove through Arling-ton, into Richmond, then back again—where would I go?—through the black, rainy night. Finally, I came home. I didn't know what else to do.

I was soaked when I stood in the middle of the liv-ing room facing Cal. I think I had been standing in the rain for quite a while. My brain ceased to work; no thoughts invaded that quiet, empty space.

"Where have you been?" His voice was nervous, wavy as the warm wind outside our door. He knew I had seen him and Francine.

I didn't answer him. I turned and climbed the stairs again, the sickening stairs. Then I was in the bath. How I got in the bath, I can't remember. I can still recall the feel of the hot oil as it caressed my body, which was thick and heavy with my expectant child. Then Cal was standing over me. I thought I had locked the door.

"Where have you been?" His voice was still nervous.

I got up and dried myself. I removed the talcum from its shelf and powdered myself. My hands shook so that I dropped the talcum on the floor, making a mess. I tried to clean it up, but my hands, my arms, my body trembled violently and I wasn't able to do it. I left it there, its aroma seeping through my quick and generous breaths like giant roses in their new bloom. I threw on a gown. Since I couldn't face that bed, I went downstairs. I could hear Cal in the bathroom cleaning out the tub. Water ran. He called my name. We must confront at some point. We must talk. I went up the stairs into the bathroom, planning on telling him what I saw. I would leave him. But we would talk first.

After all, we were civilized, intelligent people, not prone to throwing things, committing hostile acts. We were mature people. I walked into the bathroom, and Cal looked up at me from the clear water. I noticed the smile on his lips was a nervous smile, and his left eye tic was working overtime.

"Come on down." He laughed.

I did not move at first, but then I leaned over, holding onto the rim of the tub, and our eyes met. My voice began to work.

"Why, Cal?" My brain was moving.

I heard a scream as he pulled me into the water. I felt my shoulder wrench. Something in my abdomen ripped, but I could feel no pain, and I was looking into his smiling face with eyes hard and mean.

"Please, Cal, don't do this," I begged. I had no idea what he was going to do.

"Why not, Roseheart? I could use the money, you know. We're broke. No, of course you don't know. You're too dumb to know anything. You're worth a lot of money, baby, thanks to me. And who would know? Who would suspect? You're top heavy. You took a bath and fell and hit your head. Who's to know? I'm downstairs in the basement with Warren. And I find you drowned in the tub. It's perfect."

I tried to push away from him, but my God in heaven, I can still remember his iron strength. He pushed me under, and I was sucking water, gagging, not breathing. I pushed again and again. I was dying. There was nothing I could do. I would go to my God, and I cried for forgiveness for all my sins. But my baby stirred, kicked, and I knew she was in danger. I had to save my baby. This baby would live. My baby would survive. I gave one last push so that I had one arm up and over the tub, and my hand clutched a leg. I opened my eyes to see Warren staring down at us.

"Warren! Help me!" I screamed. He reached over and pulled me up—I never realized he had such strength. Cal had both his hands on my nightgown, restraining me, pulling me back, and then I was out, breathing in the dollops of magical air. Then I was running, out into the black rain, my torn nightgown clinging indecently to my trembling body, and I was in Phyllis' arms. There was a blinding light. A pain so unbearable I knew I would die ripped through my body, and then I heard the sirens. I was in a bed, Phyllis feeding me hot tea by the spoonfuls, warming my hot insides, warming my struggling baby. I caught a glimpse of John with policemen. I couldn't hear what they were saying. There were no sounds.

But the pain, I tried not to remember that awful pain. And then my world fell silent. I lay back on the pillows and went to sleep. In that sleep I gave birth to my baby girl, five pounds, six ounces—"a little small, but healthy, Rosemary. You have a beautiful baby girl." An angel was talking to me, and I didn't wake up for two days.

When I did awaken, I saw a sharp whiteness for several minutes, and then the picture came into focus. The wall was white, bare, thick—my fortress was comforting in its cleanliness, in its insulation. No other person was in the room. To the right was an IV bottle, a clear, plastic tube that ran down like pacific rivulets into my arm. Like my mother. I began to cry. I heard voices speaking to me.

"Don't cry now, Rosemary. You're going to be fine."

And then it all came back to me. My baby lived! Despite it all, my baby lived!

"Doctor, may I see her? Please?"

"In a minute." He held my hand.

"And your husband, Mrs. Bryant. Do you remember what happened?"

And with those words I was back in the water, drinking it, drowning in it. I screamed, and they stuck a needle in my arm, and I fell asleep again.

I dreamed. My mother was in her ice-blue dress with its matching hat and shoes, and she was helping me dress. I was about to be executed, but I didn't know why, and I knew I was not supposed to ask. I placed a ring that had a gigantic pearl embedded in tiny pearls on my finger. "Mother, make sure you get this when it's over." She was weeping. "I don't want you to leave me, Rosemary, don't leave me!" I walked out into a long hallway, which was black. I couldn't see anything, but I was able to walk straight ahead until I saw a dim light, and under the light was the electric chair.

I sat down in the chair, sat straight up in that large, wooden chair, shoulders back, chin forward. Wires ran from somewhere in the back of the chair to my head, as they do in an EKG. Each arm rested on the wide chair arms, and Father McLaughlin came in, praying from his black book. Then I saw the reporters with their flashbulbs and cameras, their little books and pencils, watching my every move, my every expression, in for the kill. I smiled at them—never complain, Rosemary—when the silent juices screeched through my body, each evil pore sucking it in; and when my brain was fried neatly, my head fell forward and I met my death.

When I awoke, the police questioned me.

I did not tell them everything. I did not tell them how I found Cal and Francine together. But I couldn't remember everything. They were kind and sympathetic. They asked a lot of questions, but told me nothing.

Phyllis and John and Sam came in after they had left. They told me Cal was dead. My husband was dead. The man who had made love to me. The man who was to be my partner in life. It was final. "Cal is dead, Rosemary," Sam said, holding my hand, caressing it.

"Warren killed him, did you know that?"

"What?" I was startled into clarity, my brain once more functioning.

"Warren was there. Didn't you know?" John was speaking to me.

"Yes, he saved my life."

"When we saw your condition, I knew something awful had to have happened. I ran over, the door was open, and I heard Warren screaming. By the time I reached the bathroom, it was too late. Warren was hitting him with the hammer. I know you love Warren, Rosemary, but after what he did to Cal, he had to be placed in an institution. Barbara, of course, won't talk to anyone. She took care of the funeral."

I was incapable of speaking. I was incapable of crying. I was incapable.

They kept me in the hospital for ten days. The diagnosis was pneumonia. But they let me keep my baby next to me. Oh, how beautiful my baby was. Her eyes searching, always searching. I was tempted to baby talk to her, but I wanted her to hear only clear, precise, beautiful English for the first time in her little life. My child would grow up loving words.

Phyllis and Sam came to see me every day. They brought me flowers, which cheered me, and chocolates I was content to look at and smell. They fed me when I wouldn't eat. They held my arm and walked me up and down the corridors. They washed my face and masked it with red and pink cosmetics. They combed and brushed my hair. They brought me baby things. I had not bought anything for the baby myself. But they made up for it. Dozens of little shirts and diapers. I had sleep outfits for a year if the baby didn't grow. I had blankets and crib sheets, even a magnificent silver spoon. I soon realized I did not have baby furniture, not even a bassinette or crib. I did not have to worry. Sam had the greatest time in her life buying a crib and

dresser. She told me she pretended to be the expectant mother. "They kept looking at my stomach, like
everyone shows in front, right?" That night I stopped
loving Sam and began to revere her.

Once when Phyllis was making me up and I was
lying back on my pillow, I closed my eyes and pretended it never happened. I was not bumped, I was
able to keep my appointment, I had lunch in the District, I did not go home, I did not see Cal and Francine.

I wept a lot.

Barbara did not come to see me nor did she call
me. I called her, but there was no answer. Sam and
Phyllis urged me to let it be until I was rested, until I
was home and feeling stronger.

And then one day, I was released. They told me I
could go home, although I wondered where that was.
I did not want to return to the house I shared with Cal.

"You could come and stay with me, Rosi. I'd love to
have both of you."

It would have been great to take up residence once
more with my best friend. The invitation was loving,
but I knew that part of my life was over. I was now
a mother, and I had decisions to make and a life to
create for myself and my child. There was no going

back. Sam was still a student and entitled to live unencumbered, free, and independent. Sadly, our lives had forked.

CHAPTER
9

The house was delightfully cool as we stepped in from the summer's heat.

"The police let us in when it was clear. And, of course, with your written approval." Phyllis put her arm around me. *When did I give my written approval? I* walked into the living room holding Katie close to me. Sam went straight into the kitchen.

"You're spoiling me," I complained.

"Just for a while, "Phyllis said. "Then you'll be on your own. Now I've got to go to the office and do some work, so take care. I'll be home all night if you need me." And then to Sam. "You have my office number in case, Sam."

In case what?

We were in the living room sipping iced tea. I was curled into a chair. I held Katie in my arms and smiled to myself. Sam stared down at her, grinning, unmoving, for about three minutes. "She doesn't look like you or Cal. She just looks like a baby. Oh, can I hold her?" she asked, taking her from my arms. Still grinning at my newborn, she blew out her lips to resemble a fish. While she was busy with her mock mothering, I threw out *The Universe*, Francine's macramé and the waxed red flowers. I couldn't stop. I went from room to room throwing out everything that made me uncomfortable, even his favorite corkscrew, the remains of his favorite scotch, a photograph of the two of us, a photograph of him, frames and all, went into the trash. The upstairs could wait.

"Feel better?" Sam, the grand protectress, asked me as she sank into my favorite chair.

"Uh huh." I nodded, managing a smile and settling myself onto the couch.

"Want to talk?" my best friend asked.

"Yes. But let me put Katie to bed first. Look how sleepy she is."

"Can I help?"

"You can help me make it up those stairs."

"Come on!" She gave me a huge smile and walked behind me. Carrying Katie in my arms, I had the courage to retrace those fatal steps. The reality of returning to the past was not frightening, but I hesitated when we reached the upstairs hallway.

"Lights will help, Rosi," Sam advised me. "Keep the lights on all the time."

We went to Katie's room. The crib and dresser were beautiful; the room was a bit too white.

"Phil and I will help you decorate it. We didn't want to do anything, you know. You have your own ideas."

"It's beautiful, Sam. Thanks so much." The sheet smelled of a light perfumed scent, and I laid Katie in her bed for the first time.

"She's sound asleep. I love her so much. Look at her."

"That's going to be one spoiled little kid."

"And don't I know who's going to spoil her." We both laughed. "Come on, we have a lot to talk about."

We made lunch. My friends had filled the refrigerator with loads of deli food—delicious, expensive deli food. I piled a platter high with chicken, coleslaw, and a vegetable/rice salad. Sam pulled out a cool Chablis from the refrigerator, and we made ourselves comfortable at the kitchen table.

When we had finished our lunch and had drunk most of the Chablis, I talked about that night. It felt good to talk to someone I trusted and loved, whose confidence I had. I told her how I found Cal and Francine, how I just drove until I could drive no more. I cried and Sam cried with me. She covered her face with long, slender hands, hands that should play Chopin.

"You've been through hell, Rosi." She stood up and walked in circles without stopping.

I raced to the back door and vomited over the steps. I vomited until I retched, and nothing more could come up. Sam helped me back into the living room.

But I didn't want to lie down. I had had enough bed for a lifetime. I wanted to move, I wanted to live again, to go back to that life I had before Cal, but with Katie.

"Listen to me, Rosi. Listen carefully. They did an autopsy on Cal. He had a lot of alcohol in him. He was also smoking pot. Your neck was purple the day after. You had a lot of marks on you. It looked as if someone had beaten you, as if someone was strangling you. Rosemary, it was pretty obvious what happened that night." She was holding me by my arms. "He was trying to kill you, Rosi. Can you understand that? After you got out of the house, Warren finished him off. John was a witness to that."

My mind was numb, but I managed to ask, "What home is he in? Could I see him?"

"They put him in a state institution."

My heart sank. My poor Warren. My poor, helpless Warren.

"And Barbara and Francine?"

"They won't answer the phone. We tried to contact them. We even went over there, but it's all closed up. I don't think they're there."

It took me a long time, but I finally asked the question: "Where is Cal buried? Did they have a funeral?"

"No. They had no viewing. John did a little sleuthing and discovered they had a private cremation ceremony."

I had to be close to Katie. I went up to see my daughter. It was necessary.

Sam followed me upstairs. I couldn't speak, but I needed to be alone with my Katie. She was sleeping like an angel, her tiny fists curled up, her rosebud mouth opened just slightly. She was only twelve days old, but she had a thick crown of blonde hair. Cal's hair was black, mine was brown, my mother's brown. No one in Cal's family had blonde hair. I looked closer, and I smiled when I realized whom she looked like. I knew my baby would be perfectly normal, as I thought of that beautiful, innocent young man I made love to. Yes, my Katie will have a wonderful life.

I thought of my mother when I was born, when I was the one in the crib, and she was looking down on me. What were her thoughts? I went out into the hallway. My bedroom door was closed, but I opened it and walked inside. No fear, no timidity would intrude upon my life ever again. I had a daughter now, and I would protect her. And as my mother had lived for me, I would live for her.

The room in its unused, uninhabited state took on a new perspective. The shades and drapes were open, and the dim light of the fading day illuminated what could have been a dark and gloomy space. I opened the closet door without hesitation. I would never be intimidated again. I couldn't believe what I saw or didn't see. All of Cal's clothes were gone. Not a tie or belt left. I walked over to his dresser, pulling out each drawer, wiping off his fingerprints, removing all traces. Every drawer was empty. Without hesitation I picked up the phone and dialed Barbara's number. It rang almost a dozen times before she answered. I had no intention of hanging up. I would let it ring until it roasted. Finally, I heard her voice, hoarse and empty.

"Barbara, this is Rosemary."

There was a long pause—I thought she would hang up—before she spoke. "How are you feeling?"

"Do you care? Do you know you have a grand-child?"

"No, Rosemary, I guess I don't. I lost my son. That says it all, doesn't it?"

"I lost a husband, Barbara. The father of your grandchild. Why won't you speak with me?"

Silence.

"Cal's clothes are gone. Did you take them?"

"Yes. I took them."

"Why?"

"They belong to my son."

"They belong to my husband."

I held the dead receiver in my hand for a few minutes, and then I hung up the phone. It didn't matter. I had broken the silence. I called the locksmith to come and change all the locks on every door. He would be there the next morning.

Sam and I sat in the living room with Beethoven playing low in the background. We sipped wine spritzers. And then a thought occurred to me.

"Sam. Come with me, please."

I went up to the bedroom, retrieved the secret key from the bottom of my shoe and went into the den. With Sam looking on, I opened Cal's desk. Every file, every piece of correspondence was gone. I saw no evidence of a mortgage, no evidence of any insurance. The money was gone.

"I think it's time you got yourself a lawyer," Sam advised me when I told her about the mortgage and insurance policies. I did not tell her about the money.

I opened my purse and checked my bank balance. Maybe enough for a month. Now I was really frightened. How would we live? How could we eat? Would I be thrown out into the street tomorrow? Was this history repeating itself? I recalled that dreadful time with my mother when we had not money for anything, not for rent or food. But there was no longer time left to grieve or complain. Nor did I have the desire to do so. I had a new energy in me. The time had come to fight. There was a new me, or perhaps the old me that I'd forgotten about, tucked away, hidden from view lest the enemy attack, saved for the Black Rage.

Thinking back on it now, I don't know how they thought they could get away with it. It didn't take me long to get a lawyer. With John's help I got an excellent one.

I could not have the house. Legally it belonged to Barbara. It was in her name. But I was entitled to all of his life insurance, every penny we had the day he died, his pension, and the two cars. I did not tell the lawyer about the money. I knew Barbara had it.

"Strange people," my lawyer said with a shake of his head. "I don't know how she thought she could get away with this. I've spoken to her attorney, and she'll return the insurance policies to you. You get to keep everything in the house, but the house is hers. We can't do anything about it. She is allowing you a year to find another place."

I did not care about the house. It was a relief to know that what had brought me so much unhappiness was now no longer mine, was never mine. I only needed what was necessary to raise my child and to see that she would be educated.

I was grateful for Sam's time with me. But after she left, I had to keep busy. I set up a cot in Katie's room and slept there. I was no longer frightened to go into my bedroom or my bathroom; fear no longer stalked me. Instead, I was filled with disgust and preferred not to be reminded of him, so I never again slept in that bed.

Father McLaughlin baptized Katie the end of September. Sam was her godmother, and John Wagner was her godfather. Sam had a small quiet gathering after the baptism at her house. It was a small group:

Phyllis and John, Sam's mother and father, Congress-man Barone and his wife, Father McLaughlin, and me.

For the first time—it seemed—joy rushed into my life. Katie was my joy, my reason for living. When I was underwater and not caring anymore, it was Katie who had kicked within me, Katie who had told me to live. She swept away the sadness, the loneliness. She awak-ened the silence in my soul and filled it with music. The oppression that had once weighed upon me had lifted so that I was whole again. Katie was my life, and I was, after what seemed like such a long time in com-ing—a lifetime, really—achieving happiness.

The day we settled our financial affairs, Barbara asked to see me. She appeared tired, almost drowsy. Her voice was dry and crackling. She had aged. The fine lines had furrowed deeper, so that she appeared very old.

"Rosemary…I'm sorry. For all of…this."

"I am too. Thank you, Barbara."

"I knew about Cal and Francine." She did not look at me. "Subconsciously, I tried to hide it. When I did come to grips with it, it was too late. You're a mother now, and someday I hope you'll never have to, but there are things mothers don't want to see in their children. And when those things are horrid, that's even more reason to suppress them. Francine is in counseling now." She smiled with a weariness even I had not possessed. "So am I."

"I'm happy for you. How is Warren?"

"He's well. The same. I don't think he understands what he did."

"Tell him I love him."

She smiled again. "I will."

She did not mention the money, nor did I. And then she did what she had never done. She put her two frail arms around me and placed her cheek on mine. Her hands embraced my hands.

"Good-bye, Rosemary."

"Good-bye, Barbara."

I had received all of Cal's life insurance benefits, along with all of his retirement and savings from the Hill. Although I was not a wealthy woman, I had enough to put away for Katie's college. And with my peace of mind, I was that day a very rich woman.

Sam returned to the Amazon. Phyllis and John were my constant companions; one or the other was always at my side showering me with their kindness and friendship and bestowing upon Katie all kinds of toys and affection. Phyllis told me that John did nothing but brag for weeks to anyone who'd listen about his being a godfather.

In my will I made arrangements that should anything happen to me, Katie would go to Sam; or if conditions made that impossible, she would go to Phyllis and John. Everyone wanted Katie, and I hoped I would live forever.

Congressman Barone had a full staff, but he used his influence, along with Mr. Westcott, and I obtained a great job with a New York senator. I wrote and researched. The lawyer Phyllis and John had retained for me protected my assets and interests. I was still financially comfortable, and my salary was terrific, although not as high as with Congressman Barone. But I did not put in the hours for the senator that I put in for him. It was no longer necessary to work those long hours, and I had time for my child and my novel.

Rob and I married and have three children: Katie, Ann, and Robbie. They are all grown now, married, parents themselves, and happy—or at least we think they are. Rob taught me to live again; with him I healed and I stopped worrying about poverty.

Sammy is our best friend and godmother to all our children. She writes as well, but it is nonfiction, historical, and sympathetic always to the underdog.

It took almost twenty years, but I did accomplish my dream: I became a best-selling author of several novels. With my first advance on my first book, I had Warren transferred to a private institution. Barbara allowed me to do it. Most of my royalties go to causes for mental illness.

Warren and I know what happened that night. Rob does not know, nor does Sam. No one knows but us. I remember all of it to this day with a precise clarity.

After Warren had saved me from Cal, I ran out into the hallway. I stopped to breathe. I can still remember the water dripping from me as I leaned against the wall, gasping for air. Thinking back on it today, I can't believe what I did; I should have been crazed, incapable of any functional or logical thought. I should have been out of my mind, but I know I wasn't. I saw that Warren and Cal were grappling with each other, both at a disadvantage, Cal because he was still in the water-filled tub and Warren, bless him, because he was so clumsy. I was afraid for Warren, but I was afraid for me too, and for my child. What would Cal do now? No one would believe he tried to kill me, and if they did, nothing would happen to him. I would have him always in my life, in my baby's life. I thought of my baby growing up with such a father. I was filled with such hatred—hatred coated with thick bile—and it lay heavy in my burning throat. I saw my chance to rid myself of this awful man, to rid my child of this malignant tumor in our lives. I returned to the bathroom, picked up the hammer from the floor, and tried to hit Cal on his head. I missed. He laughed. He looked up at me and laughed. I remember his eyes, those perfect, small, mean eyes, and I hit him again. That time the hammer fell straight on my target, and he stopped laughing. With a belly filled with child, I straddled my husband and hit him again and again, and I watched him slip under the water. Did my blows kill him? Of course. I know they did. Did Warren finish him off? I doubt it. My poor Warren was just doing what I had taught him to do—*"Hammer it like this, Warren."* He had no idea what he had done. When John discovered him, he was laughing and gurgling and hammering away. But all of it is irrelevant now, for having seen my future with Cal, I decided to destroy him, with malice, with hatred, with forethought, with the hope he would never live. I, who never believed in evil, had absorbed its demons.

Over the years I've grappled with the arguments. If I had admitted to my guilt, confessed everything, would they believe me? Perhaps no court of law would find me guilty of murder. If they called it self-defense, I know in my heart and mind it was murder. But is murder justified to save the psychological life of a baby? And if I had been found guilty, would I have been electrocuted? Or sent away for life? Would my baby grow up never to know me, the good side of me? Would she know that her mother had killed her father? I could not let that happen. And who would raise her? Barbara and her sick children? I could not let that happen. So I left my fate to God, and I've had to live—and continue to live—with my terrible deed. One day I'll face him, and he will be my judge. One day I'll face Warren, and I pray he will still love me enough to forgive me.

Hillsborough, N.C.
April 26, 2011

ACKNOWLEDGEMENTS:

I owe thanks to many people: to Philip Gerard, Professor of Creative Writing at the University of North Carolina at Wilmington, who read the first fifty pages of my ms. and gave me the encouragement I needed to continue; to Margaret Jennings South, *Story* consultant and producer of *Beaches*, who helped tremendously in the telling of this story; Carolyn Woods, author of *The Aardvark's Wife,* who proved to be my mainstay, Lorraine Biniek who stayed up all night to finish it; to readers – Pat Rowe, Kelly Webb Hunter, Sandra Buchin, Joy Murphy; to those hard-working, striving writers in Works in Progress (WIP) Carrboro, NC; to Ray Strother of Orange County Library in Hillsborough. I can't forget Sean Murphy who knew more about finding deleted files than all of the professionals and he was only thirteen, and to my cheering section: Trish Kehler and Kathy Gill for their constant encouragement and faith. My heartfelt thanks and gratitude to all of you for your great work.